STRENGTH
OF SIGHT

STRENGTH OF SIGHT

BOOK THREE OF THE ARMOR SERIES

BY KATARINA KYDE

Flying Squid Leaf Media

Printed in the United States of America

Second Edition: 2025
Paperback ISBN: 979-8-9918929-5-7
Ebook ISBN: 979-8-9918929-4-0
First Printing: 2018

DEDICATION

To me, adventures are more than just adrenaline-inducing activities. They're the building blocks of a fulfilling existence. They're what fill your heart, enrapture your soul, or cause you to grow as a person. Adventures can be big or small and come in all different forms such as learning something new, discovering truths, giving of yourself, making a friend, traveling, collecting personal treasures, forming connections, working hard, creating or appreciating art, embracing yourself for who you are, falling in love. We all have our favorite adventures, and one of mine has been writing this series. For everyone who joined me on this adventure by reading my books, I thank you. This book is for you.

A NOTE FOR MY READERS:

The Armor Series, at its core, is a contemporary low fantasy about the walls we put up and the armor we all don when we're scared, uncomfortable, or insecure, and moving forward through these times as best we can with self-love and self-acceptance. This central theme is woven into the backdrop of heart-pumping action. Be aware that some scenes within the series are emotionally charged and/or highly action-oriented.

This book specifically, *Strength of Sight*, contains scenes depicting kidnapping, fear, anxiety, violence, emotional, verbal, and physical abuse, blood, death, grief, sexual situations, and profanity.

"Old age brings such sight. Such powerful revelations. Why couldn't I have been older when I was young?"

-Dr. Frederick Dromly

Prologue
WHY WON'T YOU DIE?

Friday, June 14, 1963

He's lost his damn mind. That has to be the explanation. Charlie Masser slammed the journal shut with disgust. Magical necklaces, superhero strength, mind control, red-headed psychics, a piece of metal that'll bring back the dead. A complete bullshit waste of time. Was Fred Dromly trying to write a sissy diary or a comic book? And probably the most unbelievable part of all—sex with Dot. The words made her sound like a conquest and made Charlie want to puke.

He stormed down the empty hallway of Springfield University's faculty offices building, unlocked an office door, and stormed inside. Seeing the startled face of someone he didn't recognize digging through some files, he asked, "Where's Dromly? He dropped his diary." Under his light blond, mop top bangs, Charlie eyed the stranger suspiciously, turning his body to make sure the younger man could see the Chief of Security badge on his uniform.

The younger man rose quickly and closed the filing cabinet drawer. His eyes darted back and forth as if looking for an easy escape route. "Oh, his trip journal. He's been looking for that. Thanks for bringing it by." He took it gingerly out of Charlie's hand. "I'll just put it with the others."

"There's more?" Charlie scoffed.

"Professor Dromly writes in his journal every day. He's filled up a whole stack of them." The younger man opened a closet and put the journal inside.

Charlie turned to leave, but a nagging feeling in his stomach made him turn back around. "Who are you? Why are you in Dromly's office?"

"The name's Thomas Brevain, sir. Fred and I are working on a project together."

"How well do you know him?"

"Very well."

Charlie leaned forward, wanting his size and height to intimidate the younger and smaller man. "You're going to have to do better than that."

"I worked for him as a student a decade ago and then we became colleagues after I earned my PhD. I worked here at the university for several years before I got a job at the museum downtown. I'm surprised you don't remember seeing me around. I remember seeing *you* here for years."

Charlie eyed the room. Nothing seemed out of place. "I see. Has he said anything...strange lately?"

"No. Why do you ask?"

"What time is he coming back?"

"Oh, he won't be back tonight. Said he has a date with the love of his life." Thomas picked up his work bag. "I also have a wife to get home to. Is there anything else I can do for you?"

Charlie wasn't about to let this guy get away that easily. "Yeah. Did he say where he's taking his wife tonight? Mine told me if I take her to the buffet one more time, I'll be wearing it."

A small chuckle escaped Thomas's lips. "The new place on 23rd. Classy. Romantic."

"Thanks. I'll have to try it." Charlie stood in the doorway, blocking Thomas from leaving the room. "So you know him well. What do you think of him?"

"He's great," Thomas said, his fake smile making him look guilty about something. "The students love him."

"But you...not so much, right?"

"I don't know what you're talking about." Thomas shifted his bag to the other shoulder.

"I have to let the janitor in here every night. No one has keys to Freddie's office but Freddie and me. So how'd you get in?"

Thomas cleared his throat. "He was in a hurry to leave, and I needed something in here. He left it open for me."

"And so if I confirm this story with Freddie, he'll tell me the same thing? He'll tell me what it was that you needed from his filing cabinet?"

Thomas let out a small laugh and ran his hand through his jet black hair. "Look...I..."

"This offense could get you fired. Thrown in prison."

Thomas's cobalt blue eyes widened. "I can explain."

"You don't have to. I think I already know. You see, I know Freddie pretty well too. He's an arrogant piece of shit who did something to piss you off. Am I close?"

Thomas stared at the floor. "Something like that."

"I thought so." Charlie stared at the younger man. "We can help each other out, Dr. Brevain. I'm going to forget about this night until I need a favor from you. And when I come for you, you better deliver. Do we have a deal?"

Thomas's head bobbed up and down. "Yes, absolutely."

"Go then." Charlie watched Thomas disappear down the hallway. Fishing his keys out of his pocket, Charlie headed to the parking lot.

✳ ✳ ✳

FREDERICK DROMLY PUT AN ARM AROUND the petite woman in the pretty yellow dress beside him as he looked up at the stars. They were beautiful, but they couldn't compare to the sparkle radiating from her big brown eyes.

"Thanks for dinner, Fred." She put an arm around him as well as they walked through the parking lot toward his Granada red 1963 Buick Riviera.

"My pleasure, Dottie," he replied, running a hand

over her black hair and giving her a kiss. "I'm glad we were finally able to sneak away for an evening."

"Me too." She kissed him back with a passion they could only show each other when alone. "I love you."

He held her close for a moment. She was there, and there were stars, and the new car smell, and so many adventures to be had in the future. The world was indeed a magical place. "I love you, too."

She looked surprised when he handed her his keys. "You want me to drive your brand new car?"

He nodded. "I had too much wine with dinner."

"I told you so," she teased, grabbing the keys.

"And you were right!" he proclaimed loudly with a grin, his finger dramatically pointing to the sky.

She smirked as she rolled her eyes. "Let's get you home." Dot pulled out of the parking lot and onto 23rd. "It's so fast!" she exclaimed, smiling with pleasure as she accelerated through the green light.

Fred squinted as bright lights blinded him through the driver's side window. There was a loud sound of crunching, glass raining, a crushing pressure, and lots of pain before everything went black.

✳✳✳

FRED'S HAND GENTLY TOUCHED HIS THROBBING forehead. He groaned and tried to go back to sleep. Why was there noise? Who was shouting?

"Sir, can you hear me?"

Fred groaned again and felt someone touching his face. There was a bright light in one eye and then the other.

"Mr. Dromly, can you hear me?" a voice said again.

"That's Dr. Dromly to you," said a second voice.

"Dr. Dromly, can you open your eyes? Look, your wife is here."

Fred opened his eyes. There she was, looking down on him, her tears falling on the white bedsheets.

"You're finally awake."

"Helen," he said in a whisper. "What..."

The doctor explained to Fred that he'd broken an arm, both legs, a couple ribs, and fractured his spine in the accident. One surgery had already been completed, but he may need more, and it would be at least a couple months before he'd be able to leave the hospital.

"Charlie was driving home from work," Helen told him once she and Fred were alone. Her voice waivered, and her body trembled. "He drove by the accident shortly after it happened. You and my sister were unconscious on the road, covered in glass and blood."

"Is Dot okay?" Fred asked. His voice was still weak.

Helen shook her head in anger, her black bob caressing her chin. "Charlie said he's suspected something's been going on with you two. Is it true?"

"Helen, is Dot okay?"

"Is it true?" Helen asked again in a raised voice, her brows narrowing in rage.

Fred raised his one good arm to touch his aching head again, feeling his short brown curls wrap around his fingers. "I'm sorry, Helen. Yes."

"Well!" Helen sat in a nearby chair, took a deep breath in, and let it out slowly.

Dr. Waterman had taught her breathing exercises to combat her involuntary trembling and the urge to scream when she got upset. Fred was grateful that her breathing seemed to be calming her. "I'm so sorry. We never intended—"

"Of course you didn't," she replied through gritted teeth. "Dot must have been utterly charmed by your 'zest for life' as she often called it. And you were just being Fred, taking advantage of every exciting opportunity that comes your way."

"Helen..."

"I should've seen it coming. She was at the house all the time."

"She was there to help you. She was the only one who could make you feel calm."

"Yes. Such fine excuses. So fine I actually believed them."

"They weren't excuses, Helen."

"You never stopped being that little orphan who didn't matter to anyone, did you? You just can't resist an admirer. Tell me, did she make you feel important? Like you were someone who actually matters?"

"Helen..."

"Charlie said that there was alcohol involved in the accident."

"I wasn't the one driv—"

"You betrayed me!" Helen shouted. "You took advantage of my sister, and then you killed her!"

Fred tried to catch his breath. "What? Dot is dead?"

Helen started to sob. "Was your little game worth it? Did you get what you wanted from her before you carelessly threw her life away?"

"It wasn't a game!" Fred felt himself getting angry. "I loved her!"

Helen let out a wail and stood up.

"Sit down before you faint!"

"I hate you, Fred! I will never forgive you! And you can forget about ever seeing your son again!" She started to storm out of the room but fainted before she got to the door.

"Helen?" Fred called out. He wished he could get up to help her. "Help! Help!" he cried. Nurses rushed in and helped revive Helen. They ushered her to another room.

Fred looked at the suspended ceiling through his tears. They distorted his view, and the normally static pattern on the moveable tiles oozed through his vision like lava that was trying to cool but wasn't quite ready. He turned his head to the door at the sound of footsteps.

"Charlie," he said, recognizing the man entering his room. "Helen just fainted. She shouldn't drive home. Please check on her."

Charlie Masser loomed over Fred's bed, and his light blue eyes shot daggers. "You son of a bitch."

"Charlie, I'm very sorry about Dot."

"You know what the doc told me about my dead wife? He told me she was pregnant. Just about one month along. Did she tell you?"

"No. I'm so sorry."

"She may not have even known herself yet. But here's the kicker. I had a vasectomy a few years back. So the dead little bastard's yours!" His laugh was slow, soft, and pained.

Fred nervously wiggled the fingers of his uninjured hand, feeling very vulnerable in his casts. "We didn't want to hurt anyone," Fred tried to explain, "but we were in love. We didn't mean for it to happen. And it certainly wasn't supposed to end like this."

"Well, Fred, you're right about that." Charlie leaned over and looked Fred in the eye. One hand pushed his blond, mop top bangs out of his eyes while the other wrapped around Fred's throat. "I thought for sure you'd be the one driving that fancy new car of yours." His hand squeezed tighter. "It was *you* I wanted to kill in that accident!"

Fred's one good arm flailed about while he choked. His hand found a metal pole on wheels that held his IV bag. He grabbed and pulled, and it came crashing down on Charlie's head before coming to rest loudly on the floor.

A nurse ran in upon hearing the commotion. "Is everything okay in here?"

Charlie stood up and let the nurse pick up the mess. "Pardon my clumsiness, ma'am."

"Visiting hours are over," she told him firmly. "Dr. Dromly needs his rest."

"We'll finish this when you get out of here, Freddie." Charlie lingered by the door for a moment to glare at Fred before leaving.

Tuesday, September 17, 1963

THREE MONTHS LATER, FRED EXITED A taxi and gingerly walked up to his front door. "Oh, Helen," he mumbled when he discovered his key didn't fit the lock anymore. He knocked and rang the doorbell. "Helen!" he called out. "Helen, open the door!"

The door opened and a man stood on the other side of the entryway. "You have the wrong house. There's no Helen here."

"This is my house," Fred said, confused. His hand ran through his brown curls as he looked past the man and saw furniture in the living room that wasn't his.

"Not since August," the man said. That's when I bought this place. Now get off my porch." The door closed in Fred's face.

Fred held his hands out in disbelief. He headed to the next door neighbor's house. "Virginia, hello!" he greeted his elderly neighbor when she answered the door.

"Oh, hello, Fred. I was wondering when you'd come by. Helen told me everything that happened." She gave Fred a disapproving frown. "She had a nervous breakdown a few weeks later and was taken to the Willow Brook facility. Her parents came, cleaned out the house, and sold it."

Fred sighed. He knew he should never have accepted the house as a wedding present. They were just so young and the idea of living in a beautiful house they couldn't afford on their own was too tempting. "Helen is still at Willow Brook?"

Virginia shrugged. "As far as I know."

"And Kent? Where is he?"

"I don't know. Helen was out in the yard screaming, trying to set the front porch on fire. Your poor little boy was watching her and crying. I called the authorities and Willow Brook. Helen went to the hospital, and Kent went with the officers."

"Thanks for your help, Virginia. May I use your phone?"

"Go to hell, Fred." She slammed the door.

"I think I'm already there," he said aloud to no one. He felt his legs aching as he walked toward the payphone by the gas station several blocks away. So much for taking it slow like the doctor had ordered.

The cab picked him up at the gas station and took him to Willow Brook. Fred walked up the path toward the front door, well aware of the leering eyes of the patients who were strolling the campus grounds. The landscaping was beautiful with bright flowers soaking up the last of summer's warmth, their vivid colors radiating joyfulness. The residents looked anything but joyful, their facility-issued robes dancing in the breeze underneath their horrified or vacant expressions. The mismatch made Fred sad. Sad for them, sad for Helen and Kent, and sad for himself. He was okay with the sadness though. It was human, appropriate, and possibly even poetic. The slow ache of sadness can inspire the greatest works of art. It was the fear that was making this unbearable. Fear doesn't inspire. It rips the soul from your body and shits on it before shoving it back down your throat and punching you in the gut with a promise to do it all again tomorrow.

"You're welcome to see her," Dr. Waterman told Fred. "She was brought here after trying to burn down your house. Her thoughts and words were scattered at first and her fainting spells increased to several times a day. For the last month, however, she's been catatonic. We have her on sedatives to keep her calm, but there's not much else we can do for her at this time."

"Helen," said Fred softly as he entered her room. She was sitting in a chair and leaning unnaturally far over to the right. "How are you feeling? I heard about what happened."

Helen blankly stared straight ahead and didn't react when Fred sat her up straight and pushed her bobbed black hair out of her face.

"Helen? I'm here to apologize. This is all my fault. I'm so sorry." He sat in a chair across from her.

Her blank expression didn't change.

"I want you to know I don't care about the house. I don't blame you for having your parents sell it out from under me. I care about you, and I want you to get better. I also love and miss our son so much. Where is Kent?" Fred asked her.

"Kent," she said in a robotic tone. Her eyes remained staring blankly in the distance.

"Yes, Kent. Kent—where is he?"

"Kent. Kent," she parroted back.

"Where is he?" Fred asked again, trying to keep his frustration at bay.

"Where is he?" Helen whispered. Her eyes had not moved.

"Snap out of it!" Fred demanded, raising his voice. "Tell me where my son is!"

Helen's eyes blinked for the first time. They looked at Fred before Helen fainted.

Fred sighed, picked up his wife, and put her gently on the bed. "Good bye, Helen," he told her, gently stroking her hair before leaving Willow Brook.

✳ ✳ ✳

"WHAT IS THE MEANING OF THIS commotion?" shouted Helen and Dot's father after swinging open his front door. "How dare you pound on my door at this hour? After all you've put this family through?"

"Words cannot express how sorry I am for the damage I've done, Al," Fred told him. "I'm just here for my son."

"What makes you think he's here? Get off my property before I call the police!" Al started to slam the door, but Fred's foot stopped it.

"There's nowhere else Helen would leave him," Fred replied.

Helen and Dot's mother came to the door and handed Fred a large envelope. "You no longer have custody of Kent," she informed him. "And you're not welcome here."

"Daddy?" A four-year-old child with the same curly hair as Fred but black like his mother's peeked through the cracked open door.

"Kent!" Fred dropped to his knees and held out his arms. "I missed you so much!"

Kent tried to squeeze through Al's legs to get out the door but was unsuccessful.

"I told you to keep him upstairs, Madge!" roared Fred's father-in-law to his wife. She picked up Kent who screamed and called for his father while being carried upstairs.

"You can't keep my son from me! I *will* fight this!"

"If you come around here again, Fred, you'll be leaving in a body bag." The door slammed in Fred's face. "Call Charlie," Fred heard Al shouting to Madge. "He'll want to know that Fred's out of the hospital."

"Charlie. Shit." Fred was glad he had asked the cab driver to wait for him. If he wanted to live through the night, he had to get to his office at Springfield University before Charlie Masser found him.

✳✳✳

HIS BODY ACHED, HE MISSED HIS son, and a couple tears drew paths down his cheeks. Exhausted from the day's adventure, Fred huffed and puffed up the stairs, too impatient to wait for the elevator. He opened the door to his office and made a bee line for the safe. He swung it open and then felt a gun pressed to the back of his head.

"I thought you'd show up here, Freddie."

"Charlie, you don't want to do this."

"I really do. Don't move." He backed up slowly with the gun still pointed at Fred's head. He hung a rope over the office door, not seeing when Fred quickly reached into his safe and grabbed what he'd come for. "You see, your body is broken, you lost your wife, your girlfriend, your son, your unborn child. You just can't live with the pain." He waved the noose around with a victorious grin on his face and pulled a chair from Fred's conference table over to the door. "Now get over here."

Fred crossed his arms. "And what if I don't? You'll shoot me? You're willing to spend the rest of your life in prison?"

Charlie shook his head and put his gun away. "Nah, I won't shoot you. But you should know that Al has his bowling league and Madge plays bridge twice a week. I've been asked to pick up Kent after pre-school on those days which is no problem because my Barbara goes to the same school. And as you recently learned the hard way, unfortunate accidents do happen."

"You're threatening my four-year-old son?! He's an innocent child!" Fred angrily stomped toward Charlie, his fists in tight balls.

Charlie was ten inches taller and a hundred pounds heavier than Fred. He easily overpowered the smaller man, picked him up, and stood him on the chair. "It's either you or him," he said.

Fred took a deep, shaking breath. How long had it been since he'd last taken care of the contents of his safe? Three months at least. No one had touched it since then, so the black agate necklace he'd just fished out of there should still hold a charge—right? He wasn't sure, but he had no other choice than to take that chance. Putting his head in the noose, he closed his eyes.

"Are you ready to go to hell, Fred?" snarled Charlie.

"I'll save you a seat," Fred replied with a confident smirk as he saw a soft glow coming from the pendent underneath his shirt.

"Cocky bastard! Justice is gonna be sweet." Angrily, Charlie kicked the chair out from under Fred.

Fred felt a rush of fear. A moment later, his feet landed on the floor. "Oh no," he said with a laugh. "Looks like the rope came untied. How embarrassing for you."

Charlie retied the rope and secured it over the door. "A minor setback," he said. "This time, you're dead."

"We'll see about that," Fred laughed. "Your knot tying skills are surprisingly terrible. If I were going to hang someone, I'd be more prepared. Tsk, tsk." He shook his head.

"Shut up!" Again, Charlie stood Fred on the chair. He forced Fred's head in the noose and tightened it. Without saying a word, he pulled the chair out from under Fred.

Softly, Fred's feet landed on the floor once more. "Now the rope broke? This was not the time to save money on cheap supplies, Charlie." He couldn't help but laugh again. Invincibility was something he could get used to. He sat in the chair behind his desk and put his feet up.

Charlie snorted in frustration. "What the hell is happening?"

It was the perfect time to celebrate his victory. Fred lit up a cigar and held it between his teeth while he grinned at Charlie. "The finest Cuban stogie," he said. "I'd offer you one, but with the murder attempts and all... you understand."

Charlie's confused eyes pointed toward the glowing pendant under Fred's shirt. "How can you sit there with a stupid grin on your face when you're about to die?" He grabbed his gun and shot at Fred from across the office. The expression on his face grew more and more horrified as the bullet zoomed around his target and hit the wall instead. Walking closer, he leaned over the desk, put the barrel of the gun right on Fred's forehead, and pulled the trigger. Nothing happened.

Fred blew a mouthful of smoke in Charlie's face and enjoyed watching him cough.

"What the hell is wrong with this gun?" Charlie yelled.

Fred stood up when several campus security officers burst into the room. "Your boss is trying to kill me," Fred told them. "And he has really bad aim."

"Why won't you die, Dromly?!" shouted Charlie as he was taken away.

Fred collapsed back into his chair. He pulled out the amulet he wore under his shirt and ran a finger over the black agate and sardonyx stones. "Thank you, my friend," he told the piece of Jewelry.

He grabbed the envelope his mother-in-law had handed him earlier that evening. The custody paperwork claimed that he had a problem with alcohol. He *had* started drinking more than usual when he and Helen would get into fights, but he never considered it a problem. He saw how a court might feel it was, however. "I will get my son back. I will never drink again," he vowed. He pulled out the liquor bottles he had in a cabinet, opened his window, and hurled them at Charlie's car in the parking lot, cheering when he made a direct hit to the windshield.

As he sat on the chair behind his desk again, a wave of loneliness washed over him. Charlie was right. He'd lost his wife, his girlfriend, his son, and another child he'd never get to meet. He looked at the amulet again. It was one piece of Jewelry in a set called the Armor Jewelry, and according to a legend from Mallandia, an ancient civilization that he'd discovered by unearthing their ruins, it was used by ancient warriors in battles to keep them from being killed or injured. He remembered the day many years ago when he'd learned that the legend of the amulet was actually true. That had been one of his favorite adventures to date.

He flipped through a trip journal he used during his travel to Europe about ten years prior. Smiling, he remembered the newest legend he'd learned when he and his assistant Thomas Brevain had been there. According to very ancient sources, the Plate of Destiny had the secrets of life and death inlaid in gold upon it and gave directions on not only how to live your best life, but also on how to bring back the dead. There'd been a time when he'd been completely focused on finding the Plate, but with his family, teaching, symposiums, book signings, television appearances, and other trips he'd taken, Fred had almost forgotten about it. He sat up straight. What he wouldn't do to give Dottie and her unborn child their lives back.

Part 1

GO FIND HER

Chapter 1

Tuesday, October 6, 2015

Anise Viston closed her eyes and opened them again, hoping the nightmare would pass and she'd wake up. No such luck. She stared at the face of her nemesis, the old woman as notoriously resilient as a cockroach. Not even death could kill her.

"That's right, it's me. Surprised?" Grace asked her.

"Yes." *Terrified might be a better word,* Anise thought, as she pushed her wavy brown hair out of her eyes with a shaking hand. "I heard you had died in prison." Her hand moved from her hair to her forehead. It throbbed behind her palm, but her mind was starting to clear nevertheless. Turning to look out the window, she saw nothing but farmland below their plane. The two of them were the only passengers on the small private jet as far as she could tell. She eyed the amulet around Grace's aging, wrinkled neck. The beginning of an anxiety attack made her chest tighten and her stomach churn. "Why did you kidnap me?" she blurted out. "Where are you taking me?"

"Your questions can wait," snapped Grace. "First you need to heal me. Then I'll explain where we're going."

"Heal you?" Perhaps her mind wasn't as clear as she'd

thought. Anise's head still felt like she was swimming underwater in the dark. "What do you mean?"

Grace scowled. "Either you're an idiot or I hit your head harder than I thought. You are the last living descendant of the Mallandian royal line, the only one left with king's blood, remember? You are the only person who can heal me with the Armor Jewelry."

"Wait, you know about king's blood?" Anise asked with surprise.

"I've known for decades."

"Decades?" Things didn't quite make sense, and suddenly Anise had a million questions. "If you knew I had king's blood, and you knew only I could heal you, why did you try to kill me?" Anise demanded.

Grace rolled her eyes. "I wanted your blood, obviously."

"So, everything that happened three years ago—all the times you tried to take my amulet or tried to kill me—was because you wanted my blood?" Anise paused for a moment as she started to piece everything together. "Because only someone with king's blood can use the healing powers of the cuff. And you wanted to cure yourself from your headaches and hallucinations?"

"Yes," Grace replied.

"But king's blood works on intention. If you stole my blood from me, it wouldn't have been willing blood! It wouldn't have worked for you!"

"It seems you've been doing your homework," Grace commented. "But don't you think I have ways to make you willing?"

"But why threaten me? Why didn't you just ask me for my help like you are now? I would've gladly healed you, and we could've avoided the whole murderous scene!" Anise demanded as her arms flailed.

Grace silently stared at her.

"Because that's not all you want, is it?" Anise concluded, answering her own question. "You still need something else from me. What aren't you telling me?" Anise demanded.

"All you need to know is that I'm going to make you willing to heal me."

"You mean *force* me to heal you."

"No, I meant willing. You know very well that just like king's blood, the cuff and all the other Armor Jewelry work by intention. You must be willing to heal me or it won't work. You just learned that from Kent Dromly."

Anise wondered how long Grace had been following her and tried to breathe through her growing anxiety as best as she could. She let out a slow exhale and placed a hand on her aching chest. "How did you know I talked to Kent?"

"When I escaped from prison, I planted a bug in Kent's house and waited for you and Nate to show up. I heard everything the three of you talked about."

Anise was both impressed and intimidated by Grace's resourcefulness. It reminded her of Nate. He was just as resourceful. And he'd be coming for her. That thought alone made her anxiety dissipate somewhat, at least enough to let her hand relax in her lap. "How did you know we'd be going to see Kent?"

"Nate asked about him when he came to visit me," Grace explained. "I thought nothing of it at first, but the more I played it back in my head, the more important it seemed to be. Nate is very purposeful in his actions."

Nate had promised to stay away from Grace. Anise felt a pit form in her stomach. "He is," she agreed. "But when did he go to visit you?"

"He didn't tell you?" laughed Grace. "In exchange for more information about the Armor Jewelry he helped me escape."

"*What?!*" The world paused for a moment as Anise tried to take in Grace's words. *Helped me escape.* Her eyes narrowed. "You're lying. Nate would never do that."

Grace shrugged. "Believe whatever you want."

"But you tried to murder me. Even if he visited you, he'd never help you *escape*."

"I couldn't have done it without him," said Grace. "He brought me the neurotoxin I needed to pretend I was dead. I was shipped to the morgue and escaped from there as per...an agreement I had with the pathologist. In just the right dose, this neurotoxin causes you to appear dead. Your body gets cold, your breathing and heartbeat get so slow that they're undetectable, and you become temporarily paralyzed and go into a deep sleep. The guards found the rest of the toxin near my body and assumed I had committed suicide." She laughed with amusement. "I woke up in the morgue and frightened the pathologist half to death. When I informed him and he confirmed that his family had been taken hostage, he was very agreeable when it came to faking my autopsy report and keeping his mouth shut."

"How do you know he won't still talk?" Anise asked her.

"Well, if the men I hired did their jobs correctly," Grace said, "he *can't* talk."

"I don't even want to know what that means." Anise wondered how long it would be before Grace tried to murder her again. She took another deep breath to center herself, but the anxiety was coming on strong. Her arms went numb and she blinked a few times to try to stop the dizziness. She needed to think about something else to try to avoid a panic attack. She needed to keep her mind ready for whatever Grace might do to her. Usually, thoughts of Nate could calm her down. But Nate had kept something from her—a very big something—again. He had promised her she could trust him! He had looked at her soul with his damn charming blue eyes and said that he loved her. She felt angry tears looming. But...Grace wasn't a trustworthy person herself, to say the least. She was a thief and a murderer...maybe she was lying about Nate. A neurotoxin? Anise put a hand over the burning in her chest again. *Please let her be lying about Nate.* "If you want me to heal you with the Jewelry, you'll have to hand it over. What makes you think I'll be willing to help you once you do?" she snapped.

"Because you're weak," Grace answered matter-of-factly. "And you'd miss your friends if they were gone, right?"

"What are you talking about?" Anise asked, as the worry grew inside her. Her stomach and chest still felt hot, and she wished she had a soda. She often got a nervous stomach, but heartburn for her was rare.

"Joy, Vanessa, Erin," said Grace, listing Anise's three best and oldest friends. "I've hidden a bomb in each of their apartments," she explained with a smile that made Anise shiver. "They can be activated digitally from anywhere in the world." She showed Anise the screen of her laptop. "Once I click on this button, they'll self-activate in 15 minutes." She clicked the button.

"Turn it off!" Anise cried as she jumped out of her seat. Grace pushed her with the strength that the earrings from the Armor Jewelry set gave her, and Anise's body slammed against the side of the plane. She winced as she tried to catch her breath.

In a wild fit of anger as she screamed and pulled on her hair, Grace jumped and slammed her own body on the wall of the plane, causing the aircraft to pull violently to the side. Anise screamed as she held on to the seats.

INSIDE THE COCKPIT, THE PILOT BEGAN to pray as he got the plane back on course. Grabbing a small towel, he drenched it with the sweat on his wide, round face and dropped it in a pile with the others. He'd worked for Grace Brevain before and had seen things he wished he could forget. He'd promised himself never again. But somehow, no matter where in the world he went, she always found him. There was something supernatural about the evil old devil woman. He had taken this job partly because Grace wouldn't take no for an answer, partly because she'd paid him an obscene amount of money, and partly because he was scared shitless of her. He'd once transported a 350 pound murderous criminal who wasn't half as scary as this little old lady. The things she had threatened him with...he shuddered and kissed the cross he wore around his neck, grateful for the locked door that separated him from Grace.

"STUPID GIRL!" SHOUTED GRACE AS THE plane straightened out. "If you want to help your friends, you better listen!" Grace commanded.

"I'll help you!" Anise agreed quickly, still holding on to the seat in front of her.

Grace scowled at Anise. "You think that if I hand over the Jewelry, you'll be able to use the cuff's mind control powers to force me to stop the explosion without healing me first! I'm too smart to fall for that!" Grace reached into her bag and pulled out a needle.

"What's that for?" Anise demanded nervously. She stepped into the aisle and backed away from Grace.

Pulling off the cap, Grace said, "This serum works very quickly." She gave the syringe a few flicks of her finger.

"What will it do to me?" Anise choked out. She took another step backward and let out a short scream when Grace grabbed her by the arm.

"Pay attention! I'm only going to say this once," Grace barked.

Anise couldn't break Grace's grip on her arm. "Let me go!"

"I said listen!" commanded Grace. To Anise's shock, she injected the serum into her own arm.

"What?!" Anise couldn't help but exclaim. *What the hell is happening?*

"Once I pass out, you won't be able to brainwash me or threaten me in any way. The only way to stop the explosions is to heal..." Grace collapsed in the aisle.

"Shit!" Anise knelt on the floor of the plane next to Grace trying to figure out what she wanted to do. If she only healed Grace from the effects of the serum, she could then brainwash her into stopping the explosions. Quickly, Anise removed the amulet, ring, earrings, and cuff from Grace's unconscious body. Putting them on herself, she began having doubts. Knowing Grace, she likely had a plan in case Anise decided to only wake her and not cure her of the side effects of the cuff. What then? She looked at the countdown on Grace's laptop. Only a few minutes left.

Gingerly, she picked up Grace's hand. There was no time to waste. "Grace," she began, "Dr. Smithton spent years trying to brainwash you with this cuff. I've learned that when the brainwashing is attempted by someone who doesn't have king's blood, then the victim will have headaches, hallucinations, and eventually turn into what they fear the most. I can't imagine what you must fear the most, because you are by far the most fearsome person I've ever known. You must have experienced something terrible in your life, and I'm sorry for that. I honestly *do* want you to heal, not just so you'll stop terrorizing every-one, but so your demons can stop terrorizing you, too." The lapis lazuli and jasper stones on the cuff sparkled, and Anise waited.

Grace's eyes opened. She blinked a few times but said nothing.

"Turn it off!" Anise cried again.

When Grace did as she requested, Anise collapsed into a seat with relief.

"Well?" asked Anise curiously. "How do you feel?"

Grace sat down in a seat across the aisle and took a long pause before answering. "I don't know. Say something annoying."

"What?"

"Yes, like that. Keep going."

"I don't know what you want me to say."

Grace leaned back in her seat, looking deep in thought. "I'm not getting frustrated."

"Good for you. I hope you don't think you'll be getting the Jewelry back."

"Still not frustrated," Grace replied with a laugh. "No headache. I think it worked!" She looked at Anise and smiled.

Anise had never seen Grace smile so genuinely before. It was unnerving and certainly not helping the anxiety stomachache that had grown to a size of a basketball in her gut. Anise looked at her with disdain. Grace had traumatized her and had been the source of her recurring nightmares. She was the reason Anise hadn't felt safe without the protective amulet around her neck these last three years. Talking with her now, Anise was starting to see how pathetic this manipulative old hag could be. She pitied Nate for growing up with Grace and having had to deal with her nonsense daily when he was young. What he went through would be too much for an adult to deal with, much less an innocent child. *Please let her be lying about Nate.* "Well, I'm glad you're happy," Anise drawled with sarcasm. "I almost lost my best friends."

Grace rolled her eyes. "Oh, relax. There were never any bombs," she said, throwing her head back and laughing. "I just escaped from prison. When would I have had the time to set that up? I can't believe you bought such a ridiculous story!"

Her tone made Anise feel mortified. "I'm glad my friends were never in any danger," she replied. "But I wasn't about to take any chances with their lives. Knowing you and your criminal record it was fully plausible that you'd be happy to murder more innocent people for whatever the hell it is that you want!" She saw Grace eyeing her amulet. Anise put her hand on it. "And this is worth repeating—you're not getting this Jewelry back."

Grace shrugged and had an expression of amusement on her face. "You can keep it—for now. As long as one of us has it when we find the Plate of Destiny."

Anise finally understood where Grace was taking her. She remembered Kent saying the Plate of Destiny was hidden in Florida. What she didn't understand was why Grace wanted her help. "What's this 'we' stuff?" Anise demanded. She watched the older woman settle deeper in her seat with her eyes closed and a content look on her face, as if she were on a relaxing vacation. "Grace, did you hear me? I asked you what this *'we'* stuff is."

Grace sighed, her eyes still closed. "As much as I hate it, I won't be able to read the knowledge inlaid on the Plate without you. As someone with king's blood, you are meant to protect the knowledge. That's why your blood must be spilled on the Plate in order for a seer like me to be able to read it."

Anise's stomach churned. "So that's what you still want from me? You still need my blood?! That makes more sense as to why you wanted to kill me three years ago."

"Yes, but because of Nate, you're still here. You have no idea how many times he saved your life, do you?"

No. She didn't. But he wasn't there to help her now, and she had more important things to think about. "So besides the fact that I'm wearing all the Armor Jewelry, what's preventing you from killing me now?" Anise asked.

"Believe it or not, I'm glad Nate didn't let me kill you. I need you alive. Prison gives you a lot of time for research. I found more legends and learned that your blood must be *fresh* when it touches the Plate of Destiny. I had planned to harvest your blood and freeze it, but I know now that wouldn't have worked."

Anise narrowed her eyebrows. "I thought you'd be completely different after being healed from the side effects of the cuff like Jonathan was. But you haven't changed at all, have you? You still want to kill me!"

"I don't kill for fun!" Grace snarled. "And your death isn't necessary. A few drops of your blood is all I need. Then the words inlaid in gold will appear on the Plate, and we'll both have the knowledge of life and death!"

"No deal," Anise said with an air of finality. "I don't know if you're telling the truth. I'm not helping you."

"Don't you want to find the Plate?"

"Not particularly. I have more important things to do. I have somewhere else I need to go, and as soon as we land, I'll be leaving." She thought about how she'd been about to leave for Philadelphia when Grace kidnapped her. She'd had possession of all the Armor Jewelry and would've been able to heal her brother Les from his undiagnosable fainting spells, finally. But Grace went and ruined that plan. Anise felt anger rise like bile into her throat.

"I'll follow you," Grace shrugged. "As soon as the Jewelry runs out of charge, I'll get you back under my control."

Shit! Anise's chest tightened and she fought to take a breath. Grace could easily take Les's blood if she found out he also had king's blood. His existence needed to stay a secret from her.

"Besides," Grace continued, "while you were unconscious, something happened that will change your mind. You'll want to find that Plate."

"What are you talking about?" Anise asked with an edge in her voice. Ever since she'd woken, she'd been riding the edge of a panic attack, and it was exhausting. All she wanted was her own bed and for the rest of the world to disappear.

"Your friend Erin was killed in an accident today."

Anise rolled her eyes. "I'm not falling for that again."

"Look for yourself." Grace handed her the laptop. The screen showed a website of the local newspaper with a breaking article.

Anise skimmed the article that mentioned a car that had run a red light and collided with a pole. "You planted this. This is fake." Still, her stomach squeezed and her heart pounded so hard she could see a pulsating light in her eyes. With trembling fingers, she went to the websites of other reputable news sources. One had a photo of Erin's mangled car with her body halfway through the windshield, her golden-bronzy hair framing her bloody face. After taking in that visual, it was hard to concentrate on the article itself. It mentioned Erin was only a few blocks from home. Her boyfriend had told the reporter she'd been on her way to help a friend in need.

A friend in need. Anise's tears blurred the rest of the article. Shoving the laptop into the seat next to her, Anise got up to frantically pace the small aisle of the plane, twisting the garnet ring on her finger. *She* was the friend in need. Had she not called Erin while having a panic attack in Jonathan's bathroom, her friend would be alive.

"I need to get off the plane!" Her pacing turned into running and anxiety overtook her. She banged loudly on the cockpit door until her hands were red and throbbing. "I need to get off the plane! Land now! Please!" She tugged at the door, hoping the earrings would make her strong enough to pull it off.

"I had it reinforced," Grace told her with a yawn. "You can't open it, not even with the earrings."

The panic was too much. She knew she was going to faint, puke, and die, not necessarily in that order. Anise kicked the door over and over screamed loudly enough for Grace to make a face and cover her ears. Giving up on the door, she spun around, and her eyes scanned the plane. *There's more than one way to get off this fucking flying tin can.* She forcefully opened every compartment and looked under each seat.

"What the hell are you doing?" Grace wanted to know.

"I'm looking for a parachute!"

"Do you know how to use a parachute?"

"Go to hell!" A dizzying wave made Anise grasp the seats for balance. It was daytime, but stars appeared before her eyes. The light faded quickly. Desperate gasps made the air hunger worse. No feeling in her arms or legs. Her knees buckled. Her body melted. Slowly disappearing. Her mind screamed. *Breathe! In, out. Again.* Feeling came back in her limbs. *Breathe. In, out.* The anxiety lessened somewhat, and she found herself supine across the seats, staring at the ceiling of the plane, seeing nothing but Erin's bloody face.

Grace's voice unwelcomely reached Anise's ears. "So... do you want to find the Plate of Destiny now? You could use it to bring back your friend."

Anise's entire being trembled. Erin was dead because of her. She *had* to find the Plate...*if* Erin was dead. Grace had to be lying. She must've made the whole thing up. The timing was too convenient. "If the article is real and Erin is actually gone, then yes. But not with you."

"I see. And what do you plan to do about it?" Grace looked at her with a smile of slight amusement, and Anise sensed she'd already lost the battle of wits she was about to play, but she had to try.

Anise's muscles were weak and shaking, but she sat up straight. "I have all the Jewelry and the cuff. I can brainwash you. Grace, you no longer want the Plate of Destiny." As the cuff sparkled, she watched Grace's eyes glaze over for a moment before they quickly cleared.

Grace laughed condescendingly. "You can brainwash someone into believing something or doing something, but not into feeling something. Wanting is a feeling. The brainwashing can change thoughts and behavior, but not emotions or desires. You haven't figured that out yet?"

Anise narrowed her brows as she thought back to

how Dr. Smithton had tried to brainwash Jonathan into not loving her, but it didn't work. "I could brainwash you into believing the Plate isn't real."

Grace shrugged. "You could. But beliefs are easily changed, and how long do you think it would take me to realize that belief is wrong? I would come after you, and I certainly wouldn't be as nice as I am now."

"Okay," Anise said, trying to think quickly. "Then I can brainwash you into ordering the pilot to turn the plane around."

"Sure," Grace agreed. "But then Morty or Fred would most assuredly beat us to the Plate, and I think we both know they won't share. Then what?"

Anise frowned. "So we'll continue on our trip. But I could make you stay on the plane when we land."

"We're not landing at an airport. We'll be in a very remote location."

"So?"

"So I've already ordered the pilot to stay in the cockpit until we've left the plane. He can't help you if he can't hear you behind that heavy door."

"You must've ordered a driver?" Anise asked.

Grace lazily stretched her arms over her head. "Yes, but by the time we land, the Jewelry will have run out of charge and will be useless to you. He won't help you either. He only takes orders from me."

"Fine," said Anise, feeling defeated. "Once we land, I'll just go off on my own. I don't need you."

"Really?" Grace challenged her. "So when we land in Florida, you have a plan of where to go, and you have the money to get there by yourself?"

"Tell me where I have to go to find the Plate!" Anise demanded, intending to brainwash Grace into revealing information. The cuff sparkled and Grace's eyes glazed over.

"I have no idea. My plan is to follow Dromly," Grace responded before her eyes cleared.

Anise's body stiffened. "Money. No, you kidnapped me. As far as I know, my wallet is still at Jonathan's apartment. But he'll be coming after me, you know. I'm sure he's on his way right now along with Kent, Lorelei... and Nate." She spit Nate's name out quickly. *Please let her be lying about Nate.* Her stomach carried a hot coal. "Is there any soda on this plane?" She got up and found the small package of snacks and drinks in the back. Cold ginger ale was the best medicine.

"Lorelei," grumbled Grace with a frown. "Kent's been taking care of her."

Anise took a swig of her ginger ale. "That's right. Dan didn't kill her."

Grace snorted. "I should've known that Dan couldn't handle the simplest of tasks." Waving the thought away with her hand, she changed the subject. "Anyway, you're right, I have no doubt your curator friend is on his way. I'm sure you know who else will be coming for you."

Anise looked down at her hands and twisted her garnet ring around her finger. "Dr. Smithton."

"That's right," Grace told her in a disturbing and uncharacteristically calm manner. "Morty wants us to believe his plan is to find the Plate and use it to inflict his utopia fantasy on the world, but I don't buy that bullshit for a second. What the hell does that candy-ass really want?"

"I wish I knew." Anise watched as Grace started pacing up and down the aisle of the plane.

"I think you might know. You and Nate were whispering about something at one point when you were at Kent's that I couldn't hear," Grace said. "What was it?"

Les. Anise was relieved that Grace hadn't heard that part. If she knew that Les also had king's blood, who knows what she'd do to him to get it? "None of your business."

Grace dismissively waved her hand in the air. "It doesn't matter. There's no way that you know anything about Morty that I don't."

"What do *you* want with the Plate?" Anise asked boldly.

Grace spun around to face the younger woman and loomed over her. "What business is that of yours?" she snapped.

"Because I'm the last one with king's blood, I'm the protector of the Plate. If you want my help in finding it, I need to know what you were hoping to do with it. No one who knows you well—Dr. Smithton, Nate, Lorelei—would ever trust you with the kind of power the Jewelry would give you, much less the Plate. I can only imagine all the evil things they'd think you'd want to do. But I want to hear your side. Tell me. Please."

The sincerity of Anise's words seemed to calm Grace's anger, and she sat back down. "All right." She took a short pause. "The Plate of Destiny is said to have the secrets of life and death inlaid on it. Time, suffering, heartbreak—none of this would be a concern for someone who possesses the knowledge on the Plate."

Anise understood immediately what Grace was trying to say. "You lost someone," she said. "You want to bring them back."

Grace sat perfectly still, a stone-like expression on her face.

Anise could see through the flat affect that Grace was hurting. Maybe being cured of the side effects of the cuff had changed her after all. She remembered how much Jonathan had suffered from the side effects of the cuff. Grace had gone through the same experience but for much, much longer. Anise almost felt sorry for her. "You actually cared about someone like a real human being. Who was it?" she asked, her curiosity taking over.

Chapter 2

Anise's question made Grace think about Thomas. "Shut up!" she snapped. Grace felt herself tense up and willed away the tears that threatened to make an appearance. She was here to force Anise to cure her, find the Plate, bring back Thomas, and go somewhere with him where no one would ever find them. And her plan was going well so far. Tampering with Erin's brakes to ensure Anise would want to find the Plate was an excellent start. So these tears were unnecessary. She was being weak. But somehow, she felt that perhaps trying not to appear weak shouldn't be one of her main concerns anymore. Killing an innocent girl also didn't feel like the stroke of genius it had a few minutes ago. Instead, it felt like...she had no idea what it felt like, but the delight was gone. She closed her eyes in confusion as she tried to remember who she was before the brainwashing, before Thomas, before Morty, before she killed her father...

She felt Anise squeezing her hand. "Well, whoever it is, I'm sorry," Anise said.

Grace's eyes flew open at the unexpected touch. Suddenly she was blind and falling backward, and she reached her arms out to grab on to anything, but they found nothing. Then everything was very still. Colors started appearing. Rapidly, the scene before her eyes began changing from one location to another. Where the plane had gone, she didn't know, but she was standing in a tiny apartment watching a giant throw a lamp at Anise. A heartbeat later, the giant lay dead on a white tile floor, a bullet hole between his eyes. Then there was a woman ridiculing Anise and a man ignoring her. The man and woman then lay dead and bloody in a car at the bottom of a cliff.

"Grace? Are you okay?"

Grace suddenly found herself back on the plane with Anise's hazel eyes staring at her. She ripped her hand away from Anise's. "What the hell did you do to me?" she demanded.

"What are you talking about?"

"You said you cured me! You lied! I just had another hallucination!" She put her hand to her head but surprisingly still didn't feel the need to pull on her hair.

"I didn't lie! I did cure you!" Anise insisted. "You didn't seem to be hallucinating to me. There was no hair pulling that I saw."

"Oh, and you're the expert?" Grace snarled.

"No, but I've seen both you and Jonathan have hallucinations, and this didn't look the same at all. Your eyes were darting back and forth. You also seemed to be in no pain. Am I right?"

"I was in no pain," agreed Grace. "But I saw things that weren't here!" Breathing angrily, she gave Anise a stare that she hoped would haunt the annoying girl for the rest of her life. "How dare you lie to me?! Fix it! Now! Or else one phone call from me can guarantee that your curator friend will never make it to Florida alive!"

"There's no need for threats," Anise told Grace. She stood and glared as if trying to appear brave.

Grace rolled her eyes. With her wavering voice, the girl sounded anything but.

"I'll try to cure you again," Anise added.

"You won't try," insisted Grace. "You'll *do it.*"

Anise glared at Grace again but grabbed her hand and closed her eyes. "Heal from the side effects of the cuff," she whispered.

As soon as she felt Anise's hand on hers, Grace felt like she was falling again and grabbed on to her seat's armrest. She was standing on a mountain pass and saw a car being pushed off the road by another vehicle. The first car rolled down a small cliff. Looking inside, she saw a man and a woman, bloody and dying. Suddenly she was back on the plane, looking at the silly girl in front of her, her eyes closed and her face intense. "Let go of me!" she snapped, ripping her hand out of Anise's grasp. "What are you doing to me? I had another hallucination! As soon as you grabbed my hand!"

"I'm not doing anything to you!" cried Anise. "I'm trying to cure you, but you're not making it easy. And again, it didn't seem like you were hallucinating, at least not in the same way you used to. Before, you would pull on your hair and look like you were in a lot of pain. These last two times your eyes were moving back and forth rapidly like you were looking at something. Maybe you're experiencing something else."

"Don't tell me what I am or am not experiencing. I'm the one experiencing it!" yelled Grace.

"Okay, that's fair," agreed Anise. "But you do have to admit, it's different from your prior hallucinations, am I right?"

Grace narrowed her eyes. "Yes."

"Let's try to figure this out," Anise offered. "Are you comfortable sharing what you saw just now?"

Comfortable sharing? This girl sounded like the irritating prison counselor she'd been made to talk to. Ignoring her instinct to smack the girl across her face, Grace explained what she had seen. "I saw a car go off a cliff on a mountain pass. There was a man and a woman inside dying. During the first hallucination I had after you *supposedly* cured me, I saw almost the same scene. I also saw a giant man throw a lamp at you, then he lay dead on a tile floor." She looked at Anise and saw her fighting off some tears. "What are you blubbering about?"

"I told you I'm doing the best I can. I'm honestly trying to cure you. There's no need for you to bring up the worst times in my life. Haven't you tried to hurt me enough already?" Anise complained.

"What the hell are you talking about?"

"The giant that lay dead on the tile floor—that was Brian Houser, my ex-boyfriend three years ago. You're the one who shot him between the eyes in the Springfield Museum!"

"Oh, that's right," Grace said thoughtfully. "I almost forgot about him."

"How did you know he threw a lamp at me?" Anise demanded. "Only my friends know about that, and I know none of them would ever tell you or anyone else about it."

"I told you, I just saw it when you touched my hand." Grace got up and paced the aisle of the plane in confusion. "Am I seeing your memories instead of my own? Do you know a couple who died in a car crash?"

"Yes! They were my parents!" snapped Anise. "But I never saw them in the car, so it can't be my memories you're seeing."

"Interesting. Were you thinking about them just before you touched my hand?"

"No, but they're always there in the back of my mind," Anise replied. "Brian, too." She looked down at her hands.

Grace glared at the young woman who was sitting very still. "What is it? What are you remembering?"

"My garnet ring," Anise said about the tiny red stone on her finger. "It was a gift from Brian for my 23rd birthday, and I can't bring myself to take it off. Not when I'm responsible for his death. The ring is a good reminder that my actions have consequences."

Grace rolled her eyes. *Such a drama queen.* "Whatever. Let's try it again," said Grace, grabbing the young woman's hand. Grace had the falling sensation again, but it was getting less and less frightening each time. She was back in the small apartment. Brian took a swing at Anise's face and missed. Her mother scolded her. Her father ignored her questions. Grace felt a sense of sorrow and unworthiness that she knew was not her own. Suddenly, she was looking up into a pair of cobalt blue eyes, and it made her think of Thomas. But these eyes didn't belong to her deceased husband. They were her grandson's. Another emotion was coming through. Grace laughed out loud. Love. Lust. Excitement. That was something she hadn't felt for a very long time. There was also anger and heartbreak when she looked into those eyes. The feeling was so uncomfortable that Grace turned around. She saw arms holding her. Tilting her head back up, she saw light green eyes and dark rimmed glasses. It was Anise's museum curator friend. Love. Comfort. Friendship. She hadn't felt that for a long time either. Her fingers felt cold as she realized Anise had taken her hand away.

"It's been several minutes," Anise told her. "Your eyes were moving rapidly again. What did you see?"

Experiencing the depth of Anise's emotions left Grace feeling uncomfortably empty. She had forgotten everything that life had to offer. All she had felt for the last fifty or sixty years had been pain, rage, fear, and hate. She looked at the young woman and would've given anything to trade places with her at that moment. She frowned. "Brian was abusive to you," she said and watched her young companion tear up again. "I would've *ended* him. Why didn't *you*?"

"He was my first long-term boyfriend," Anise admitted. "I had loved him, and he wasn't abusive when we first got together. He'd always had an anger problem, but he was gentle with *me*. But things changed. He tried to hit me once and threw a lamp at me. I left him right after that."

"It was good that you left him, but I still would've ended him," said Grace through a clenched jaw. "Your parents too. Your mother was too harsh on you, and your father ignored you."

"You saw that?" Anise asked, her eyes wide.

Grace nodded. "Your parents disrespected you until the day they died. Why didn't you do something to change that, or cut them out of your life? If you don't respect yourself, no one else will either. There's no reason for you to be so weak." Grace looked at her with disgust and was surprised to see her smile.

"Thank you," Anise replied. "That's good advice." After a short but somewhat awkward silence, Anise asked, "You were laughing at one point during your vision. What else did you see?"

"You're in love with my grandson," Grace answered, suppressing a laugh. Why she found that funny, she wasn't sure. Maybe because she still saw Nate as the wide-eyed child who'd constantly annoyed her.

"Yes, I am," Anise confirmed.

"You also love your curator friend."

"Jonathan. Yes." Anise's hands began to fidget. "Have *you* ever been in love with two men at the same time?"

Thomas. Morty. Grace paused, remembering the old emotions. "I have."

"What did *you* do?"

It had been so long ago it felt like a dream to her, but when all the memories and feelings came rushing back, she felt like she had woken up. "My situation was a little different. My relationship with one was over before I met the other. But I still loved him."

"Did you ever think about going back to him?"

"No."

"Why not?"

"Because as much as I loved him...I loved the other

man more."

Anise's face lit up. "I'm thrilled to know that you were an actual human being before you became a..."

"A monster?"

Anise looked at her but said nothing.

Grace was surprised at how much she was opening up to this young woman. Anise reminded Grace very much of her mother. Annie Polk, just like Anise, was loving and kind, more so than anyone else she'd ever met. They both saw the best in others and forgave very quickly, sometimes too quickly. They wanted nothing more than to help others, give others the love they needed to heal, and always try to do what's right. They were like angels on earth. Grace had always thought of Anise as weak, but on second thought, perhaps she had a different kind of strength. Being strong doesn't mean being alpha, or fearless, or a bully. Continuously trying to make the world better instead of something that fueled hate, jealousy, greed, violence, sadness, or even indifference took a strength, awareness, and dedication that Grace knew she'd never have. She began to have a new respect for the young woman. Perhaps Anise was the strongest of them all.

Anise had another question for Grace. "So, Kent told us that one of Professor Dromly's students wrote a report about a European archeologist who found a seer's jewel in a cave. Do you know what the seer's jewel is?"

"*I* was the student who wrote that report." Grace thought as hard as she could about the report she had written in college sixty years ago. She looked at Anise when she remembered. "Since you're going to help me find the Plate of Destiny, you might as well know."

After listening to the whole story, Anise asked, "So, let me make sure I understand. The seer's jewel is an obsidian attached to a wand. When you were in college, your professor initiated you with the seer's jewel because you had red hair, and only a redheaded woman can be a seer. Now you're the only person in the world who can see the symbols on the Plate of Destiny because they're invisible to everyone except seers?"

Grace ignored her to concentrate on her racing mind.

Anise spoke up again, "Do you think these visions you just had might have something to do with you being initiated as a seer? And if so, why would they start now when you were initiated decades ago?"

Grace had been wondering the same thing. Her eyes narrowed as she thought about who might be responsible for this fresh hell. "Good question."

Chapter 3

Jonathan followed Nate down the hallway of their hotel toward their rooms and glared at the back of Nate's head. They'd never have known that Grace was taking Anise to Florida to find the Plate of Destiny if Nate hadn't gotten it out of Dr. S. And they'd never have made it to Florida so quickly if Nate hadn't been there to charter the private jet with no notice—and also somehow book four hotel rooms in a nice hotel that had no vacancy according to the website. Jonathan couldn't stand how Nate got whatever he wanted. Just thinking about it made him want to ask with genuine interest how he did it but also find a way to cut his insufferable arrogance down a notch or two. Not that Nate had bragged about it, but he'd acted as if it was an everyday task that was no big deal. *Cocky prick.*

Jonathan found himself worrying about Anise and what being with Grace might be doing to her. She was too anxious a person to have to deal with all this stress. She couldn't even leave her apartment without wearing the amulet or else she'd get panic attacks. When that happened, he'd frantically try to convince her to take medication or at least talk to someone, but she'd only get annoyed and tell him to stop. But it frightened him every time she freaked out. Jonathan firmly believed that

Nate and his violent grandmother and everything they'd put her through had been the reasons for Anise's declining mental health over the last three years. After all, she hadn't had agoraphobia when they'd first met.

Jonathan wished there was more he could do to help Anise. He glared at the back of Nate's head again. Keeping her away from the criminal psychopath would be a good start. After all the arguing he and Nate had done on the plane, Jonathan knew he should keep his mouth shut, but he found himself saying the words anyway. "Once we find Anise and get her home, you need to stay away from her. You've gotten her into too many dangerous situations, and I won't let that happen anymore."

"Fuck you, Boy Scout," Nate shot back over his shoulder. "She's had the amulet around her neck the entire time I've known her. Even if she hadn't, I would've protected her with my life."

"Yeah, right," Jonathan scoffed. He had an urge to kick the tray with a half-eaten meal on it that someone left in the hallway.

"The times she wasn't safe, she was with *you*," Nate shot back.

"That's not fair!" complained Jonathan. "That's when I was brainwashed!"

Nate turned around to glare at him. "Okay, fine. Three years ago you took her to the Springfield Museum to try to fight me, Dan, and Grace for the earrings. You weren't brainwashed then. Just stupid. If I hadn't saved your asses, you'd both be rotting in prison right now, or else Grace would've killed you."

"She was wearing the amulet then, too," said Jonathan, using Nate's excuse. "I also would've protected her with my life."

"And you would've had to if I hadn't traded three years of my life to save yours!"

"You're so full of shit!" exclaimed Jonathan. "Anise believes you went to prison to protect her even though it's a lie. I keep trying to show her you're not the big hero she thinks you are. I know the truth."

Nate's mouth raised into a prideful smirk, presumably getting a charge out of Anise thinking he's a hero. Jonathan took a deep breath and made himself stare at the beachy art on the wall, trying to calm the visceral reaction that crooked grin always gave him. *What an ass.*

"And what *is* the truth?" Nate asked.

"You wanted to be rid of Dan and Grace. You wanted to take them down, but the only way you could do that is to go down with them. You just made sure most of the blame got pinned on them so you could be released and infect Anise's life with your presence again as soon as possible." Jonathan's voice got louder as he continued unloading his pile of anger on Nate. "You're a selfish, arrogant liar! You're a criminal, and you're untrustworthy. You're not good enough for her!" His cheeks burst into flames.

Nate flashed the cocky sideways grin again as if he knew how much Jonathan hated it. "And you think you are?" Nate asked him calmly. "I know I don't have to remind you who she chose to be with."

"Like I said before," Jonathan snarled, "don't get used to it. We both know you're going to fuck it up. All I have to do is sit back and wait." He was a little disappointed that his comment didn't seem to upset Nate at all.

"Good luck with that," Nate replied, his eyes laughing at Jonathan. He stuck his key card in his door.

"We need to leave to find Anise right away," Jonathan said from a few doors down. "I still can't believe you wanted to check in first."

"I didn't *want* to check in first," Nate argued. "Kent was so motion sick from the plane that he could barely walk. And my mother's been through a lot. I had to make sure they had a place to rest before I left them. I was hoping we could split up so at least one of us could start looking for Anise, but there were no more cars available."

"Fine. I get that," Jonathan conceded. "But we still need to leave right away. I'm just dropping my bag in my room and then grabbing the car keys from Kent."

"I need a few minutes," Nate said.

"For what? We have no idea where Anise is! We're going to be driving around all night. We need to leave now!" Jonathan opened his door, threw his bag inside, and let it shut again.

"No, we need to be smart, not drive around all night. Just give me a few minutes. I'll meet you at Kent's room."

"What does a few minutes mean? For what? We don't have a few minutes!" Jonathan cried with annoyance as Nate ignored him and disappeared into his room.

Jonathan cursed at the bright red hexagons on the carpet. He'd give Nate three minutes, but that's it. There was no way he could wait any longer.

✳✳✳

"JONATHAN, HELLO," LORELEI SAID, TRYING TO hide her disappointment that her son hadn't been the one to knock on her hotel door.

"I'm sorry about how heated things got between Nate and me on the plane," Jonathan apologized. "Normally I wouldn't speak that way to anyone. It's not an excuse, but I'm really worried about Anise, and I'm on edge."

"I'm sure Nate feels the same," Lorelei said to the polite young man. When Jonathan stared at the floor instead of agreeing with her, she continued. "I remember him as such a loving child. Being raised by Grace has made him angry. My heart hurts for him. I wish I knew what to do to help him."

Jonathan gave her a kind response that she barely heard. She couldn't stop thinking about Nate and hoping he was okay. Jonathan excused himself, and she shut the door. The plane ride had been long and full of ugliness between the two young men. They couldn't seem to get along and had both said some horrible things to each other. She'd attempted to get Nate to stop and cool down, but for some reason, that seemed to make things worse. Taking a deep breath, she let it out slowly. Hopefully there'd be time for her to have a good talk with her son soon.

NATE PUT HIS PHONE DOWN AND rubbed his eyes. It'd taken longer than he'd thought, but he finally found the information he needed and knew exactly where to start searching. Boy Scout would have a fit that they hadn't left yet, but he'd have to get over it. Nate had no doubt they'd find Anise within the hour. Maybe two, tops.

He tapped on his mother's door and watched her eyes light up at the sight of him. "I'm fine, thank you," she told him when he asked if she was okay. "Go find her."

Nate turned around and found Kent standing there with a stack of trip journals piled up in his arms. It was so tall, he couldn't see over the top.

"Oh my goodness, how many are there?" Lorelei asked him as she grabbed some of the books.

"About two more stacks like this," he replied.

"Feeling better?" Nate asked him.

"Yes, finally. Thanks."

"Are you ready to go look for Anise?" Nate was feeling as impatient as Boy Scout had been.

"We thought it might be more productive if we split up," Kent said. "We ordered another car. It should be here any minute. In the meantime, we're going to continue reading these trip journals of my father's and hopefully find some helpful information about the location of the Plate of Destiny."

"Okay. Can I get the keys to the rental? I want to head out now," Nate asked Kent, eager to see Anise again. "And where's Boy Scout?"

"Jonathan grabbed them from me about fifteen minutes ago," Kent told him. "I figured the two of you were going together."

"So did I." Nate looked out the window of his mother's room. "The car is gone." He wanted to say more, but held his tongue. He hadn't liked the look on Lorelei's face when he'd gotten angry on the plane and shouted some choice words at Boy Scout. He didn't want her to think he was anything like Grace. "I'll see you later," he mumbled, walking quickly out the door and getting on his phone.

GRACE'S PILOT STEPPED OUT OF A touristy bar, somewhat satisfied with the drink he'd had. Another few would've been nice to calm his nerves after working for the scary old devil woman. Usually he needed to get drunk after any interaction with her, but this time he'd booked a flight to somewhere where he hoped she wouldn't be able to find him again. He'd need to hurry to make the flight. He could drink on the plane.

As he took a shortcut through an alley toward the bus stop, he heard footsteps behind him. Casually looking over his shoulder, he saw a tall, dark-haired man entering the alley. A tiny spark of fear ignited his gut. Even though it was probably just a lost tourist, he picked up the pace of his steps nevertheless. The footsteps behind him grew quicker and louder. He glanced over his shoulder again and saw that the man was gaining on him. Something was familiar about him, but he couldn't remember what. Where had he seen this man before?

The pilot attempted an awkward movement of something between a trot and a power walk as the whisky he'd tasted sloshed around in his stomach. The footsteps behind him grew louder and quicker still, and he looked behind him to see the man break into a run like a tomcat hunting a petrified mouse. The spark of fear was now a full blown fire. The pilot bolted forward, and suddenly the place where the alley met the street felt much further away than it did a moment ago. He looked over his shoulder again. The man was almost on him.

"Stay away!" the pilot huffed and puffed. "I have a knife!"

The warning didn't deter his pursuer at all. He felt his shoulders being grabbed and his back and skull slammed against the brick wall in the shadows of the alley.

"Please," the pilot begged, "I don't want any trouble."

"There won't be any if you tell me what I want to know. Where did she go?"

"She wh-who?" stammered the pilot.

"You know who."

The pilot looked up into the taller man's face and remembered what felt familiar about him. It was the devil woman's grandson with those unnaturally blue eyes, their glare so demonically warning him that dragging him to hell would be a pleasure. The pilot quickly weighed his options. He *could* provide the information that'd been demanded of him, but if the devil woman knew he'd given away her location what would she do to him? She'd warned him to keep his mouth shut, or else, and he decided he'd better do as she'd asked. "How do you people always know how to find me?" he asked. It was like they had a supernatural power of always knowing where he was no matter where he went.

"Tell me where she is!"

"I don't know!" the pilot replied, wishing he could stop shaking.

The demon tightened his grip on the pilot's collar. "I don't believe you. You flew her all the way to Florida.

You've must've heard something."

The pilot shook his head and continued to tremble.

"Okay." The devil woman's grandson took an envelope out of an inner pocket in his jacket and showed the pilot the contents. "Do you remember now?"

The pilot drew in a sharp breath. His eyes grew as he looked at the stack of large bills. That amount of money could help him disappear. Hide on an island. Change his name. He'd be rid of these evil beings forever. But what if the scary old woman found out he'd betrayed her before his flight took off? His fingers gingerly traced the outline of the knife handle in his pants.

"Well?" the demon demanded, pulling him forward only to slam his back against the wall again.

The pilot grabbed the envelope with one hand and tried to stab the man with his pocket knife with the other. He was quick, however, and grabbed the pilot's wrist. Looking down, the pilot saw he'd only superficially sliced the man's waist as a small amount of blood began seeping through the man's fingers of his other hand as he grabbed his wound.

The blue-eyed monster snarled at him. "You shouldn't have done that."

Panicking, the pilot dropped the knife while pulling his wrist free and tried to run, shoving the envelope in his shirt pocket. He managed a few steps before he felt himself being tackled, and his face was on the pavement before he had time to put his hands out to catch himself. He was forcefully turned over and saw his own pocket knife in the monster's hand. It lowered to threaten his neck, the point freeing a trickle of blood that ran down behind his ear. The pilot opened his mouth to apologize, but words were replaced by a high-pitched squeal.

"Don't be stupid," the demon warned him. "Tell me where she is, and I might let you live."

The pilot felt his bowels loosen. He could either die now by this evil being's hand in a puddle of his own shit, or give him what he wanted and at least try to hide from the devil woman. With the amount of money in that envelope, he at least had a chance. "I heard her making a hotel reservation." He gave up the location of where the old woman was staying.

"Was there anyone with her?" the nightmare demanded, pressing the knife a little further into the pilot's neck.

The stream of his blood warmed the chill running up and down his spine. Nodding, the pilot answered in the affirmative. "A...a young lady."

"She was alive?"

"Yes. I watched through the window as she stepped off the plane." To his great relief, the knife was removed from his throat. The pilot closed his eyes and let out a deep, shaky breath. He never saw the punch coming. And because his hand then covered his aching eye, he never saw the second one. Or the third. He lost count after that. Right before he passed out, he felt the envelope of money along with his hopes and dreams being pulled out of his pocket and heard the demon's footsteps fade into the distance.

JONATHAN RUBBED HIS EYES AND LEANED back in the seat of the car in the parking lot of the fifth hotel he'd been to. No one had recognized Anise or Grace from the pictures he'd shown them. He started the engine. Nothing would stop him until he found her.

As he drove to the next hotel on his list, he wondered how he'd confront Grace if this was the one. The thought of meeting Grace again made him shiver. Maybe he should've waited for Nate. He really didn't want Nate with him, but it would've been smart to bring him along. Nate knew Grace and most assuredly had a better idea of how to handle her. Plus, Jonathan was starting to feel guilty for purposely leaving him behind. If *Nate* had left without *him*, he'd have been livid.

Pulling into the parking lot of the next hotel, he tried not to picture Anise in Grace's clutches and what Grace might be doing to her. Was she okay? The worry made him feel sick. He wondered again how Anise was doing with her agoraphobia. Could she handle the panic attacks she was probably having?

Chapter 4

Anise felt her wrists burning as she struggled against the ropes. Unlike Jonathan and Dr. Smithton, Grace knew how to immobilize her victims. Escape would be much harder than it was the last time Anise had been tied up. Just like Grace had said it would, the Jewelry had lost its charge. With a gun near her skull, she'd had no choice but to accompany Grace to her hotel room. Once there, Grace had bound her wrists and ankles to a chair and removed the Armor Jewelry, placing it in her purse. Grace had then left the room without a word.

Three hours later, Anise's cries for help had gone unheard through the gag Grace had placed in her mouth. Ignoring the pain, she kept struggling. Anise sighed with relief as the rope that had bound her wrists to the chair finally fell to the floor. She removed the gag and then bent over and untied each ankle as well. As soon as she was free, she heard the key in the door. *Shit!* She loosely looped the ropes around her ankles, put the gag back in her mouth, and held her hands behind her back, her heart beating loudly in her chest.

"I brought food," Grace announced, placing a brown paper bag on the desk and her purse next to it. "Do you want some?" She ripped the gag from Anise's mouth, causing her to wince in pain.

"Untie me!" Anise demanded.

Grace gave her a smirk. "I'll take that as a no." She took her cell phone out of her purse and squinted at the screen.

In one swift motion, Anise stood and punched her captor in the throat, grabbed Grace's purse, and ran. She opened the hotel room door and peeked over her shoulder. Even though Grace was on her hands and knees wheezing, she was also trying to stand up as she crawled toward the door. Anise sprinted for the stairwell at the end of the hall. She heard the elevator door open, and looked back to see Grace stumbling into it. Anise's heart pounded as her footsteps echoed down five flights of concrete stairs. What if the elevator was faster than she was? She felt a wave of hope when she rounded the last turn in the stairwell and saw the door to the lobby. Bolting down the last flight, she leapt for the door and stopped dead in her tracks.

Grace pushed open the door in front of her and stepped into the stairwell. Anise turned and tried to run back up the stairs, but felt Grace catch her shoulder. She let out a cry of pain and couldn't help but sink to her knees as she weakly pulled on the old woman's fingers that were pressing into a spot near her neck. Seeing stars, Anise felt her body slowly sliding down the two steps she'd managed to climb.

"Stupid girl!" Grace sneered. Suddenly, she let out a cry and her fingers released Anise's neck.

As the stars cleared from her eyes, Anise looked up to see two large men with tight grips on each of Grace's arms. She picked up Grace's purse as Grace struggled against the two behemoths.

"Let me go!" Grace screamed, kicking the men in the knees. They barely seemed to notice.

"Are you Anise Viston?" one of the men demanded of Anise.

"No," Anise replied, rapidly shaking her head. She ran past the men, narrowly averting the reach of one of them. Darting into the crowded lobby, she wove her way through the mass of people trying to check in or gathering near the restaurant for dinner. Pushing through the front door, she took in a breath of city air.

Now what? Knowing she had no charged Armor Jewelry to assist her, she felt a panic attack coming on. Standing on the sidewalk, she frantically looked around the busy street while digging in the purse for Grace's wallet. There were shops and people and restaurants and traffic she could hide in, but she had no money to find someplace to stay. All that was in the purse was the Armor Jewelry and Grace's gun which she knew she'd never use. Headlights glared in her eyes in the evening dusk. It would be dark soon; she'd need a place to hide out, and she was exhausted even though her panic attack made her start running away as fast as she could. The sidewalk was busy and her attempt at running was more like a series of continuously interrupted jogging as she avoided collisions with people. Maybe she'd have a little luck and pass a police station and get some help. Forcing her way through the crowded downtown, her anxiety grew exponentially. Her arms went numb, and the world started spinning as her heart pounded so loudly she could hear it above the street noise. Looking around, her eyes attempted to find a trash can to vomit into, just in case. She wondered if anyone could point her in the right direction of a police station. Peering behind her, she saw one of Grace's large captors step out of the hotel and look around. Keeping her head low, she gasped for air as her stomach tightened, and she put a hand on a street lamp to keep herself from passing out.

Her breath caught when she heard a familiar male voice call her name. She turned around and saw Nate getting off of a beat-up, ancient motorcycle that looked like it might fall apart if the wind started blowing. She darted in his direction, and he ran toward her. She forgot for the moment that she was angry with him as she threw her arms around his neck, and he held her tightly.

"Are you okay?" he asked with concern in his eyes. She was trembling violently.

She turned her head and saw Grace's captor still searching for her. "I'm okay. Just get me out of here. We have to hurry."

They rode off, and she held him from behind tightly, leaning her head on his back and closing her eyes. Watching Nate zipping through the lines of cars in heavy traffic would only make her anxiety worse. After the panic attack began to wane somewhat, her empty stomach started to ache. "Can we stop somewhere? I haven't eaten since I don't know when," she said by his ear.

"Of course," he replied and pulled over in front of a café. "Are you sure you're okay, honey? You're still shaking. And your wrists are bleeding."

"Oh, shit, I'm sorry," she said, as she noticed she'd bled all over his clothes from holding on to him while they were on the motorcycle.

He shook his head. "I don't care about that. I care about you. What happened?"

"Grace had a gun and tied me up when the Jewelry lost its charge. I had to fight my way out." She told him of the two men and how they'd unintentionally helped her escape.

His eyes narrowed and his mouth frowned. "Fucking Grace."

Memories of what Grace had said on the plane about Nate visiting her in prison were rushing back. She was too tired and hungry to confront him at the moment though and was grateful when the host showed them to their table.

After they ordered, and Anise had washed her wrists in the restroom, she relaxed into her chair next to Nate. His presence was still comforting, and her anxiety was at a manageable level, even as she thought about how she wanted to confront him.

"I'm so relieved you're okay. I've never been so worried in my life." He took her hand. "I love you, honey."

Even though she loved him too, she didn't feel like saying it. Not when he may have lied to her again. Luckily, their food came at that moment, and she dug in hungrily.

"Listen, I need to tell you something." His voice sounded hesitant, almost like it didn't want to work at all. "I got voicemails from both Vanessa and Joy when they couldn't reach you. Erin was in an accident."

"Oh, god, so it's true?" Anise put down her fork, suddenly nauseated.

"You heard?"

"Grace told me. I thought she was lying."

"I'm sorry, honey." Nate handed her a couple of his napkins. "What can I do?"

She dabbed her eyes with the napkins. "Nothing."

"If you want, I can call for another plane. We can go straight to the airport and on to Philadelphia so you can heal Les."

"Thanks, but no," she declined. "Now that I know Erin is really gone, I need to find the Plate of Destiny before anyone else does." She picked up her fork again. As nauseated as she was, she was also famished and hoped that food might help.

As she ate, she told him about how she'd healed Grace with the Jewelry, the seer abilities, and that Grace was planning to follow Fred Dromly to look for the Plate of Destiny. "You wouldn't believe how much she changed," Anise told him as she stabbed the last bite of her food with her fork. "Granted she was still cold, unfeeling, and manipulative, but there were moments there when she was acting like a real person."

He scoffed. "I'll never trust her."

Anise frowned. "Speaking of Grace and trust...there are some things I want to know. I was alone in Jonathan's bathroom when she kidnapped me. How did you know it was Grace who had me?"

"We didn't at first. Smithton told us."

"Dr. Smithton? How did *he* know?"

Nate shrugged. "He was the only one who wasn't fooled when she faked her own death. He's known her since they were younger than us. He might be the only person in the world who knows her better than I do."

While Nate paid the bill, Anise wondered if there was anything else besides their mutual desire to find the Plate of Destiny that made Grace and Dr. Smithton hate each other so much. She looked at Nate and grew angry again. The not knowing if he'd helped Grace escape was killing her, and there were already too many things killing her. She had to confront him, and it had to be now. "Grace told me you were the one who gave her the neurotoxin that allowed her to fake her death and escape from prison."

He grimaced. "Shit," he said under his breath. "I wanted to tell you."

Everything around her grew dark. "So it's true?" Anise demanded.

"I know how much Grace terrifies you; she terrifies everybody," he continued. "I know it looks like—"

"Did you give her the neurotoxin or not, Nate?" Anise demanded, cutting him off.

"Yes. But—"

"No!" she said firmly. "I don't want to hear it! Grace tried to kill me when we were fighting over the amulet three years ago. Have you forgotten that?"

"No, but—"

"By giving her that neurotoxin, you freed the person who wanted me dead! I don't know what your reasons were as to why you did it, but you gave absolutely no thought as to how this might affect me and my chances to stay alive! Or maybe you did and you didn't care!"

He gave her a confused look. "It's not like that. I

didn't know what she was planning to do with it."

"Nate, you're one of the smartest people I know. I have a hard time believing that you had no idea what she might do with the neurotoxin. Plus, that stuff is lethal. Did it even cross your mind that she might've wanted it to try to kill me?"

"I meant I didn't know she was planning to use it to escape. It wasn't a lethal dose, so I knew she couldn't kill anyone with it. I thought—"

While he was speaking, Anise opened her mouth, speechless for a moment before she interrupted Nate again. "Do you *hear* yourself? You knew you provided Grace with a toxic substance, whether it was lethal or not, and you had no reservations about it whatsoever?"

"I *knew* it wasn't lethal. And I did have reservations, but—"

"But you did it anyway. Your grandmother is a murderer, and you gave her something she could hurt people with! Does human life mean nothing to you? You can't claim innocence here, Nate. You knew you were doing something wrong because you lied to me about it!"

"I didn't lie. I just—"

"Right, I know. It wasn't a lie, you just kept it a secret from me that the woman who tried to kill me was about to get every opportunity to try it again! Don't patronize me with nuances!" She crossed her arms and sat back in her chair with a huff.

"I didn't help her escape!" he insisted. "On its own, the neurotoxin wasn't strong enough to make her seem dead. She must've mixed it with someth—"

"There's nothing you can say that will make this okay," she said, on the verge of tears.

He sighed in frustration. "If you remember, I was trying to tell you something before this whole shit went down. I asked to talk to you in the car and then again at Boy Scout's apartment. This is what I wanted to tell you."

She narrowed her eyes. "When exactly did you go

visit Grace?"

He thought for a moment. "Right after we got back from trying to find my mother in Nevada."

"So about two weeks ago?! But you didn't try to tell me until yesterday. Why did you wait?"

Nate took a deep breath. "Grace told me that Smithton was using the cuff to form a cult. He wants to use his cult to find the Plate of Destiny. I was afraid that as soon as I told you all that, you'd tell Boy Scout, who would then tell Smithton. And if Smithton had any idea how much we knew about his plans, it might prompt him to come after you. He's already tried to take your blood! So I hesitated. It wouldn't have been the first time your mouth got you into trouble. But I did want to tell you, and I did try."

"That excuses nothing. You still gave Grace a means to escape from prison, putting my life in danger! She wouldn't have been able to kidnap me if it hadn't been for you!"

"I got them to put Grace in solitary until they could get her a transfer to another prison. I made sure there was no way she could use it to hurt anyone."

Anise leaned forward to hiss at him. "You think you're so smart and that you have everything under control all the time. But you don't. Grace easily outsmarts you. How could you not even consider the fact that she'd be able to use it to escape? Who knows who she's killed since she's been out? I think the only reason she didn't kill me is because she needed me to cure her. But if she manages to get the Jewelry back somehow, I doubt I'll survive much longer." She sat back in her chair, fuming. "She told me straight out that she needed to spill my blood on the Plate of Destiny in order to read it. She said it has to be fresh blood so she's glad you didn't let her kill me."

Nate's eyes widened. "Grace still wants your blood?"

"She said she only needs a few drops, but I don't believe it. As soon as we find the Plate, she'll be after me, and she'll kill me."

"I won't let that happen," Nate told her, taking her hand. "I'm calling the cops right now. They'll take her back to prison. She won't get out again."

Anise ripped her hand away. "You can't fix this! It's Grace. She'll figure out how to escape again."

"I won't let that happen," he repeated.

"Oh, shut up! You can't beat her. Every time you've tried, she's bested you. And even though she tried to kill me, you still helped her! Do you not see how much of a betrayal that is? You were wrong about how she was planning to use the neurotoxin, and you're probably wrong about everything else you think too!" She glared at him. "You obviously didn't care what happened to me when you helped Grace. You didn't give me a second thought. You said you *loved* me!"

"I was *only* thinking about you!" he shot back. "I didn't help her; I was trying to get information from her. And I *do* love you!"

"That has to be another lie," she argued, dabbing her eyes with her napkin. "You're just like Grace. You're a monster and incapable of love."

Anise watched as Nate got up from the table and left the restaurant. Through the front window, she saw him sit on the motorcycle to wait for her. His expression turned from angry to relaxed and far away in less than a minute. She wondered if he was dissociating and what he might be thinking about. She told herself she didn't care and joined him on the bike. "Let's go," she ordered.

ANISE FOLLOWED NATE DOWN THE HALLWAY of the hotel, grateful as hell that he'd found her, but still too livid to say a word to him.

"Anise!" exclaimed Kent when she and Nate entered

the hotel room. He dropped the trip journal he'd been reading on the small table next to his chair as he got up. "Thanks for texting us," he added to Nate. "We were so relieved when you found her."

Lorelei gave Anise a hug. "Are you okay?"

"I'm fine, thanks," Anise replied, hugging her back. "Grateful to be here with you, finally."

"Do you need anything?"

"No. Well, a shower and a change of clothes would be nice. Oh..." She remembered she didn't have any luggage since Grace had knocked her out and brought her to Florida against her will.

"I brought your bag that you packed," Nate told her. "It's in our room."

She nodded in his direction, looking at the floor. She told Kent and Lorelei she'd see them soon to let them know what happened and stepped out into the hallway. Her body was still exhausted from the panic attack she'd had on the street, and her stomach ached. The hotel felt safe, but she knew she wouldn't feel completely better until the amulet was charged again.

"I want my own room," she announced to Nate. "I don't want to be anywhere near you right now."

"The hotel is full," Nate responded without looking at her.

"Well then...you can sleep on the floor." She walked with Nate down the hall wondering what he'd say to that, but he kept his mouth shut. After a moment of silence she asked, "Where's Jonathan?"

Nate shrugged. "I don't know."

"What do you mean, you don't know? Did he come to Florida with you? Is he at the hotel?"

"He's probably still out looking for you."

"You haven't called him yet to tell him you found me?!"

"No," Nate replied matter-of-factly as he stuck the key in the door and entered their room.

"Why not?! *He'd* never do something like that to *you*."

He turned around to look at her for the first time since the restaurant.

"He wouldn't!" she confirmed after he raised his eyebrows at her questioningly. Grabbing her phone from her bag, she saw she didn't have much battery left, so she sent Jonathan a text instead of calling. Scrolling through her notifications, she saw she had voicemails from Vanessa and Joy that must be about Erin, but she felt like she'd die herself if she listened to them. Almost immediately, Jonathan texted back that he couldn't wait to see her and that he'd be there soon.

Without a word, she took her bag into the bathroom. She took all of the Armor Jewelry out of Grace's purse, rinsed them under the faucet, and set them on a towel next to the sink. Healing Grace took up a lot of their energy and they'd lost their charge before their plane had landed. If only they'd kept a charge a little longer, she could've made her escape after they landed in the middle of nowhere, far from the airport.

Even in the hotel room behind a locked door, she was a little uncomfortable with not having the amulet charged. She couldn't wait for the sun to come up the next morning. "It's just one night," she told herself. She reached into her bag and pulled out the affirmation card she needed. "I can do this. I can do this."

After her shower, Anise came out of the bathroom to find herself alone, and she figured Nate was with his mother and Kent. She then forced her mind to go anywhere but to him. Nate and his lies were the last things she wanted to think about.

Someone lightly tapped on her door, and she was thrilled to see Jonathan on the other side. He gave her a big hug. "I'm so glad you're safe! I was so worried about you!"

"Thank you," she told him, not wanting their hug to end. "And thank you for coming all the way out here and helping to look for me."

"I wouldn't be anywhere else," he confirmed, finally ending their embrace. "Tell me everything! What happened?"

"I will," she promised, "but I want to tell everyone else at the same time. I think they're all in Lorelei's room."

"Let's go!"

ANISE MADE HERSELF COMFORTABLE ON THE small couch in Lorelei's room. She told everyone about how she had cured Grace from the side effects of the cuff and how Grace began having visions about Anise's life. She accepted the tea Jonathan was handing her as he sat next to her.

"Visions?" said Lorelei. "I just read about that in one of the trip journals. Did she say anything about a seer's wand?"

Anise nodded. "She did. As you know, Kent's father, Fred Dromly, was Grace's professor when she was in school. He initiated her with the seer's wand at that time, but strangely, she didn't have any visions until I cured her."

"We just read about that too," said Kent. "When a redheaded woman is initiated with the wand, her seer powers must be activated with all four pieces of Armor Jewelry before she can have any visions. Going off the dates of the journal entries, my father didn't know that when he first initiated her. He didn't find out until quite recently when Morty told him."

Anise saw Jonathan hang his head at the mention of his formerly beloved mentor's name. She imagined how betrayed he must feel. Betrayal was something she knew well. She glared in Nate's direction, but he didn't notice.

"Morty recently told my father about how someone

with king's blood is needed to activate the seer's abilities." Kent looked at Anise. "Grace may have kidnapped you for that purpose per my father's order."

"I doubt it," Nate said. "Grace doesn't work for anyone but herself."

"I have to agree with Nate," Anise told Kent. "Grace didn't know what was happening at first when her seer abilities started. She just wanted me to heal her from the side effects of the brainwashing. But she quickly figured out that Fred Dromly will be relying on her to read the Plate of Destiny once he finds it. She said that since she's the seer, only she can read it."

"In that case, you're still in danger, Anise," Kent fretted, a concerned look spreading across his face. "My father knows he'll need you to activate Grace's seer abilities since you're the only one left with king's blood. Since he doesn't know that's already happened, he'll be coming after you."

"Don't worry," Jonathan told her. "All of us will protect you. Plus, you have the Jewelry."

"Fred Dromly has the Jewelry, too. Several sets of it, actually, according to what I read in his trip journals. We'll need to be especially careful," Lorelei warned.

"We will be," Anise agreed.

"Maybe you should go into hiding until the rest of us find the Plate," Jonathan suggested to Anise. "I don't want anything to happen to you."

"She's not weak and helpless," Nate spat. "She's smart and capable, and we'll find the Plate faster with her help. Besides, we can all better protect her when she's with us."

"You have a habit of putting her in dangerous situations," Jonathan snapped back. "How can we protect her if whoever comes for her has a set of the Jewelry and guns?"

"I have a habit of protecting her far better than you ever could," Nate countered, his blue eyes flashing. "I'm the one that found her tonight. Where the hell were you anyway?"

"I was out looking for her! You were taking your sweet time, and I wasn't going to wait for you."

"Well, great job, Boy Scout. You were a huge help," Nate said, his voice dripping with sarcasm.

"Stop it! Both of you!" Anise commanded. "I'm not going into hiding, and I will help find the Plate. End of story." She took a deep breath in an attempt to calm her anger. Looking at Kent and Lorelei, she asked, "Did you find anything in the trip journals about the Plate's location?"

"Sort of," Lorelei confirmed. "Fred mentions having found some journals by a scientist he calls W. S. who found the Plate of Destiny in Europe in a cave back in the early 1800's. For some reason, Fred believes the Plate is now hidden in a cave in northern Florida. He's looked extensively in the caves around this area. He didn't find the Plate, but he talked about the cave art he found on the wall of one of the local caves that he believes was drawn not by local ancient people, but by W. S. He was the last known person who had the Plate, and Fred believes the cave art is actually a map that leads to the Plate."

"My father doesn't really go into any more detail in the journals that we've read so far," Kent added, "so we thought the best place to start would be to visit the caverns in the area. We should join a tour, so we'll need to get on the road early in the morning. I'm hoping the tour guide can answer any questions we might have."

"That sounds good to me," Anise agreed. "Thank you both for combing through that stack of journals."

"Of course," Lorelei told her. "Anything we can do to help. Now that you're safe and sound, Grace is my biggest concern. Where is she now? And how did you get away from her?"

"It was really strange," Anise answered. "I had to fight her, but I didn't get away until two men grabbed her. They knew my name, and I was afraid they'd grab me too, so I ran away as fast as I could. I didn't have a plan for what to do next except maybe try to find someone to direct me to the police station. Luckily for me, that's when Nate found me."

"Wait a minute. So he just *happened* to know where you were while I was driving around the entire city not knowing where to start," Jonathan said to Anise. "And when Grace kidnapped you, she just *happened* to know that you were at my apartment." He glared at Nate.

"Just what the hell are you accusing me of?" Nate said, standing up threateningly.

"Sit down!" Anise barked at Nate. "Jonathan, it's not like that. Grace had been following us for some time after escaping prison. She admitted to it herself."

"How does someone escape from a maximum security prison anyway?" Jonathan demanded.

"It's Grace," Anise muttered. "She knows how to make things happen." She uncomfortably shifted around where she was sitting on the floor.

"I don't buy it. How did you find Anise?" Jonathan asked Nate directly.

"I found Grace's pilot. He told me what hotel she was staying at. That's the first and only place I had to look."

"How very convenient," Jonathan said, venom dripping from his words. "You knew exactly where her pilot would be?"

"Actually, yeah," Nate shot back. "Not that I owe you an explanation, but Grace tracks everyone who works for her. I figured out how to hack the app she uses."

"You're full of shit," Jonathan snapped. "Like it's that easy."

"Maybe not for *you*," Nate replied arrogantly.

Anise sighed with exasperation. The constant bickering between Nate and Jonathan wasn't something she had the energy to deal with just then. "And on that note, I'm going to bed."

***

"Do *you* think I'm working with Grace?" Nate asked Anise in a quiet voice as they walked down the hall to their room. Boy Scout had made him look guilty. He was almost afraid to hear her answer.

"Of course not."

"Good. You do know you can trust me, right?"

"I'm too exhausted to do this now," Anise told him. She got into bed as soon as they entered the room. "What happened to your hand?" she asked, pointing to his swollen fingers. "Wait, are you bleeding?" she added, motioning to his shirt.

He shook his head. "That's from your wrists." He grabbed his bag and headed to the bathroom, hoping she would drop it.

"No, it's fresh," she insisted. She got up, walked over to him, and lifted his shirt. "What happened? It looks like you were cut."

He shrugged. "I'll wash it. It'll be fine."

"What happened?" she asked again, a little louder.

"I got into a fight. It's not a big deal."

"So you *were* cut? Who did this? Why didn't you say something?" she demanded angrily.

"Because it's not a big deal. I'll be fine."

She sighed. "Yeah, not a big deal. Just something *else* you kept from me."

"Come on, honey. It's not like that and you know it," he said gently, trying to pull her close.

"Don't." She pushed him away. "I'll heal you tomorrow after the Jewelry charges." She got back in bed and fell asleep moments later.

Her rejection gnawed at him, and Nate knew that would keep him awake. He left the room and went for a ride to try to clear his head, but his mind wouldn't leave him alone. He thought about how much he hated Grace.

He'd never work with her again, and it pissed him off that anyone might think that he would. But Boy Scout had been right about one thing—he'd fucked everything up with Anise.

Chapter 5

"What's the matter, Morty? Don't you like your room?"

Morty looked around the hotel room Fred Dromly had booked for him. It boasted fine furnishings and linens, a kitchenette, a separate bedroom, a white marble bathroom, and a city view. The main living area was large enough for his brainwashed army of forty-seven co-workers to sit comfortably on the furniture and floor. Their bodies appeared relaxed, but their eyes stared straight ahead as if they were catatonic. He tried not to look directly at their faces which reminded him of a horror movie he'd watched against his better judgment that'd kept him awake for a week. "It's exquisite," Morty replied. "But I don't need all this. Something more frugal would've suited me fine."

"It's time to relax about that," Fred insisted. "Your parents left you a fortune. You've been earning a good living your whole life. You've worked 15 years past retirement age. Never had a wife. Never had kids. Lived in the same small house for...four or five decades? I'd say you're set. And how on earth do you still have all of your hair? It sits there in perfect waves mocking me." He touched the top of his head where only a few stubborn hairs were still stalwartly hanging on.

"One can never be too cautious," Morty argued. "What if something bad happens?"

Fred's brown eyes sparkled. "Have I ever told you about the time I got thrown through a saloon window?"

Morty sensed he was about to be the recipient of a "Dromlyism," as he'd secretly dubbed them. He'd heard them since college but was never sure whether to believe his Professor's absurd yet marvelous allegories. "Saloons still exist?"

"Yes! Quaint tourist attractions, but there're a handful of them out there. I walked in and joined a card game with some other gentlemen. I'd nearly relieved them of their life savings when one of them figured out how I was cheating. You see, his wife was standing behind him, letting me know what he held using a code we'd created earlier. It was remuneration for the immense pleasure I'd bestowed on her, and naturally she was exceedingly grateful." Dromly laughed with pure joy. "Her husband picked me up. Then through the window I flew. You haven't *lived* until you've had shards of glass embedded in your face!"

Morty figured his expression showed his horror and confusion because Dromly laughed again.

"My point," Dromly continued, his eyes still sparkling, "is that when you take risks once in a while, some will work out and others will end badly. But either way, they make you feel far more alive than doing nothing! We must each go forth and write our own stories, and I'm telling you Morty, you don't want to end up with a book full of blank pages."

"You're right, of course," agreed Morty quickly with a slight nod of his head. He looked out the window at the city lights. His whole life he had been preparing to deal with what was starting to happen at this moment. All the lies he had told, all the people he had hurt, it all led up to now. When he looked back on it all and saw how out of hand it had gotten, he was ashamed. Ashamed wasn't a strong enough word though. He couldn't think of a word harsh enough to describe the depth of his sorrow and self-loathing. He couldn't stop, however. He didn't want all the terrible things he had done to be in vain. And if he *hadn't* done them...he shuddered at the thought and pushed it quickly from his mind. *I must succeed,* he told himself.

"Then tell me what's wrong," Dromly insisted. "I've known you long enough to know you're unhappy about something."

"Was it really necessary to have your two giant hooligans escort me from my home to the airport, on the plane, and directly to the hotel?" Morty looked at the two large men who had delivered him to Dromly. They stood by the front door with their arms crossed as if they were angry at the world and more than happy to take it out on anyone at all. "Big Ears and Crooked Nose weren't exactly patient travel companions," he added in a whisper. "They wouldn't even let me use the restroom at the airport. Nor would they tell me their names. It was a highly uncomfortable situation."

Fred adjusted the cape that sat on his shoulders. "I'm surprised I needed them to help convince you to charter the jet. You *are* still on board with this, right?"

"Of course," Morty lied. "Like I said, I'm frugal."

"Right. Well, I want you to know you did a great job at creating the army I asked for," Fred told him, looking at the unblinking mass of former museum employees scattered throughout Morty's living area. "They're brainwashed to the point of unquestioned loyalty."

Morty's stomach burned. "I'm glad you're pleased."

"No, you're not. I can tell by that look. Are you still feeling guilty?"

"Of course I'm feeling guilty! How are you not?"

"Morty, what do I keep saying?"

"That you can fix it. I just wish you would tell me when. Their lives have been turned upside down, and they're not getting any younger."

Dromly frowned. "Speaking of youth, it would've been nice to have some younger bodies in my army. Everyone you've sent me is of retirement age."

"It was easier to explain it that way. If anyone asked, I told them that their former co-worker retired and went to Florida to participate in an archeology project. Besides, I did brainwash everyone else I work with, and I had them buy plane tickets. They're on their way to you as we speak."

"Good work. Someone wants me dead, Morty. The army of your co-workers you created will protect me physically. And since they all have the necessary experience and knowledge, they're also helping greatly on my searches for the Plate of Destiny."

Dromly had said someone wanted him dead before, but he'd never given a name. Morty wondered who it could be. "How close are you to finding the Plate of Destiny?"

"I know where it is, I just have to retrieve it. Listen carefully, Morty. You'll need to understand this if you're going to help me. You know how we suspect that Thomas Brevain knew the entirety of the legend of the Armor Jewelry, the seer's wand, and the Plate but was keeping it from us for some reason?"

"Yes, of course."

"And then two years ago, you'd discovered that king's blood is needed to use the cuff properly. Not just king's blood, but *willing* king's blood."

"Yes."

"Well, I was inspired by your new discovery and motivated by Thomas's secret successes. I found the rest of the legend."

"Really? That's incredible!"

"I know. Now listen here. King's blood is needed for more than just use of the cuff. The words on the Plate of Destiny are supposedly inlaid in gold, and only a seer can see them. However, I learned the words are also hidden from the view of seers."

Morty narrowed his brows in confusion. "Then how does a seer read the words on the Plate?"

"I learned that *king's blood must be spilled directly on the Plate in order for a seer to read it.*"

"What?!" Morty cried, pressing his hand to his heart to make sure it was still beating. He wondered what Dromly might want to do to Anise to get her blood to spill on the Plate in order to read its wisdom. Flashes of Thomas Brevain lying dead on his office floor pulsed in his mind. If Dromly had no problem murdering Thomas...

"Yes. So we'll need Anise Viston to activate Grace's seer powers. Once that's happened, we'll need to spill Anise's blood on the Plate. At that point, Grace should start to see the golden writing appear."

Morty thought about his former best friend. "But was it necessary to keep all of this from Grace? Why couldn't we have all worked together on this?"

"Because I always knew she wasn't one to be trusted. I think *you* learned that the hard way."

Morty nodded. "Indeed I did." *I learned the hard way that you can't be trusted either*, Morty thought.

"Just like I learned that Thomas couldn't be trusted when I found half-burned Plate of Destiny research in a dumpster after his murder," Dromly added.

"Unfortunately not," agreed Morty, once again picturing Thomas dead on the floor of his office at the Springfield Museum fifty-three years earlier. "What if we find the Plate, and Grace refuses to read it?" asked Morty. "She has no reason to want to help us."

"I fully expect that's what'll happen. But you already know the answer to that, Morty. We need to possess her eyes. You know her best, so I'll leave it up to you to fig-ure out a way to do it," Dromly said, pointing a finger at Morty.

Morty swallowed, already turning green. Possess

her eyes? What was that supposed to mean? Did Dromly want him to harvest her eyes?

Fred continued, "So start with Grace. Then we'll find Anise."

The knot in Morty's stomach grew. "Speaking of Anise, how much of her blood is needed to spill on the Plate of Destiny?"

"A lot. Enough to completely drench the Plate several times over."

Dromly killed Thomas. Now, he's going to kill Anise and expects me to kill Grace for her eyes. Morty rooted through his bag, found his antacids, and popped them in his mouth. His ears perked up when he heard stirring in the next room, and he paused his chewing to listen. *Grace is waking up.*

GRACE WOKE FROM A DEEP SLEEP and felt groggy. She kept her eyes closed and hoped to fall back asleep. However, someone far away was speaking, and it was keeping her awake. She tried to listen but couldn't understand the words. Her mind was lost in a fog, and she wondered if she'd been drugged. She struggled against the drowsiness and finally was able to open her lids. Her eyes scanned the dimly lit room. The television set had been moved and the corner lamp was missing. "This is not my room," she realized. "Who's here? Where am I?" Her arms shook from weakness, but she managed to push herself into a seated position on the bed even though her hands were bound together.

"Grace, you're awake," said a tall man coming into the small bedroom. "How are you feeling?"

"Morty?" she asked in disbelief.

"Hello, Grace," said a much shorter man coming up behind Morty. He leaned on his cane.

Grace glared at the old man. "Professor Dromly. So you've been working with Morty behind my back."

"Behind your back?" Morty sputtered with confusion. He looked at the professor. "*You've* been working with Grace?"

"She says it as if I betrayed her," Fred said. "It was really the other way around, wasn't it, Grace? You despised me because Thomas did."

"He had good reason," Grace informed him.

"Yet you pretended everything was good between us. You got all the latest information about the Plate of Destiny from me in Europe or here in Florida when you weren't back home searching for a way to get a complete set of Armor Jewelry in the meantime. Don't think I didn't know what you were up to." Dromly turned back to Morty. "I didn't mind. Grace volunteered her services at each of my excavation sites for decades up until she got arrested. Not only was she very helpful, but it was also a great way to keep tabs on her whereabouts. And of course, I didn't tell her everything."

Glaring at Fred, Grace asked, "And why have I been brought here against my will?"

"We have big plans, and you're going to help."

"I know why you need me. You can't read the Plate of Destiny without me because only a seer can do that."

"You know about that?" Morty said, looking shocked. "So you're willing to help?"

"The hell I am!" she snarled at him. "I don't care what your plans are! I have my own, and nothing you do is going to stop me! You underestimate me if you think you can keep me here!"

Fred frowned. "I'm sorry you feel that way, Grace. Morty, I'm afraid I don't have the time to deal with this. You do what you have to do." He straightened the cape on his shoulders and left.

"You're an idiot if you think you can keep me here," Grace barked.

"So you've informed me," Morty replied.

Grace stood up and tried to take a step before she realized her ankles were also tied together.

Morty caught her and placed her back on the bed. "Be careful," he told her. "It's not just you and me in this hotel room. Part of my army is out in the main living area."

"Your brainwashed co-workers?"

"Yes. Unlike you, they all responded to the cuff's brainwashing effects. You know they'll do anything I tell them." He got up and closed the door to the bedroom.

"And what are you going to tell your army to do?" Grace demanded.

He looked at her, took a deep breath as if he were nervous about something, and told her about a lock box he'd found decades ago under the floorboards in Dromly's office which had contained a plan to find the Plate of Destiny. "Dromly hired me to help Thomas figure out the language that had been used on the Plate of Destiny. Your part as the seer was to see the writing on the Plate."

Grace shook her head. "I haven't had any visions of the Plate's writings."

"You wouldn't have for two reasons," Morty answered. "First, for a seer to see the Plate's writings, you have to be *looking at* and *touching* the Plate itself. Second, the seer's powers have to be activated. To do so—"

"Yes, I know all about the activation and needing someone with king's blood to do it," Grace interrupted, remembering how Anise had accidentally activated her seer's powers on the plane. "So Dromly wants me to see and describe the symbols on the Plate and you to read and interpret them. I don't care. You both betrayed me and Thomas! There's no way I'm helping you or Dromly read what's on the Plate. I can find it before either of you—"

"Stop." Morty interrupted her and narrowed his eyes. To her surprise, he fell to his knees in front of her. "Grace,

I've worked my derriere off my entire life to keep you safe. I didn't want you to have any of the Armor Jewelry so Dromly wouldn't see you as a threat. When you managed to obtain some of the pieces, I lied to Dromly about where they were and told him I had them. I didn't want him to hurt you."

She glared at him. She didn't believe a word, but now that he'd started confessing, she knew him well enough to know he wouldn't be able to stop. His pained voice continued. "I'm so sorry about your headaches and hallucinations. I didn't mean for that to happen. When I followed you around trying to use the Jewelry on you all those years ago, I wasn't actually trying to brainwash you. I was trying to invoke your seer's abilities so you'd see the truth on your own because I knew you wouldn't believe me if I told you, just like you don't believe me now."

It was obvious he still knew her well. Her memories of how close they used to be was the only reason she kept listening to him now as he droned on.

"I obeyed when Dromly told me to initiate other red-headed women in the hopes the focus would be taken off of you and for some reason they ended up dead." Morty's face turned red. "I lied to Jonathan and Anise and put them in danger, two people I care about and respect very much, in an attempt to keep you safe from Dromly."

His words began coming out quicker. "I brainwashed my colleagues per Dromly's orders, but I kept many of them with me instead of sending them to Dromly for years longer than was necessary to brainwash them. I wanted them to help me find the Jewelry before you did so Dromly wouldn't come after you. They all now have headaches and hallucinations and their spouses have all left them due to their extreme personality changes. Anise's parents were accidentally *killed*..." He paused to wipe the tears from his eyes with his fingers. "They were killed in my attempt to get king's blood from her mother so I could try again to invoke your seer's powers."

His voice raised with emotion. "I didn't mean for any-one to get hurt! It started getting more and more out of hand, and I didn't want to keep going, but I couldn't stop or it would all have been for naught. All I ever wanted was for *you* to be safe. I've spent my entire waking life working to keep you safe, Grace! You are not going to negate everything I've done!" He sat back on his heels and hung his head.

"What the hell are you talking about, Morty?" His blubbering was getting annoying.

Morty pushed himself up from the floor and sat next to her on the bed, rubbing his knees. "Thomas knew far more about the Plate of Destiny than Dromly or I ever did. He was keeping things from Dromly—from all of us—and Dromly must've seen him as a threat. That's why he killed Thomas. I didn't want the same thing to happen to you."

"*Dromly* killed Thomas?" *Could that be?* It did make more sense than Morty being the killer. Morty simply didn't have it in him.

"He sees *you* as a threat, too. The solution to this problem is your death, Grace. Dromly doesn't need *you* to see the words on the Plate. All he needs is to possess the eyes of a seer. He expects me to kill you and harvest your eyes."

"And is that what you're going to do?"

He stared at her for a moment, his nostrils flared and mouth agape. "Of course not! I'm going to let you go." He untied her and verbally dismissed the army of co-work-ers. Grace heard a thundering of footsteps leaving out the front door. "Go do what you need to do," he said qui-etly to her once the door to the suite slammed shut after the last brainwashed co-worker had left. "I'll tell Dromly that you bested me somehow."

Grace stood up, brushed the wrinkles out of her clothes, and walked out of the suite. Before the door closed completely behind her, she walked back into the room. Morty was sitting on a chair with his head in his hands. She was beginning to think there might be at least some truth in his claim of trying to keep her safe. After all, he'd had her and let her go. "Come *with* me," she demanded.

Part 2
THE CAVE

Chapter 6

Wednesday, October 7, 2015

Before sunrise, Lorelei waited for everyone downstairs in the lobby for breakfast. After going through the buffet line, they sat at a large round table. Lorelei noticed that Anise purposely did not sit next to Nate. She wondered what was going on between the two of them.

Jonathan chattered on happily about how amazing the cavern tour was going to be, and Lorelei noticed Anise smiling at Jonathan's excitement.

Nate remained silent throughout the entire meal.

"Are we ready to go?" asked Kent when everyone was finished eating.

The others responded in the affirmative.

"Mom, wanna ride with me?" Nate asked.

Lorelei smiled at her son. She still couldn't believe they were finally together again. Being away from him during her years in captivity had been worse than hell. "I'd love to. Let's go."

On the car ride over, and after some heavy prodding, Lorelei finally got her son to confess to her why he was upset. He didn't go into too many details about his fight with Anise, but Lorelei heard enough to understand.

"It's just a fight with a girlfriend. I usually wouldn't even care," Nate said. "But for some reason, I do."

"You love her."

He nodded. "I feel bad that I lied and pissed her off. How do I get that feeling to go away?"

Lorelei was surprised that her son had no understanding of how to cope with everyday human emotions. What had Grace done to him? "Talk to her. Apologize."

He shrugged. "There's no point. I don't think she'll forgive me this time."

"It's not about her forgiving you. It's about you doing the right thing. She deserves to know that you're sorry and to hear your apology even if she won't accept it." Her son was quiet, and she wondered what he was thinking. Ever since the plane, he'd recoiled every time she tried to touch him. He'd spoken to her almost robotically. Not coldly, but not warmly and with love like he used to when he was a child, either. He must be upset with her for having been gone so long and leaving him alone to deal with Grace. Her eyes welled up. It had been hard for her to deal with Grace as an adult. She could only imagine how a small child would feel alone in that toxic environment. "Speaking of apologies, I want to apologize to you," she began. "For being gone. I know things could've been so much better for you if I hadn't—"

"Don't apologize," he said, cutting her off. "It wasn't your fault."

She tried to talk to him further, but that had been the extent of what he was willing to expose regarding his emotional state. Instead, she asked him questions about other areas of his life, her ears hungrily absorbing all the information she'd longed to know when she was held captive.

When they finally arrived at the park where the caverns were located, she was grateful to get out of the car and stretch her legs. They began walking toward the entrance with Anise, Kent, and Jonathan a few steps ahead of them. "Go talk to her," Lorelei urged in a hushed tone.

"Here? Now?" Nate said, looking around at the other tourists.

"Find a time when she's away from Jonathan and Kent," Lorelei insisted, "and talk to her. You can't keep holding on to your anger, and neither can she."

As she followed him through the parking lot, Lorelei hoped he'd open up more to her in the future. Today had at least been a start.

✳✳✳

As they entered the Visitor's Center, Anise took notice of the displays behind glass walls teaching about the formation of the caverns. She purchased her ticket and walked outside with the others to wait for the cave tour.

"This is going to be so amazing!" Jonathan exclaimed.

Anise found herself looking forward to their tour also. Jonathan's excitement had always been contagious. Even though it was October, the temperature was still high, and Anise wiped some sweat off her brow.

"Here's the tour leader," said Kent.

"Hello!" chirped a female voice to the group of about twenty visitors gathered for the tour.

Anise looked up. A young woman in a park ranger uniform looked directly at her and smiled. Her dark eyes were bright, and her black, silky hair hung down almost to her waist. *She's stunning*, Anise thought, feeling a little disheveled in her loose clothing and ponytail.

"Welcome," the guide said. "My name is Raina. I'll be your guide for the tour. I'll tell you about what we see when we walk through the caverns, and I'm happy to answer any questions you may have along the way."

Anise followed Raina on a paved path that led through

trees and brush. She glanced at her companions on the way. Jonathan and Kent looked excited about what they might see in the cave. Nate's gaze went everywhere except to her. Lorelei kept stealing small glances at her son as if she couldn't believe he was actually there next to her. Anise wanted to be more excited about what information they might find out about the Plate of Destiny but was nauseated from the heat and could only look forward to the cooler temperature the cave would provide.

Raina stopped before a narrow cement staircase that led down to the entrance of the caverns. "Before we go in, there are a few rules. The most important one is to not touch anything. There are oils on your skin that can stop the formations from growing. No food or drinks are allowed. Photography is allowed, but please make sure your flash is off. The bats don't like it." She led the group down the stairs where she unlocked a door and motioned for everyone to step inside.

The sudden change of temperature made Anise shiver happily. Her nausea dissipated quickly as she looked around in wonder. The underground room was wide and filled with rock formations.

"This area used to be underwater," Raina announced. "Shells, coral, and other skeletal sediments collected on the seafloor and turned to limestone once the water levels dropped. Groundwater dissolved some of the limestone underneath the surface which created the caverns." She shined a flashlight on the ceiling. "As water drips through the ceiling, the dissolved calcium from the limestone solidifies and creates this icicle-shaped formation. Anyone know what this is called?"

"A stalagmite?" guessed Jonathan.

"No," came a voice from behind. "It's a stalactite."

Anise and Jonathan looked over their shoulders with curiosity. The voice belonged to a woman about their age. She wore skinny jeans, a t-shirt, and sneakers and stood just a couple inches shorter than Jonathan. Her blonde hair hung in loose, beachy waves to the middle of her back, and her light blue eyes as well as her pink lips smiled at him.

Raina nodded. "She's right! Stalagmites grow from the ground up. Stalactites grow from the top down. Once the stalactites and stalagmites meet in the middle, they become a column."

Anise watched as Jonathan turned around to say something to the blonde woman, but she'd already made her way to the other side of the room, looking completely entranced by the cave formations.

They ducked through a short tunnel into another room. Raina shined her flashlight on a part of the wall that looked white in comparison to the surrounding rock. "Here you can see calcite."

Anise touched Jonathan's arm. "Have you seen anything resembling cave art?" she whispered.

"No." He shook his head. "I doubt it'll be in this cave where all the tourists are. I'm hoping maybe Raina will know where it is. And if she knows about the cave art, maybe she's even heard of Mallandia and the Plate of Destiny."

At the mention of Mallandia, Anise touched the amulet that she'd tucked under her loose tank top. She'd let the sun shine on it during the car ride and felt safe now that it had a full charge. She also had the cuff, earrings, and ring with her, but kept them in her cross-body bag. The pieces were large, and she didn't want to draw unnecessary attention to herself—what if Dr. Smithton was wrong, and there were others who knew about the legend? Fighting off more people who wanted the Armor Jewelry was not what she needed right now.

She glanced over at Nate and saw him wandering the cave, his deep blue eyes looking at the rock formations and his handsome face set in a look of concentration. Part of her wished he'd come over and talk to her. But the ease with which he could lie or keep things from her loomed over her head like a cloud.

"If everyone's ready," Raina called out, "I'm going to turn out all the lights so you can experience what it's like in the cavern in complete darkness."

After Raina flipped the switch, there was silence for a brief moment until the other guests began making jokes or reassuring their children. For Anise, the complete blackness was novel at first and then somewhat unsettling. Her eyes were wide open and scanned desperately for anything at all, completely offended at being robbed of their only purpose. She began hearing the drips of water echoing through the cave, every little shuffle by the other guests in the group, and her own breathing. The cool air on her skin became more prominent, and her hands longed to reach out and touch something so she could get her bearings.

The lights came back on, and Anise saw Jonathan grinning at her.

"That was incredible!" His eyes were wide with excitement.

"Yeah." She agreed with him but was also glad it was over. Her head turned to look at Nate who was staring off into a distant part of the cave, seemingly unaffected by the sensory experience.

Raina led the group down a few concrete stairs into the next room. Thick columns filled much of the space and had colored lights shining up on them from the smooth, man-made floor. "This is the one part of the cavern that you're allowed to touch. Feel free to explore this room."

Anise watched as Nate, Lorelei, and Kent strolled the room, running their fingers over the wall and formations. She turned and followed Jonathan to the other side of the room.

Jonathan pointed to a stalagmite that hadn't quite grown tall enough to reach the stalactite above it yet. "I wonder if you can tell the age of a stalagmite by its height," he pondered out loud.

"There's a lot more that goes into that calculation than height alone," came a voice from behind them.

They turned around and saw the blonde woman that had corrected Jonathan earlier. Anise could tell from his focused attention that he was already fascinated by what this woman might have to say.

"Like what?" he asked her.

A manicured finger pointed to the ceiling. "The drip rate of the water. The concentration of minerals. The air flow and quality."

"That makes sense." He returned the smile she was giving him. "Thanks for the lesson."

"My pleasure," she replied. "It's fun to meet someone who's actually interested in that kind of thing."

"I've studied ancient history and archaeology," he told her. "So my knowledge about caves is limited to what artifacts have been found in them. But understanding how caves formed is just as interesting to me."

"Where did you go to school?" she asked him with another smile.

Anise smiled to herself as Jonathan answered the woman. She obviously found him attractive, but he seemed to have no idea.

"I'm Jonathan, by the way," he said, offering her his name. "And this is Anise."

"I'm Selina," the blonde woman replied.

Raina directed everyone to look at various formations that had developed into shapes resembling cartoon characters or famous figures.

"What a pretty garnet," Selina said to Anise, motioning to her finger.

"Oh, thanks," Anise replied, lifting her right hand so they could both get a better look at the ring she wore. "I'm surprised you noticed it. No one's ever commented on it before." She thought about her ex-boyfriend Brian who had given it to her. When the guilt that accompanied every thought about him started to tear apart her stomach, she pushed Brian and all negative feelings out of her mind.

"I'm a geologist, so I notice every stone," Selina replied. "The color is exquisite."

"Your ring is beautiful, too. What stone is that?" Anise admired the dark, mossy green stone with bright red spots.

"Thank you. It's a bloodstone," Selina responded, bringing her hand closer to their view.

"Does it mean anything?" Anise asked. She thought about her friend Erin who'd used gemstones for metaphysical purposes. For a moment, she'd forgotten Erin was gone. The memories roared back and punched her in the gut.

Selina nodded. "Yes, it's for good health and courage."

"Has it worked?"

"I like to think so," Selina said.

"I wonder if there were any artifacts found in this cavern," Jonathan said.

"I'd love to know that, too!" Selina replied.

"We should ask Raina," he suggested.

"Definitely," she agreed.

"I actually have a lot of questions I'd like to ask her," Jonathan said to Anise. He motioned toward Raina who was ahead of them answering questions from Kent.

"I know you do," Anise answered with a little laugh.

"I'll find you in a few minutes," Jonathan told her as he and Selina trotted ahead.

Anise turned to look at the walls and tried to imagine what the cave art they were searching for might look like. She wondered how Fred Dromly discovered that the art was actually a map in disguise and if he was able to read it.

"Anise."

She spun around at the sound of her name behind

her. "Nate," she said, greeting him. She'd wanted him to come talk to her all morning, but now that he was, she felt a pit of sadness in her stomach. His presence felt different and distant. It was heartbreaking and infuriating. Anise wasn't sure if she wanted to scream at him or kiss him. She did neither. "Are you enjoying the tour?"

"Very much," he said. "It's interesting stuff. Have you seen anything that might be cave art?"

"Not yet," she admitted. "You?"

"No," he replied. "But we need to talk about something else, too. I know you're pissed at me, and I don't blame you. I want to apologize."

"We do need to talk; you're right. But I'd prefer to have privacy. Let's talk tonight." Anise turned away from him. She hadn't meant to blow him off, but there was so much to say, she didn't know where to start. If she had poured her heart out to him, she might've said something like: *I can't stand the sight of you, and I don't want to go another day without you.* She needed to focus her thoughts before they spoke.

"Anise, get this," Jonathan said, rejoining her. Kent, Lorelei, Raina, and Selina were right behind him. "Raina was telling us that there are dozens of other caves around here and that cave art was found in some of them."

"Yes," agreed Raina. "And since they both have so many questions still, I've invited Jonathan and Selina to meet me for lunch today. I hope all of you will come as well. I'd be happy to answer any questions about the caves you still have."

"That's very kind of you," said Kent. "We'll be there!"

Chapter 7

"Why did you bring me here?" Morty sat across from Grace at the small table in her hotel suite. "It certainly can't be to beat you at gin rummy."

Grace finished dealing the cards. She hoped Morty wasn't going to whine all night. "Because I knew you could help me. I figured Anise had escaped, and together we found her. We now know which hotel she's staying at, and we know where Dromly is also. Dromly thinks he still needs Anise to activate my seer's abilities. He'll be looking for her. There's no need to act right now, but if Dromly finds that Plate before we do—and we know he's close—we'll hide Anise from him."

"Why?"

"Because I don't believe for a second that he doesn't have another initiated redhead somewhere that you don't know about. I need to make sure that he needs *me* when he finds that Plate or he might succeed at hiding it away from me forever. If Anise is missing, he'll come looking for me."

"If he has another redheaded woman initiated, she's probably already dead," Morty lamented. "They each died so quickly after initiation with the seer's wand. So many unnecessary deaths, and they're all my fault."

"You candy-ass," she said, shaking her head.

"What?"

"You didn't kill those redheaded women. I did." For the first time ever, a nonchalant admission of murder didn't sit well with her. *I can't change the past,* she reasoned with herself, trying to will away the uncomfortable feelings.

"What?!" Morty's horrified face looked at her in surprise.

"I wanted to make sure that Dromly needed *me* when the time came, not some other initiated redhead. I didn't want him finding the Plate without me!"

Morty was quivering. "I know the real you. You're not a cold-hearted killer. If I hadn't tried to brainwash you in the first place, you wouldn't have murdered those women."

Grace thought about his words and how different she felt now that Anise had cured her from the side effects of the cuff. She thought about something she'd said to her father right before she'd killed him—that the only way she'd ever kill anyone is if they left her no choice. It was hard to know if she would've felt she had no choice regarding the redheaded women had she not been brainwashed by Morty and the cuff, so she wasn't sure if Morty's statement was true or not. Also, she was aware her desire to find the Plate of Destiny had turned into a full-blown obsession, and it had become difficult to think of anything else. That pull she felt to the Plate was so strong it influenced every choice she felt she had—or didn't have. "Maybe. Maybe not. Either way, we're both guilty."

Morty hung his head. "Yes."

Grace looked at her former friend intensely. "You robbed me of my life with Thomas. You robbed me of my life with you. You robbed me of my health and mental well-being for decades. Helping me find the Plate before Dromly is the least you could do."

Morty lifted his head to face her, and she could see

him tearing up.

"You owe me," she added.

Morty wore a crestfallen expression. "I'm sorry for all that. I was trying to protect you. And I certainly didn't want you to antagonize Dromly and get yourself killed like Thomas did."

Wanting him to look at her so she could make sure he knew how upset she was, she rested her hand on his until his eyes turned upward. "I don't want to hear it or any other lies about my husband! Thomas may have hated Dromly, but he wouldn't have kept anything from him. He certainly wouldn't have kept secrets from *me*!" She stared at their hands on the table and felt herself falling backward. Her eyes went blind before colors began swirling. As the pieces of rainbow came together, she saw a caped figure enter Morty's old office at the Springfield Museum and shoot Thomas twice in the chest. Quickly retracting her hand, she looked up at her former friend, her breath shallow.

"You see it, don't you?" he asked her. "You see the truth through visions. Anise has already cured you of the brainwashing effects of the cuff and has awakened your seer's abilities. Hasn't she?"

Grace nodded at him.

"Put your hand back, Grace. Let your vision finish."

She did as he suggested and felt herself falling.

"I have to get Grace out of the country," Thomas said to Morty.

"Why?" Morty asked.

"I know everything there is to know about the Armor Jewelry. And the Plate, too, except for the words written on it," Thomas replied in a whisper. *"If I don't leave tonight, I won't survive much longer."*

"What are you talking about? We've been doing research together for years. What did you learn that you haven't told me and Dromly?"

"A lot. Listen, Morty, I don't have time to explain, but please, I need your help. If anyone asks where I am, and I mean anyone, just say that Grace and I are taking a vacation to California. That should give us a head start. Can you do that?"

"If it keeps Grace safe, then yes. But don't think I won't look for you myself, you despicable piece of shit. Grace deserves better than you. She deserves someone who loves her. All you've ever done is use her." Morty's angry face glared at Thomas.

Thomas ignored Morty's accusation. "There's one more thing Morty. In my office closet is a large duffel. I need you to burn—"

The lights went out.

With his hood up and his face covered in shadow, a man in a cape of Fred Dromly's size and build stepped into the dark office and shot Thomas twice in the chest. Thomas fell in a crumpled heap.

The look of shock and horror on Morty's face convinced Grace of his innocence in Thomas's murder. "No!" Morty managed to choke out. Grace heard her own voice shouting Thomas's name from down the hall and watched as the armed figure ran out of Morty's office and through the door to the stairwell, his cape flapping behind him.

Grace took her hand back and looked at Morty. She noticed the playing cards had scattered across the table and onto the tile floor. Taking a slow, deep breath, she fought the moisture forming in her eyes. Fifty-three years had passed since she'd last cried, and she would've rather rolled naked on an ant hill than start over at day one. The unborn tears dissipated, and she leaned back in her chair.

"I'm so sorry," Morty said softly. "I—"

"You were right," she interrupted. "I would've reacted with rage and gotten myself killed, and I'd have never seen it coming. Dromly is a lot of things, but I never thought him capable of murder. You were just trying to protect me." She shook her head at him. "But *why*? You hated me."

"I never hated you a day in my life."

"Yes, you did."

"Not true. I never stopped loving you."

"No, you hated me. But Morty, I swear I didn't abort our child. I—"

"I know," he said, interrupting *her* this time.

"You know?" she asked, confused.

"After I got notice that you had died in prison, I flew out to Springfield right away. I wanted to see you one last time to say good-bye. While I was there, I managed to sneak into the hospital's old record repository and stole your medical file."

"You did?" Grace asked with a big, surprised smile. "That's so unlike you."

He chuckled at her reaction. "Yes. I couldn't help myself; all I could think about was how you had denied it all those years, and I had to find out for certain, once and for all. The report for the night I rushed you there said that you had been badly bruised all over your body, you had a concussion, and that you had a miscarriage, despite attempts to save the fetus. There was no mention of signs of an abortion."

She frowned at him. "I *told* you."

Morty hung his head. "That you did, and I'm so sorry—so *very* sorry—that I didn't believe you."

"I'm sorry I didn't believe you about Thomas's murder. I knew you didn't have it in you to kill anyone; I just couldn't imagine who else would want to kill him. Dromly must've found out Thomas was keeping things from him." She frowned again. It was a shock to find out Thomas had kept his discoveries about the Armor Jewelry and Plate of Destiny a secret from her. *He must've had a good reason to do it though.* He'd loved her more than anything and wouldn't have done that to her unless he had to.

"I don't want us to be sorry anymore," Morty said, taking her hand. "I miss my best friend."

To her surprise and relief, Grace found it easier than she thought it would be to fight off the urge to fall into a vision from his touch. "I miss mine, too," she admitted.

They stood up from the table, and he held her for several minutes in the glow of the single-bulb light fixture above their heads. They said nothing and just stood there in each other's embrace, grateful for the opportunity to salvage the friendship they had lost so many years ago.

"What duffel was Thomas talking about?" Grace asked her friend.

"I don't know. I looked for it, but there was nothing in his closet. I think I saw Dromly running off with it that evening. But listen, more importantly, you already know Dromly wants to kill you for your eyes. He also will kill Anise for her blood."

"Why would he kill her? He just needs a little of her blood. A few drops should do it, right?"

"No. Not a little. A lot. The Plate must be drenched with it. Anise will not survive. We have to prevent it from happening. If she dies, Jonathan would never forgive me. I'd never forgive myself."

"But that means *we* won't be able to read the Plate either!" She felt like she had just lost Thomas all over again. "I've been working to get back to Thomas my whole life, and now I find out it's impossible unless I kill that girl."

"You're not that murderous person anymore," Morty reminded her. "You've been cured from the effects of the cuff."

Grace knew he was right. Killing a person used to be as easy as squashing a bug. Now the thought of it made her stomach churn. "This would be easier if I hadn't been cured," she said, scowling. "Then I'd just kill her and take what I need."

"Don't talk that way," he scolded. "Because now you're back to being the Grace I used to know. And that Grace is a good person."

"I still need to read what's on the Plate. I *have* to. How am I going to do that?"

"We'll find another way," he reassured her.

What she had wanted from him the most when they were younger was for him to stick up for her in confrontational situations. When he had instead shied away from conflict, she had called him a candy-ass. The last thing she ever expected to find out now was that he'd actually been protecting her for most of their lives. She wrapped her arms around his torso again. "Thank you," she said as she felt him hugging her back. "So now that neither of us will willingly help Dromly, what do you think he'll do?"

Morty looked at her. "He won't let that stand in his way. He'll kill Anise. He'll cut your eyes out and read the symbols on the Plate for himself. He'll threaten my life and yours and possibly Jonathan's as well to make me interpret them for him."

"Unless we stop him. And we can do it. Together." She held out her hand.

Morty took it in his. "Together."

Chapter 8

They sat at a large wooden table next to windows that looked out to a small town street lined with shops and restaurants. Jonathan hadn't realized how much of an appetite he'd worked up and was devouring his salad and tuna fish sandwich.

"So have you always wanted to be a park ranger?" Anise asked Raina.

"Pretty much," said Raina. She'd changed clothes and looked equally comfortable in her sundress as she had in her uniform. "Growing up, my parents took us camping and hiking all the time. My dad is a botanist and my mom an herbalist, so I know a lot about practically any plant that grows native to the area and how to take care of it. I volunteered at the park in high school and loved it. I knew it was something I wanted to do long term."

"What kind of training does it take to be a park ranger?" Kent wanted to know.

"I had to take the park's training course," Raina explained. "But I also have a degree in park management with a minor in speleology."

"What's speleology?" Lorelei asked.

"The study of caves," Raina told her. "Spelunking is a favorite hobby of mine, and I'm lucky to be able to work inside caves now."

"There's nothing better than turning a hobby into a career," Selina agreed.

"Did you do that too?" Raina asked.

Selina nodded. "My childhood rock collection led me into geology."

Jonathan glanced to his left at Anise who was staring at her lap. He wondered if she was cursing herself again for not going to art school when she had the chance.

"So, what questions do y'all have for me?" Raina asked the table.

"We were hoping you could help us find something," Jonathan spoke up. "We're in search of an ancient artifact from Bronze Age Europe called the Plate of Destiny. We have reason to believe it's hidden somewhere in northern Florida."

"Oh! I've heard of that!" Raina replied.

"Really?" Jonathan asked, surprised.

"My family has lived in this area for a long time," Raina explained. "I've heard all of the local folklore, including the story of the Plate of Destiny."

"We'd love to hear it," Lorelei said. "Even though we're looking for it, we don't know that much about it."

Raina began her story. "In the 1810's there was a German archeologist named Wilhelm Schwartz who liked to explore caves for artifacts along with his friend and co-worker Karl Meier."

"Wilhelm Schwartz! He must be the W. S. that Dromly mentioned in his journal!" Jonathan hissed excitedly to Anise.

"Oh yeah! Good catch," she whispered back.

"Wilhelm Schwartz is the one who discovered the Mallandian king's remains!" Jonathan added in an excited whisper.

"While on a dig in northern Germany," Raina continued, "Schwartz and Meier discovered some bones from a Bronze Age king. The king was buried with Jewelry that had gemstones from faraway places and a stone tablet engraved with curly and wavy symbols. After years of study, Schwartz figured out how to read the language on the tablet. It talked about some magical jewelry and a round, metal disc called the Plate of Destiny that supposedly had the secrets of life and death inlaid in gold writing on it.

"Following the instructions on how to find the Plate of Destiny from the tablet, Schwartz discovered it in a cave along with some other artifacts. He spent the next several years of his life trying to read it. His friend Karl Meier grew concerned about him because all it's made of is bronze. There was no writing, no gold inlay. Just a patina that made it a greenish color. There was nothing to indicate that the Plate had anything written on it at all, but Schwartz didn't give up. He became obsessed with it, forgetting to eat, bathe, or go to work. Meier, out of concern for his friend, tried to have him committed, so Schwartz took the Plate and fled to the United States in 1825.

"Florida had just become a U.S. territory a few years earlier, and since there are plenty of caves here, he decided it would be a great place to hide not only the Plate of Destiny, but also all the other artifacts he found that belonged to the same kingdom. On the ship over, he met a red-headed woman who somehow helped him figure out how to read the secrets on the Plate. After hiding the Plate and his other artifacts in separate caves, he went home spouting the worldly knowledge he'd learned from reading the Plate—but only the secrets of life. If anyone asked him about the secrets of death, he refused to tell them. Half of the people called him selfish, and the other half called him crazy. His friends forced him into a sanitarium where he was kept medicated for the rest of his life."

"That's so sad," Anise commented.

"It's just a story," Raina shrugged. "Probably not a word of truth in it. I doubt the Plate of Destiny even exists."

"My father is an archaeologist," Kent began. "He discovered a battlefield from the small kingdom that was ruled by the king in your story. We know it's the same kingdom because the fallen soldiers each kept a stone with them that had a curly or wavy symbol engraved on it, just like on the tablet that was found with the king. The symbols stood for inspiring words like honor or courage."

Anise leaned over and whispered to Jonathan, "Those stones remind me of my affirmation cards."

He smiled at her and agreed.

"He named the kingdom Mallandia," Kent continued, "which is Old German for small land. He kept journals of his digs, travels, and all the artifacts he found there. He also included his thoughts about the Mallandian myths he'd uncovered and how they were related to some of the artifacts. He believes the Plate of Destiny is a real object, and he's been looking for it, but his journals didn't contain enough details of where he still plans to search or anything else about it. They read more like novels than a scientist's notebook, so we were hoping you might be able to fill in some of the blanks."

"Whoa, that's incredible!" exclaimed Raina. "May I ask who your father is?"

"His name is Frederick Dromly. He was a professor at Springfield University and then quit to devote his time to fieldwork."

"Wait," spoke up Selina. "Your father is *the* Dr. Frederick Dromly? The world famous archeologist?"

"That would be him," agreed Kent, a small frown forming on his lips.

Jonathan remembered Kent mentioning his strained relationship with his father. He hoped Kent wouldn't start acting curmudgeonly toward Selina for being a fan of Fred Dromly's. She wouldn't deserve that.

"No way!" Selina beamed at Kent excitedly. "The one time I met him he was so mesmerizing when he began speaking. You could tell his work was his passion. Haven't you tried to ask *him* about his journals?"

"I haven't," Kent said curtly, "and that's a long story."

"I'm so sorry; I shouldn't have asked. That's none of my business," Selina said quickly, her cheeks turning red.

Jonathan leaned over to his right. "No worries," he whispered to her. "Anyone would have done the same."

"Thank you," she whispered back, a look of gratitude crossing her face. "You're very kind."

From the moment she corrected him in the cave, Jonathan's mind had started composing a song about her, and it continued playing. He grabbed one of his paper napkins and quickly jotted down a few lyrics and a chord progression. Shoving the napkin in his pocket, he glanced at her, eager to learn more about her. "So how did you meet Dr. Dromly?"

"I was wondering the same thing," Nate piped up for the first time.

"Dr. Dromly and his team were starting a new dig," Selina began. "They were expecting to find artifacts I assume—I don't really know the whole story. Instead, they uncovered some fossils and rare minerals. So I was one of the lucky ones who got to travel to the site with several other geologists and a few paleontologists. Dr. Dromly was still there when we arrived and spoke with all of us. He told us some stories of his adventures that had everyone on the edge of their seat. He's like a real-live action hero!"

Kent rolled his eyes. "He'd love to know that's the impression he made."

Selina looked down at her hands and squirmed in her seat.

Kent and Lorelei began asking Raina questions about cave art. Jonathan took that opportunity to turn to his right and tell Selina so only she could hear, "I've read all of Dr. Dromly's books and some of the entries in his journals. They really are remarkable. I was a huge fan of his too at first until Kent told us how neglectful of a father he was and how arrogant he is."

"I'm sorry, I didn't know," she whispered back.

"Of course not; how could you know?"

Her shoulders shrugged slightly. "Nothing I've said seems to be okay with Kent. I'm sorry I intruded on your group. I think I should excuse myself and leave."

Jonathan found himself hoping she wouldn't go. "Don't do that. And don't feel bad about anything you've said. You've done nothing wrong."

"Thank you," she told him, the corners of her pink lips turning upward as she discretely reached over and gave his hand a slight squeeze under the table. Her touch was tender and her fingers cold.

"Do you want to borrow my jacket?" Jonathan asked, taking off his sweat jacket and handing it to her.

"That's so nice of you," she said, rewarding him with another smile. "I should know better than to have a cold salad and ice water when the air conditioning is blasting." She put on his jacket and rubbed her arms.

His jacket had never looked better. A sudden urge to take her hands in his to warm them made him force his attention back to the table's conversation instead.

"So we believe that Dr. Dromly thinks there's a map disguised as cave art drawings," Lorelei told Raina.

"A map for what?" Raina wondered out loud.

"According to what we've read in Dr. Dromly's journals so far, he seems to think it leads to where the Plate of Destiny is hidden," Lorelei replied.

"Interesting," Raina said with a thoughtful look.

"Do you think my father could be right? Have you seen any cave art that maybe looked more like a map?" Kent asked.

Raina paused while the table was being served dessert. Jonathan dug in to his slice of chocolate cake while Raina answered Kent. "I haven't seen it myself, but I've heard of a few caves where ancient cave art has been found. There's one in particular that has drawings that appear to be newer based on the sharpness of the lines."

"Do you know which cave?" Anise asked.

"I do!" Raina said, nodding her head enthusiastically. "I've been wanting to explore it for a while now. I have the afternoon off, and I'd be happy to take y'all spelunking if you'd like!"

"I'm game," Nate replied.

"Me too!" Jonathan said excitedly.

"We'd appreciate that, thank you," Lorelei said as Anise and Kent voiced their agreement as well.

"This is great," Jonathan said in between bites. "We're getting somewhere, but we know that Dromly has already seen this map. If he hasn't found the Plate by now, he's missing something. We need to figure out what that is."

"I'd love to help," Selina spoke up. "I was going to go to the library in Tallahassee tomorrow to do some research on the minerals they have in the area, but your questions are far more interesting. I'll see if there's anything I can find."

"I'll go with you," Jonathan volunteered. He looked forward to seeing her again. "Two heads are better than one."

"Kent and I will read more of the trip journals," Lorelei said to Anise. "Maybe there's something in there we missed. We'll figure this out one way or another."

"I look forward to seeing you tomorrow," Selina whispered to Jonathan while the others listened to the driving instructions Raina was giving them. "But I should get going now. You didn't expect to have another person tagging along on your trip to the cave, and I don't want to intrude on your group any further."

"It's not an intrusion," Jonathan told her. "Come with us. It'd be interesting to see what a geologist thinks of the cave art we'll see."

✳ ✳ ✳

ANISE ADJUSTED THE COVER-ALLS RAINA HAD lent her and put on a helmet that had a light over the forehead. The hike to the mouth of the cave hadn't been long, and with the amulet around her neck, she felt safe and ready for the next part of the adventure.

"This is a good cave for beginners," Raina told them. She showed them the map of the cave she'd brought. "Although we will have to crawl through one part, it's not too difficult. Remember to stay together, and for the sake of the cave, please be careful where you step, and make sure the only thing you take away from it is pictures. Is everyone ready?"

"I'm a little nervous," Selina admitted to the group.

"Really?" Jonathan asked. "What are you nervous about?"

Selina shrugged shyly. "The darkness. The tight spaces. The bugs in the tight spaces."

"You seemed fine in the tour we took this morning," he commented with a concerned expression.

"That was different," Selina admitted. "There were lights and paths and..." She looked at the ground as her cheeks flushed.

Anise stepped over to her and said warmly, "If there's one thing I understand, it's anxiety. If you don't want to do this, you don't have to. But if you do, we'll all be with you."

Selina's eyes shined with gratitude. "Thank you for that. I'll be fine. What kind of geologist would I be if I said no to this opportunity?"

Anise admired the confidence Selina found without the need to prepare herself mentally with affirmations or protective amulets. Anise hoped to be there too someday.

"Great," Raina told Selina. "If you start to feel claustrophobic at any time though, just let me know."

Anise followed Raina inside and switched on her helmet light. The darkness came quickly once the cave swallowed them whole. She walked slowly through the narrow corridor, trying to avoid tripping or bumping her head on a stalactite. She followed behind Raina closely and heard the others' footsteps behind her. Jonathan seemed to have made a fast friend of Selina and they could be heard oohing and aahing at the back of the line together and taking pictures of the rock formations that had them so enchanted.

"Here's where we'll have to crawl a little bit," Raina warned them. "These caves can flood during storms, and it rained recently so it's probably pretty muddy."

Anise watched as Raina ducked down into a small passageway and disappeared. She followed suit and soon found she needed to drop to her hands and knees and then push herself along on her stomach.

"It's a little tight!" Raina called out. "But keep going, it won't be for long!"

Anise paused for a moment to blink when some mud from Raina's boot was accidentally kicked into her eye. Trying not to follow Raina quite as closely anymore, she took her time getting through the tunnel and felt a sense of accomplishment when she was able to stand up in an underground room. Mud dropped from her knees and chest to the ground. The floors weren't smooth and flat like they were in the cavern they'd toured earlier that day, and she stepped carefully forward over a trickling stream to where Raina was standing.

"How's everyone doing?" Raina asked, looking right at Selina.

"I'm great!" Selina replied, her smile making her mud-smeared cheeks raise. "This is so cool!"

"You're not anxious at all?" Jonathan asked her.

Selina shrugged. "Maybe a little. That crawl was a tight squeeze, but it wasn't as bad as I thought it was going to be. I'm glad I'm doing this."

"This is the room where some cave art was found," Raina announced. "But I'm not sure where exactly it is. We'll have to search for it." She began shining her flashlight slowly over a part of the wall and the others joined her.

Anise looked over at Nate who grinned sideways at her. She couldn't help but smile back at him and hated herself for it. *Why is that grin so charming every damn time?* She considered turning away but noticed her legs carrying her over to him. "How's your cut?"

"It came open a little," he admitted, putting his hand over where he'd been sliced. "But it'll be okay."

"Let me heal you now," she said. "I have the Jewelry in my backpack. It's going to rip open more when we have to crawl back through that tunnel. And uphill this time." Grabbing his hand, she led him around a corner where Selina and Raina wouldn't see her putting on the Jewelry. Lifting his shirt and placing her hands over the cut on his abdomen, she willed for him to heal. The cuff sparkled, and within moments, the cut grew back together with new, healthy skin. She put the Armor Jewelry back in her bag while he resituated his clothes.

"Thanks, honey," Nate said. He stepped out of the dark corner, took her in his arms, and kissed her forehead.

"You're muddy," she complained, pushing him away.

"So are you," he replied, enveloping her into a tighter hug.

The mud on their chests and stomachs squished and puckered between them, the ridiculous noises making Anise laugh as she strained her neck to not let her semi-clean face be besmirched by the filth on his arms and chest. He kissed her mouth, and she pushed him away again. "Not here," she whispered.

"Okay," he agreed. His eyes sparkled brighter than the cuff had a moment earlier. "Later then. In the shower." He walked back to the others and joined them in searching for the cave art.

Anise saw Raina smiling at the two of them and their playful antics. She returned Raina's smile but then frowned at the back of Nate's head, not willing to admit to herself how much she wanted to meet him in the shower and let her anger run down the drain with the warm, caressing water. But he had lied, put her life in danger, and she had to stay mad at him, no matter how many times he made her laugh or feel happy and loved. Pushing aside her thoughts, she shined her flashlight on the wall to search for the map.

"What's it supposed to look like exactly?" Nate called out.

"Nice work, you found it!" Jonathan exclaimed, checking out the spot Nate was staring at.

"Are you sure?" Nate asked him. "It's just a few lines. Doesn't look like anything."

"Definitely. I don't know what it's supposed to be, but those lines are man-made."

Anise wondered why the guys couldn't get along that well all the time. She joined the others to see what Nate had found. The lines carved into the cave wall formed a few squares and some were further divided into smaller squares or triangles.

"Are those Schwartz's markings or actual ancient drawings?" Nate asked Jonathan.

"I'm not sure. What do you think?" Jonathan asked Raina and Selina.

"Those look like the ancient drawings I saw in pictures," Raina commented.

"I'd have to agree," Selina chimed in. "Look how worn the edges of the carvings are. My guess is this drawing was here a very long time. Which means that Wilhelm Schwartz's drawing is probably near here somewhere."

"I think I found it!" Jonathan exclaimed. He'd wandered a few feet away and was staring intently at the wall illuminated by his flashlight.

"It looks like an 'L,'" Nate commented. "Did that letter have any significance in Dromly's journals?"

"Not that I read," his mother replied.

"Same," Kent agreed.

Anise stood on her tiptoes to see over Raina's shoulder. The drawing Jonathan had found did look like the letter L and the vertical line had two short horizontal lines dividing it into three equal parts.

Jonathan took several pictures of both drawings. "Let's see if we can find out anything more about them in the journals," he said to Kent and Lorelei, "and at the library," he added to Selina. "Maybe the meaning of this drawing is what Dromly is missing. Maybe that's why he hasn't found the Plate of Destiny yet."

Chapter 9

Thursday, October 8, 2015

Really?" Lorelei asked. She looked at Nate, unable to hide her amazement. "You can make a beef Wellington?" She was thoroughly enjoying her son's company on the car ride back to the hotel. Even though it was after midnight, she was wide awake. It was almost surreal getting to know him as the man he'd become when her last memory of him was as a small child.

"Yeah," Nate confirmed. "I made it once. It turned out pretty good."

"That's impressive," she told him. "Where'd you learn to cook?"

"I spent a lot of time at my friends Scott and Peter's house when I was a kid. I never wanted to go home, so I'd volunteer to help their mom with dinner. I don't know how much I actually helped, but she was always gracious and let me stay as long as I wanted."

"She was a good cook?"

"Yeah. The best. A good teacher, too. I learned a lot from her."

"That's great." Lorelei was happy for him but wished it could've been her teaching him to cook. Or anything at all. "I never tried to make anything that ambitious. I made steaks once for Grace and Dan on his birthday. I was nervous because I knew Grace would tear me apart if I didn't get a perfect medium-rare."

"Did you get it?" Nate wanted to know.

"Yes! But I dropped one on the ground, and I didn't have any extra." Lorelei let out a small laugh. "I was so upset with myself."

"So what did you do?"

"I picked it up, brushed it off, and served it to Grace."

THE DRIVE BACK TO THEIR HOTEL droned on and on as if they were going backward. From her shotgun position next to Kent, Anise could see Nate and Lorelei in the car in front of them talking and laughing, and she couldn't help glaring at him the entire time. How could he laugh right now as if he hadn't done anything wrong?

When they finally arrived back at the hotel, it was in the very early morning hours. She headed straight for the shower—alone, at her insistence and Nate's great disappointment—and all she wanted was to close her eyes and dream about her own bed. After washing away all the mud, she came out of the bathroom wrapped in a towel. She realized she'd never asked more questions about the fight he got into. Her curiosity grew as she thought about it. Who would he have to fight here? She hoped to bring up the topic without actually asking outright so he wouldn't think that she cared. "Do you have any more cuts you didn't tell me about?"

"No, just the one."

"Are you sure? Any bruises? Pain of any kind? The Jewelry still has a strong charge. I can heal you."

He grinned and held out his arms as if to give his body over to her. "If you don't believe me, you're welcome to check."

She looked away, not wanting to see his stupid, charming grins anymore. "No. If you don't want to tell me about the fight, then any pain you still have is *your* problem."

He shrugged. "It really wasn't that bad."

She gave him a look of disbelief.

"I've had worse," he said.

She rolled her eyes. "Fine. Whatever." She walked around him, grabbed her pajamas, and started putting them on. *Clueless fucking man*. It was the details she wanted. The who, what, when, where, and mostly the goddamn why.

"You were right, honey," he conceded. "I should've told you about it. If something like that happened to you, I would want to know about it."

"Thank you," Anise said, putting her bag on the desk and digging through it to look for an antacid. She felt his arms wrap around her from behind.

"It happened when I was—"

"It doesn't matter anymore," she interrupted him. He'd finally understood what she wanted and was about to explain it. Good. But if she listened, he'd know she still cared. And she didn't care. Or at least, she wouldn't soon enough.

Even though she was doing her best to brush him off, his arms held her closer. She could feel his breath on her neck. The comforting warmth from his arms made her want to melt into them, to wrap her own arms around them so he wouldn't let go, but her anger wouldn't allow it. Instead, she stepped out of his embrace and sat on the bed holding her stomach.

"Are you okay?" Nate asked Anise.

"I'll be fine. It's just some heartburn. And I'm so tired. It was a long day." But it wasn't just exhaustion. She missed her friends, especially Erin. She missed feeling safe. She missed when she and Nate were happy. She'd missed another day of work, and she wondered if her boss would buy that she had the flu again.

"You're stressed," Nate concluded.

"Yes," she replied. "But I'm ready to talk."

"Good," he said. "Then you can finally let me explain."

"You helped Grace escape from prison and armed her with a neurotoxin knowing full well she's tried to kill me in the past. How can you possibly explain?" She looked at the floor still holding her stomach.

He sat next to her on the bed. "I knew she wouldn't be able to kill anyone, and I had no idea she'd be able to use it to escape."

"How did you know she wasn't going to kill anyone with it? What else did you think she'd want it for?" Anise demanded.

"Like I said before, the dose wasn't strong enough to kill anyone. I did my research before I brought it to her. She must've somehow gotten someone else to bring her more of it or else she got her hands on something to mix with it to make it stronger."

"Why didn't you think of that first?" Anise demanded.

"Because Grace doesn't need a toxic substance to kill anyone. I've seen her take down someone way bigger than her really easily. People misjudge her because she's a little old lady, so they don't expect her to be violent or physically capable. The truth is that she has an extensive working knowledge of pressure points and can hurt people with it, paralyze them, or even kill them. She keeps herself in good shape and is stronger than she looks. So if she wanted to hurt someone, she'd just do it. She doesn't need anyone's help."

"Well obviously she wanted it for something. Why didn't you consider the possibilities?"

"I did. She's had me and Dan steal drugs for her before, including that specific one. I thought she wanted it for pain like every other time."

"Why wouldn't she just go to the doctor like a normal

person?"

"She hates being poked and prodded by doctors. Her words. She thinks getting help from anyone including doctors is weak, and she won't do it."

Anise narrowed her brows, thinking back to when she was at the Springfield Museum trying to get the chalcedony earrings before Grace did. The night Grace had planned to kill her. "That's not true. I saw Dan giving her pills once when she was having an episode of hallucinations."

"Yeah, Dan stole those for her and tried to shove them down her throat. We both thought she belonged in a mental institution. But she wouldn't take them because she knew that her hallucinations were caused by Smithton trying to brainwash her with the cuff without having king's blood. She didn't actually have any psychoses."

Nate's explanations made sense—so much sense that she almost had no reason to be angry with him anymore. But she was. The anger filled her like a water balloon about to burst. "All these perfect little justifications," her sarcasm oozed.

"You think I'm making this up?" Nate looked hurt.

Anise didn't care. "You still stole something for her, and you promised me no more illegal activity. You still gave her a toxic substance that could've hurt someone. You still kept it from me."

"I offered a bribe to have her put in solitary confinement so she couldn't use it to hurt anyone until they could get her a transfer to another prison. That way if she'd hidden it, she wouldn't have access to it."

Anise sighed. "Fine. So you tried. But it wasn't good enough. You still helped her escape and put my life in danger."

"Honey, if I had known what she was planning to do with the toxin, I would've never gotten it for her. No one wanted to be rid of her more than I did. I let myself get caught and go to prison so I could take her down with me."

Anise looked up at him, her stomach suddenly hurting even more. "So Jonathan was *right*. All this time I've been believing that you went to prison because you stayed behind to cover my tracks. He told me it was only because you wanted Grace and Dan to be locked away so you could rid yourself of them. He was right all along. This is the second time I've found out you're not who I thought you were." She shook her head sadly at him and got up to walk to the bathroom. Her stomach had never hurt so badly before.

"He's not right," Nate insisted.

She turned back. "You just said yourself you got caught so you could take Grace down!"

"That's only part of it," he explained. "The other part *was* to keep you out of prison. *And* to save your life. If I hadn't taken down Grace she would've come after you again."

She glared at him. A murderer who wants her blood was walking free because of him. "Nice try," she said with snarling lips and began walking toward the bathroom again.

"It's true," he insisted. "Anise."

She stopped to listen to him but didn't turn back around to face him. Tears were starting to form in her eyes, and she didn't want him to see.

"I..." he started. "You..." He sighed in frustration as he seemed to struggle for the right words. "When we first met, getting you alone so I could steal your amulet was just a way for me to prevent another person from getting killed by Grace. But you were so genuine and trusting and innocent..." The bed creaked when he stood up. "I've never been in love before, but with you it happened so fast."

She dabbed her eyes with her sleeve and turned around to look at him.

Nate continued, his eyes intense but his voice gentle.

"You're the most beautiful person I've ever met, inside and out, and I knew I wanted to protect you. I had no plans to keep helping Grace, but she poisoned me with the ring when I told her I wanted out. I had to pretend I was still on her side so she wouldn't kill me, but everything I did from that point on was to protect you from her. I admit I wanted to protect myself too, but you wouldn't blame me if you knew what it was like growing up with her. And as far as bringing Grace the neurotoxin...she said she had some information that might help us, and of course she wanted something in return. I wanted to do anything I could to help you, so I took a chance. I'd do anything to help you, and I'm not sorry about that. But I should've told you about it. I know I fucked that part up, and for that, I'm sorry."

Anise recalled her psychologist friend Corinne telling her how Nate had experienced mental, emotional, and possibly physical abuse from Grace on a daily basis as a child. His pained expression convinced her of what he was saying. She stepped over to him and wrapped her arms around him. "I believe you."

He hugged her back. "Thank you. And I'm sorry. For everything." He nuzzled her hair. "I love you, honey."

She stepped back when he tried to kiss her. "No. I forgive you, but I can't do this anymore."

"What are you saying?"

"We can't be together anymore." Her stomach pains grew worse.

He looked at her with a confused expression.

"Nate, I've never met anyone that makes me feel like you do—and I mean that in a good way. I feel so *alive* when I'm around you. You're determined and confident and generous and smart and dangerous and sexy and rebellious, and I love all those things about you. But you *lie*, Nate. You've lied to me so much, I can't trust you anymore. I can't be with someone I don't trust. And what I loved most about you is that you used to make me feel so safe, but that's gone now. And before you ask, no, I don't want to give you another chance. You've had more than your share of second chances."

He was quiet for a moment, rubbing his head with his hand. "I didn't lie. And I didn't want to keep anything from you either. Like I said before, I tried to tell you—twice."

"During two very inappropriate times! You had plenty of opportunity to tell me before, but you didn't. I can't believe I had to find out from Grace. It was so humiliating!"

"It's not the kind of thing you interject into a casual conversation," Nate insisted.

Anise's mouth opened in disbelief. "I get that some things are scary to say to someone when you know they won't be happy, but that's just part of being an adult. Seriously, grow the fuck up!"

Nate's eyes narrowed. "What about what you did? You promised me you'd stay away from Smithton, but then you snuck out of my house when I was sleeping to go to the museum."

"*My* actions didn't put *your* life in danger!" she shot back.

"No, worse! They put *your* life in danger!"

"Oh, please," she moaned, rolling her eyes again.

"But *now* your life *isn't* in danger," Nate argued. "Grace said herself she was relieved I didn't let her kill you."

"Because she wants my fresh blood! She still wants to hurt me! And she might kill me if blood is all she wants."

"I told you I won't let that happen!"

"She outsmarted you once. She can do it again." She crossed her arms over her chest. "And at least I told you about the times I went to see Dr. Smithton at the museum! You told me nothing about going to see Grace!" She sat down on the bed and grabbing a pillow, hugged it to her chest.

"I didn't tell you because I wanted to protect you

from your own mouth. You would've run right to Boy Scout to tell him all about what I heard from Grace. He would've gone straight to Smithton. And I don't have to remind you how he tied you up, tried to brainwash you, and threatened to turn you over to the cops!"

"Well then, I guess neither one of us can trust the other," she concluded. "Your kind of protection I don't need. I'm so disappointed in you and so angry at myself for thinking that being with you would be a good idea." She stood up and slammed the pillow back on the bed. "I should've listened to Jonathan," she mumbled to herself.

"So you're going back to Boy Scout now?" he demanded.

Anise could see the hurt in his eyes and rubbed her forehead. "I shouldn't have brought him up. Jonathan has nothing to do with this. I have no idea what, if anything, is going to happen with me and Jonathan from here on out. But I know that nothing more is going to happen between you and I, and I wanted to tell you now instead of later."

His scowling face gave her a quick nod, and he walked around her, heading for the door.

"Where are you going?" she called after him. "It's the middle of the night!"

He left the room letting the door slam behind him.

Anise sat on the bed again and let her blinding tears fall onto her lap as she doubled over, cradling her stomach. She heard him start his motorcycle and speed away. Wanting to be alone, she groaned softly to herself and wiped her tears away when she heard a light tapping on her door. "Hey," she said quietly when she answered it.

"Hey," replied Jonathan. "I passed Nate in the hall a couple minutes ago, and he stormed right by me. Are you okay?"

She shook her head no as she opened her door wider and waved him in.

"Talk to me," he said as he sat in her desk chair.

"I'd feel weird talking to you about this," she replied

as she sat on the end of her bed.

"You had a fight?"

She nodded.

"We may have broken up, but that doesn't have to mean our friendship is over too," he said.

"I would *love* to get our friendship back."

"Good, it's settled then. Now, talk to me."

"Okay," she agreed, still a little uncomfortable. "Whatever it was that Nate and I had, it's over. I just ended it. He lied to me over and over again. You were right. I'm an idiot for letting myself get so involved with him."

"I never called you an idiot," protested Jonathan. "But I'm glad you're finally seeing him for who he really is."

"I am. It sucks though because there's so much about him that's amazing."

Jonathan remained silent and looked at the floor.

Anise continued. "I miss him already. And I *hate* that I miss him. It hurts. And I hate that I really hurt him," she lamented.

"He'll be okay," said Jonathan, moving to the bed to sit next to her. "And so will you. We've all had a broken heart at some point in our lives."

"I know," she said. "But Nate has had more than his share. His mother disappeared when he was a little kid. His father and grandmother were nothing but abusive. His heart was broken every day and when he finally got the courage to open it to someone, I stomp all over it." Her tears started to flow again.

Jonathan got up and brought her a box of tissues from the bathroom. "That's unfortunate, but it's no reason to stay with someone who keeps lying to you."

She dabbed her eyes. "You're right, I know. I should never have let this happen. I should never have let myself fall in love with him."

He put an arm around her shoulder in an attempt to comfort her. "It's partly my fault. I should've never broken up with you in the first place. I've regretted it ever since it happened."

She looked at him. "Then why did it happen?"

His cheeks turned red. "I was jealous of the time you were spending with Nate. I could tell you still had feelings for him."

"I did," she admitted. "But I never would've acted on them. I should've not hung out with him so much until I could get over my feelings for him. I should've never given you any reason to doubt me."

"I know you wouldn't have acted on your feelings, and I never should've doubted you. If I had believed in you and in us a little more, everything would've been okay."

"You were also brainwashed," said Anise. "I know that didn't help matters."

"No," agreed Jonathan. "I had these scary violent urges, and I wanted you to stay away from me so you'd be safe."

"Well, none of that is anything we have to worry about anymore," Anise said. A few more tears found their way down her cheeks.

"That's right," Jonathan agreed. He grabbed another tissue and wiped away her tears. "And I'm glad we're friends again."

"Me too." Anise gave Jonathan a serious look. "Do you think I need to change?"

"Not at all. I think pajamas are completely appropriate this time of night."

It felt good to laugh, and she looked at him with gratitude. "What I mean is that my friends have always told me that I see only the good in other people which opens me up to being hurt and taken advantage of. How my parents and Brian treated me, for example. Am I really that naïve?"

Jonathan shook his head. "You do always see the good in people," he agreed. "And that's not an easy thing to do. Even when they do something wrong, you treat them with love and kindness. But no way are you naïve about it. When you've had enough of bad behavior, you put your foot down. You broke up with Brian, and I was there a few times when you told your parents off. Now you broke up with Nate. You have an open heart, and you freely give your love and trust until someone gives you a reason not to. Most people are too scared to do that, but that's just who you are. It's strong, and it's amazing, and it's one of the many reasons why I fell in love with you."

"Thank you." With her eyes misty, she gave him a quick hug. "I want you to know that after you broke up with me, I didn't run right to Nate with the intention of being with him. I was heartbroken over you, and jumping into another relationship was the furthest thing from my mind. My biggest priorities were helping you get better from your brainwashing symptoms and helping Nate find Lorelei. I considered him to be a friend, someone I had gone through a life-changing experience with. I *never* expected I'd feel what I do for him."

"You don't have to explain, Anise," Jonathan told her. "I know these things are always more complicated than they might seem to people outside the relationship."

"They are!" Anise exclaimed, happy that he understood. "I just don't want you to think that you were easily replaced or something. You could never be replaced in my life. I am so lucky to know you, and I will always love you, and I miss you. When we were together, I—"

"I really...don't want to talk about this," Jonathan said, interrupting her while staring at the floor.

"Oh. Sorry." She looked down at her fidgeting hands and wondered what she had said that was so wrong. She twisted her garnet ring around her finger.

"Let's just move forward. We make great friends," he said.

"Of course," she replied, uncomfortable during the silence that followed. "I should get some sleep. Thanks for checking in on me."

"HAVE A GOOD NIGHT," JONATHAN SAID to Anise. He left, closing her hotel room door behind him. His face grimaced as he walked down the hallway toward his own room. Could he live with himself if he let their conversation end that way? He paused, turned around, and headed back in Anise's direction. She said she loved and missed him. Did they still have a chance? His fist raised to knock on her door, but he stopped himself. He wondered what she'd meant when she said there were so many things about Nate that are amazing. He tried to imagine what those things might be but came up with nothing. For some reason, she seemed to believe that Nate had some redeeming qualities, enough to make her love him. His chest ached when he realized the muffled sounds he was hearing were her sobs. And from the conversation they'd just had, it was obvious that her tears were for Nate, not for him. Sighing, he hurried toward his room and wondered if he'd be able to sleep that night.

* * *

ANISE WOKE A FEW HOURS LATER from the intense burning in her esophagus. She held her chest and sat up straight. Nate wasn't in the bed next to her as she hoped he might be by that time of night. She felt worry creep up inside her. Was he out doing something reckless? Switching on the lamp next to the bed, she saw that he'd been back in the room while she had been asleep. His jacket was on the chair. His motorcycle key was on the desk. A bottle of Sprite was in the ice bucket surrounded by ice that was only partly melted. Grateful, she opened the cold soda and took a swig. Nothing helped her more than soda when her stomach was upset. Tears fell again.

After everything she'd said to him, after breaking up with him, he'd still brought her soda. She tried to push aside her thoughts and pulled the covers up to her chin. Her eyebrows narrowed at his jacket. She wanted to put it on so she could pretend he was behind her holding her tight almost as much as she wanted to throw it in the bathtub with gasoline and a match. Damn him for making her doubt her decision, even if just for a moment.

NATE WALKED DOWN THE HALLWAY OF the hotel. His plan had been to get some sleep, but his racing mind told him it was going to be another sleepless night. He'd felt numb during his ride, but now that some time had passed, his chest was suddenly tight, and he noticed an aching that felt like a punch to the gut yet seemed to have no bodily origin. All he had wanted was to help. To continue to be the hero Anise used to think he was. But nothing was good enough. He had never been good enough. Not for Grace or Dan, not for Lorelei with her disapproving looks, and not for Anise, the only woman he'd ever cared about. Anise didn't even ask what it was that Grace told him—the whole reason he went to see her in the first place—the reason they were fighting now. *Fuck them all.*

Passing by Lorelei's room, he saw a light on underneath her door. He knew he was angry and almost walked by, but another emotion popped up. He stood in the hallway and mentally went through the list of emotions the prison shrink had given him. This was exhausting. *Do most people have this many feelings all at once?* He wished he could be numb again. Was it guilt? He wasn't sure, but for some reason, he knew that if he didn't knock on his mother's door to check on her, he'd feel bad. He tapped softly in case she'd fallen asleep with the light on. He thought about how Anise said she should've listened to Boy Scout. There was an emotion surrounding that, too. What was it? Jealousy?

Lorelei opened the door. "Hi! Come in!" Her eyes lit up at the sight of him. "What are you doing up at this hour?"

"I could ask you the same question."

"I couldn't sleep. I'm reading trip journals," she said, pointing to the stack of books on her dresser. When he just stood there and stared at her, she prompted him, "Are you okay?"

Nate barely noticed her words or that she'd taken his arm and pulled him into her room. *It wasn't jealousy*, he thought. *It's worse. It's grief.* He didn't move as he tried to turn off the bombarding emotions. He thought about the new Ducati Monster 1200 S in an attempt to banish Anise from his mind.

"Nate?" his mother said.

"Sorry I bothered you. I should go to sleep."

"No," she said. "Don't go." She sat on the bed, grabbed his arm and pulled him into a seated position next to her.

His arm tensed up at her touch, and she let go immediately.

"Sorry," she said.

He rotated his shoulder, wondering if there was something wrong with the muscles in his arm. They usually didn't contract that way. "It's okay. What's going on?"

"That's what I'd like to know. You look upset."

He wasn't sure what to say. Nate had never talked to anyone about his problems before. Well, except for the prison psychiatrist, but she was just doing her job. She didn't actually care. Not like his mother did.

Lorelei spoke again when he remained silent. "You don't have to tell me what happened; that's none of my business. I just want to be there for you when you're hurting. Especially since I wasn't able to be there for so long."

Nate shrugged. "Don't worry about it. I'll be fine.

And it wasn't your fault you were gone. You have nothing to make up for, Mom."

It was obvious from her face that Lorelei disagreed, but she didn't argue. "Okay," she said softly as she rose. "Why don't you hang out and rest then? I'll just be over here reading if you change your mind." She gave him a weak smile before she turned to walk back to the easy chair.

Nate watched her walk away while her sad expression made him feel an uncomfortable emotion he couldn't quite place. "How are you okay?" he asked.

She looked at him and slightly cocked her head. "What do you mean?"

"You were held captive for 26 years. I was locked away for only three, and sometimes I feel like I'm still not out yet. If people know I'm an ex-con, I get judged before they even know me. I can't get rehired at my old job. And I have these nightmares where I have to go back to prison. So...how are you okay? How do you not hate Dan and Grace for everything you missed out on?"

"Who says I don't?" she replied, sitting on the bed next to him again. "I had dreams of things I wanted to do in my life. And I have nightmares, just like you. I've been mourning what I lost ever since I woke up from the coma. But I remind myself of all the wonderful things that I do still have. I also have plenty of life left. And thanks to you, Kent, and Anise, I still get a chance to live my dreams."

"What do you want to do?" Nate asked, interested in learning more about her.

Lorelei's far-away gaze was wistful. "Travel the world," she replied. "There are places on every continent I'd love to see."

"I want to take you. If that's okay."

Her face lit up with delight. "I'd love that! You could bring Anise, too."

Nate looked at the floor. "No. It's over," he mumbled.

"You and Anise?"

He nodded.

Lorelei frowned with a sad-looking expression. "I'm so sorry."

Nate felt another overwhelming emotion building up. He had no idea what it was or if it was positive or negative. He just knew that no one had ever looked at him like they cared about what he was going through before. At least, not like Lorelei was. Her face looked like his pain was causing her to hurt just as much as he was. He'd never seen such a thing before. His mother must be a very empathic person. He wondered how long it had taken her to get used to feeling everyone else's emotions. He couldn't even handle his own.

"If it's okay, I'd like to give you a hug." His mother opened her arms to him.

He allowed her to embrace him while he leaned his forehead on her shoulder.

"My little prince," Lorelei said. "I love you, and everything is going to be okay."

The comforting way she said it made him believe her. Almost.

Chapter 10

Nate opened his eyes when he heard a gentle voice. He lifted his head off the pillow and realized he was still in his mother's room. "Why didn't you wake me up?"

"I just did," Lorelei told him.

"I mean last night. Where did *you* sleep?" He sat up and put his feet on the floor.

"In the chair."

"Mom, why?" He groaned, rubbing the grogginess out of his eyes.

"You were sleeping so soundly. I'm fine. I slept well. The chair reclines."

"I can't believe I slept all night," he said. "I didn't wake up once. That hasn't happened in...a long time."

A big smile spread over her face. "When you were little, you would hug all of your stuffed animals before going to bed. You couldn't sleep unless you had one to cuddle with. Last night, you fell asleep quickly, but you were moving around a lot. I put a pillow by your chest and you settled down right away."

He felt a new emotion. Was it comforting? Was it sad? He wasn't sure, and he wasn't in the mood to try to figure it out. Memories of Anise and their conversation from the night before flooded his mind. He put head in his hands and rubbed his face. "Why am I even still here?" Nate grumbled. "I should be on my way back home. Come with me. Or even better, we can start our trip around the world." The disapproving expression on Lorelei's face made him sense an emotion that caused his heart physical pain, but again, he couldn't name it.

"Absolutely not. We made a commitment to help Anise, and that's what we're going to do. Come on now, go wash your face. Then we're all meeting in Kent's room to talk about the trip journals."

Nate knew she was right, and he knew he wouldn't have left anyway. It'd been his shitty mood talking. He did as he was told and followed her to Kent's room even though it was the last place he wanted to be. Anise and Boy Scout were already there and were seated next to each other on one of the two queen beds.

"Good morning!" Kent greeted them.

"Good morning," Lorelei replied.

Nate sat on the floor and leaned against Kent's dresser without giving Anise a glance.

"So what did you learn from the trip journals last night?" Kent asked Lorelei.

She sat on the other queen bed while Kent took the desk chair. "Your father mentions the map a lot in the journals I read last night. He says that he has several ideas about how to find it which is strange because in previous journals he already knew that the cave art he'd found was the map."

"So there's a second map," Nate concluded. His eyes felt droopy, and he was exhausted despite the sleep that managed to find him in Lorelei's room.

"You may be on to something there," Kent said. "Maybe the first map leads to a second map which leads to the Plate of Destiny."

"Kind of like a scavenger hunt," Anise commented.

"That's what I'll focus on when I do research today," Jonathan said. "I'm meeting Selina at the library this morning. We'll see if we can find anything about both maps and how to read them."

"Did you find anything new?" Lorelei asked Kent.

"Yes, actually, quite a bit. In the trip journals I read, there was a lot about the Armor Jewelry," Kent said. "I learned that all four pieces are needed to recognize the Plate. Apparently without wearing all four pieces of Jewelry, the Plate would look like nothing more than a round piece of metal. If all four pieces are worn, the amplified strength and health your body would receive would allow your eyes to see a certain sheen on the surface of the Plate that normal human eyes wouldn't be able to see."

"That's why Grace wanted all four pieces of Jewelry so badly," Anise said. "Now I have them. She's going to be after me again."

"Grace knows where you are, and she knows you have all the Jewelry," Nate told her without looking at her. "She's going to let you keep it safe for her for now while she looks for the Plate. Once she finds it, she'll show up. Just keep it charged, and it'll be easy enough to keep it away from her." He felt his mind wanting to drift, to go somewhere more pleasant, but he forced himself to focus.

"There's more," Kent said. "It seems, according to a legend, that in Mallandia in the Bronze Age, a disgruntled Jewelry engineer had a revenge plot to kill the king who'd had his father executed. This Jewelry engineer did a great job of hiding the Plate of Destiny, not to mention the words written on it."

"What do you mean?" Jonathan asked.

"Even if someone had been able to find the Plate of Destiny because they had all four pieces of Armor Jewelry and saw the sheen on it, they wouldn't have seen anything *written* on it. The words of wisdom supposedly inlaid in gold were hidden from everyone, including most seers, by hiding them in various phases of time. Some of the words existed in the past, others in the present, and the rest in the future. Only a special seer, a beautiful woman with hair of flame that was initiated with the seer's wand, would be able to read it."

"Grace had flame red hair when she was young," Lorelei said. "Fred Dromly must've initiated her with the seer's wand at some point."

Kent continued, "The journals also talked about the importance of the reigning Mallandian royal having a royal Jewelry engineer. They didn't give a reason why, but it got me thinking. Anise, since you're the last one with king's blood, you'd be the reigning royal if Mallandia were still around today."

She smiled. "Maybe I should choose one then. Jonathan, I hereby appoint you my official royal Jewelry engineer."

He smiled back. "I humbly accept this great honor, my queen."

Nate rolled his eyes and then saw his mother giving him a look of warning.

"I read about a legend in one of the journals where the disgruntled Jewelry engineer made a second cuff," Lorelei said. "Maybe Fred or Grace has it. Maybe there're more cuffs than we know."

"Do you remember more about the legend?" Jonathan asked with fascination.

"I read so much last night," she replied apologetically. "I'll look for it again today, and I'll read it to everyone later."

"Great!" Jonathan said. "I need to get going anyway."

"That doesn't make any sense," Nate said, his eyes narrowed.

"What doesn't?" Lorelei asked.

"That Anise is the only descendent left of that Mallandian king. Didn't he live around the same time that King Tut did?"

"Yeah. So what?" Jonathan asked.

"So aren't most Europeans supposed to be genetically related to Tut somehow? And he came much later, but *all* Europeans are related to Charlemagne somehow, right? It just doesn't make sense that Anise would be the *only one* still alive with king's blood."

"You're right," Jonathan said, furrowing his brow in thought.

"The legend I mentioned actually offers an explanation for that, too," Lorelei told the young men.

"I can't wait to hear this one!" Jonathan said. "But I really need to get going now. Tell us tonight?"

"Of course," Lorelei told him.

"Are you ready for another stack of journals?" Kent asked Lorelei, handing her a pile of books.

Nate took them from Kent instead. "She was rubbing her eyes a lot last night. She needs a break. I'll read them."

"And I'll read your pile, Kent," Anise offered. "I'm sure you could use a break, too."

"Much appreciated," Kent told her. "Let's go down to the lobby for some breakfast," he added to Lorelei.

"Thank you," Lorelei told Nate. "I'll be back up to help you read in a little while."

"Take your time," he said. He ducked out before he'd have to make small talk with Anise.

ANISE WISHED JONATHAN GOOD LUCK WITH his research and looked around for Nate but saw that he had already left. She said good bye to the others and headed back to her room. Nate was in the shower when she got there, so she perched on a chair, cracked open a journal, and began to read. She hadn't gotten far when he came out wrapped in a towel, his wet hair dripping onto his sinewy shoulders. "Thank you for the soda you left me last night," she said, trying to ease some of the tension between them. "It really helped."

He nodded slightly at her and quickly got dressed. Grabbing the stack of journals he had promised to read, he headed for the door.

"Nate? Can we talk?"

Without a word, he sat on the bed and stared at her.

"I don't want to fight anymore," she said. She waited, but when the look on his face didn't change, she continued. "I'm sorry. I said some things in anger that I didn't mean. I want us to be friends again."

"Friends."

She couldn't tell if it was a statement or a question from the way he said it. "Yes, friends. I can't be anything more to you because you—"

He interrupted her. "I know, I'm a liar."

"I know you're still hurting too, but I really think—"

"I'm fine," he said coldly, interrupting her again.

"Oh," she said, trying not to get frustrated with him for lying again. "Good. Then you have no reason to not want to make up."

"No reason at all," he confirmed, his face still flat.

"Good, I'm glad to hear it."

He got up to leave.

She stood up before he got too far and wrapped her arms around him. "I'm really glad we're friends again," she told him.

"Me too," he said, returning her hug.

His short, loose hug didn't feel the same, and she fought back the tears that threatened to spill over. Without another word, Nate left the room and closed the door behind him.

She reached into her bag and pulled out her stack of affirmation cards, shuffling through them until she found the one that fit. "I did the right thing," she read out loud. "I did the right thing. I did the right thing." She sighed as she put her cards away. "He just can't stop lying."

✳✳✳

JONATHAN WALKED INTO THE LIBRARY AND found Selina sitting at a table near the door waiting for him. She waved as he headed toward her.

"I hope I haven't kept you waiting long," he said.

She shook her head, and her blonde waves danced around her face. "Not at all. I just got here." Rising from her seat, she motioned toward the back of the library. "Come with me."

He watched her lavender maxi dress lightly brush against her hips, legs, and ankles as she led him into a large room lined with computers.

"These computers are connected to the database of every major library in the world," she told him. "We can see anything from any library as long as it's in the database."

"That's awesome," Jonathan said, sitting next to her at a computer station.

"So where would you like to start?"

"This morning, my friends and I were discussing the possibility of there being two maps."

"Two?" Selina asked, looking intrigued.

"Yeah, so in his journals, Dr. Dromly kept talking about searching for the map after he'd already found the map that Wilhelm Schwartz disguised as cave art. That's why we think there's another map."

"That makes sense...somewhat. Why split the maps up? Where would this second map lead?"

"We don't know. That's what I'd like to search for today."

"Great, I'm excited to get started!"

✳✳✳

ANISE HEARD NATE ENTER THEIR ROOM and looked up. He had the stack of journals under his arm, his room key in his hand, and a half of a blueberry muffin between his teeth. He let the door slam behind him and set everything on the dresser. Grabbing his duffel bag, he began stuffing his clothes and other belongings inside of it.

Anise closed the trip journal she was reading. "What are you doing?"

"I'm gonna get my own room."

She put the book down. "That's probably for the best, but...these rooms are expensive, and I can't afford to pay for my own right now."

"They'll both be on my credit card. You don't owe me anything." He walked into the bathroom to grab his razor, comb, and toothbrush.

She followed him. "I don't feel comfortable with that."

With his packing complete, he swung his bag over his shoulder and headed for the door.

"Nate, listen, I got—" Anise started to say. The door closed in her face, and he was gone. She sighed and went back to her chair. Staring at the journal on the arm of the chair, she wanted to pick it back up and continue reading but found it hard to concentrate. She grabbed a tissue, dabbed her eyes, and picked up her sketchbook instead.

In his hurry to leave, Nate hadn't noticed when his bag knocked his sunglasses off of the dresser and onto the floor. They sat sadly on the carpet with one temple extended and the other folded, lonely and forgotten about. Abandoned by the person they used to be so close to. Wondering if they'd ever touch his face again. It didn't take her long to sketch them. Feeling better, she picked up the journal and found concentrating much easier this time.

A few minutes later, Nate returned. "I forgot my sunglasses," he said without looking at her. His eyes spotted them on the floor. Bending over, he grabbed the glasses and turned to leave again.

"Nate, I got fired today," Anise blurted out as she stood and walked over to him.

He turned to look at her. "What happened?"

She felt her face burning with embarrassment. "My boss called. She told me that I've been calling in too much lately. With all that's been going on though I had to. She wanted me to come in tomorrow so we could discuss it and put me on a performance improvement plan. Obviously I can't go in to work tomorrow, so she let me go." She looked at the ground, unable to stop her shoulders from slumping. Her eyes lifted to face him.

He stood motionless for a moment but then his expression softened. He placed his duffel bag on the floor and put his arms around her. "I'm sorry."

She hugged him back and squeezed him tightly. "This is why I can't pay for my own room right now. I have inheritance money from my parents, but it's all tied up in investments, and it'll be a while before I can look through the paperwork and decide which one to liquidate so I can pay you back. I feel like I've lost control over every part of my life. So I want to pay for my own room. I'll pay you back as soon as I can. That would let me hold on to the small amount of pride I have left."

"Okay," he agreed.

"Thank you," she said, still holding on to him. He felt so good. Her face leaned against his chest. "How much do I owe you?"

"Fifty bucks a night."

She kept her arms around him but took her head off his chest to look up at him. "That's it? This is a really nice hotel."

He shrugged. "I got a really good deal."

She glared at him. "Are you lying to me again?"

His cobalt eyes sparkled, and he gave her the mischievous sideways grin she was trying not to find irresistible anymore.

"Nate!" She wanted to be angry but found herself

laughing instead.

He laughed along with her. "Okay, you're the one who's getting a really good deal. You wanted to be friends again. So let me help you. Isn't that what friends are supposed to do?"

"Thank you for your offer. But once we get back home, I'm paying you back, full price."

"Fine," he agreed. "I tried to get another room, but there're conventions and other events going on. The hotel is full. I called some nearby hotels, same thing. I'm going to see if Kent would mind a roommate."

"Later," she told him. "Right now we need to put more time into reading these journals."

She hadn't let him go yet, and for a moment, the way he looked at her made it seem like he wanted to kiss her. Instead, he removed his arms from around her and picked up the stack of journals he'd left on the dresser. "Have you found anything worthwhile in here yet?"

"Not yet," she admitted, finally releasing her grip around him. "You?"

"I barely started. I have doubts as to whether sitting around reading is the best plan of action." He set the journals on the desk. "Lorelei and Kent want us all to meet for lunch today to discuss what we find."

"Great! Let's get back to it then. I'll text Jonathan and let him know about our plans." She sat in the easy chair, and he took the desk chair. She watched him start to read through a journal. Damn him for making her laugh and feel better.

✳✳✳

"WE'LL HAVE TO BE VERY CAREFUL," Morty said as he slowly walked along the crowded city street. "Dromly has his army with him at all times." He pulled the brim of his hat down further over his face in case any of the army members should turn around. Someone as tall as he was would be easy to recognize.

"We'll be fine," Grace told him. She motioned ahead to Dromly and the team of brainwashed co-workers Morty had supplied him with. "But why is it *his* army? I thought they were loyal to *you*?"

"They were always meant to be his. He had me command them to be loyal to only him unless he specifically puts me in command of them. Otherwise, they won't listen to me anymore."

"What's he doing anyway? All he's done today is go shopping."

"I know he's close to finding the second map. My guess is he's collecting supplies. So far we've seen him purchase rope, flashlights, canteens, special shoes of some kind."

"Where the hell is this map?" Grace wondered out loud.

"Wherever it is, we'll find out soon."

"I MADE A LIST OF BOOKS that've been completely digitized and put on the system that might be of some help," Selina said to Jonathan after a few hours of research.

"I did the same thing," he told her. "We'll compare lists. But first, I could use a break. Are your eyes as tired as mine are?"

She nodded. "They are."

"How about some lunch?" he asked her. "It'll be my treat as a thank you for helping me."

"I'd love to!"

Jonathan held the door for Selina as they exited the library. They walked together along the busy city street passing hotels, restaurants, and other businesses while trying to speak above the noise of the traffic.

"So do you live around here?" Jonathan asked her.

"No, just visiting. You?"

"Same. Are you here for business or pleasure?"

"Both," she answered. "My grandfather brought me here as a present for my thirtieth birthday. He knew I've always wanted to come here and learn about the minerals in the area. But I'm also participating in some digs while I'm here. We're planning on staying a couple of months."

"When's your birthday?"

Selina looked down and shrugged. "It's today, actually."

Jonathan raised his eyebrows in surprise. "Happy birthday!"

"Thanks!"

"Why are you spending it at the library with me when you could be out living it up?"

She shrugged again. "I love being at the library learning about...anything at all. And I'm enjoying hanging out with you."

They found a small café and sat across from each other at a tiny, round table near the window.

"So where are you from?" Jonathan asked.

"Chicago. I lived in the city for a while, but I'm in the suburbs now." As Selina hung her bag on the back of her chair, a thin book with Japanese writing and a picture of a beach on the cover fell out.

Jonathan picked it up for her. "Can you read this?"

She gave a little laugh as she put the book back in her bag. "Sort of. I'm trying to. Japan has a lot of interesting geologic formations, and I hope to visit one day soon. I'm told this is the book with the best information. I couldn't find an English translation, and I took several Japanese classes in college, so I'm slowly making my way through it."

"That's impressive! Is Japanese hard to learn?"

"It's very different from English, so yes, it's pretty challenging. But I enjoy a challenge. Do you speak any other languages?"

"I took a couple years of Spanish in high school, but I don't remember much. It wasn't my best subject." He shook his head. "Kent speaks seven languages. I don't know how he keeps it all straight."

"Seven?!" she exclaimed. "Wow. Genius must run in his family." She looked down at her lap and her cheeks turned red. "Sorry. I didn't mean to bring up Fred Dromly."

"Don't be," Jonathan reassured her. "Kent's a little sensitive about his relationship with his dad, but I'm with you. Like I said, I've read a few of Fred Dromly's journals, and I'm hooked. He may not have been a good father, but it's hard not to admire him for the work he's done. He's had an amazing, adventurous life."

"I'd love to have that kind of life," she sighed. "I went into geology partly because I've always loved rocks, but I also wanted to be able to travel to interesting places. And I have, but not as much as I'd like."

"So what makes a person fall in love with rocks?" Jonathan asked, excited to learn more about this intelligent, accomplished woman.

"When I was a kid, I was really into solo activities like reading, and I had several collections—dolls, stamps, postcards. While the other kids were running around playing tag or whatever, I was constantly on the ground digging up rocks with my bare hands. I had shelves and shelves of them in my room. They were my favorite collection by far. Each one was different, and it was exciting to find one that was unique in some way. Some had interesting colors or a metallic shine, and those got the place of honor on my shelves."

Her voice was pure and clear with a sparkling quality like a pristine mountain lake on a sunny day. He detected only a slight Chicago accent. He had friends from that area with much heavier accents, and he wondered if she grew up somewhere else. His eyes fixated on her pink lips when she spoke again.

"When my grandfather would buy me books about rocks, I loved them even more with every turn of the page. Rocks are like books themselves—they tell stories about the earth that we wouldn't know otherwise. Plus, they're beautiful," she added, looking at her ring. "This is a bloodstone," she said, showing Jonathan her perfectly manicured hand. A dainty gold bracelet circling her wrist drifted slightly forward from the motion and seemed to echo her careful and understated mannerisms. "My grandfather gave it to me. They're supposedly for good health and courage. I don't buy into the metaphysical properties people assign to gemstones, but I try to stay open-minded. After all, the vibration of quartz crystals are so precise they're used in watches, which I find so fascinating. Maybe with future studies we'll be able to find more amazing uses for them."

"It sounds like you're close with your grandfather."

She nodded. "My parents both died young. I don't remember either one of them. My grandfather raised me by himself."

Jonathan could've listened to her talk all day. "Do you have a favorite rock or mineral?"

"Fluorite," she responded immediately. "I went on a night dig once in college, and the fluorite was glowing this gorgeous indigo color under the UV lights we brought. It was the most magical thing I've ever seen, and indigo has been my favorite color ever since." She brought up a picture on her phone and showed it to him. "This was from that night."

"Wow, that's incredible!" he told her. "I hope you posted that on social media. Something like that should be shared with the world."

"Not from that night; it was too long ago, before people took as many pictures as they do now. But I posted some more recent pictures of digs," she replied.

"I'd love to see them. Text me where I can follow you."

"Okay, but I'm not very active on social media. I've never posted a picture of myself. All my pictures are of rocks, so it's not very exciting to most people. And I don't think I've posted in over a year."

"Really?" Jonathan thought pictures of Selina should be shared with the world, too.

"I don't like being on my phone too much. Honestly, I'd rather be reading a book."

"What's the last thing you posted?"

Selina grabbed her phone and showed him a picture of a rock with a scruffy little dog sitting next to it.

"Aw, who's this cute little guy?" he asked.

"That's my sweet girl Opal," Selina replied with a smile. "I've had her since she was a puppy. She's staying with one of my grandpa's friends while we're here. I miss her."

"Opal. A gemstone name," Jonathan commented.

Selina laughed. "Of course!"

"This is Max," Jonathan said, showing Selina a picture of his dog.

"Oh, a husky!" she exclaimed. "He's so beautiful!"

Their food came at that moment, and their conversation continued with questions about their schools, employment, and what they like to do for fun.

"Travel is what I'm enjoying most right now," Selina told him. "Besides reading, of course. What about you?"

Jonathan noticed that Selina couldn't stop smiling when he told her about his band, guitars, and how much he loved songwriting.

"I love the passion you have for your music!" she gushed. "Is any of it online? I'd love to hear some."

"We have some live performances posted. But I think I have a CD we made in my bag. I used to keep the extras in there, and I didn't take all of them out. I'll have to check."

"Please tell me you have pictures of you and your band on stage," she said, clasping her hands in hope.

"I have a ton!" he replied enthusiastically. Reaching into his pocket, he pulled out his phone and opened one of his social media accounts. He saw he had a text from Anise and made a mental note to answer it after lunch. He handed the phone to Selina, and she scrolled through the pictures slowly as he gave her a short explanation of each one.

"You look so different in these photos," she said, the corners of her lips turning up. "It's like you're a completely different person. Your demeanor, your body language, not to mention your clothes. You're not wearing your glasses—and is that eyeliner?" She pointed to the screen.

He felt his cheeks burning. "It is," he confirmed, uncomfortably knowing that his embarrassment showed in his face. "I don't normally wear eyeliner. But we were playing some punk rock covers that night."

"I love it! You look amazing!" She laughed with delight. "Not that you don't look good now, too," she added.

"Sure," he replied. "If you like the nerdy look." He looked down at his clothes and regretted wearing an old pair of jeans and an embarrassing novelty t-shirt that made a joke about how curators were so valuable that they belonged in museums.

"I've always liked nerds," she told him, her lips forming a coquettish pout. "And museum curators."

Jonathan was fully aware of how awkward his smile must look to her, but he had no idea what to say. It had been a while since a woman had looked at him like that. The way Anise looked at Nate. It felt good. "Can I buy you dessert?"

She smiled back. "I'd love dessert."

✳ ✳ ✳

NATE CHECKED HIS BEEPING PHONE AND was thrilled when the address of Dromly's hotel appeared in the text message he'd been waiting on. He knew what he wanted to do next and hoped this lunch wouldn't take too long.

"Where's Jonathan?" Kent asked as they waited to order in a restaurant around the corner from the hotel.

"I don't know," Anise replied, checking her phone. "I texted him this morning, but I never heard back. That's not like him."

"He's in a library; it's possible he may be in a basement or another area with poor reception," Kent said.

"That could be," Anise agreed. "Or he could just be so involved in his research that he forgot to check his phone."

Nate resisted the urge to roll his eyes. Who cares if Boy Scout was late to lunch? "Has anyone found anything in Dromly's journals that can help us?" he asked impatiently. He wanted to get up and leave but knew that Lorelei would grill him on why he wasn't staying, what he was going to do, and tell him it might be dangerous. For some reason, the thought of that alone made him angry. Or maybe some other emotion that he didn't care to identify.

"Not really," his mother told him. "There're a lot of interesting stories, and Fred mentions places that he's searched, but so far I've found nothing about the second map or details about how to read either of them."

"Same for me," Kent confirmed.

"This is a waste of time," Nate told them. "We need to act, not sit around reading." He dropped the journal he'd been flipping through on the table.

"We need to get to the Plate of Destiny before Grace or my father," Kent said. "The only way to do that is to figure out what they know and then get one step ahead of them."

Nate closed his eyes and rubbed the bridge of his nose. "We can't know everything they know. They've both dedicated their lives to finding this Plate. There's no way we can get one step ahead of them."

"I'd be all for going out and searching for it," Kent said, "but we have no idea where to even start looking. The only clues we have are in these journals."

"I have to agree with Kent," Lorelei piped up. "I know it's a slow process, but we need to stay the course."

Nate ate the rest of his lunch in silence while his three companions discussed what they had read which wasn't anything of value. A complete waste of time.

"I want to get some tea," Anise said after lunch, pointing at a coffee shop across the street. "Come with me?" she asked Nate.

He wanted to leave and put his plan into action right away, but for some reason he couldn't tell her no. He set aside his impatience, gave in to her request, and walked with her across the street as Kent and Lorelei made their way back to the hotel. She ordered a ginger tea while he got a cup of coffee.

"I agree with you," she told him. "I think we need to act, and I think you have a plan. I also think you didn't want to share it with Kent and Lorelei for some reason."

Something about her comment made a wave of sadness wash over Nate until he shoved it aside. "You know me well."

"You think they'd disapprove of not only your plan but also of you for coming up with it."

He looked at her, surprised. He didn't realize that's exactly what he'd been feeling until Anise verbalized it. *How did she know?* "Yeah," he replied uncomfortably. When he'd seen the disappointment in Lorelei's eyes from things he had said or how he had behaved, it bothered him in a way he couldn't explain to himself.

"Whatever it is, I think we should do it," Anise said. "You're right, there's no way we can beat Fred Dromly or Grace by trying to know more than they do about their field of expertise. You're brilliant, Nate, and whatever you're thinking, I'm in."

He looked at her again, wanting to say something about how she could always calm him down, but not knowing exactly how to do it.

"That must be Jonathan," she said when her phone beeped. She took it out of her tote bag. "Oh, it's Raina. I forgot I texted her this morning, too. I told her about your idea of a second map, and she says she has some information we might be interested in."

"You meet with her," Nate suggested as he stood up to leave. "I have to go."

"Okay," she agreed. "Whatever your plan is, good luck."

✳✳✳

IT WASN'T LONG BEFORE ANISE SAW Raina walk into the coffee shop. They exchanged pleasantries.

"Are you *really*?" Raina asked her, her deep brown eyes obviously not buying it, after Anise told her she was doing fine.

"Well, I've been having an upset stomach all day," Anise admitted. "That happens when I get stressed out."

"Ginger tea is a good remedy," Raina said, motioning to Anise's drink.

Anise nodded. "It's helping already."

Raina pushed her long black hair over her shoulders. "But is it more than that? Forgive me, I don't know you well, but you seem sad."

As if on cue, the sadness Anise was trying to forget rushed back into the forefront of her mind. A few tears made their way down her cheeks, and Raina went to fetch her some napkins.

"Thank you," Anise said, gently touching a napkin to her cheeks and eyes.

"You can talk to me...if you want," Raina told her.

Anise missed Vanessa, Erin, and Joy so much at that moment. She longed for a friend and Raina was being so kind that Anise decided to open up to her. "I broke up with Nate," she sighed.

"Really? You two looked so cute together in the cave yesterday," Raina replied.

"I didn't want to, but I feel like he didn't give me any other choice."

"Then *he* should be the one who's sad," Raina said.

Anise took a sip of her tea. "He is. I can tell. But I am too. I was so in love with him, and he lied to me multiple times."

"That's not good," Raina agreed. "But you're not glad to be rid of a liar?"

"I know I should be. It's just that...when things are good with us, they're *really good*."

"How so?"

Anise smiled as she thought about Nate. "I told him recently that I feel so *alive* when I'm with him. He's smart and adventurous and fearless, and he nudges me outside of my comfort zone which is so good for me, but he also doesn't push *too* hard which is also good. He makes me feel so safe, like I'm okay the way I am regardless of my flaws. And strong too—like I can do more than I thought I could." Her smile grew. "When he's happy, he gets playful and silly, and he makes me laugh like no one else ever could. He can come across as intimidating to others, but with me he's gentle and loving and protective and passionate...I don't know that I've ever felt so much about anyone before. I'm constantly smiling with him, and I have more fun with him than anyone else. He makes me feel happy and loved and desirable...being with him is so...intoxicating. I don't know if I can even describe it fully."

Raina beamed. "It was exciting, intense, magical!"

"Yes! But it was a lot more than that. Even in the quiet moments, maybe especially then, I found myself feeling so content and...so happy. Even when we were doing something mundane, it was fun because I was doing it with him."

"It sounds wonderful."

"It was! For a while there I thought he was the one. But the *lies*. He's apologized, and explained himself, and he's being sweet and charming and making me doubt my choice which is pissing me off."

"Why are you doubting yourself?"

"I don't know. I just miss him." Another tear ran down Anise's cheek. "His explanations even made sense, and I believe him. But I'm still so angry."

"It sounds like being kept in the dark about things really gets to you, even if you feel there were understandable reasons for it. Maybe you should explore that."

There seemed to be wisdom packed into Raina's statement, but Anise wasn't sure how to siphon it. She was too angry to even try. "Maybe," she shrugged.

Raina gave her a sympathetic look. "If he's really sorry, and convinces you it won't happen again, is there any chance you could forgive him?"

Anise shook her head. "He's apologized before, and I forgave him, and then he lied again. As much as I want to, I just can't trust him."

"Then you made the right choice," Raina assured her. "You deserve someone who makes you feel all those things *and* who's trustworthy."

"You're right," Anise agreed. "I'm just sad and disappointed to put it mildly. This isn't how I wanted things to be. So when he's acting like nothing's changed, it feels so good and so right, and I miss him so much it hurts. What's *wrong* with me?" She put her head in her hands.

"Nothing is wrong with you, and I understand," Raina said. "I've been there, too."

"Really?" Anise asked, giving her eyes another dab with the napkin.

"Of course. You can't fall out of love that quickly,

even when someone hurts you. Give it time, and things will get better. Maybe you need to make a clean break to help you get over him. Stop seeing him, and it'll be easier. I know that helped me."

"You're right, and I will. As soon as we get back home." The thought of not seeing Nate at all anymore made her stomach twinge. "Tell me the truth though. Is cutting all ties as hard as it sounds?"

Raina nodded. "It was at first. Especially because I couldn't cut *all* ties. He's my daughter's father. But it gets easier with time."

"You have a daughter?"

Raina's face beamed as she grabbed her phone and scrolled through a few pictures for Anise. "This is Lily. She's almost three."

Anise's heart melted when she saw the little girl in the frilly dress with dark, curly pigtails and a bright smile. "Aw, she's so cute!"

"Thanks!"

"Why aren't you with her father anymore?" Anise asked, unable to contain her curiosity.

"He's irresponsible and drinks too much," Raina replied matter-of-factly.

"Ugh, been there," Anise groaned. "That exactly describes my first long-term relationship," she added, thinking about Brian.

"With him, I was right where you are with Nate. He was the love of my life, but I won't put up with that. At least you don't have any kids with him. Give it a few months and you'll feel so much better, I promise."

"I agree completely," Anise said. "And now I don't want to think about him anymore. Thank you for listening."

"Anytime!"

"So let's get to the reason we're here," Anise said, feeling stronger after confiding in her new friend.

"Yes! I thought your idea of there being two maps

was intriguing."

Anise frowned. "I get that Wilhelm Schwartz needed the first map to show where he hid the Plate of Destiny. That's the map disguised as ancient cave art. But what would be the purpose of the second map?"

"I think having two maps would be a security feature. I believe the Plate of Destiny can't be found with the first map," Raina replied. "I would bet the first map leads to the second map. The second map leads to the Plate."

"So the purpose would be to make it harder for who-ever is looking for the Plate of Destiny."

"Exactly," Raina confirmed. "Schwartz wanted to keep the Plate hidden from everyone."

Anise frowned in thought. "If he wanted to keep it hidden, why have a map that leads to it at all?"

Raina shrugged. "That I can't answer. But we don't need to let questions like that slow us down in finding the Plate."

"I agree," said Anise. "The fact that the first map is pretending to be cave art was supposed to fool people. Do you think there's a secret surrounding the second map as well?"

"My guess would be yes. A secret or a disguise or an additional security feature of some kind."

"A security feature? Do you mean it might be behind a physical barrier that would be hard to break through?"

Raina shrugged. "Possibly. Your guess is as good as mine."

"I wish we knew how to read Wilhelm Schwartz's map," Anise said. "That 'L' that was carved on the cave wall must mean something."

"I've actually been thinking about that, and I don't believe it's an 'L.' My guess is that the second map is buried very deep somewhere. I think the vertical line of the 'L' means we'd have to repel down a vertical tunnel in another cave. I think the two horizontal lines on the vertical part of the 'L' are depth markers."

"Okay...so how do we know which caves to look in?"

"I have an idea about that too. There was a new cave recently discovered that has deep shafts, but get this. Outside the entrance, there's a marking that looks just like the 'L' with the two horizontal lines carved into the rock."

"So that's where the second map could be!" Anise said excitedly. "Did anyone discover any cave art in this new cave?"

Raina shrugged. "I haven't heard of that, but it's still a very new discovery. Much of it still hasn't been explored yet because it could be treacherous."

"Is it in danger of collapsing?" Anise asked.

Raina shook her head. "No, it's stable, but sometimes caves that can only be accessed by a vertical shaft flood easily. The terrain could be hazardous, and there might be venomous creatures that live there."

Anise made a face of disgust. "Okay...but how would one access these caves?"

"It's not a cave that the public has access to. It's on government-owned park land. You'd have to get permission to explore it," Raina explained.

"Would *you* be able to get permission?"

"Unfortunately, no. As much as I'd love to explore it, you'd have to be part of a research group, or a professional cave diver, or work for the National Park Service or one of their partnering organizations."

"Oh, okay." Anise stared off into the distance as she thought about the cave and what it would take to explore it. She wondered if Fred Dromly had found it yet.

After a few moments of silence, Raina asked, "Anise, you're not planning on going down into the cave, are you? You could be arrested or seriously injured. Or worse!"

"I was just curious." Anise looked down at the table. Lying to Raina made her very uncomfortable. She began to wonder how Nate could lie so easily over and over before she pushed him out of her mind again.

After they had finished their beverages, Raina grabbed her purse from the back of her chair. "I need to get going. My sister is off work today too, and we're taking Lily and her cousins to the zoo."

"That sounds fun," Anise told her. "Have a great time!"

"Would you like to join us?"

"I'd love to," Anise said, grateful for the invitation, "but my stomach is still feeling off. I think I could use a nap instead."

"Okay, feel better soon!" Raina said, giving Anise a hug before she left.

Thinking about what she'd learned from Raina about the cave with the vertical shaft, Anise excitedly raced back to the hotel. She knocked on her friends' doors but got no responses. Nate was still out doing whatever he said he had to do, Kent and Lorelei weren't in their rooms, and Jonathan hadn't yet come back from the library. Disappointed that she couldn't share her news yet with anyone, Anise lay on the bed and stared at the ceiling. She hadn't realized how tired she was and fell asleep quickly.

✶✶✶

SEVERAL HOURS LATER, JONATHAN STARTED RUBBING his eyes. He and Selina still hadn't found anything of value, but he didn't want to give up. He had no idea what time it was but was committed to stay and research as long as it took.

"Jonathan, get this," Selina whispered as she sat down beside him. "The last book on my list is actually in this library! I tried to find it, but it's locked away in a special section due to its age. Let's go ask someone for help."

Excitement and hope bubbled up inside him. "Sounds good!" He walked next to her and admired her confident stride as her slingback woven flats softly tapped the floor with each step. Her intelligence exuded from her eyes and her speech as she pointed a manicured nail to her list and politely asked for help from the librarian.

They were led to a locked room. The librarian handed them each a pair of white gloves, let them in, and found the book Selina had asked for. They were made to leave their cell phones outside the room as no photography of the book was permitted. Selina placed the book on a small table and carefully started turning pages.

"So tell me about this book," Jonathan requested.

"I know this isn't very scientific, but I have a hunch. Go with me on this."

"Okay..."

"It's a book about local folklore."

"Folklore?" He was surprised that a scientist like Selina would put any faith into a work of fiction.

"I know what you're thinking," she said as her sky blue eyes commanded him to have an open mind. "But look at this." She pointed to a passage. "This says something about Mallandia."

Jonathan's ears perked up. "Really?"

"It says these artifacts were found there by Wilhelm Schwartz and brought to Florida."

When Jonathan saw the drawings on the page, he didn't mean to make his noise of surprise so loudly. "Sorry," he said when Selina looked at him questioningly.

"It's okay," she said, laughing. "Does this mean something to you?" She looked at the drawings inquisitively.

"It's the Armor Jewelry of Mallandia!" he exclaimed. "Anise has...uh, I mean, Anise and I discovered this legend a few years ago at the museum where I work."

"See? It can't just be a coincidence. But I thought it would say something about the Plate of Destiny." She turned the page again.

"What does that say?" Jonathan asked, pointing to a caption under a drawing of some oval shaped stones with Mallandian writing on them.

"Carnelian beads were used to lock away treasure."

"What's that supposed to mean?" Jonathan wondered out loud. "How can you lock away treasure with oval stone beads?"

Selina pursed her lips in thought. "No idea."

Jonathan couldn't keep his eyes off of the drawings of the beads. "I wish I could take a picture of this to show the others."

The librarian walked into the room at that moment and held the door open for them. "The library is closing."

"That's unfortunate timing," Selina commented to Jonathan under her breath.

"I didn't realize we'd been here all day," Jonathan said, reluctantly getting up. He led the way out of the room, and Selina walked beside him as they exited the library. "I'm going to have to come back tomorrow. I think we stumbled on something in that book. I need to know more about those beads. I hate to ask since you already dedicated your entire birthday to this..."

"I would love to help you again tomorrow!" Selina told him, her voice full of delight. "Today was fascinating...and fun."

"I agree," Jonathan said. He found himself not wanting to wait until the next day to spend more time with her. "So do you have birthday plans with your grandfather tonight?"

Selina shook her head. "He's almost ninety and goes to bed pretty early. I'm just going to curl up with a good book tonight."

"Can I persuade you to push your plans back for a couple hours?" he asked hopefully. "I'd like to take you out to dinner to celebrate."

Her face lit up. "I'd love that!"

Chapter 11

"Where's Anise? And Jonathan?" Lorelei asked, ready to read the legend she'd found in the trip journals. She picked up a plastic fork even though she didn't have much of an appetite. Kent and Nate were already helping themselves to the take out they'd picked up. She was glad. They might not want to eat after hearing the legend.

"Sorry I'm late," Jonathan announced, breezing in the door that had been left ajar for him. He shook his head when Lorelei offered him some food. "No, thanks. I already ate."

"I just checked on Anise," Nate said. "She's fast asleep, and I didn't want to wake her. She's been having stress stomachaches lately."

"That's probably for the best anyway," Lorelei said. "This legend is pretty upsetting." Her memory of the first time she'd read it made her skin prickle.

"How so?" Jonathan asked, sounding intrigued.

"I'll read it to you," Lorelei replied, opening Fred Dromly's journal. "It's about a man in ancient Mallandia named Frondok who was the son of Dagan, the original Jewelry engineer. Dagan is the one who created the Armor Jewelry and was apparently executed by the king. The journal entry is dated Friday, March 27, 2015. Just about seven months ago. It says:

The legend of Frondok and the Curse: Frondok was devastated after his father Dagan was executed. He was expected to take over Dagan's duties as Jewelry Engineer immediately, leaving him no time to grieve. He did, however, make time to plot his revenge. After Frondok avenged his father by killing the king and framing the seer who had fled for her life, the king's son was put on the throne. Frondok's wife, a seer who'd been initiated with the seer's wand, had seen the writing on the Plate of Destiny, but she didn't fully understand how to apply its teachings. Most of Frondok's time was devoted to studying and seeking council from those wiser than himself with hope that one day he'd be able to bring Dagan back from the dead. He was angry when he discovered that the Plate of Destiny that he had hidden in a cave to keep it safe had been stolen. As the current Jewelry engineer, and with wishes to keep the Plate safe, Frondok decided to make an Armor cuff for himself in order to be able to take charge of the king's army by way of mind control.

His father Dagan had designed the cuff so that only someone with king's blood could control the army with their minds by putting drops of blood underneath the lapis lazuli and jasper stones that decorated the cuff. Frondok tried making a cuff with his own blood, but it had no immediate results. For years, Frondok attempted to brainwash the army anyway, and even though each army member suffered of "disease of the head," he was eventually able to command the army via mind control.

The new king and his siblings began to suspect Frondok when the royal army was going on missions that the king hadn't ordered to look for the Plate of Destiny. In order to protect himself, Frondok placed a curse on the king's family and all their future descendants. Only one descendant at a time would live to procreate. The procreation was necessary for Frondok to stay sup-

plied in willing king's blood in order to make new cuffs, otherwise he simply would've killed the entire royal family. He needed an unending supply of cuffs because at the time, the royals of Mallandia weren't aware they could charge the stones and reuse the Jewelry. Once the stones ran out of charge, the Jewelry was abandoned and more was made.

The curse worked just as Frondok had planned. Once the sole living descendant of the king had children, that descendant would die at any time before their first grandchild was born. Only one of the descendant's children would live to procreate. This would be their destiny until the end of time.

The king's wife was pregnant, and all of the king's siblings perished within the next few months to years. Once the child was born, the king lived a few more years and passed from an unknown sleeping disease. Frondok managed to become advisor to the queen regent until the child grew up. The army was sent out time and time again, but the Plate of Destiny was never discovered. Frondok died a bitter and angry man of old age. The Plate of Destiny remained hidden until it was found by Wilhelm Schwartz and brought to Florida to rest in its new hiding spot.

"Wait, these royals are Anise's ancestors," Jonathan said. "Only one descendent at a time can live to procreate and once they do, they could die at any time? Is this saying that Anise is going to die early?" His mouth hung open in horror. He stood up and sat back down again as if he didn't know what to do with himself.

"We don't know that for sure," Kent told him.

"All the other legends are true," Nate said quietly, staring at the floor with a serious face. "Why should this one be any different?"

"We have to tell her!" Jonathan exclaimed, standing up again.

Nate stood up. "I'll go wake her up."

"Wait a minute," Lorelei said, holding her hands up to stop them. "This is a delicate matter. This news is devastating. Let's at least think of what we're going to say first to break it to her as gently as possible. Okay?"

To her relief, the men agreed.

"At least we know she's safe until she's had a child," Kent said.

"No we don't," Nate argued.

"Did you not hear the legend?" Jonathan asked him. "It said that only one royal would live to procreate, and—"

"I heard it," Nate replied, sitting back down. "She told me this in confidence, so understand I'm only telling you this so that you don't falsely believe she's invincible until she has a baby."

"Okay," Lorelei said to her son. Kent was staring at him, and Jonathan looked confused and horrified.

"Well, what is it?" Jonathan demanded.

"Anise has a brother who was given up for adoption. He's still alive, so she's not the only one with king's blood. And since he's alive, she could still die. So we have to continue protecting her. She's not safe from death. In fact, Les is a lot older than she is. I don't think he has a family, but if he has a kid out there that he doesn't know about, she might be closer to death than we know."

Everyone turned their heads when they heard a knock at the door. Kent opened it and let Anise in.

"Sorry, I fell asleep. What did I miss?" Anise asked. She looked around at the quiet room and worry crossed her face.

Lorelei got up to greet the poor girl warmly with a hug. "I'm glad you're here. We're just exchanging stories about what we discovered today." Feeling like she needed more time to figure out the best way to break the awful news to Anise, she handed Anise a plate. "Have some food. You must be hungry." She looked directly at Jonathan for help.

He took the hint. "That's right! I was about to tell everyone what Selina and I found at the library today!" Jonathan said with excitement as Lorelei sat next to Anise on the bed.

"Did they look like these?" Lorelei asked Jonathan after he told the others of the oval carnelian beads. She flipped a few pages in one of Fred's journals. "I had no idea what these were when I saw them drawn in this journal, so I didn't put much stock in them. They're just ovals with Mallandian writing on them. Fred wrote down what words are engraved into the beads, but otherwise they have no explanation whatsoever." She showed him the journal once she found the correct page.

"Yes!" Jonathan confirmed. "That's the same thing we saw in the book!"

"What are the beads for?" Anise asked.

"I don't know yet," Jonathan replied. "Selina and I are going back to the library tomorrow to figure that out. But I really think we stumbled onto something big."

"I met with Raina today, and I think we stumbled onto something big, too!" Anise said. She explained Raina's idea that the second map would be hidden in a cave with a vertical tunnel.

"That's a big lead!" Jonathan exclaimed, his eyes wide.

"Let's get up early tomorrow and try to find that cave before the sun comes up," Nate said to Kent.

"Let's do it," Kent agreed.

"I'm coming with you," Anise told them.

"I wish I could go, too!" Jonathan lamented. "But I need to learn more about those beads."

"Need to or want to?" Nate challenged him.

"What's that supposed to mean?" Jonathan asked defensively.

"You're going to be sitting around looking at old books with a pretty girl while the rest of us are risking our lives in the caves. Are you trying to get out of the real work?"

"Of course not!" Jonathan said, getting miffed. "And Selina's more than just a pretty girl. She's a friend who's interested in historical artifacts. And she's been really helpful—she's great at doing research. She followed a hunch I never would have, and it's what led us to finding the information about the beads."

"Friend?" Nate scoffed. "You've known her what—for two days?"

"Maybe if you *had* friends you'd understand. I'm not the one here who's trying to get out of doing work. What have *you* done today besides sit around and mope? Have you been scheming with Grace again?"

Nate stood up with anger in his eyes. Lorelei was relieved when all he did was drop a book on the table.

"I got this," he sneered at Jonathan. His eyes then met with Lorelei's and Kent's. "Since you two want to read the trip journals, I figured this one might be the most helpful." He sat next to Kent on the couch.

Lorelei picked it up and looked at the last entry. "October 7, 2015. That's yesterday!" She looked at her son with surprise. "How did you get this?"

"So that was your plan," Anise said, looking pleased.

"Great work!" Kent told Nate with a proud slap on the back.

"Nate?" Lorelei said. *Did he put himself in danger?*

"I stole it from Dromly's hotel room," he replied with annoyance.

"Well I figured that," Lorelei said softly, her heart sinking. "I just meant...never mind. Please don't get angry. I was just concerned for your safety."

"You're even an asshole to your mom," Jonathan said, judgmentally shaking his head at Nate. "What's wrong with you?"

Nate stood up again, his eyes narrowed at Jonathan.

"Nate, leave," Anise demanded.

Kent stood up, too. "Go get some sleep," he told Nate

with a pat on the shoulder. "We have an early day ahead of us."

Nate looked at Lorelei, and she could tell from his face that something in her expression seemed to upset him more. Without a word, he walked out of the room.

"Why do you have to antagonize him all the time?" Anise asked Jonathan with frustration.

"He started it," protested Jonathan. "He's an asshole, and somebody needs to call him out on it. Why do you always defend his bullshit behavior?"

"I don't!" Anise insisted. "And I'm not now. But you provoking him is just making things worse. So I'm calling you out on *your* bullshit behavior."

Jonathan laughed and gave her a warm smile. "You're right. I'm sorry. I shouldn't let him get to me. Thanks for keeping me on the right path."

"I should find Nate," Lorelei said. Her worry for him grew. Both Dan and Grace were hurtful monsters when they were angry. They both held on to their anger and let it eat them alive. *But Nate can't possibly be the same way...right?* She hoped he was okay, wherever he'd gone.

"It's probably best to let him cool off for a while," Anise advised her.

Lorelei nodded her agreement and said good night. When she got to her room, she allowed her tears to flow freely. Where was the kind, loving boy Nate used to be? Her heart ached. Her son was hurting, and she had no idea how to help him. But she couldn't just sit there and not do anything. He came by her room as soon as she texted him.

"I know you're angry," Lorelei said to Nate as he sat in her chair. She paced slowly back and forth in front of him. "And you have every right to be. I can't even imagine what it was like for you to be subjected to Grace and Dan for all those years with no one on your side."

"Mom..." Nate let out a sigh. "That's the last thing I want to talk about."

"I get it. But it needs to be talked about. I want you to know that it's okay you're angry with me because I wasn't there."

"I'm not angry with you," he replied. "I'm just...angry at the situation. It wasn't fair to you."

"Or to you," she added. "But if you're not angry with me, why do you pull away from me like my touch is toxic?"

"I'm thirty years old," he snapped at her. "I don't need mothering anymore."

"Of course," she said softly, raising a hand to her face. "I forget sometimes that I'm a virtual stranger to you. You were so young when I was kidnapped. You must barely remember me if at all. I'm sorry."

Nate shook his head. "You have nothing to be sorry for. It's not that."

"What is it?" She watched her son's eyes stare at her. "Tell me, please."

He looked at his lap. "Anise thinks I'm afraid you're judging me."

Lorelei thought about all the times Grace had been overly critical with Nate. She wondered how bad the criticism got while she was gone. "And what do *you* think?"

Nate's gaze went to the floor, and he shrugged. "I don't know."

His response made Lorelei remember all the looks and words of reprimand she'd given him on this trip as if he were still a child, and a tear ran down her cheek. "There's something I need to ask of you."

"What?" he asked softly, leaning back in the chair.

"I ask you to remember that everything I say, I say out of love. I wasn't judging you earlier. I was worried."

He looked confused. "Why?"

"You broke into Fred Dromly's room. What if you had gotten caught?"

Nate scoffed. "I'm a professional. I don't get caught."

"You were in prison for three years."

"That's different. I chose that."

Lorelei got comfortable on her couch while she listened to her son tell her the entire story of how he was arrested at the Springfield Museum. "You did all that for Anise?"

"For her, but also for everyone involved, including myself. Grace needed to be taken down. I didn't want anyone else getting hurt."

Lorelei smiled. *There* was the boy she remembered. "I'd like to give you some advice, but I want you to keep in mind that it's only because I want to help. Is that okay?"

He nodded.

"When someone says something to you that seems judgmental or critical, try to think about where they're coming from. And I mean anyone. If it's me, Anise, or even Jonathan. If you consider their words, you can then choose to dismiss them, or if you think they have a point, you can use their comments constructively. Let these experiences help you instead of making you angry. Can you try that?"

He nodded again. "I'm sorry about earlier," he told her. "I won't speak to you like that again." He stood and walked over to her.

Her heart soared when he hugged her, and she wrapped her arms around him. Having her little prince back was all she'd ever wanted.

WHEN ANISE ENTERED HER ROOM, SHE looked around for Nate, but he wasn't there. Disappointed, she frowned and wondered where he'd gone. She'd wanted to thank him for stealing the most recent trip journal. If anything had the potential to lead them closer to the Plate of Destiny, that would be it. She was surprised at how tired and ready for sleep she was too, considering the long nap she'd taken that afternoon. Twisting the cap off of a bottle of soda, she washed down a few antacid pills and pulled the bed covers up to her chin.

Chapter 12

Friday, October 9, 2015

Fred Dromly looked up at the starry sky. "Billions and billions of brilliant beings of light. Tonight team, during the witching hour, they illuminate our path as we boldly step into our destiny. *This* is the cave."

"Are you sure, boss?" asked Fred's most helpful member of the brainwashed army. He wiped the beads of sweat that had collected above his bushy gray eyebrows and lowered the pack he was carrying to the ground. His hands reached up to rub his shoulders and then yanked at his t-shirt to make sure it was still covering his round belly.

"Yes, George, this time I'm sure."

George stepped forward and shined a flashlight into the entrance of the cave and through a large crack in the wall. "I don't mean to rain on your parade, but it's what you said last time. And the time before that."

"Ah, but last time, I didn't mention the stars, nor was it the witching hour."

George nodded politely. "Sure, boss. Makes sense."

Fred sighed as he looked around at the brainwashed

members of his team that Morty had sent him over the years plus the newer members that still worked under Morty at the museum. All in different stages of adulthood, all with advanced degrees in archeology or history or anthropology, none with any excited anticipation of what was about to happen. Such beauty, such adventure awaited them, and they were falling asleep on their feet! Fred frowned at them.

A gunshot rang out and echoed through the quiet dark of the forest. Fred's team let out cries of fear and dropped to the ground.

"Everyone in the cave! Hurry!" Fred commanded. He lit the way with his flashlight and made sure all of them were safe and accounted for as another shot rang out.

"Is that you, Buffalo Bill?" shouted Fred at the top of his lungs into the darkness. He made sure all four pieces of Armor Jewelry were fastened securely before running as fast as his 88-year-old legs could carry him out into a nearby clearing. The amulet around his neck glowed. He heard another shot whiz by his head. "What's the matter, Annie Oakley? I'm right here! Shoot me! Do it!" He laughed heartily when another bullet flew over his St. Louis Cardinals baseball cap. "You couldn't hit the ground if your gun was pointed straight down!" Two more shots ricocheted off nearby rocks. "I'd tell you to swallow your gun, but you'd miss the back of your own head! Fucker!"

Several more bullets headed in his direction. This time, he could see by the light of the glowing amulet and his flashlight that they had to change their direction at the last moment to avoid hitting him. "Looks like you got some help!" Fred shouted. "I know that wasn't you! You're a bad shot and you always were!"

Fred returned to the cave entrance where his team was hiding. "Every night for months!" he said with amusement, shaking his head and laughing to himself.

He led the others through the wide open crack in

the limestone wall and down a narrow corridor. They reached their destination in under ten minutes. His team helped Fred get into the harness and strapped an oxygen tank to his back.

"Slowly now," he said, as they lowered him down thirty feet through a vertical tunnel into an open room of rock. He turned on the lantern he had brought with him and marveled at the sight. The floor reached up toward the ceiling in a few places, and the room was narrow but long. He could see the far wall in front of him and the one behind him, but the sides of the cave were much further away and hidden in the darkness. But what struck Fred the most was the feeling he got while down there. It was a hope and a knowing and a comfort all in one. There was something different about this cave. "Not today, madam," he said, as he brushed a white arachnid off of the arm of his utility jacket. The spider ran off and hid under a rock.

George and a few of the other team members joined Fred in the subterranean room. They each took a hit of oxygen as they slowly wandered around, tripping on the uneven floor and upsetting a colony of bats that had taken up residence on a part of the low ceiling. They could hear shouts of surprise from their teammates that had stayed above as the bats flew up the tunnel and out of the cave.

"Look!" Fred exclaimed. "It's the keystone lock!" He shined a flashlight on the wall where there were four oval-shaped indentations. He laughed with disbelief and joy at the same time. "We found it! We finally found it!" George and the others happily celebrated and shouted the good news up the tunnel.

"The camera, the camera!" Fred demanded, as he reached into his pocket and closed his hand around the four keys to the lock.

George aimed his video camera at Fred.

His hand twitching in anticipation, Fred pushed an oval carnelian bead into each of the indentations in the stone wall. He stepped back and waited.

Several silent seconds passed.

"So...where's the second map?" George asked.

Fred shined his flashlight around the entire room. "I don't know." He tried pushing on the beads to make sure they were firmly in place, but that changed nothing.

"Maybe we have the wrong cave again?" George wondered out loud.

"Impossible," said Fred with confidence. "The lock is right here. The beads fit perfectly into the lock. This is the cave."

"Maybe it takes some time," George said.

"Doubtful," Fred replied as he furrowed his brow in confusion. "When you put the right key in a lock, it unlocks right away. That's how locks work."

"Right, but this is no ordinary lock."

Fred frowned, trying to figure out what to do next.

"Maybe you have to turn the beads," George suggested. "You have to turn a key, maybe you have to turn the keystones."

"The legend said nothing about turning the beads," Fred stated with frustration but tried George's suggestion anyway. "They're not turning. The wall is solid rock." He rubbed his chin. "I'm doing something wrong." He collected the beads from their places in the wall. He cursed quietly, then as loudly as he could, and he stood with his eyes shut letting the sound waves bombard him, the echoing expletives reaching his ears over and over. "I have to do more research to figure this out. We'll try again another night."

As they left the cave and took deep breaths in the fresh night air, George gave Fred's shoulder a pat. "Sorry the keys didn't work, boss."

"No sorrys needed," Fred told him. "At least we know for sure we found the right cave. Let's go get some well-deserved sleep."

***

THEY HID AROUND THE SIDE OF the cave entrance, squatting uncomfortably in the shrubbery, attempting to avoid the face-scratching twigs, waiting until Fred and his team drove away in their van.

"Come on, Morty, you heard him. He's sure this is the cave!"

Morty lingered by the narrow crack in the cave wall. He didn't want Grace entering into such a dangerous situation, however, he also knew he wouldn't be able to stop her.

"Well, come *on*, Morty!"

"What makes you think you're going to find anything down there when it seems like Dromly didn't?" Morty asked her as they walked up to the tunnel.

"What are you saying? That I shouldn't even try?"

"Perhaps not. You could die down there. Maybe I should be the one to go down there. It'll be very easy to fall when you can't see where you're going and climbing over uneven ground. You could get bitten by a venomous spider. You could—"

"Enough!" Grace told him. "You're twice as big as I am," she told him matter-of-factly. "I can't lower you down. I have to be the one who goes down there."

He strategically wrapped a rope around her, and with his stomach tied in knots, Morty slowly began lowering her down the tunnel. His aging back muscles flared up angrily. "Are you down?" he asked her.

"Not yet," said her voice drifting up the tunnel. "Give me more rope."

Morty stepped forward and released more rope. His foot landed on something that moved, and he slipped, landing face first on the ground. A wail escaped his lips as the rope fell out of his hands and down the tunnel. He heard a scream and a thump. "Grace? Grace?" he called frantically.

"Morty, you idiot!" he heard her yelling. "What the hell happened?"

He breathed a sigh of relief. She was alive. "It's dark! I slipped on something!" He looked and saw what it was. "I think Dromly left his video camera here! Are you okay?"

"No, you moron! I think I broke my leg! And the rope is down here with me! How the hell are you going to pull me back up?"

He heard her gasping. "Hook up to your oxygen tank!" he called out. "I'll get another rope! I'll be back right away!" Morty picked up the video camera, ran out of the cave, into the dark forest, and toward their car. When he was almost there, he stopped short, turned, and ran the other way. Panting and wheezing, he looked around for a place to hide or something that could be used as a weapon. He felt hands on his back pushing him forward, and he felt himself falling onto a floor of fallen leaves.

"Looks like you have something of mine, Morty," he heard George say before everything went black.

Chapter 13

Anise yawned and pulled her hair into a ponytail before opening the hotel room door. It was still dark out, and she wanted nothing more than to go back to bed.

"Good morning," Lorelei said to Anise when they stepped into the hallway at the same time.

"Good morning," Anise replied sleepily. She'd spent half the night wondering where Nate was sleeping, worrying about him, and hoping to hear him come in the room. He never did.

They lightly tapped on Kent's door, and he waved them inside. Anise saw Nate putting on his jacket and was relieved to know he was okay.

"We've already packed our boots, ropes, flashlights, food and water, and a first aid kit in the trunk. Are you ready to go look for these caves?" Kent asked the women.

"More than ready," Anise replied.

Lorelei held up the trip journal that Nate had stolen from Dromly. "Fred gave us a description of how to get to a thirty foot vertical tunnel once we find the right entrance. If we can find where the opening of this cave is, we should be able to find where the second map is hidden."

"I know exactly where we have to go," Nate said to his

mother.

"Really? That's great! How did you find out?" Lorelei exclaimed, beaming at her son.

"Grace and Smithton have been working together," he explained. "I've been having them followed, and my source called me last night with exact directions on how to get to the cave where he spotted them a few hours ago."

Anise followed the others out to the car. A waxing crescent moon lit their way through the parking lot.

"Since they were there, it's possible Morty and Grace may have already found the second map," Kent speculated.

"Maybe," Anise said. "But maybe not. There may be a security measure associated with this cave. Raina believes the map won't be in plain sight and that we'll have to get past barriers of some kind if we're going to find it."

"She could be right," Kent said with a shrug. "We'll find out when we get there!"

✳✳✳

"So according to Fred's journal, it's thirty feet down," Lorelei told her companions as they peered into the black abyss of the vertical tunnel in the cave. She worried about Nate who'd volunteered to go down first.

Kent began tying a rope around Nate strategically. "I'm sorry I won't be able to join you down there like we'd planned," Kent told him.

"Your ankle still hurts?" Anise asked him, adjusting the armor ring and earrings she wore.

Kent put more weight on the foot he'd been babying and grimaced. "I think I may have sprained it."

"Your leg is still bleeding," Lorelei told him, watching the blood slowly stain his pant leg.

"The rock I fell on was sharp," Kent said. "But I'll be

okay. Just be careful down there. As treacherous as is it up here, it'll be worse down there."

"Let me heal you with the Jewelry," Anise said.

Kent waved away her offer. "No, not yet. We don't want to use up the Jewelry's charge on that. We need to make sure there's enough strength for us to pull Nate back up."

"After we lower Nate down, will you still be able to lower *me* down?" Anise asked hopefully.

"Ready," Nate said, stepping over the entrance to the tunnel.

"I think so," Kent told her.

"Tie the rope to that stalagmite over there," Nate suggested. "Just in case the Jewelry loses charge. Make sure the rope stays attached to it, and I should be fine."

"Be careful!" Lorelei called after him as Anise began lowering Nate down the tunnel slowly using the strength the earrings gave her. Watching her son disappear into the dark hole made Lorelei's chest tighten. She paced back and forth, hoping he wouldn't have to be down there too long.

"Made it!" Nate's voice shouted up the tunnel and into Lorelei's happy ears.

"My turn!" Anise said excitedly to Kent as he tied another rope around her waist.

Kent let out a cry of pain when Anise put some of her weight on the rope. "I'm sorry, I don't think I can do this."

"That's okay." Anise pointed to a large rock. "If we tie the rope around that rock, I should be able to lower myself down with no problem. I am wearing the Armor Jewelry after all, so I'm more than strong enough."

"I'm not comfortable with that," Lorelei argued. "What if the Jewelry loses charge and you fall?"

"It shouldn't. I charged it yesterday before dusk."

"Not for long enough. It doesn't have as much charge as it should. I want you and Nate to be able to get back out."

"I should be down there!" Anise exclaimed. "It's dangerous. Nate shouldn't be there by himself. And with two of us looking, we'll be more likely to find what we're looking for."

"Absolutely not!" Lorelei insisted. "We're not taking that risk." She gasped when they heard Nate's voice let out a yell of fear from deep inside the cave.

***

"GOOD MORNING!" JONATHAN SAID. HE'D PUT on a polo shirt and a nicer pair of jeans than the pair he'd worn yesterday and hoped he didn't look too tired. He'd spent half the night tossing and turning. Thinking about Selina's beautiful face and brilliant mind had kept him awake and counting down the hours until he'd get to spend time with her again.

Selina looked perfect in a white, pleated sundress, white cardigan, and her flaxen hair in a crown of braids on the top of her head with some front pieces left out to frame her face. She wore a few delicate gold chains around her neck that matched the bracelet on her wrist. On her feet were gold sandals with thin straps that stopped at the vamp to reveal pretty, polished toes. The song about her continued playing in his head. Verse two lyrics began unfolding and his mind searched for rhymes and near rhymes. The chord progression. G, E minor, C, D.

She stood up from her seat on the stairs that led to the library. "Good morning," she said. "That's a nice shirt. Green suits you. It brings out your eyes."

"Thanks!" He smiled shyly. He wanted to give her a compliment as well, but she had already turned around and was headed inside.

Selina found a librarian to retrieve the book they needed and unlock the same room they were in the day before. They left their phones outside, and Selina opened the book to the page with the Armor Jewelry. Sitting next to each other at the table, they stared at the drawings.

"I can't wait to hear more about this Jewelry," she said. "Tell me about the legend you mentioned yesterday."

Jonathan described each piece of Armor Jewelry to her, using the drawings in the book as visual aids, and told her about the powers each granted to the wearer. He explained the legend of how each piece was used in battle and that they were stronger when used together. His excitement for the story grew with every detail he remembered, and he felt encouraged to express it from the attentiveness of his audience. "Anise even named me, uh, well, jokingly said if she was Mallandian royalty and had a set of Armor Jewelry, I'd be her Jewelry engineer."

"So the carnelian beads discussed in this book are connected to the Armor Jewelry somehow?" Selina asked. She pointed at the four ovals that were drawn in the book. All of them had a word in the curly, wavy Mallandian writing engraved near each end.

"That's what it seems like," Jonathan replied. He took his phone out of his pocket. "And today I'll be able to show the others exactly what I've found. Dr. Dromly had drawn ovals in one of his journals, but without an explanation of what they're for."

"I thought I saw you leave your phone outside the door," Selina said, confused.

"That was Anise's phone," he told her. "She let me borrow it."

"Bad boy," Selina purred jokingly.

Jonathan laughed. "Normally, I wouldn't break the rules. I actually couldn't sleep last night because I was wrestling with myself about whether I should do it or not." He frowned, still not completely comfortable with his decision. It was something Nate would do. "Are you comfortable with this?"

"Of course," she told him. "I know you won't publicize these photos. You just want to be able to show your friends without having to bring them here."

Having her approval made him feel better. "Okay, good. And I'm going to delete them as soon as they've seen them." He hovered the phone over the caption under the beads and snapped a shot. "It says these were found in a local cave!"

"Really?" She moved her chair closer to his and stared at the pages.

"These four carnelian beads were originally found by Wilhelm Schwartz in Germany. It says they're keystones from the Bronze Age meant to guard a treasure of the Mallandian king. They were originally created by a Mallandian craftsman."

"Keystones?" said Selina, confused. "You mean like the stone on the top of an archway? Is the guarded treasure under four arches?"

Jonathan took a thoughtful pause. "Maybe?" he replied. "But I'm wondering if the translation is more literal in this case."

"You mean stones that act as keys?"

"Yes. Look at this next picture." He pointed a finger at a drawing that consisted of lines, arrows, and tiny ovals.

"I have no idea what that's supposed to be," she told him, shaking her head.

"I didn't either until just now." He pointed at the drawing. "This line is supposed to be a wall, and the arrows are pointing to four parts that've been carved out. Look how the beads are the same shape as the indentations in the wall."

"Oh!" she said, understanding. "It's kind of like a combination lock. You put the beads in the slots in the wall, probably in a certain order, and then you can open... what? A hidden door maybe?"

"I'm guessing so," he said.

"That's incredible!" she bubbled over. "What else

does it say?"

"The symbols written on the beads each have a meaning. They could be combined to form a sentence, idea, code, or passphrase."

"Like the numbers in a combination!"

"Exactly! The code could also be changed at will if the original combination was ever compromised."

"Wait, what? That doesn't make any sense," Selina said, her brows narrowing. "The lock was obviously mechanical. To change the combination of the beads means you'd have to change the mechanical workings of the entire lock of the hidden door. That seems like an absurd amount of work. Work that needs to be very precise since these beads look like they're practically the same size and shape."

"True," Jonathan said. He thought for a moment, and his eyes suddenly lit up. "Oh, I get it! The Mallandian Armor Jewelry worked on intention. The craftsman who worked for the king was almost assuredly the royal Jewelry engineer, the same official tasked with making the Jewelry. We already know that Wilhelm Schwartz had a set of the Jewelry because he was able to find the Plate of Destiny, and no one can recognize it without wearing the Jewelry. So, if the beads were meant to work with someone who had a set of Jewelry, the lock wouldn't need to be mechanical at all!"

Selina's face crinkled in confusion. "I don't follow."

Jonathan was awe-struck by what he'd just figured out. The lock was simple, yet complex and brilliant all at the same time. "There're two parts to cracking this hidden safe door. The first part would be figuring out the correct order of the beads."

"Okay, I get that. But there are only four beads. Even if you had no idea, it wouldn't take that long to try every combination. That doesn't seem very secure, does it?"

Jonathan felt himself getting overwhelmed with excitement by the wonder of it all. "That's where the intention part comes in! The Armor Jewelry works on intention and so do the beads. So even if you guessed the correct order, it wouldn't work unless you understood the meaning of the order. You'd have to know what each symbol on the beads means and what Wilhelm was trying to say through his passcode."

Selina narrowed her brows. "Weird, but okay. What's the second part to cracking the safe?"

"The second part would be wearing a complete set of Armor Jewelry. Since you can't recognize the Plate of Destiny without the Armor Jewelry, there's no point in finding the map to the Plate if you don't have the Jewelry. Part of the intention to open the safe would be to know this and be prepared by wearing the Jewelry. That's what makes this lock so genius. Even if figuring out the right code from the beads was easy to crack, and even if the code was understood and not just a lucky guess, it was unlikely that anyone besides the Mallandian army would have a set of *Mallandian* Armor Jewelry. It's almost foolproof!"

"I don't get it." Selina looked confused. "You're saying the entire Mallandian army could've opened a lock with the keystones? That still doesn't seem secure."

Jonathan shook his head. "No. Back in the Bronze Age, the army was kept under mind control with the cuff. If they came across the keystone beads and the hiding spot of the hidden door, they could be ordered not to open it. The Plate would be safe inside the door if no one could open it but the royal family."

"Okay...so how does this translate to Wilhelm Schwartz and how he used the keystones?"

"In Wilhelm Schwartz's time, absolutely no one but a handful of archaeologists would've found some of the Armor Jewelry, and none of them were American. The U.S. was the perfect place to hide the Plate of Destiny using a hidden door because no one in the entire country would've had access to the Armor Jewelry. Plus, Wilhelm hid the keystones in a separate cave. At that time, it would've been impossible for anyone to find the keystones, have access to the Armor Jewelry, find the hidden door in a separate cave, understand that the keystone beads were actually keys to a lock, put the stones in the right order, *and* understand the meaning that Wilhelm gave the keystone passcode when he created it!"

Selina gave Jonathan a doubtful look. "I know this is an old legend based in myth. But you and your friends are serious about finding a very real map. According to this book, the lock and the carnelian keystone beads are also real. But you came up with a very...metaphysical interpretation. And it sounds like you actually believe it," she said.

He noticed her uncomfortable expression and realizing he had said too much out of excitement, forced himself to laugh. "That's what *Wilhelm Schwartz* would've believed anyway. But remember, his friends tried to have him committed. In reality, you're right. The lock would've been mechanical and changing the combination would've been a lot of work." He wanted to kick himself for forgetting who he was talking to. "I'd love to see if there's any more information about these beads," he added, trying to change the subject.

"Keep reading," Selina suggested. "Maybe we'll find something."

IT WAS PITCH BLACK, AND THERE was noticeably less oxygen in the air. Dripping water could be heard every few seconds or so along with the occasional scurry of a cave-dwelling creature. Nate was searching in his backpack for a flashlight when he felt something grab his ankle. Letting out a yell, he jumped backward and shined the flashlight in front of him with a shaking hand, ready to fight whatever demon might be lurking in this entrance to hell.

"What the fuck, Grace?!" he cried, recognizing the demon. "What are you doing here?"

"Having a picnic," she said, sarcasm dripping from her lips.

Nate heard Anise yelling down the tunnel. "Are you okay? I'm on my way down."

"No!" Nate shouted back up. The last thing he wanted was Anise to be in a scary cave with Grace, who made it all the more horrifying. "I'm fine. Stay up there. I'll be back up soon."

"What do you *think* I'm doing here?!" Grace continued. "Morty and I know the map to the Plate of Destiny is somewhere in this cave. I fell when he was lowering me down here, and now I can't stand. He went off to get another rope."

"How long have you been down here?" he asked, checking out the injury on her leg.

"A few hours," she replied, looking at her watch. "Ouch!" She swatted his hand away when he touched her bruise.

"That's where it hurts?"

"Obviously!"

"Fuck you," he told her. "I was just trying to help."

"That kind of help I don't need!"

Nate started to feel emotionally numb and wanted nothing more than to get out of there. He couldn't leave though until he found what he was looking for, so he changed the subject instead. "Smithton's been gone for a few hours? It doesn't take that long to find a rope."

"It does in the middle of the night!"

"You always have rope with you," Nate reminded his grandmother. "I bet you have extra in your room. And if you're working with Smithton then he'd know that too."

Grace glared at him. "So what are you saying? That Morty's not coming back? That something happened to him?"

"Maybe he got wise and decided to leave you here to die. I should do the same thing." He ran the beam of the flashlight around the cave. It had a low ceiling and a floor where each step would be like climbing or descending stairs—and that was the smooth part. He looked back at Grace. The thought of her being trapped in the cave forever felt freeing. "No one would ever find you. These fucking spiders would eat you alive." He brushed a white spider off of his chest. "They're everywhere."

"You're not looking in the right place," she told him as she crushed a couple of spiders under her fist. "Give me that," she said with annoyance, reaching for his flashlight.

He handed it over. "What did you find?"

She took a hit of oxygen before she responded. "I was able to crawl around a little before my leg started to swell. Look at the wall." She pointed the beam of light on the wall of the far side of the cave.

Nate grabbed another flashlight and carefully made his way to where she was pointing. He ran his fingers over the four oval indentations in the rock. "What is it?"

"Morty and I saw Dromly leaving the cave right before we came in. He was saying something about keys and how they weren't working. Those four indentations look man-made to me."

Nate nodded. "To me too. They're too perfectly shaped to be natural."

"Exactly. I think Dromly has the keys that fit inside those...locks or whatever they're supposed to be. The map is here somewhere, but we need Dromly's keys to find it."

"Did he say what these keys look like?"

Grace shook her head. "No."

Nate walked slowly around the cave, but saw nothing else of interest. He carefully made his way back to Grace with suspicion looming in his mind. "Why did you tell me all that?"

"Because you're right. I think Dromly has Morty, and Morty won't be coming for me. If I can't have the Plate of Destiny, I want you to have it."

"You really believe I'm going to leave you here?"

"Of course," she said. "It's what I would've done."

"And it's what you deserve, you old hag. But I'm not leaving you here. I'm nothing like you." He pulled on the rope to make sure it was still fastened securely to the stalagmite above.

She tugged on his arm. "Sit here a minute before we go. I have something to tell you."

"Is it about how to find the Plate?"

"No."

"Then I'm not interested."

"Sit down and shut up!" she ordered. "I need to tell you this."

He ignored her and thought about the best way to carry her up the thirty foot tunnel.

"Please," she begged him.

He looked at her with surprise. She'd never said the word please to him before. "Fine," he agreed, sitting on a raised part of the floor. "What is it?"

"I never told you about Joseph," Grace said to her grandson.

"Who?"

"Joseph Polk. Your great-grandfather."

"I don't care. We have more important things to do right now."

Grace glared at him. "Just hear me out. I need to say this. I was ten when my baby brother Danny was born."

Nate sighed, stared at the ground, and wondered how much of his time she was going to waste.

Grace continued her story. "I loved him with all my heart. I took care of him when Joseph was beating my mother or trying to run her over with the car while my older sisters and I were made to watch. One night my mother dropped our dinner on the floor, and he hit her with a cast iron skillet until she died. My sisters wouldn't stop screaming, so he shot them."

Nate turned his eyes up from the floor and looked at her.

"When I was fourteen, Danny came down with the flu. He cried too much, and Joseph killed him while I was at school. When I screamed at him, he threatened my life. I shot him twice and left. I was homeless until I moved into my college dormitory."

Nate had never heard any of this. "Shit."

"Morty and I got engaged when I became pregnant with his child. I was afraid to be a mother and scheduled an abortion—which was illegal back then—without telling Morty. When I got there, however, I changed my mind. The doctor propositioned me as payment for his time, and when I refused him, he got irate and threw me down a flight of stairs. Back home, Morty had found out about my plan and was upset, but he forgave me when I told him I had a change of heart. I started bleeding, and he took me to the hospital. I lost the baby due to the fall, but Morty thought I had gone through with the abortion and lied to him about it. I had lied about other things previously, so his trust in me was already shaky. He took back the engagement ring, and he's hated me ever since. Several years later, Thomas, my husband, your grandfather, was shot to death in Morty's office. I thought Morty had hired a hitman to get even with me, and we were mortal enemies after that. I dedicated my entire life to finding the Plate of Destiny so I could bring Thomas back. However, it was on this trip that I found out *Dromly* had shot Thomas, not Morty. Thomas hated Dromly and wanted to beat him in finding the Plate. According to Morty, Thomas had only married me to keep a watch on me because unknown to me, I was to be his seer when he found the Plate of Destiny, but I know that's not true. Thomas loved me. He was planning to hide me for my safety. Morty had brainwashed me only to use all the Armor Jewelry on me in an attempt to activate my seer's abilities and for me to learn the entire truth. He couldn't come out and tell me because he thought I'd antagonize Dromly and get myself killed, which is true. Morty was just trying to keep me safe this entire time."

Nate's full attention was on his grandmother. "Why are you telling me all this?"

"Because I want you to know I understand. I know how unfair life can be. I know that lying to someone you love is sometimes easier but never ends well, even if you meant no harm. I know how it feels to be betrayed by those who are supposed to love and protect you. I know how horrible it was to have grown up with me as your guardian because I had Joseph as mine."

"Sounds like he was worse than you," Nate said quietly.

"Not by much," Grace admitted. "I'm lucky you didn't kill me like I killed Joseph. Not that I could blame you if you had. I also wouldn't blame you if you decided to leave me to the spiders in this cave. But now you know everything. I know this doesn't change anything, but my hope is that by being truthful and open with you, I can help to start to repair the damage I inflicted between us. If you're not open to that, I understand. I just ask you to remember that I'm sorry and that I *do* love you."

Nate was silent for several moments, trying to feel something—anything—about what his grandmother had just told him. He felt nothing, not even numbness, and he realized he just didn't care. Her apology was too little, too late. "We don't have time for this right now," he said, picking her up. "Hold on to my neck. I'm going to need both hands to climb this rope."

✶✶✶

SELINA ENJOYED FEELING THE WARMTH OF the sun on her face as she and Jonathan walked along the city street passing shops, offices, and restaurants. She thought about what she'd learned from him over the past two days and how interested her grandfather had been when she told him everything she and Jonathan had discovered the day before. He'd also said he wanted to hear more after she got back from the library today. Her grandpa had never had any desire to hear about things she'd learned before, and it had been fun to share it with him, finally. She looked forward to telling him what she'd discovered today as well.

Her eyes turned to Jonathan, and she found herself hoping he'd worn the nicer shirt for the same reason she'd spent an hour on her hairdo. Their arms occasionally brushed against each other as they walked, and she was pleased he hadn't moved further away. "You know what I just realized?" Selina said when a thought popped into her head.

"What's that?" Jonathan asked.

"Every piece of the Armor Jewelry has chalcedony on it."

Jonathan shook his head. "Only the earrings are made of chalcedony."

"Yes, but each piece includes a stone that's a *type* of chalcedony. The ring has carnelian, the amulet has sardonyx and black agate, and the cuff has jasper."

"All those stones are actually types of chalcedony?" Jonathan asked.

"Yes. I wonder if that meant anything to the Mallandians."

"You're the geologist. You tell me," he teased her with a smirk.

"You're the historian," she teased back.

He laughed and gave her an adorable grin. His arm moved, and she thought he was going to drape it over her shoulder before he quickly shoved his hands in his pockets.

"Thanks for walking me back to my hotel," she said as they reached the parking lot and stood facing each other.

"Had I known your hotel was right next to mine, I would've done so yesterday too. And we could've walked there together in the mornings."

"Maybe tomorrow?" she asked, hopefully. "We didn't find out anything else about those carnelian beads."

"As much as I'd like that, I think my research is done. At least for now. And I couldn't ask you to give up any more of your time."

Selina found it strange that Jonathan wouldn't want to keep searching for more answers, but she tried to give him the benefit of the doubt. After a short silence, she asked, "So did you find the CD you promised me?"

"The CD," he groaned. "I forgot to look."

"I've got some time now," she said.

"Sure! Come on up."

He led her to his room, and she shut the door behind them, watching as he rooted through his travel bag.

"Found it!" He handed it to her. "I hope you like it."

"Thanks! I'm sure I will." She took a step closer to him. Being almost as tall as he was allowed her to look directly into his light green eyes. "When we were outside you said you couldn't ask me to give up any more of my time. I want you to know I don't see it that way. I got to do fascinating research with an amazing man that I can't stop thinking about. I hope you're not planning on flying back home anytime soon, because I'd really like to get to know you better."

His cheeks turned bright red. "You're amazing too," he told her, shyly looking at the floor. "I've been more than impressed with everything you know, your willingness to help out, your confidence, your—"

Selina stopped his speech by gently putting her lips on his. He seemed to enjoy her affection by the way his soft lips tenderly returned her kiss and his hands claiming her lower back to pull her closer. She opened her mouth slightly to make room for his tongue and let her hands wander over his chest. He looked mesmerized for a moment when she paused to look in his gorgeous green eyes. When she tried to kiss him again, however, he stopped her.

"I want you to know I think everything about you is incredible," Jonathan said softly. "But right now...there's someone I'm just not over."

"I'm sorry," Selina said quickly. She looked at her feet while her cheeks grew hot.

"Don't be," he told her. "I like you, and I'm sure I'm going to kick myself for this later, but the timing just isn't right for me."

Still feeling embarrassed, she didn't want to ask but *had* to know. "It's Anise, isn't it?"

He nodded.

"So, wait. Isn't she with Nate?" Selina asked, feeling more and more hurt by his rejection as she thought about the situation. "She leaves you for your friend, and you're still carrying a torch for her?"

"That's not how it happened," Jonathan explained. "I broke up with her which I shouldn't have done. And I wouldn't call Nate my friend."

"I'm sorry, this is none of my business," she said, looking down again. "I just keep embarrassing myself." She wondered why she kept saying the wrong thing. First with Kent, now with Jonathan. Maybe she should head back to the library and find a book on how to be socially intuitive. "I should go." She hurried out of his room and down the hall to the stairwell, ignoring the fact that he was calling her name. She shoved through the door at the end of the hall and fled down the stairs.

He caught up to her in the lobby. "Selina, wait. You have nothing to be embarrassed about. I'm honored you think that highly of me, and believe me, the feeling is mutual. If the timing were different..."

"It's fine, Jonathan." She stepped outside with him right behind her and headed toward her hotel next door.

They both turned their heads when they saw a car pull in to the parking lot. Anise waved at them from the backseat. They waved back and headed over.

"Hi Selina, good to see you again!" Anise said.

"You too," Selina told her. She couldn't help but notice that the outline of whatever necklace Anise was wearing under her loose cotton shirt was square-shaped and large, and it reminded Selina of the drawings of the amulet in the book.

"How did it go?" Jonathan asked.

"We have a lot to tell you," Anise said. "Meet us upstairs." She looked at Selina and then back at Jonathan. "When you're ready."

There was a brief moment of silence and Selina sensed whatever Anise and the others had to say was not for her ears. Feeling awkward once again, she gave a half-wave to everyone. "It was nice to see you all. It's time for me to get going." She turned and started walking quickly, eager to get away and go somewhere to lick her wounds. Trying not to think about how much humiliation she had experienced in the last few minutes, she thought about the Armor Jewelry. Whatever necklace Anise was wearing was the right size and shape, but she wouldn't actually wear such a valuable piece that belonged in a museum, would she? Jonathan would be horrified by the thought, and he'd tell her so.

"Selina, wait," Jonathan called out. "We didn't get a chance to finish our conversation." She could hear his footsteps as he ran after her.

"We could use your help with the equipment, Boy Scout," Nate called out.

"I'll be right there!" Jonathan said loudly over his shoulder, sounding annoyed.

Selina stopped walking and turned around to face him. "I don't think there's anything left to say. I just misread you, that's all."

"But you didn't," Jonathan insisted. "You really didn't. I just think it wouldn't be fair to you if I...if we...um...—"

"I understand that," she said, interrupting him. "It's fine, really. Go help your friends. Or your non-friends. Whoever they are to you." She could tell by his frown that he didn't like the way the conversation was ending, but all she wanted was to leave.

"I'd really like for us to be friends. I'll call you later," he promised her, and jogged back to the car.

Selina watched him take a few things out of the trunk. The chain on the necklace Anise wore glistened in the sun and looked like it could've been the alloy metal that Jonathan had talked about. Something about this seemed off. She needed to get a better look at it. Waiting for a moment, she saw her chance and took it. Anise looked up as she began heading toward the hotel and waved good-bye to Selina. Selina waved back and pretended to trip over something. She sat on the ground and held her ankle.

Anise rushed over to her. "Are you okay? That looked like a nasty fall."

"I'll be fine," Selina said, faking a smile. "But could you help me up?"

"Of course," Anise told her, and bending over, offered Selina her hands.

As Anise's loose top fell away from her chest when she bent down, Selina was in the perfect position to see the necklace that also fell forward and out from behind the shield of the top. It had a large black stone with five smaller orange and white stones around it. It *was* the amulet! She felt her mouth open in surprise. There's no way that anyone would wear this piece knowing how valuable it was. Unless...no. Impossible and ridiculous to even think such a thing.

"Thank you, Anise," Selina said as she stood up, pretending she hadn't seen anything of interest. She watched as Anise quickly tucked the amulet underneath her top again.

"Are you hurt?" Jonathan asked, running up behind them.

"Only my pride," Selina answered honestly.

"Why don't you walk her back to her hotel?" Anise suggested to Jonathan.

"No," Selina snapped. "I'm fine." She turned around and walked away. After a moment, Selina turned around and saw Anise and Jonathan heading back to the car. She stooped to pick up a rock, and hurled it at the back of Anise's head as hard as she could. The rock stopped short of the brown, wavy mane and headed back toward Selina, landing at her feet. She let out an involuntary squeak. "Anise!" she called out, and ran after her.

Anise turned around, and Selina tried not to let out another noise of shock. Anise seemed to be oblivious of the additional light as she squinted in the sun. Selina's shadow fell on Anise's top and there was no question in her mind—the amulet was glowing, just as Jonathan had described from the legend. She realized they were waiting for her to speak and she spit out, "I'm sorry if I came across as rude just now. I've...been having a strange day."

"No worries," Anise told her gently. "You're shaking... are you sure you're okay?"

Selina shook her head and tucked a blonde strand that had come loose behind her ear. "Actually, I'm not feeling very well. I'm going to lie down for a while."

"I'll check on you later," Jonathan said, the concern evident in his voice.

"Feel better!" Anise added.

SELINA COLLAPSED ON THE SOFA IN the two bedroom suite she shared with her grandfather and curled up in a ball.

She wiped a few tears of embarrassment off her cheeks.

"You're back?" Charlie Masser asked her, coming out of the bathroom dressed in a button-down shirt and khaki pants that were a little too short for a man almost six-and-a-half feet tall. "It's still morning. I thought you were spending the day with that boy you told me about. What's his name again?"

"Jonathan. I thought so too."

"What happened?" He towel dried the few hairs his liver-spotted head had left and looked around for his glasses. He grabbed them and looked to her, waiting for her answer.

Selina groaned. "I made a fool out of myself. I can't seem to say anything right."

"Did he say something to you?" He put on his glasses and squinted at his pill bottles.

"No, it's not him. It's his friends. They act like they don't want me around. It's weird. The women are nice enough, but kind of distant. And the men don't seem to like me at all."

"How could anyone not like you?" He sat down beside her and put an arm around her.

Selina laughed. "It's not that simple, Grandpa. I know I pissed off Kent when I talked to him about his father. And for some reason, Nate barely even acknowledges my presence. Lorelei hasn't said much to me either. Anise seems like someone I'd like to be friends with, but Jonathan is her ex and...I don't know. Maybe she resents me or something."

"That's just speculation," he told her. "I thought you said Jonathan was a very nice boy."

"He is. But if his friends don't like me...I'm sure their opinions mean something to him."

"Then you need to change their opinions."

"No, I'm done. Today was humiliating. I don't want to see any of them again."

"Don't say that." He squeezed her shoulders.

"There's no point, Grandpa."

"What do you mean?"

"Jonathan told me he's not over Anise. But even if he were, we live three states away from each other. How would that even work?"

He chuckled. "Who says it has to be long term? Enjoy each other now."

Selina hung her head. "No. I'm not the type to have a fling," she said, "and I don't think Jonathan is either."

"You really like this boy," he concluded.

Selina let out a small, embarrassed laugh. "I do. But I'll get over it."

He squeezed her shoulders. "Why don't you tell me about what you discovered today?"

She told him everything she and Jonathan had learned while her grandpa listened without interruption. "But there's more. I saw that Anise was wearing the amulet which I thought was really strange because it's priceless. It shouldn't be worn. Which got me thinking. And please don't call me delusional, but I think the legends are true."

After Selina told him about the glowing amulet and how the rock she'd thrown at Anise impossibly changed directions in the air, he looked her right in the eyes. "I believe you."

She raised her eyebrows doubtfully at him. "Really?"

"Of course. There are things in this world that no one understands. That doesn't mean you're delusional for finding one of them."

"Grandpa, you're amazing!" She gave him a hug. "But, should I do anything with this knowledge? I feel like I should tell at least Anise and Jonathan what I know."

"Why?"

"That way we don't have to keep secrets from each other anymore. Wouldn't it be better that way?" She sighed with indecision. "But I don't know. I'd like to tell them I figured it out and offer to help, but they've made it clear they don't want me involved." Her face lit up with a thought. "But maybe that's only because—"

"No," Charlie interrupted. "If they don't want your help, they don't deserve it. Let's keep this information between us. What you're going to do is go see Jonathan and make him realize that he'd be an idiot to turn you away."

She hung her head. "No. He made his decision, and I'm going to respect it."

He patted her hand. "That's very mature of you, but at least go talk to him instead of hiding here feeling sorry for yourself. Perhaps you can make a good friend out of him. Wouldn't that be nice? I bet things aren't as bad as you think."

"Maybe. He said he'd call me later. And he did say something about wanting to be friends."

"You see? It sounds like he does care."

"I don't know. He's such a good guy; I think he'd do that for anyone."

"Enough of this. You're going over there. Right now. Well, after you make a run to the drug store. I need you to pick something up for me."

"But I still don't want to see him," she argued.

Charlie stood and held out his hands to her. "You're going. You'll see that I'm right."

She allowed him to pull her to a standing position. "Okay. Fine. But I need a shower first."

THIS WOULDN'T DO AT ALL. THESE new people in Selina's life needed to like her. Charlie's entire plan, the reason he was in Florida, depended on it. As soon as he heard the water running in the shower, Charlie got on the phone. "Shawn. I need you and Dave for a very special project. Now."

Part 3

THE DEAD

Chapter 14

S o where is Grace now?" Jonathan asked Nate to fill the awkward silence. Anise had gone to the lobby to purchase a soda, and Lorelei and Kent were on the other side of the room digging through the trip journals, trying to find anything more Fred Dromly may have written about the carnelian beads.

"We dropped her off at a hospital," he replied.

"You just left her there?"

"She doesn't need a baby-sitter."

"That's not what I mean. She wants the Plate of Destiny. She'll be coming after Anise and the Jewelry, and we promised each other we'd keep her safe. Keep her from dying early."

Nate shook his head. "Grace won't get that far. Dromly and his brainwashed army are after her for her seer powers. They'll catch her long before Grace can come after Anise."

"How do you know?"

"Because I told them where she is. They already have Smithton. I called his phone and one of his brainwashed co-workers answered. If Dromly has Grace, she can't hurt Anise."

Jonathan felt his mouth open in horror. "They have Dr. S.?" Mixed emotions about his former mentor and friend bubbled up in his mind.

"Don't even think about going after him," Nate warned. "Anise needs you here."

"I won't go after him," Jonathan promised. "My loyalty is with Anise, not Dr. S."

Anise reentered the room with her bottle of soda. "Any luck?" she asked Lorelei and Kent.

"Yes," Lorelei replied. "I just found something!" She showed them a page in a trip journal.

"That's the same picture I saw in the book at the library today!" Jonathan exclaimed.

They all looked at the drawing in Dromly's journal. Four ovals represented the carnelian keystone beads. Each bead had two curly Mallandian symbols on them— one near each tapered end.

"What does it say?" Jonathan asked.

"In this entry, Fred wrote an interpretation of the writing on each bead," Lorelei said. "He says that the oval-shaped beads are supposed to be placed vertically and the symbols are sideways so as not to indicate if the bead is right-side-up or upside-down. He put them in order to create a sentence which is a code to open the lock Jonathan read about. When you put the four beads next to each other with the tapered ends of the ovals pointing up and down, not side to side, they form a phrase in two lines—the upper line and the lower line—and they're read left to right. The four beads, in order, basically say 'Protection of the life and death knowledge from the world for me,' meaning he's protecting the knowledge on the Plate of Destiny for himself."

Jonathan looked at the drawing in the journal again to read the two lines as Lorelei had said.

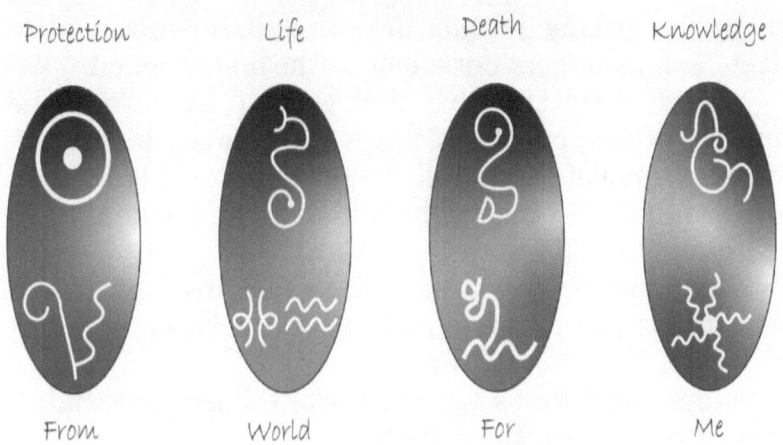

Protection — Life — Death — Knowledge

From — World — For — Me

"We need to get our hands on those beads," Anise declared.

"I think I have a plan for that," Kent told her. "I need you and Nate to come with me."

"You're sure you can get in?" Kent asked, taking a deep breath to calm himself.

"Piece of cake," Nate responded. "I already broke in once, remember?"

"He'll get us in," Anise responded confidently.

"Okay." Kent stepped out of the stairwell and walked down the hall toward his father's hotel room. Butterflies fluttered in his stomach. This, right now, was a big reason he was here. Could he and his father actually come to some kind of understanding about what happened between them? What would happen if they could? Would a relationship be possible after all these years? Tricking Fred into leaving his room so Nate and Anise could break in wasn't exactly how Kent imagined the father-son reunion going down, but under the circumstances, it was necessary. Taking another deep breath, he knocked. He stretched his fingers nervously as the door opened.

"Kent!" Fred Dromly's eyes grew to the size of the saucer he gripped in his fingers to balance his cup of tea. An aroma of chamomile, mint, and rose filled the air. "You found me! Come in," he said, holding the door open as wide as his smile.

Kent pointed down the hallway with his thumb. "No. Let's go for a drink or something. We have some things to discuss."

"I see. As long as we can make the drink a walk. I haven't had a drop since 1963."

"Oh. Yeah, fine."

"One moment while I grab my wallet."

When Fred reemerged from his room, Kent led him to the elevator at the opposite end of the hall from where his two young companions were hiding.

ONCE THE HALLWAY WAS CLEAR, ANISE glided silently down the colorful carpet right behind Nate. She watched as he pulled a key card out of his pocket. Within seconds, Nate had the door open and they were inside. He closed it behind them and locked it.

"You had a key?" she asked, almost disappointed. "I thought you'd have a fancy way of picking it open."

"It's an electronic lock," he replied. "Much easier to steal a key from the front desk."

"Mmmhmm," she agreed, nodding.

She could tell he knew what she was thinking when he smirked at her and said, "The point is to get in as quickly and discreetly as possible, not to be fancy, right?"

"Of course," she answered, feeling immature at romanticizing his criminal knowledge. Her fidgety fingers hid inside the pockets of her knee-length, purple sundress, and she dug the toe of a silver sandal into the carpet. Disturbed by her own emotions, she silently scolded herself, vowing to stop feeling turned on by him when he easily succeeded at doing something illegal. *It's not the fact that he's doing something wrong*, she reasoned, trying to be compassionate with herself. *It's that nothing can stop him, no matter what it is. It's the power, the skill, the knowledge.* But it didn't matter. They were broken up. It still had to stop.

"Check all the drawers," he told her. "I'll start working on the safe."

"Fred has a really nice room," Anise commented. "This little hotel kitchen is nicer than the one in my apartment." She carefully rooted through all the drawers and cabinets in the kitchenette, the bathroom, the bedroom, and the living area. "No beads," she said, walking up to the closet where Nate was sitting on the floor trying to crack the small in-room safe. "I did find a new trip journal he started."

"Let's take that, too," he said as the safe door popped open. He reached in and pulled out a small leather bag that was closed and tied with a string. Nate opened the top of the bag and poured the contents into his hand.

"They're beautiful!" Anise exclaimed. The orange, oval-shaped carnelian beads were polished, and the curly Mallandian writing was prominently etched in them, still legible despite their age. Each bead was about two inches long and had two symbols, one near each end. A hole ran vertically through each bead so they could be connected with string if desired.

Nate put them back in their bag and dropped it in his backpack. Anise added the trip journal and zipped it up.

"You know," she said, frowning as she looked around the room, "because of Fred Dromly, Kent has been through so much pain. And Dromly's obsession with the Jewelry and the Plate of Destiny led to a series of events that's caused a shit-ton of trouble for me and people I love. And now we're alone in his room. I just feel like..."

Nate grinned at her as he closed the safe and put it back in the closet. "What'd you have in mind, honey?"

She shrugged. "I don't know. Nothing. I'm not the vengeful type. I just wish I could make him understand how much hurt he's caused."

"If it's revenge you want, I've got a great idea," Nate said. Still sitting on the floor by the closet, he grabbed a pair of Dromly's shoes and handed one to her. "Let's tie all his shoelaces in knots."

Anise laughed out loud. Taking the shoe, she sat down beside Nate. "Yeah," she said, "'cause that'll teach him."

"The fucking bastard won't know what hit him," Nate said with passion as he quickly tied several knots which made Anise laugh again. "Make sure you get 'em nice and tight."

"Yes, sir," she promised, pulling her knot as tightly as she could.

"Come on," he said, grabbing her hand, pulling her to her feet, and leading her across the room.

"Why are we in the kitchen?" she asked.

Nate opened the drawer that held the silverware and grabbed all the spoons. He handed one to her. "We lick them and put them back," he explained with a serious face.

Anise watched with horror as he put the spoon in his mouth and then back in the silverware tray. "This is disgusting," she announced, but she followed suit anyway, and her giggles of revulsion made him start laughing as well.

"Now *you* think of one," he encouraged her.

"Oh, I don't know," she said, looking around. "We could...jump on his bed with our shoes on?"

"Great one!" he told her enthusiastically. "Don't forget to stomp on the pillows!"

Darting into the bedroom, Nate leapt onto the bed

and held out his hand. Laughing again, Anise allowed him to pull her up. They bounced around, and Nate dramatically called out, "Take *that* Dromly! You rat bastard! What are you gonna do now? Huh? *Nothing*, you little bitch! You can't do a damn fucking thing about it!"

The old bed had taken more than it could stand, and the footboard collapsed under the weight of the two gamboling adults, sending them tumbling to the floor. Anise heard Nate scrambling over to her. "Are you okay? Are you hurt?" he asked.

Her hands covered her face, and she was laughing so hard at the absurdity of it all that the only sounds she made were heavy, wheezing inhales. She leaned back against the lopsided bed, still laughing uncontrollably, and Nate sat beside her as he started to laugh as well. She buried her face in his chest until she could calm herself down. When she lifted her head to look at him, she felt his fingers touch her face and gently wipe away the tears of laughter that were making their way down her cheeks. She basked in the loving look he was giving her. Then his lips were on hers, and she eagerly kissed him back. Everything felt right again. He swept her up in his arms, and they lay together on the lop-sided bed as their kisses became more intense and their passion grew. She grabbed his wrists and directed his hands under her sundress where she needed them. She held his face as she kissed his mouth and pressed herself against where his fingers were ravishing her. She let out a sigh of pleasure and began unzipping his pants, but reality came back to her in a flash.

"No, stop." Her hands pushed him away. "We're broken up," she reminded the both of them. She sat up and tried to collect herself.

Nate sat up too. "Don't do this, Anise. We're so good together. I love you."

Anger bubbled up inside her again. "Yes! We *were* good together. It was so good I stupidly thought you were the one. And I loved you so much until you fucked everything up!"

He looked at her with a pained expression on his face. "I know I fucked up. And I *know* you're the one. It's not stupid. I feel it too."

"I'm so *mad* at you!" she cried. "You *ruined* something so beautiful. How could you do that? And I'm so mad at myself for letting you get to me just now." She sighed and stood up.

He stood as well but gently pulled her back down until they were both sitting on the bed again. "We have a connection," he reminded her. "We always have. Anise, I've never been in a relationship like this before, and I know I have a lot to learn. I want to change into the man that you deserve. I'm trying."

Her expression softened. "I know you are. And I have no doubt that someday you'll make a great partner for a very lucky woman. But I'm not going to wait around for that, giving you infinite chances to get things right, and getting my heart broken over and over again along the way."

"Honey—"

"No!" she said, cutting him off. "I need to get over you. And today has taught me that I obviously can't do that with you still in my life. When we get back home, I'll need to break off all contact with you."

"None?" he asked, looking surprised. "You don't even want to be friends anymore?"

Her voice was shaky and her response came out in a whisper. "I can't."

He put his elbows on his knees and his head in his hands for a few seconds. "We have the beads. We should go." He got up, grabbed the backpack, and waited for her by the front door.

She put the broken footboard back in place as best as she could before following him out into the hallway.

***

THE DROMLY MEN WALKED SIDE BY side along the busy street until they arrived at a park. Fred stole small glances at his son, marveling at the masterpiece time had created. If only he'd had the pleasure of watching it happen. He remembered how his wife Helen never made it out of the mental health facility she'd been placed in. She was making some progress but then passed. Her parents had full custody of Kent, and they took immense pleasure in telling Fred that his son didn't want to see him. Fred was in Europe searching for the Plate of Destiny much of the time, but came back multiple times a year—for every birthday, for Christmas, for his school plays, for as many of his baseball games as he could. He just had to sneak into each event or watch from afar. He wrote Kent letters several times a month, but they all remained unanswered.

Fred couldn't help but think of the time when Kent was a teenager, and Fred waited in the lobby of a movie theater where his son was watching a film with his friends. He'd had enough of keeping his distance, and it was time to ask his son why he never wanted to see him, why he wouldn't want to at least try to know each other. When he came out, Fred tried to talk to him, but Kent angrily dismissed him. When Fred kept trying to engage with him, it started a big scene. Kent had felt abandoned because they hadn't seen each other in so long. The night ended with Fred's arrest and Kent's hatred for Fred growing larger.

When Kent became an adult, Fred attempted to reach out again. Some of his journals had been stolen, and he needed a safe place to keep them. This gave him the brilliant idea of sharing them with his son. Kent could keep them safe for him, and Fred could keep the lines of communication open. Every time Fred filled a trip journal, he'd send it to his son with a personal letter. Fred never heard back from him but sincerely hoped he read them.

They'd been walking for several minutes in silence. Kent found a bench and sat on one end of it while Fred sat on the other end. Each stared straight ahead. "I've often thought of what I'd say to you if I ever saw you again, but none of it's coming to mind," Kent said.

Several moments passed before Fred commented, "You look well."

"So do you," Kent replied.

"I've been wearing the earrings quite often. They're keeping me young."

"Ah."

A few more minutes ticked by.

"Have you ever noticed," Fred said as a small breeze blew over his skin, "that although you can never see the wind, you can see its consequences by the reactions of what it touches?"

His son gave him the same inquisitive look as when he was a child and Fred was trying to teach him something. "What do you mean?"

"Wind can cause grass to bow, a sail to proudly puff out its chest, and leaves to dance. On the other hand, it can also cause trucks to tip over, neighborhoods to be flattened, and trees to be ripped from the only place they've ever called home. You never saw much of me, but I can see the effects my actions have had on you. I was a tornado in your life."

Kent nodded. "Yes. You were."

"For that, son, I am truly sorry." This surprise reunion was making his heart long to reach out to Kent, to nurture and grow the bond one can only feel with a child or parent.

✳✳✳

KENT STARED AT HIS FATHER, EYEING his ridiculous cape that was far too warm for the Florida heat. He had wanted to hear Fred's apology for most of his life. But for some reason, instead of wanting to apologize for his own role in their estrangement, he found himself growing angry. "Are you really sorry though?"

"Truly," Fred repeated.

"You know," Kent began, "when I was 32 years old, I met a woman and her young son Nate. The woman was later kidnapped and hidden away by her husband." Kent showed his father a current picture of Nate and Lorelei he had on his phone. "Nate, who was just a small child at the time, asked if he could live with me instead of his father. I probably wouldn't have been able to get custody of him, but I promised him I'd never stop looking for his mother. And I never did. I found her. Alive. And I have to admit, I've regretted not even trying for custody. It haunts me to this day. I felt more fatherly toward a virtual stranger's child than you ever did toward me."

"You saw yourself in him and his situation."

"Are you trying to say I was feeling sorry for myself and not for him?"

"No, it was just a comment. I'm sure you felt sorry for the both of you. We tend to empathize more with those with whom we have something in common."

Kent frowned. "I'm beginning to understand. You left for good when I was a young teen. I was never to hear from you again besides the trip journals you'd send me. But you had no empathy for me because we had nothing in common."

"Not true. I loved you. I still do. And I reached out *many* times, but you had no desire to see me."

Kent narrowed his eyebrows thinking of all his disappointing childhood birthdays with no word from his father. "Do you even know when my birthday is?"

"Of course! How could I ever forget the nones of July?"

Kent sighed. "Why can't you say 'the seventh' like a

normal person?"

"Many reasons!" his father began. "First, saying 'the nones' is far more poetic and special. And your birthday was very special indeed. Second, being a normal person must be the worst fate I—"

"Yeah, okay. Fine," Kent interrupted.

"I don't understand. What more was I to do?"

"Keep trying to reach out to me! That's what you should've done. I may have pushed you away that *one time* you tried to talk to me after mom died, but that didn't mean I never wanted to see you again. We must have a different definition of what 'many times' means." No calls, no letters, no visits. Only the trip journals. It wasn't good enough.

"I made mistakes that I regret. Parenting isn't easy."

"I guess I wouldn't know," Kent grumbled. His father had hit a nerve.

"You would've made a great parent, I'm sure. Why is it you didn't ever have kids?"

Kent winced internally at the bad memories that question evoked. "Because I couldn't even though I wanted to. My wife left me for it. I wanted to adopt, but she wanted her own."

"I'm sorry," Fred told him. "That must've been difficult."

Kent stewed in silence.

"Maybe if you had become a father, you'd understand me a little better."

"You abandoned me, and you think the problem is that I don't understand you?"

It was Fred's turn to be silent.

"I can't believe how arrogant and selfish you still are," Kent said as he heard his phone beep. Taking a quick glance at the screen, he saw he'd received a one-word text from Nate that read *OK*. Kent felt relieved that his conversation with his father could now end. "This was a mistake." He got up to leave.

"Wait," his father said, reaching out and touching Kent's arm. "Don't go. Let's start over."

"Start over how?" Kent asked doubtfully.

"Join me! I'm so close to finding the Plate of Destiny! We can find it together."

"Why do you want the Plate so badly? What was it about the Plate that kept you away constantly?"

"You know it can bring back the dead?"

"So the legend goes," Kent replied.

"The love of my life, Dot, was killed in an automobile accident."

Kent waited a moment before speaking. "That's it?"

"That's not enough?"

"No! You don't care about bringing Mom back? And you didn't care about your son being in your life who was very much alive and still is? You just devoted your entire existence to a dead woman? Oh, excuse me, *and* the fame and publicity you'd receive when you find another amazing artifact." Kent started walking away.

Fred came up behind him. "Hate me all you want, but there's something you need to know. For the Plate to work, Anise Viston's blood must be spilled directly on it."

Kent turned to look at him. "So you don't just need Anise to activate Grace's seer powers? You also want to kill her so you can bring back your precious corpse love? Well, there's something you need to know too. Nate and I and the rest of us won't let that happen!"

Fred shook his head. "No, that's not what I'm saying at all! Besides, once I gain the knowledge of resurrection, I'd be happy to bring back your mother and anyone else you want to see again. Join me, son. Bring me Anise and—"

"No!" Kent shouted at the old man. "I won't let you harm a hair on that girl's head!" Kent stared at his father, wondering if he should kill him and end the entire thing here and now.

Fred looked down at the amulet glowing underneath

his shirt. "Now, that's not very nice," he told Kent. "Even if you did kill me, you'd still have Grace and Morty to deal with."

Kent began walking away again.

"Please wait!" Fred begged as he reached out and grabbed Kent's arm. "You remember I loved to travel the world and find artifacts, especially those connected to legends and incantations. Even more than the artifacts, my trip journals were—are—my prized possessions. Have you read them? They're my written compilation of the moments in my life that I truly *lived*. This is what I wanted to share with you. Having those moments of being so alive are what make life worth living. I just want to know that you have those moments. Please. Tell me."

Kent glared at Fred as he ripped his arm out of the old man's grasp. "We're done here."

FRED SAT BACK ON THE BENCH as he watched his son storm away. "Confusion is the most uncomfortable feeling," he whispered to himself. Grace accused him of killing Thomas. Morty believed he wanted to kill Grace. Kent thought he wanted Anise to die. Why was everyone so convinced he was a murderer? He'd never killed anyone in his life and had no intention to do so. Anise wouldn't have to die. He'd planned several controlled bleeds with short pauses for her to use the Jewelry to heal herself in between. He'd solicit her help in exchange for something she wants. Surely she had someone she'd like to bring back from the realm of the dead.

He reminded himself that the fear reactions he elicited from others was exactly what he'd wanted originally. It's often easier to get what you want when others are afraid of you, and his plan was certainly working thus far. But it had a side effect. The loneliness and longing for true companionship or partnerships could eat you alive when you're seen as a monster.

Fred's thoughts turned to his son's other accusation that he hadn't reached out enough during Kent's formative years. But it wasn't true. He remembered again all the birthday cards and gifts he'd sent, letters he'd written, all the times he'd tried to call, all the times that Kent's grandparents turned Fred away from the door because they said Kent had refused to see him. They must indeed have a very different definition of what 'many times' means.

Fred got up and leaned on his cane. He didn't need it to walk, but there was something comforting about it. "Thank you," he told the cane, "for offering me the support that I haven't found with another human being in a very long time."

Chapter 15

T his is the order that Fred has in the journal," Lorelei explained, arranging the beads on the desk in
Anise's room as she sat with the journal open in
front of her. "The first bead has the words 'protection'
and 'from' on each end. The second one has 'life' and
'world.' And so on." When she was finished putting them
in their proper places, they read:

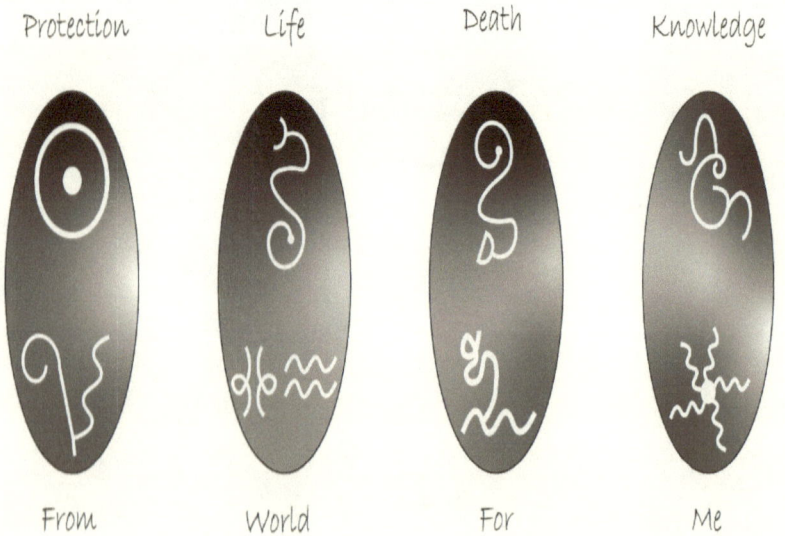

Protection   Life   Death   Knowledge

From   World   For   Me

Nate looked at the beads over Lorelei's shoulder. "I guess that could make sense. Wilhelm Schwartz hid the Plate because he wanted to protect it, and he refused to share the secrets of death with anyone. But what doesn't make sense is this entry in the new journal Anise found today in Dromly's room. Dromly says he already tried putting the beads in the lock and it did nothing."

Anise was looking over Lorelei's other shoulder. "So that means it's either the wrong code or the wrong lock. Jonathan just told us that having all four pieces of the original Armor Jewelry set is needed to open the lock as well, so maybe Dromly doesn't have them all."

"It's probably not the wrong lock," Lorelei said. "Fred hasn't found any other locks and he's been searching for most of his life."

"And we know that Dromly likely has all the pieces of Armor Jewelry," added Anise.

"So we just need to figure out the right code," Lorelei added. "By the way, where is Jonathan? He's supposed to be here."

JONATHAN DIDN'T WANT TO OPEN HIS eyes. He was so groggy; maybe he could sleep for just a few more minutes. His head pounded. Maybe he could sleep for a few more hours. The pillow wasn't under his head and there was a crick in his neck. His body tried to turn, but it couldn't. His head fell backward and then forward. *Where is my pillow?* Moments of lucidity flashed in and out. He had been dreaming he was going to check on Selina. No, wait, that wasn't a dream.

His eyes flew open, and he found himself looking at his lap. Head turning, his eyes darted back and forth. His wrists, ankles, and chest were bound tightly to a chair that stood on a concrete floor. A sole light flickered on the high ceiling above. Stacked boxes surrounded him. Stale air. He turned his head as far as it would go. Far behind him, a large metal door and one small window to its left. There was complete silence until he spoke aloud to himself. "Where the hell am I?"

"Finally, you're awake," said a deep voice.

Jonathan looked toward the sound and saw a single dark-haired figure walking toward him. "Who are you?" he demanded. "Do you work for Dromly?" He saw another man with light hair standing next to a pile of boxes staring at him.

Silently, the dark-haired man pulled a small card table in front of Jonathan and placed a full set of Armor Jewelry on it.

"Where did you get that?" Jonathan demanded. His heart pounded. "Do you work for Grace? Wait, did Nate put you up to this?"

"Shut up, four-eyes." The man pointed at the amulet, ring, and earrings. "I'm supposed to tell you these are replicas. I hear you're the Jewelry engineer."

"You want me to engrave them with the incantation," Jonathan said, finally understanding.

"Yes. Now get to it." The man put a sharp tool on the table that Jonathan could use to scratch the Mallandian symbols on the Jewelry's settings. He showed Jonathan that the gun he held was fully loaded. "Just in case you get any ideas."

Jonathan saw the light-haired man showing him his gun as well.

The man untied Jonathan's hands so he could complete the task.

WITH HER HEART PUMMELING HER CHEST, Selina stood on a couple of wooden pallets she'd piled up and peered into the small warehouse window where she'd witnessed Jonathan being dragged inside. She saw him sitting at a card table and two men with guns watching him. Frantically, she started running back toward the hotel in the sweltering Florida sun. As she got there, she saw Kent pulling into the parking lot at the hotel next door. "Kent!" she yelled, waving her arms. "Kent!"

Kent looked up as he got out of the car. Selina ran over to him at full speed, sweat dripping down her face.

"Selina! Are you okay?"

She pointed in the direction of the warehouse as she tried to catch her breath. "It's Jonathan! I need your help!" She got into the passenger's seat of his car. "Drive!" She explained that she had seen Jonathan being taken into a warehouse not far from there by men she didn't recognize. Both of them had guns.

"We need to call the police!" Kent exclaimed, reaching for his phone.

Kent parked on the street and followed her to the window where they both stood on the wooden pallets and peered inside.

"He's tied to that chair," Kent whispered to her.

"What do we do?" she asked him. "Why aren't the police here?"

"I don't know. They said they'd get here as soon as they can."

"That's not reassuring." She felt sick.

"No, it's not. We'll need more help. I'm calling Nate," he told her. Grabbing his cell phone again, he explained the situation as quickly as possible. "It's too dangerous for Anise," Kent said. "Remember how we promised to keep her safe." He hung up and stared into the window again.

"What should we do?" Selina asked Kent as she wrung her hands. *Poor Jonathan!*

"See if you can find something we might be able to use as a weapon just in case," Kent directed her.

She darted around the other side of the building to search for whatever her imagination would be able to turn into protection. A few minutes later, she heard a motorcycle. She saw Nate pull up and felt relieved. Surely the three of them could figure something out. She grabbed what she could find and headed back.

"So what's the plan, boys?" Selina asked as she rounded the corner of the building with a filthy, used broom, a bent metal pipe, and a 2 x 4 with a nail sticking out of it that had come loose from another wooden pallet.

Nate was standing on the pallets and peering in the window. He reached out for the pipe, and she handed it to him. "Is there another door to this place?" he asked.

"Yeah, there's one in the back," she replied. "I just saw it when I found this stuff."

"Go to that door," he said to Selina. "Stand as far away as you can while throwing rocks or whatever you can find at it. Make as much noise as possible. When it opens, run like hell. Don't let them catch you. I'll pick the lock on this door," he said, motioning to the front door. "Kent, you watch through the window. If they leave to check out the noise, you and I will get a chance to go in and get Boy Scout."

"Which one do you want?" Selina asked Kent, holding up the broom and the 2 x 4.

He shrugged. "Lady's choice."

She shrugged too. "I guess I'll keep the broom." Her gaze turned to Nate as she handed Kent the 2 x 4. "When they hear the noise I'm going to make on the back door, they'll probably check it out right away. Won't you need more time to pick that lock?"

"No," Nate said matter-of-factly.

"Okay," she replied, feeling both impressed and curious as to where he might've learned such a skill. "Here we go." She ran around the side of the building.

Selina threw rocks at the door as Nate had suggested. Shortly, she became impatient. She rattled the door handle and pounded on the large metal door. It opened and a light-haired man stepped out. "What do you need, blondie?"

NATE TOOK HIS LOCK PICK OUT of his pocket. *Who the hell would want Boy Scout and why?*

Kent peered into the window. "They just looked up. They heard something."

Nate started working on the lock.

"One is headed toward the back door," Kent continued.

"How do we get the other one out of there?"

"I don't know. How's the lock coming?"

"Got it." Nate put his lock pick back in his pocket. He wondered how Selina was doing. She should've been running toward them by now.

"ARE YOU LOST?" THE LIGHT-HAIRED MAN asked Selina. He stepped out of the warehouse and squinted at her in the bright sun.

Selina's heart started beating rapidly. "No!" she spat at him with all the bravery she could muster. "I just thought you should know that I know what you're doing in there." She hoped the man couldn't tell that she was shaking.

"Is that so?" He couldn't have looked more disinterested if he'd tried.

"Yes! You...you have someone kidnapped in there. And you should let him go. Right now!"

"Yeah, I'll get right on that," he told her. He opened the door and stepped back inside.

"The police are on their way!" Selina yelled after him. Placing her broom handle in between the door and the jam, she prevented it from closing and followed him. "I won't let you get away with this!" She swung the broom as hard as she could.

The light-haired man turned around when the broom handle smacked him on the side of the head. When Selina swung the handle at his head a second time, he caught it. Giving it a strong shove, his force slammed Selina's body into the door. It opened and she stumbled backward, landing hard in a seated position with her hands in the gravel. She let out a shriek as the man came out after her, drawing his gun.

"WHO WAS THAT?" JONATHAN DEMANDED. A woman was screaming.

"What the hell?" the dark-haired man said, looking over his shoulder toward the back of the warehouse. "Are you done, kid?"

"I..."

Before Jonathan could answer, the man briefly inspected the Jewelry. "Looks like every piece has an engraving to me." He gathered up the Jewelry, put it in his pocket, and retied Jonathan's hands. "I have to go check this out. Don't get any ideas. When we get back, we have plans for you."

I'm going to die! Jonathan struggled against his ropes. It was hard to breathe. When he heard footsteps behind him, he let out an involuntary moan of fear and whipped his head around to meet his doom.

"Quiet, Boy Scout."

Jonathan had never been so happy to see Nate in his life. Kent began working on the knots in the rope.

"They're gonna come back and kill me!" Jonathan

told them.

"We won't let that happen," Kent assured him.

They loosened the ropes to free him, and the three of them ran out the door. Jonathan felt dizzy, but kept up with his rescuers. Squinting in the bright, noontime sunlight, Kent and Nate looked around the parking lot.

"Go," Nate said to Kent. "Get him outta here. I'll look for Selina."

"Selina's here?" Jonathan asked with surprise.

SCRAMBLING TO HER FEET, SELINA TURNED and ran so fast that she tripped, landing on her hands and knees. Her head snapped backward as the man grabbed her by the hair.

"You need to learn to mind your own business," he said in her ear with the gun on her temple.

As hard as she could, she kicked him in the shin. She felt him let go of her, and she ran. She hadn't gotten far when she heard his pounding footsteps behind her. He tackled her, and the wind was knocked out of her as she landed face first on the gravel.

"What the hell is going on here, Dave?" demanded a deep voice.

Selina and her attacker both turned their heads in time to see a dark-haired man suddenly fall to the ground. Nate stood behind him with his metal pipe, set his eyes on Dave, and headed toward them.

Dave quickly got to his feet and pulled his gun but was too late. The pipe hit him on the wrist, and the gun landed on the ground just as the pipe smacked his jaw.

Nate picked up the gun and helped Selina to her feet. "Let's go," he said.

The dark-haired man got up and fired a shot in the direction of the two younger people hurrying away.

"Start the car!" Selina shouted, seeing familiar faces up ahead. "They're shooting at us!"

Kent started the car but then tossed the keys to Selina as Jonathan dove into the backseat and Nate revved the motorcycle's engine. "You'll need to drive. Do you know where the hospital is?"

Selina took a deep breath in as she caught the keys and dashed for the driver's seat. Kent was holding his side as he climbed into the car gingerly with blood dripping through his fingers.

"Oh my god! What happened? I have no idea where a hospital is!" She took off to get them away from the warehouse and tossed her phone to Jonathan in the backseat. "Can you look it up?" she asked him.

"Turn here," Jonathan said after a moment. "It's about a mile down on the right."

Selina looked over at Kent's wincing face and pressed on the gas, speeding through a red light while angry drivers blasted their horns at her. She pulled up to the emergency room entrance, and Nate pulled up behind them.

"What's going on?" Nate called out as he got off his motorcycle.

"Kent was shot!" Jonathan called back.

Nate raced over and helped Jonathan pull Kent out of the car. They each put one of Kent's arms around their shoulders as he labored to walk to the door. Selina ran ahead to fetch a nurse and a wheelchair.

"You're going to be okay," Nate told Kent as he was wheeled away.

Kent gave a weak smile and nod in reply.

Selina sat in the nearest plastic waiting room chair and wrapped her arms around herself in an attempt to stop her trembling. Only then did she notice the knees of her pants were torn, and her skin was a salad of scrapes, blood, and gravel.

"What the hell happened to Kent?" Nate wanted to

know.

"We were running to the car and a bullet hit a piece of metal that was leaning up against the fence. I think it ricocheted off and hit Kent," Jonathan explained.

"That was the shot they fired at us!" Selina lamented to Nate. "Do you think he's going to be okay?"

"Yeah," Nate told her. "I'm sure he'll be fine." She frowned. Nate didn't look very sure.

"How did you know where I was?" Jonathan asked them both, sitting in the chair next to Selina.

"Selina saw you," Nate explained. "She and Kent called me."

"Thank you," Jonathan told her, touching her arm.

She turned to look at him, tears streaming down her face. "I'm glad you're okay. I was so scared!"

"Are *you* okay?" Jonathan asked her.

"I will be," she answered, trying to sound as brave as possible even though she felt anything but.

"We need to figure out who did this and why," Jonathan growled.

Selina felt his eyes on her and wished she could stop her shaking. It was embarrassing.

"Let me take you home," Jonathan said to her kindly. He turned to Nate. "Can you stay? I'll be right back." He stood quickly and stumbled on his first step. He reached out to grab something, but his hand found nothing but air. Suddenly, he was on the floor with his eyes squeezed shut.

"Dizzy?" Nate asked him, helping him to his feet.

"A little," Jonathan admitted. "But I'll be fine."

"You stay and get checked out yourself. I'll take Selina home." Nate held his hand out to help Selina up, and she handed him the car keys. "Call if you get any news about Kent."

✳✳✳

"WHAT ARE WE MISSING?" ANISE WONDERED out loud. The keystone beads sat on the desktop in front of her. She'd arranged them in the order Dromly had said they should be in his journals. She stared at the beads, willing them to tell her their secret.

"I can't think of what else Wilhelm Schwartz might have wanted to say," Lorelei sighed. She got up and headed toward Anise's door. "I'm going to go back to my room to search through the journals I haven't read yet. Maybe there's something more about these beads and the order they should be in. Maybe Dromly has different interpretations he's considering. Do you want to join me?"

"I'll be over in a little while," Anise responded, still staring at the beads as Lorelei left the room. Playing with their order proved futile and frustrating. There was no other order that made any sense at all. Having an idea, she grabbed her phone and dialed.

"Anise! Hi!" came the voice through the phone.

"Les, how are you?" she asked her brother.

"I'm okay for now," he replied. "I'm on the bed though...feeling dizzy. I might have another unconscious spell soon. So if I suddenly don't answer you, that's why."

"Sorry to bother you."

"No! I'm happy to hear from you. What are you up to?"

"I remembered that you like puzzles, so I was hoping you could help me with something. We saw these artifacts today that were found by my friend Kent's father—he's an archaeologist. They contain a message by the person who made them, but we have to solve the puzzle to read it." She described the beads, the words that were carved onto them, and that she needed to find a new solution. She longed to tell him the entire story, but since he didn't even know about the Armor Jewelry yet, that would have to wait for another time. "The order that they're in now...I don't think it's right. What do you think?"

"I think you should trust your instincts," Les told her. "If this puzzle was created to be a message, put yourself in the mind of the person that created it. What would he want to say? How would he feel about the situation? How would he feel about himself in the situation?"

"Okay, I'll give it a try." She thought about how she'd managed to escape from Grace and wanted to thank him for the lesson he'd given her in how to get out of constraints the last time she'd visited him, but now was not the time. She looked at the beads and ideas formed in her mind from Les's prompts. "How has everything else been? How's Olivia?"

No answer.

"Les?"

Still nothing.

"I don't know if you can hear me during your unconscious spells, but if you can, thank you, and I'll talk to you soon."

She hung up the phone, more determined than ever to solve this puzzle. The faster she could find the Plate of Destiny, the faster she could get to Les.

Turning the beads this way and that, Anise thought about Wilhelm Schwartz. "Dromly and everyone else believe you stole the Plate of Destiny to hide it away for yourself," she said out loud. "That you were greedy. And opportunistic. Selfish. That you lost your mind." The beads rotated and changed positions under the direction of her fingers. "But you were a scientist. You knew about the Armor Jewelry. You figured out the secrets on the Plate about life and death. You were hardworking. You were smart. You took incredible care to travel to a different country and enter a dangerous cave by yourself to hide the Plate. You returned to Europe and tried to share the Plate's secrets of life with others. But if you were selfish, why would you have tried to share the secrets of life?" Her hands spun and switched the beads. "Were you actually selfish? Or did you see yourself as altruistic? Were you trying to *protect* the Plate instead of hoarding it for yourself? Did you want to hide the Plate from everyone, or did you leave a map because you actually wanted the *right* person to find it? I think you knew that someone who wants the Plate for the right reasons would also see that you took it for the right reasons."

Finally she had the beads in the position she wanted. "You're not protecting the knowledge *from* others like Fred Dromly said. The protection is *coming from* you. Like a gift you're giving." She looked at the new message the beads spelled out and she smiled to herself.

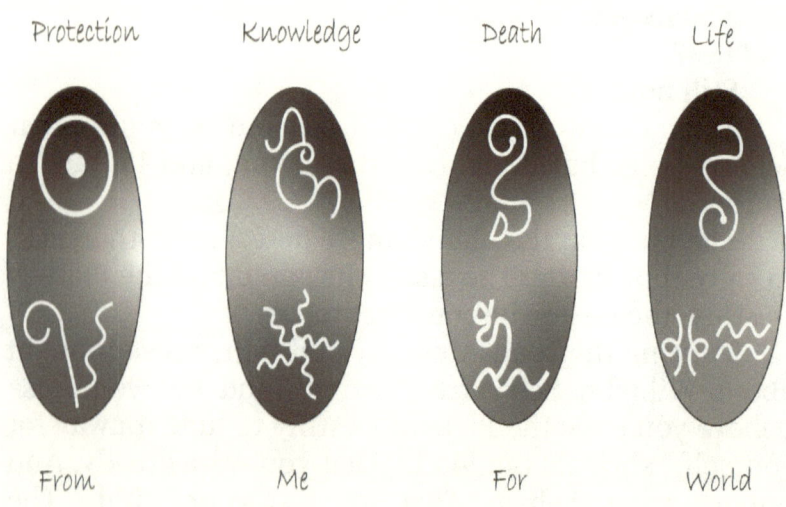

"Protection of the knowledge of death and life. From me, for the world."

"THANK YOU SO MUCH," SELINA GUSHED as Nate helped her to the sofa in her hotel room. "You saved my life and Jonathan's today. Please thank Kent for me too once he's out of the hospital."

"How are you doing?" he asked her.

"I'll be fine. I just need to wash up." She winced and let out a cry of pain when she pulled a piece of gravel out of her knee.

"Sit. I'll help you," Nate offered. He got a few fresh towels from the bathroom and filled a bowl from the kitchenette with water. Kneeling on the floor in front of her, he gently cleaned her knees and then her hands.

"You were really incredible back there," Selina said, trying to concentrate on anything but the pain. "Where did you learn to fight like that? And to pick locks?"

Nate just shrugged and dabbed a wet towel on the scrape on her chin.

"Don't be so modest! I was petrified, and you made our escape look easy. Seriously, where did you learn all that? It was really impressive and—" She stopped talking when he lifted his gaze and stared at her. His face was so close to her own, and she felt an intensity coming from his dark blue eyes as they looked into hers. Watching his lips give her an alluring lopsided smirk, she couldn't help but smile back.

"I picked it up here and there," was all he said. He got up and dumped the bloody water into the kitchenette sink.

"You expect me to believe that?" she asked him as she followed him to the front door, her curiosity piqued. "Who *are* you?"

"I'll have Boy Scout call you later," he told her and walked out the door.

The door closed behind him, and she stood there with her mouth hanging open as if that would help her think. She closed it and sat on the couch again. Her shaking had almost stopped, and she curled herself into a ball with her arms wrapped around her legs. She let her mind try to organize what had just happened.

If Nate's intention with that mesmerizing look he

gave her was to shut her up, it had certainly been effective. She considered the possibility that he'd been flirting, in which case she'd be flattered, but she greatly preferred someone more outgoing and talkative. Someone she could geek out with about nerdy things. Jonathan. If Jonathan thought something, it came out of his mouth, and that made her comfortable. Nate was the opposite. He had secrets. Secrets beyond the magical Armor Jewelry his entire group didn't want her to know about. Someone must know something about their secrets, or else Jonathan wouldn't have been kidnapped. Was he still in danger? There was more to this story than met the eye. The uncomfortable amount of questions she still had made her either want to know more or to run away from all of it and find somewhere peaceful to hunt for rocks. She wasn't sure yet.

"WHAT HAPPENED?" ANISE DEMANDED AS SHE handed Jonathan a cold washcloth for his head. He had a lump over his eyebrow, and she felt bad for not having known he'd been in trouble.

"I was walking over to check on Selina when everything went black," Jonathan explained to Anise and Lorelei. "When I came to, I was tied up in a warehouse and Kent, Nate, and Selina came for me. Kent was shot."

"Shot?!" Lorelei exclaimed. "Where's Kent now? The hospital?"

Nate and Jonathan looked at each other. "That's what we wanted to talk to you about," Nate choked out in a whisper. "Kent didn't make it."

"What?" Anise cried. "He's dead?" She put her hands on her stomach and sat on her bed. *Kent was here for me. This is my fault.* She accepted a soda that Jonathan grabbed from the mini fridge and handed to her.

Lorelei stood with a hand over her mouth and tears flooding her eyes. Nate put his arms around her, and she let out a few sobs into his chest. When she composed herself, she looked up and wiped away the couple of silent tears on her son's cheeks. "Did you call the police?" she asked.

"Yes," Jonathan said. "They spoke to us at the hospital."

"Why didn't you tell us where you were going?" Anise demanded of Nate, getting angry at him again. "We could've helped you."

"Kent asked me not to bring you, and I agreed with him. I didn't want either of you to be in any unnecessary danger," Nate told her.

Anise rolled her eyes. *Hopeless. Fucking hopeless!* "I have the Jewelry. They couldn't have hurt me! And I could've helped to protect Kent!"

Lorelei hugged her son again and then Jonathan. "I'm glad both of you are safe." She sat on Anise's couch with her eyes continuing to overflow with grief. Nate sat next to her and held her hand.

"Nate did the right thing, Anise," Jonathan said. "We don't know who they were, but they knew about the Jewelry. They had a set of their own."

"What?" Anise asked, confusion taking over her mind. "They did?"

"They were replicas," Jonathan explained. "They wanted me to engrave the Jewelry with the incantation to give them the powers of the original Jewelry."

"Why you?" Anise wondered out loud.

"Somehow they knew that you named me the Jewelry engineer."

"You mean yesterday morning when we were in Kent's room? We were joking around."

"How would they have known that?" Lorelei asked, dabbing her eyes with a tissue.

"That's a good question," Jonathan said, looking

directly at Nate. "I was wondering that myself."

"And you think it was me?" Nate said, glaring at Jonathan.

"Well it wouldn't have been anyone else in this room," Jonathan sneered. "And no one else knew."

"That's enough!" Lorelei scolded. "Nate wouldn't do anything to compromise Anise's mission here, and you know that as well as I do. I'll hear no more accusations against him!"

"With all due respect, Lorelei," Jonathan said softly, "you don't know him like I do. He's not the innocent child he may have once been."

Nate stood up. "Don't talk to her like that," he warned.

Anise stood up and got between the two men. "Stop it," she ordered, frustrated with the both of them. "Jonathan, I know Nate better than you do. I don't believe for a second that it was him. What we should be worried about is that some stranger now has a working set of Armor Jewelry."

"Maybe," Jonathan said. "I was finished with almost all of the engraving except for one of the earrings. I had only part of one symbol left to carve when Kent and Nate came for me. Will it work if the engraving isn't finished?"

"It doesn't matter," Lorelei explained. "I read in one of the journals that the Jewelry engineer was told the meaning of the incantation so he could carve it with intention. Since we don't know what the incantation says, much less what it means, Jonathan couldn't have carved it with intention. Therefore, the Jewelry won't work."

"That's a relief!" sighed Jonathan.

"I know what the incantation says," Nate spoke up.

Anise swung her head around to look at him, rage bubbling up deep inside her once more. "You do?! So it's another thing you kept from me?"

"Yeah," he agreed. "It was the information I got from Grace when I visited her. You never bothered to ask me what I learned from her, so get over it."

She glared at him, so angry she couldn't think of anything to say.

He took out a pocket knife, sat at the desk, and reached out his hand to her. "Give me that ring," he said, gesturing to the garnet on her finger.

"Why?" she demanded.

"I'll engrave it with intention while I explain what the incantation says. Then we'll see if it has any powers."

Anise handed him the garnet ring and stood over him with her arms crossed and a look that dared him to impress her.

"I need you to name me one of your Jewelry engineers," Nate said.

"Fine," Anise said with annoyance. "You're one of my Jewelry engineers."

As Nate engraved the inside of the tiny band, he began explaining. "The incantation says: Power by one, more by many. Protectors united, destroyers divided."

Jonathan took a moment to think about it. "That mostly makes sense. Each piece of Armor Jewelry is powerful by itself, but they're more powerful when used together. The Mallandian warriors used the united sets of Jewelry as protection...but what does 'destroyers divided' mean?"

"Dr. Smithton talked about this that day in his office three years ago!" Anise exclaimed. "When we were first learning about the Jewelry."

"Oh, that's right!" Jonathan agreed, remembering. "When the pieces of Jewelry are used against each other for some undetermined length of time, they cause destruction."

"We just don't know what kind of destruction or how much," Anise said, finishing his thought.

Nate finished the engraving and handed the ring back to Anise. "Test it out."

She slipped it back on her finger. "What are garnets supposed to do?" she asked no one in particular. Her eyes welled up when she thought about Erin who knew a lot about the magical properties of gemstones. If only she could call her. Pushing her grief out of the way, she tried to pick up Lorelei's desk with no luck. "No super strength." She looked down when she felt a paper airplane hit her collarbone.

"No protection," Jonathan said.

Anise grabbed Lorelei's hand. "I'm not getting any visions. I don't feel any different either. Maybe garnets don't do anything."

"Maybe they make you more vulnerable somehow. Maybe they counteract the effects of the Armor Jewelry, and maybe *he* knows that." Jonathan glared at Nate. "This could be a trick. Take that ring off, Anise!"

"Jonathan, just stop!" Anise commanded him.

He narrowed his eyebrows. "Somebody in this room let it slip that you named me Jewelry engineer. I think we can all agree on that. And my life was in danger today because of it!" He gave Nate a glare.

"You have every right to be angry about what happened to you," Anise told him. "But Nate didn't tell anyone."

"How do you know?" Jonathan demanded with a yell. "You broke up with him because he lies! How can you defend him now? How do you know he's not working against us?"

"Because I know!" she yelled back.

The room was silent as the thick tension hung above their heads.

"I have news," Anise said, changing the subject. "I believe that Fred Dromly made a mistake when he thought he'd figured out the right order for the keystone beads. I think I figured out the right combination. I want to go back to the cave tonight and try it out."

"No," said the three others in unison.

"Excuse me?" As her ire grew, Anise began to wonder if she'd ever feel anything besides anger again. Why would each one of them be so against her suggestion? Did they all know something she didn't? Were they keeping something from her?

"We're all on edge from the news of Kent's death," Lorelei announced. "I think we all need to retreat to our own space for a while. Jonathan, Anise, go to your rooms. And you," she said to Nate, "come with me."

Chapter 16

"W hat happened to you?" Horrified, Charlie Masser hurried over to his teary-eyed granddaughter and stared at her. The holes in her linen
pants framed her scraped knees. She dabbed ointment
on her hands and chin.

Her red, puffy eyes looked up at him from where
she slumped on the hotel room couch. "I had a bad day,
Grandpa."

"I can see that. What happened?"

She curled into a ball, bringing her knees to her
chest and gingerly resting her chin on them. Her blonde
hair fell around her shoulders. "I was on my way to the
drugstore like you asked, and I saw Jonathan being kidnapped. Long story short, Kent, Nate, and I rescued him,
but I was attacked by the kidnappers. They tried to kill
us."

"What?!" Charlie felt his face crinkle up in anger. He
sat next to her and gave her a tender hug. "Are you okay?
Should I take you to the hospital?"

"No, I'll be fine." She rested her head on his shoulder
as a few of her tears dropped onto his shirt.

He let a few minutes go by before he got up. "I'm
sorry, I have a phone call to make. We'll talk about this
more, just give me two minutes."

"Take your time."

Charlie left the hotel and started his car. "I put my two best men on this job, and you completely screwed it up!" he yelled into the phone.

"What are you talking about, Charlie?" Dave asked him. "It was a success! You needed those people to like and trust your granddaughter. She bravely came to that kid's rescue, just like you thought she would. There's no way she's not in good with them now. Plus we got that Jewelry engraved at the same time like you wanted. It looks good, right? Two birds and all that."

"My little girl is bloody and traumatized!" He pulled out of the hotel's parking lot and headed down the street. "What did you do to her? And where the hell was Shawn? Was he there with you?"

"Yeah, I was there. I'm sorry, Charlie," Shawn said, coming on the line. "Dave wasn't supposed to do that."

"Hey, wait a minute!" Dave fired back. "You told me to make it realistic, Charlie. I was just following orders!"

"If you ever harm a hair on that girl's angel head again, I swear to god you'll spend the rest of your tortured days begging me to kill you to put you out of your misery!"

"All right, all right," Dave said. "It won't happen again."

"And that's not the only thing you two did wrong. One of the earrings doesn't have the complete inscription," Charlie informed them.

"So what?" Shawn asked.

"So what? You wouldn't believe me if I told you."

"So you want us to grab the kid again?"

"No! No. Just follow orders next time."

When he finally returned to the room, Charlie found Selina exactly where he'd left her. "Sorry I took so long. I made a run to the market and picked up some ice cream. I know that always makes you feel better."

"Butter pecan?"

"Of course." He handed her the ice cream and a spoon.

She accepted his offering and took a bite. "I've been doing a lot of thinking today. Why are we here, Grandpa?"

"What do you mean?" He grabbed the pint of chocolate he'd bought for himself and a spoon and sat down next to her.

"I mean you hate traveling. You never had any interest in going anywhere before and then suddenly you ask me to come with you to Florida. You tell me to go do research and find out everything I can about some ancient Bronze Age artifact called the Plate of Destiny which is supposedly just a myth anyway. You woke me up in the early morning to get me on a bus to go to a tour in a cave and encourage me to 'talk to the other tourists and make friends.' When I do, I find that strangely enough, the people I talk to know quite a lot about Bronze Age artifacts." Her frustration reflected in the increasing volume of her voice. "When I don't want to talk to them anymore, you push me to go see them again. Meanwhile, you sleep during the day, and I hear you getting up and leaving in the middle of the night. Every night! Where do you go? What are you doing? And who did you have to call just now? What the hell is going on?"

He frowned. "I know how much *you* enjoy travel, and I took you to that symposium you'd been wanting to attend for years now. I wanted my girl to have a great 30th birthday. I thought you'd enjoy the trip, and I'd enjoy spending time with my granddaughter."

"I am enjoying my research, and I loved the symposium, but we're not spending any time together. What aren't you telling me?"

Charlie looked down at his ice cream wondering what to tell her. If he were lucky, the answer would be swimming in the melting chocolate and cream.

"I'm not going to let this go," she informed him firmly.

Charlie sighed. His granddaughter was too smart. She'd see right through anything he'd be able to make up on the spot. "Alright," he agreed solemnly. "The story starts with some family history. You know that your mother Barbara, my precious daughter, died during childbirth. It had been her greatest wish her entire life that she would have a daughter." He smiled through the sadness. "She would've loved you as much as I do."

Selina nodded. "I know, Grandpa. You've told me this a million times."

"You also know your father was in prison for some terrible things he had done. Dean died of natural causes one night in his cell."

"What does this have to do with the Plate of Destiny?" Selina asked.

"I'm getting there," Charlie promised. "After your mother passed, your father's parents wanted to raise you. But I was awarded custody. Not only did I have practice raising a little girl all on my own, but I also had the means to provide for you where they did not. *They* had practice raising a menace to society which the judge didn't forget."

"I know. Grandma Dot died when Mom was just a little girl and you raised her on your own," Selina said.

"Yes. But what I haven't told you is how your Grandma Dot left this earth." His last few words were said with a catch in his throat. He took out a handkerchief and squeezed it in his hands. "She was seeing another man. They were out, and he had too much to drink. As he was driving her home, he pulled out in front of another vehicle and they were hit. He survived, she did not."

"Oh, my god. I'm so sorry, Grandpa," Selina sympathized. She put her hand on his arm. "I've never heard this before. Who was the other man? Did you confront him?"

"He was the husband of Dot's sister Helen."

"Really? Great Aunt Helen who died in the mental hospital? She had a husband?"

"Yes. I've never mentioned him before because I hate talking about him, but the man's name is Frederick Dromly."

Her eyes opened wide. "Wait, what?! I'm related to Dr. Frederick Dromly?" Her mouth hung open for a few seconds in shock. "He's my..." Selina narrowed her brow in thought. "By marriage my first cousin twice removed?"

"I don't know how all that works," Charlie admitted with a shrug. "But yes, something like that."

"So we're actually here to see the Dromly's," Selina concluded, a look of disgust wrinkling her nose. "You're using me to get to Fred Dromly through his son Kent! My cousin! Oh my god!"

Charlie looked down at the ground and pressed his eyes with his handkerchief. Dot's memory still hurt so much.

"But why after all these years? Are you bent on revenge you never got? It's been so long I would think you'd want nothing to do with them anymore." She stood up and walked to the window, her arms tightly crossed. "And again, what on earth does this have to do with the Plate of Destiny?"

Charlie grunted with frustration. "Fred Dromly took away my Dot! Her death didn't even phase him. He went about his business. Going to work, traveling, and trying to find this Plate of Destiny, whatever the hell it is. He bragged to anyone who'd listen that he'd be world famous when he found it, even more than he already was. He devoted his entire life to finding it. It was his reason for living. Dot was mine. He took away my reason for living, and all I want to do is return the favor."

"You want to take away the Plate? He doesn't even have it. No one's found it yet."

"When he finds it, I want to take it, and I want to smash it."

Selina cocked her her head at him. "Grandpa...I get that you're upset, but it's been decades. Maybe we can honor Grandma Dot another way. We could put flowers on her grave, or plant a tree, or dedicate a bench or a piece of art in her honor..."

"Fred Dromly is the most arrogant, evil man I've ever known!" Charlie cried. "He doesn't care about anyone else but himself. He didn't care for his son. Refused to raise him. Kent went to live with Al and Madge—Dot and Helen's parents—after Helen was admitted. They told me he went overseas and never visited, never called. A terrible father. He didn't care for his wife Helen either. He just stuck her in that miserable psychiatric home and let her rot in there. He didn't care that he broke up my marriage, and he didn't care that his tomcatting led to Dot's death. Justice must be done!" He felt her eyes on him as tears streamed down his face. "Say you'll help me," he begged her. "Please."

He watched Selina's own tears begin flowing. Sitting beside him again, she embraced him until he stopped crying. "Of course I'll help you find the Plate of Destiny," she told him.

"Thank you," he said, wiping his eyes.

"As long as you stop using me against my knowledge," she added.

"I'm very sorry for that," Charlie told her. "I admit I'm desperate. We've come so far I couldn't bear to fail now. At first, all I wanted was to beat Freddie to his stupid Plate so I could watch his dream die. But after you told me what you discovered from Jonathan and that book at the library, everything changed. You told me how the amulet around Anise's neck was glowing, and how you thought the legends were real. I couldn't stop thinking about how the Plate of Destiny is fabled to resurrect the dead. For the first time in my life, I felt hope that I might actually get to see my Dot again."

"I'm still surprised that you chose to believe me so quickly," Selina said. "Those legends are pretty out there."

"Of course I believe you! You're my granddaughter. I don't need a better reason than that!" Hopefully, she'd buy that. He thought about the night in Fred's office when Fred simply wouldn't die no matter what. Charlie had tried to hang him and shoot him, but nothing worked. Fred and that ugly, glowing necklace. The same ugly, glowing necklace he wore when the useless snipers Charlie had hired couldn't seem to do anything but miss their target at the mouth of the caves for the last several months. But now Selina was learning more than he ever could on his own. With her on his side, Charlie felt confident he could get what he wanted. *I'll be coming for you, Freddie.*

"Thanks for saying that, Grandpa." She gave him another hug. "That means a lot. I don't think I could've blindly believed those stories without proof, no matter who told me."

Charlie frowned. He hadn't believed it either when he had first read about the Jewelry and Plate of Destiny in Freddie's journal. He'd needed the proof. And since Thomas Brevain hadn't willingly given it up, he'd had no other choice than to hire an assassin to dress up as Freddie and kill Brevain to steal the research he'd kept a secret. If only Brevain hadn't burnt most of it. And if only Freddie had been blamed for the murder like he'd hoped. But now he had his brilliant granddaughter to fill in the blanks from the missing research.

"You're sure you'll help with whatever I need?" Charlie asked Selina.

"I said I would, and I meant it."

"Good."

"I think we should join forces with Jonathan and the others," Selina suggested. "They're looking for the Plate, too. I bet they'd welcome our help, and we'd all have a better chance at finding it before Fred Dromly if we work together."

"So Kent can then hand over the Plate to his father? Absolutely not!"

"Kent isn't a fan of Fred to put it mildly," Selina told him. "We don't have to worry about that."

"Has Jonathan told you why they want the Plate?"

Charlie asked.

"No." She pursed her lips in thought. "I really don't know why they're looking for it. But does it matter?"

"If they haven't told you why, then we can't trust them. Didn't you say they're hiding things from you?"

"Yeah, but I get it now. They're looking for a magical artifact. We just met. Why would they have told me about that?"

"But we still don't know what they plan to do with it, and I don't trust them!" Charlie said with an air of finality. "Now, you told me that to find the Plate of Destiny, we'd need all of the Armor Jewelry."

"That's right. There's a sheen on the Plate that you can only see when you're wearing the full set of Armor Jewelry. Without wearing the Jewelry, it would only look like a round piece of bronze. You can't identify the Plate without the Jewelry."

"And your friend Anise has a full set, doesn't she?"

"Yes, all the more reason to join forces with them."

"No. I have a better plan."

"What are you getting at?" Selina's phone beeped, and she checked her text messages. "It's Anise."

Charlie chuckled. "Well, now. Speak of the devil."

"She wants me to meet her outside of her hotel in fifteen minutes. She doesn't say why."

"And you'll do it," Charlie commanded. "You'll use that time with her to find out where she keeps the Armor Jewelry and then you'll take it."

"What?!" Selina's face contorted with a look of shock. "No. Why? No!"

Charlie sighed. He'd figured it'd be a struggle. "Because it's the only way, Selina. Unless you have a better idea?"

"Yes!" she exclaimed. "For starters, I won't steal from my friend. Instead, we join forces with them like I said before."

"And like I said before, I don't trust them!" he shot back as he started to feel his frustration with her getting stronger. "You promised to help."

Selina shook her head. "Not like this."

Charlie looked at the floor and with sadness played the card he'd hoped he wouldn't have to use. "You will help me and do it my way or else Opal won't be there when you get back home."

His granddaughter looked at him in a way that made him feel two inches tall, but he stood behind his threat.

"What's that supposed to mean?" she asked.

"You're a smart girl. You know what it means."

To his surprise, she took his hand. "Are you okay? Are you feeling numb in your limbs? Can you see straight? Headache?"

He ripped his hand from her grasp. "For Pete's sake, I'm not having a stroke!"

"Well something's going on!" Selina argued. "Do you hear yourself? You just threatened the life of my pet that I've loved for years! If she were killed purposely to hurt me by the one person who's supposed to love me more than anyone...you must know how devastating that would be for me. This isn't you, Grandpa." She wiped her teary eyes with her index fingers. "This can't be real."

"It's real," he insisted.

"It can't be! Why are you so obsessed with this Plate of Destiny when we know practically nothing about it? Why are you willing to destroy your relationship with me over it? Grandma has been gone for decades. You don't ever have to stop feeling sad about that, but it's taking over your entire personality in an unhealthy way. Let me make an appointment for you. If you talked with a professional about it, maybe—"

"Stop!" he commanded, interrupting her. He didn't know how to answer her perfectly valid questions because he couldn't understand what was happening to him either. All he knew was that there was a possibility he could bring back Dot, and he couldn't resist the temptation to try everything he could to accomplish it. "I've made my choice, Selina. Now you have to make yours."

ANISE STAYED QUIET WHEN SHE HEARD a knock on her door. Maybe whoever it was would go away.

"Anise?" Lorelei called, opening the door.

"Over here," Anise called out from the far end of the room. She stopped texting and hid her phone under the covers. She sat in bed, letting the tears stream down her face.

Lorelei walked over to her and brought the box of tissues that were sitting on the dresser. "Nate lent me your room key; I hope that's all right. I just wanted to check on you."

"It's fine. You're always welcome," Anise told her, accepting the box of tissues and using one to dab her eyes. "I just can't believe Kent's gone."

"Me either," Lorelei said, sitting on the edge of the bed. "The boys are going to get some take-out for lunch. They wanted to know if you'd like to go. Maybe getting out of this stuffy room would do you some good."

Anise looked out the window at the early afternoon sun. "No. I just...need to be here right now."

"I understand."

"Are you going?"

"No. But I am going out to run an errand. Can I bring you anything?"

Anise squeezed Lorelei's hand with gratitude for her kindness. "No, but thank you. I just want to get some sleep."

"Okay. I'll let you know when the boys are back with the food."

As soon as Lorelei was gone, Anise threw off the covers. She grabbed her phone and three backpacks full of supplies and hurried out the door.

Chapter 17

Selina walked down the hallway of her hotel on her way to meet Anise and thought about her conversation with her grandpa. She'd looked at his face, tears streaming down his wrinkled skin. She'd never seen him cry before. His formerly tall and strong frame had then seemed so fragile, hunched over and trembling like a baby bird who'd fallen from the nest. The only parent she had ever known, the only person who had given her comfort and protected her, the only one who had loved her unconditionally now needed comfort, protection, and unconditional love from her. But what he'd asked of her was disgusting and atrocious. To keep him from going through with his heinous threat to kill her beloved dog, she had to play along until she could figure out how to stop his sudden madness—and she had an idea.

Grabbing her phone, she called the only person who might be able to help. "Hi, it's me. Can you please do me a favor?...I left Opal with my grandpa's friend in Springfield. Can you go get her?"

"Selina!" Anise called, waving at her while she walked across the parking lot.

Selina returned her wave, her phone still pressed against her ear. "Hi Anise," she greeted her. "I know it's a three hour drive," she said into the phone, "but I don't trust this person. I shouldn't have left her with him! I'm worried! Please go get her...I don't know anyone in Springfield anymore. I didn't keep in contact with anyone...You can't go today? When then?...Fine. But let me know when you have her. Please!"

"What was that about?" Anise asked as Selina put her phone back in her bag.

"I stupidly left my dog with my grandpa's friend at his insistence so I could save money. But now I don't think he's trustworthy to watch her, and I called my friend who's a cop to go pick her up, and..." Her eyebrows narrowed when she took a closer look at Anise's tear-stained face. "What's wrong?"

Anise's eyes welled up. "Kent died this afternoon."

"What?!" Selina felt light-headed while the shock sank in. "He didn't make it?"

Anise shook her head, and her tears started streaming.

"Oh, Anise. I'm so sorry." Selina grabbed Anise's hands. "Do you need help with arrangements? Is that why you asked me to meet you?"

"No," Anise told her, gently squeezing Selina's hands and then motioning behind her to the three backpacks filled with supplies. "We're waiting on Raina. The three of us are going to the hidden cave to retrieve the map that leads to the Plate of Destiny."

Selina paused for a moment to take in all the information being thrown at her. "Okay, wait a minute. Why now? Don't you have to take care of things regarding Kent's death?"

"Jonathan, Nate, and Lorelei are handling all that," Anise replied. "They think I'm in bed feeling sick and sad. And I am feeling sick and sad. But that's why I need to do this now. Kent died because he was here helping me. I need to find this Plate as soon as possible so we can all go home before someone else gets hurt."

"The kidnappers shot him...it had nothing at all to do

with you, Anise," Selina told her gently.

"Maybe." Anise wiped her eyes.

"Why don't you and your friends go home? The Plate can't be worth all this," Selina said, hoping Anise might leave and then she wouldn't have to go through with her grandfather's plan. Maybe then she'd have time to talk some sense into him.

Anise narrowed her eyes. "Can I trust you?"

Selina's guilt began eating her gut from the inside. "Of course."

"Then I'll tell you this. I can't explain why, but if I don't get that Plate, more people will get hurt. I have to find it. I can't risk anyone else dying because of me."

"I don't understand. How could Kent have died because of you?"

Anise gave Selina a serious look. "There are other people besides us and Fred Dromly who want the Plate. People who are willing to kill for it. I'm surprised they haven't killed each other already. Maybe there's even more people who know about it that I'm not aware of. They could be watching me as we speak."

Selina pursed her lips together, trying to think of a gentle way to respond. "Anise, please don't take this the wrong way, but that sounds a little paranoid. Are you sure that's not just your grief talking?"

"Like I said, I can't take that chance. I understand if you don't want to help me today. We have to repel down a thirty foot hole in the cave and trust a pulley system that I've never constructed before to help pull ourselves back up. There's less oxygen down there and maybe some venomous spiders. I just ask that you don't tell anyone what I'm doing. No one else knows."

"Don't worry about that," Selina said. "I'm totally in. But why wouldn't you tell your friends where you're going? This sounds dangerous and like they'd want to come with you."

"I tried. They were completely against it." Anise

frowned angrily.

"Okay. Well, if there are spiders you won't want to wear your hair open like that."

"I've got helmets for us."

"Still. May I?" Selina took a spare hair tie and some bobby pins out of her bag.

Anise nodded. "Thank you."

As Selina was finishing braiding and pinning up Anise's hair, Raina pulled up in her car. She rolled down the passenger-side window. "Let's go, ladies! We've got a map to find!"

A LOUD KNOCK ON HIS DOOR woke Charlie from his nap. "I'm coming!" he shouted at the ceaseless banging. He swung open the door and saw a woman with dark, silver-streaked hair. "Yes, ma'am?"

"I'm sorry to disturb you; I'm looking for someone named Selina Hanlon."

Charlie narrowed his eyes. "She's my granddaughter. What is this about?"

"My name is Lorelei Brevain. My son and his friends have befriended her."

"I see. And what can I do for you, Ms. Brevain?" Charlie eyed her suspiciously.

"I was hoping to speak with Selina and make sure she's okay. I hear she helped my son's friend Jonathan escape from a dangerous situation."

"Thank you, she's fine," Charlie said. "Now if you don't mind..." He motioned for her to leave.

"I'm glad to hear that," Lorelei told him. "But there were some other things I'd like to ask her as well. May I speak with her please?"

Charlie grunted. "She's not here. Haven't heard from her all day. Don't know when she's coming back." He began to shut the door.

Charlie snorted when the woman stuck her foot in the door jam and pushed the door back open enough to see him. "Except that's not true, is it? She came back here after she helped Jonathan."

"I must've been out, ma'am," he said. "I'll tell Selina you stopped by."

"If you haven't heard from her, how did you know about what she did today? And that she's fine?"

"Just what is it that you want here?" Charlie demanded.

"Well since you won't let me see Selina, I'd like to ask *you* a question." She positioned herself between the door jam and the partially opened door so he couldn't shut it. "And I'm not leaving here until you give me an answer."

Charlie just glared at her, not letting her push open the door fully.

"I assume Selina told you about the research she and Jonathan have been doing?"

Charlie continued to glare and stayed silent.

"I'll take that as a yes. So when Selina told you..." Her words trailed off when her eyes focused on the carnelian Armor ring on his finger. "I'm so sorry; I'm being rude. Please forgive me." She hurried off.

"Shit," Charlie said as he closed the door. He looked at the ring and grew angry at himself for falling asleep with it on. He then grew angrier that this replica he'd tried to create didn't work, otherwise he could've used it on this woman just now. He stepped into the hallway and knocked on the door directly across from his room. A dark-haired man answered it. "Shawn, the woman that just left my room. She knows. Follow her. Fix this." Charlie pointed in the direction Lorelei had gone and watched Shawn and Dave run down the hall after her. Exhausted, he went back to his bed and fell asleep again.

**

SOMETHING TOLD LORELEI SHE SHOULD RUN. She'd had a strange feeling about Selina ever since the news about Jonathan being the Jewelry engineer had leaked and had only wanted to figure out if Selina knew something. Now, she'd gotten more than she'd bargained for. That old man had a carnelian Armor ring! It was too coincidental. That could only mean one thing. Darting down the hall, she grabbed her phone from her purse and called Nate. He needed to know that Selina's grandfather was dangerous—that he'd been the one who'd had Jonathan kidnapped. The phone rang and rang. No answer. Her footsteps thundered down the stairs. She called again. Still no answer. Through the lobby and outside. Her heart pounding, she started a text. Across the parking lot. Through the lobby of her own hotel and up the stairs. She heard heavy shoes on the stairs below her, fast and pounding, getting closer. She reached her door and typed as quickly as she could while unlocking the door at the same time. Her heart was louder than the nearing footsteps as she turned the door handle. Her instinct was to look behind her at her pursuers, but she forced herself to keep her eyes on the screen of her phone to continue her text before it was too late.

Lorelei: Js kidnapper selinas g

She let out a scream as someone pushed her from behind into her own room. Her phone flew from her hands and slid under the dresser as she fell to the floor face-first. The two men that had followed her into the room flipped her over as she screamed again.

**

"ARE YOU SURE THIS'LL WORK?" RAINA asked doubtfully, looking at the system of ropes and metal contraptions Anise had rigged. "This isn't how I've done it in the past." She peered down the hole into the blackness.

"This is what we used when Nate went down there the last time I was here," Anise replied. "It kept him from sliding back down once he started climbing."

Raina had been shocked when Anise called to tell her she'd illegally been to the hidden cave they'd talked about in the coffee shop and wanted to go back. Upset that her warnings had been ignored, Raina had started another speech about the dangers of the situation, but when Anise begged for her help, Raina's curiosity about what they might find wouldn't allow her to refuse. Something was still nagging her though. "Yeah, but we still have to climb up on our own, and thirty vertical feet is a long way up. Have you ever tried to do that? I have, and it's not easy."

"I'll climb up first and help you," Anise told her. "If I pull here, it helps by lifting the rope. Even if you can't climb at all, I'd still be able to lift you out of there."

Raina looked at Anise's small arms and her doubt grew.

"That's good enough for me," Selina said. "Who's going down first?"

"I'll go last," Anise said, "so I can be here to pull you back up if you need help."

"Great! Let's do this," Selina exclaimed. Anise helped her into the harness and Selina began lowering herself down the tunnel.

"I'm very impressed with your bravery, Selina," Raina called after her. Something was off with Selina, too. She had none of the fear she had when they last went spelunking, and this cave was far more hazardous.

"You do *not* have to go down there," Anise told Raina. "I really appreciate you giving us a ride and helping me set up the ropes. Not to mention all the information you gave me. We would never have found this place if it weren't for you. So you've already helped more than you know."

Raina frowned and expected this stupid plan would get them into more trouble than they could handle. But if there really was a secret, hidden map down there... "I don't think this is safe, or a good idea, but I'm here, and there's no way I'm missing this!" She grabbed her phone from her pocket. "But I'm texting my sister with our exact location and telling her to come looking for us if she doesn't hear from me in a couple hours."

They heard a shout of surprise from Selina as she was descending the tunnel. A bat flew out of the tunnel and straight for Anise. Stepping backward to get out of the bat's flight path, Anise tripped over a loose rock and landed flat on her back.

"Are you okay?" Raina asked her, helping her up.

Anise brushed herself off. "I'm fine. But did you hear something?"

"Like what?"

"I don't know. Never mind. It was probably just the bat."

"I'm down!" Selina's voice carried her message up the tunnel.

"Your turn!" Anise told Raina.

Raina took a deep breath and let it out. She hoped she wouldn't regret this. "Okay. I'm ready."

"I CAN'T BELIEVE THIS IS HOW I'm going to die."

Grace wanted to smack him to stop his moaning. "Oh, grow a pair, Morty! They're not going to kill us. I'm the seer. They need me to see the symbols on the Plate of Destiny."

"They do need you, Grace. But they don't need *me*."

"Yes, they do. They need you to interpret the symbols after I see them." She listened to Morty sigh pitifully and rolled her eyes at him. "Stop your bellyaching, you candy-ass."

"Is that supposed to be comforting?" he asked in a huff.

"No, but this is. We're getting out of here tonight."

"How? We're on the floor in chains." He lifted his arms and rattled the metal links that bound them to the concrete floor.

"You need to get my hands untied and get the guard to come close enough so I can grab him. Then leave the rest to me."

ANISE LOOKED AROUND, TRYING TO GET her bearings in the dark. She turned on her helmet's light and brushed a spider off her shoulder. The air was very still, and she found it a little hard to breathe. Switching on her flashlight, she ran the beam of light over the walls of the cave. It was a large room, about thirty feet wide and so long that her flashlight couldn't find the far ends.

"So what are we looking for exactly?" Raina asked as the three women wandered around the underground room slowly, carefully maneuvering over and around the treacherous and uneven rocky cave floor and hopping over puddles.

"Four indentations in the wall that are the exact size and shape of the four keystones Anise showed us," Selina answered her.

"Nate said it was on the far side of the cave," Anise added as they headed carefully to the back wall.

"And how exactly are these keystones supposed to help us find the map?" asked Raina.

"They're supposed to unlock a door," Anise explained.

"A door?" Raina said doubtfully. "I only see rock walls. What kind of door?"

"I don't know," Anise replied, wishing she had more information.

"We'll know it when we find it!" Selina chimed in.

After a long while of staring at rock, tripping on the uneven floor, and running her hand over dents in the walls, Anise noticed some indentations that didn't look natural. "I think this is it!" she exclaimed. She ran her fingers over the indentations as Raina and Selina joined her.

"That definitely looks man-made," Raina confirmed.

"What are you waiting for?" Selina asked excitedly. "See if the beads fit!"

As her friends watched, Anise pulled out the keystones and inserted them one-by-one into their respective indentations, making sure to place them according to the code she believed was correct. Once she was done, the three women looked at each other in silence, waiting.

"Do you hear something?" Anise asked her friends.

They looked toward the tunnel they had climbed down but saw nothing. Moments later, all three heads swiveled in the other direction as a four foot section of the wall that contained the keystones began moving backward, as if on a hinge at one end.

Anise felt herself start to tremble.

"Whoa," Raina said under her breath.

Slowly, the rock wall opened. The cave shook slightly, and the noise of tons of rock sliding on a bumpy rock floor was even louder than the expressions of excitement coming from the women as they held on to each other and peered into the hidden room. When the door finally stopped moving, they stepped inside.

"Holy shit, this is incredible!" Raina said, looking at the two-foot square, hand-carved stone box that stood before them.

"I completely agree."

The three women jumped at the sound of the male voice behind them and spun around.

"Dr. Dromly." Anise's eyes narrowed and her heart-beat echoed in her ears.

"Ms. Viston. Dr. Hanlon." He turned to Raina. "And friend," Fred said, greeting the women.

"Um, Anise?" said Raina in a shaking voice. "Are we in trouble?"

Jonathan's former co-worker George was next to come down the tunnel. One after another of Dromly's brainwashed army dropped down into the cave. Anise counted about forty. She wore the ring under her gloves, the amulet under her shirt, the earrings under her helmet, and the cuff under her sleeve, but they wouldn't help her enough now. Dromly's army was too big. She looked down at her chest when the amulet started flashing, the light shining undeterred through her shirt in the darkness of the cave.

"What the hell is that?" Raina asked, staring questioningly at the flashing light of the amulet.

"A flashlight," Anise blurted out.

"What's going on here?" Selina asked Fred.

Fred looked at the flashing of Anise's amulet. "Stand down," he told his army. "No one is getting hurt here today." He looked directly at Anise. "I wish you and your friends no harm."

"Why are ya'll here?" Raina demanded of Fred. "This cave is off-limits to anyone who hasn't obtained the proper authorization."

Anise touched Raina's arm. "Not now," she mumbled.

"All I want is the map," Fred told them.

Anise looked down and noticed the amulet had stopped flashing. Dr. Dromly was being honest. He had no intention of hurting them. Her heartbeat slowed to an almost-normal speed.

"Anise is the one who found it," Raina declared. "The map is hers."

"Anise stole the keystones from me," Fred replied. "That makes the map mine." He waved his army over and pointed to the open door. "Let's get that map!"

"You weren't the one who figured out the code," Anise reminded him.

"No, and for that, I humbly admire your brilliance, Ms. Viston." He stepped up to her.

"Don't get any closer," Selina snapped at him.

"I could use someone like you on my team," Fred said to Anise. "All three of you," he added, extending the invitation to Selina and Raina. "Intelligent, adventurous young people. Join us, and together we'll find the Plate of Destiny."

"I don't trust you," Anise told him.

"Suit yourself," Fred replied with a shrug. "But you came all this way to get the map." He took another step forward. "It would be a shame if you gave up now."

"Back off!" came Selina's loud warning. She took a step toward him and glared down at him as she pulled a pocket knife out of her backpack.

Fred turned so that Anise was the only one who saw the amulet under his shirt and jacket glowing after Selina's threat. She saw he was wearing the earrings and assumed he had on the ring under his glove. "It's okay," Anise told Selina. "Put the knife away."

Selina narrowed her brows in doubt but did as Anise asked.

"Have you ever jumped out of a plane?" Fred asked the ladies once his amulet stopped glowing. "Not regular skydiving, I mean, but out of necessity?"

"No," Anise said carefully, wondering if this was going to be a threat or if Fred was trying to make a point. She eyed the rope hanging from the open shaft in the ceiling and wondered how she could get Dromly to let her and her friends leave.

"I once hired a pilot to fly me to and from a site containing ancient ruins. The ruins had a hidden compartment that one could only find on the solstice when the sun would shine on the otherwise hidden latch. Something about direct sunlight was needed to open the compartment. My wife was unfortunately in the hospital at the time, and I didn't want to wait for the next solstice, so I'd brought my infant son with me. He rode in a carrier around my chest."

Anise flashed confused looks at Selina and Raina which they returned. She wondered where Fred was going with this story.

"Anyway," Fred continued, "to my unbelievable luck, I'd found an artifact that had been under debate as to whether or not it even existed. Excitedly, I told the pilot how valuable this artifact was and how much more famous I'd be than I already was. I promised him a mention in the book I planned to write. Little did I know he was already well aware of the artifact's value. We then took off to head for home, and in the air, he demanded the artifact. I, of course, refused to give it to him and we fought. He was larger and stronger and tore the artifact from my grasp. I'm sure you can imagine how shocked I was when he opened the door to the plane and tossed it out. Well, I did what anyone would do in my position. I grabbed a parachute pack in one arm, my infant son in the other, and I jumped out after it."

Anise gave him a look of disbelief. He appeared not to notice.

"I could barely see the artifact falling ahead of me as I struggled to put the parachute on my back. When I pulled the ripcord, I saw the artifact falling toward a large square shape on the ground that'd been outlined with hundreds of logs spray painted red to stand out from the green field. It was at that moment I realized the pilot had thrown the artifact out of the plane at certain coordinates to ensure it would land within the square. When I reached the ground, I was met by a guard donkey."

"Okay," Selina said, her annoyance obvious in her voice. "What the hell is your point?"

"My point is that donkeys bite!" Fred exclaimed. "They can also deliver crushing blows with their legs. He was not pleased that I'd dropped in on him, quite literally. I suppose I could've fought him and won, but I didn't want to hurt him. I tried to maneuver around him instead but then several more angry donkeys showed up. I had Kent with me, and nothing was worth risking his life, so I ran. He slept through the entire ordeal."

"Great," Selina shot back sarcastically. "You're not getting the map."

"*You* may not understand," Fred said to Selina, "but Anise knows what I'm trying to tell her. Even though she and I may be evenly matched, my associates far outnumber yours." He looked directly at Anise. "I may not be a donkey, but I wouldn't try anything reckless if I were you."

"You may not be a donkey, but you are an ass!" Selina spat.

Anise ignored Selina and nodded at Fred, understanding his point no matter how strangely it was delivered. They both had a set of the Armor Jewelry and would have about the same amount of strength. But Fred's advantage was his army members who would join in the fighting if need be. She knew she didn't stand a chance. Unless...

Anise grabbed Fred's arm and pulled him aside. "I'd like to give you the same warning," she hissed at him. "You may have an army that's loyal to you, but I have king's blood and the cuff. I can turn their loyalty to my side in a split second."

Fred laughed, almost as if he were enjoying their banter. "And since they've spent years being trained to be loyal to me, I can turn them back in a split second. We could go back and forth, but is that truly how you'd like to spend the afternoon?"

Anise pressed her lips together in frustration. "Being trained? At least call it what it is. Brainwashing." She knew he was right that he could easily bring his army back to his side even if she brainwashed them instantly to follow her. After all, Jonathan used to display effects of brainwashing at the mere mention of Dr. Smithton's name.

"Hey boss," George called out. "I know you wanted me to film you finding the map, but given these new circumstances, want me to grab the map and get it out of here? Then you can be free to keep these young ladies under control? We can stash them with Morty and Grace."

Fred glanced at George and then back at Anise, almost like his mind was elsewhere.

Anise's heart raced. *Shit!* Captured and no one knew where she was. Her mind desperately fought to think of a plan.

"Start filming, George." Fred replied.

"But boss, she's right there," George argued, pointing at Anise. "And you need her. You know...for later."

"We're going to film," Fred said again, sounding unsure as he looked from George to Anise.

"But boss, you were so concerned about finding her and trapping her. Now here she is! It's perfect! Why would you want to—"

"George," Fred interrupted. "I said we're filming." He walked into the room where the stone box was waiting.

George's eyes glazed over. He followed Fred. "Yes, boss."

Anise's mouth opened in shock. She knew he needed her blood to spill on the Plate of Destiny in order to read it. Why would he walk away, allowing her time to escape?

"How on earth was I ever a fan of his?" Selina lamented. "He's not an exciting adventurer at all! He's just an old man who lies. He embellishes his stories to the point of ridiculousness, and I fell for it. I can't believe I was ever so stupid. They say you shouldn't meet your heroes and—"

"We have more important things to worry about," Raina interrupted her, flashing Selina an incredulous look.

"Right," Anise agreed. "I don't know why he's not trying to keep us here, but we need to leave before he changes his mind. Let's go!"

"We can't leave! We haven't gotten the map," Selina argued.

"Do you have a plan?" Anise asked her.

"Well, no. But we can't leave without it."

"We have to," Anise argued. "There's forty of them and three of us. The only thing we can do now is protect ourselves by leaving. We'll figure out another plan later. At least we'll know where the map is."

"What about the keystones?" Selina asked.

"Let Dromly have them," Anise responded with a wave of her hand. "We don't need them anymore anyway." She climbed up the rope easily with the strength given to her by the earrings and intensified by the other Jewelry. Quickly, she pulled up Raina and then Selina.

During the car ride home, Raina and Selina were both strangely quiet. Anise thought she'd have to answer a pile of questions from them, but neither said a word. When Raina pulled up to Anise's hotel, they all got out of the car and helped bring the supplies to the front door.

"I have to go check on my grandfather," Selina said. "I'll come see you tomorrow, Anise."

Anise gave her friend a hug. "Thanks for your help tonight. And don't be too upset. We'll find a way to get that map."

"Yes, we will," Selina affirmed. She gave Raina a hug too before she left.

"Anise," Raina said, once Selina was gone. "The Armor Jewelry...you're wearing it. And the legends I've read are real, aren't they? I saw the amulet glowing. And that's why you were so confident and so quick at climbing thirty vertical feet."

Anise frowned in concern. "Please don't tell anyone," she begged. "For years now I've had to deal with people who've been after me for the Armor Jewelry besides Fred Dromly. There may even be others who know. I'm not sure. But the more people who know, the less safe we are."

"I won't tell anyone."

"Thank you." Anise felt her stomach twinging. She should've been more careful to keep the Armor Jewelry a secret. "The others are going to be upset with me that I told you."

"Were they upset when you told Selina?"

Anise shook her head. "She doesn't know."

"She absolutely knows."

"What? Did she say something to you?" Anise asked with worry.

"No," Raina replied. "But she saw your amulet flashing in the cave and didn't seem phased by it at all while I was doing my best not to act shocked."

"Maybe she bought that it was my flashlight."

"I don't think so. She had no concern about going into that deep, dangerous hole when last time we were in a cave she was clinging to Jonathan for dear life. She also seemed to think Fred Dromly might be intimidated by us if she stood up to him."

"Shit." As Anise and Raina walked up to Anise's room, Anise thought about Selina. "How would she have found out?" she wondered.

"She's your friend, right? Is it a problem that she knows?"

Anise shrugged. "I'm sure not, just like it's fine that you know, too. But..." Her face crinkled with an uncomfortable twinge from her gut-residing intuition.

"But what?" Raina prompted her.

"Why wouldn't she have said something once she figured it out like you just did? Isn't it kind of weird that she'd keep it to herself? I need to tell the others."

They knocked on Jonathan's door and Kent's door in case Nate was in there after Anise checked her own room. After no response anywhere, they went to Lorelei's room.

"Why isn't she answering? Her light's on." Anise knocked harder and the heavy door moved. "Her door's not closed all the way." The two women stepped inside. "Lorelei?"

"She's sleeping," Raina whispered, pointing to the bed.

Anise walked over and placed a hand on Lorelei's arm to wake her.

"ANSWER YOUR PHONE," JONATHAN SAID, ANNOYED, as he shifted his weight from one foot to the other. They'd had to go back to the hospital and spent a long time there taking care of miscellaneous paperwork regarding Kent's death before heading to grab some take-out. The restaurant was packed and understaffed, it would be a while before their food was ready, and he was sick of watching Nate pace up and down through the crowd of people who were waiting for a table. "That's the third time it's rung in the last two minutes."

Nate took his phone out of his pocket and looked at the screen. "It's Anise," he told Jonathan. "What?" he said into the phone. Nate's face turned pale, and he let his body slowly tilt backward until his shoulders hit the wall with a thud. He put his phone back in his pocket and said nothing.

"What is it?" Jonathan asked him.

Nate stared straight ahead. "We have to go now."

"Right now? Why? Our food should be ready soon."

"My mother is dead."

Chapter 18

"What are you waiting for?" Grace hissed impatiently. She narrowed her eyes with annoyance but was still thrilled that she didn't feel the need to pull on her hair anymore.

"Are you sure this is going to work?" Morty whispered.

"Just do it." Grace groaned loudly and collapsed in a heap.

"What's wrong with her, Dr. Smithton?" A middle-aged man hurried over to the two of them. He eyed Grace with a worried expression.

"Where are the others, Bradley?" Morty demanded of him.

"Out. I'm on guard duty tonight." Bradley smirked. "I drew the short straw."

"Release us!" Morty demanded again. "You can see she's not okay."

Grace took that opportunity to groan dramatically.

"I can't do that, Dr. Smithton, I'm sorry. You know, at first it seemed wrong to have my former boss sit on the floor with his wrists and ankles bound in chains, but for some reason when Dr. Dromly explained it, it made complete sense."

Grace resisted the urge to call the brainwashed idiot a candy-ass and groaned again instead.

"We haven't been fed all day!" Morty complained. "She's weak and feeble Bradley; can't you tell?"

"I wasn't given instructions to provide a meal," Bradley said, scratching his head.

"Were you given instructions to let her get deathly ill? She's a diabetic!" Morty yelled.

"No, Dr. Smithton, I'm sorry. I'll get some food right away!" He hurried off.

"Nice work!" Grace praised him with a big grin as she sat up.

Morty chuckled quietly. "He'll be back soon. Don't let him catch you sitting up."

Bradley returned after a few minutes. "I'm sorry, Mrs. Brevain. We didn't have much food. I hope you like peanut butter and jelly." He knelt in front of her and held the sandwich to her lips.

"My god, man! She's not a child. Untie her hands so she can eat with dignity! And that's *Dr*. Brevain to you!" Morty barked.

Bradley looked flustered, and he tripped over his words. "I—I'm sorry, Dr. Smithton, Dr. Brevain." He fumbled in his pocket for the key and unlocked Grace's wrists. He helped her sit and handed her the sandwich.

"Thank you, young man," Grace said in a weak, pathetic voice, touching Bradley's face with false gratitude. Her fingers wandered down his neck.

Bradley let out a cry of pain. He sank to the floor under Grace's knowledge of pressure points. Once he'd passed out, Grace took his key, unlocked her ankle binds, and freed Morty. They locked Bradley in the constraints and walked out the door to find themselves in a driveway in a small residential neighborhood. Most of the houses seemed empty.

"Now what?" Grace wondered out loud.

"I purloined Dromly's car keys," Morty replied, holding them up. "He must've driven here and carpooled with the rest of the army in the vans."

"Why weren't you always this helpful and resourceful?" Grace asked. She wondered what her life would've been like if their engagement had lasted.

"It took a while for your bad influence to rub off on me." He opened the car door for her.

She sat, and as they drove off, she took a bite of the peanut butter and jelly sandwich. "Well, it's about goddamn time."

AFTER SHOOING EVERYONE OUT OF LORELEI'S room, Nate sat next to his mother's body and held her cold hand. His entire being was numb, inside and out. He tried to feel something—sadness, anger, horror, anything. The only emotion that managed to squeeze through his tight walls was remorse. He'd just gotten her back, and now she was gone again. He hadn't spent enough time with her. He should've been here to protect her. He should've known she was just trying to love him, not judge him. He should've made the most of the time they had together instead of being angry about the time they'd missed. His grief was soon interrupted by a soft glow he noticed coming from under the dresser. Kneeling on the floor, he reached for the glow and pulled out Lorelei's phone. A spam call was coming through. He rejected the call, and the screen changed, its display punching Nate in the gut. "She was texting me right before..." He looked carefully at the words she'd been typing.

Js kidnapper selinas g

Selina? What did she have to do with Boy Scout's kidnapping? His eyes narrowed as he tried to interpret Lorelei's words in the text that never got sent, but his brain had turned to mush, making concentration impossible. Erasing the text, he slid the phone back under the dresser where he found it. He opened the door after a tap-tap-tap startled him out of his fog. Sitting in the chair she'd slept in when she let him have the bed, he talked to the police, answering their questions, but keeping the existence of the text to himself. Anise, Raina, and Boy Scout answered questions next.

Nate watched the coroner take his mother away in a body bag. The police sealed off her room with yellow tape and left. He stood silently in the hallway, feeling nothing but an emptiness so heavy he could barely move. Anise, Boy Scout, and Raina approached him.

"What did they tell you?" Anise asked him.

"She was strangled," Nate replied in a quiet voice. "The cameras in the lobby show her entering the hotel and two men following behind her. They showed the footage to me, but I don't recognize them. They had caps on. I couldn't see their faces."

"Who would do this?" Anise wondered, holding her stomach.

"I'm really sorry," Boy Scout said. "Is there anything I can do?"

Nate shook his head. The next several minutes consisted of Anise, Raina, and Boy Scout trying to comfort him or offering him things until he asked to be alone.

"I can't find my room key," Anise announced as her hands dug in her pockets.

"Take mine. I don't need it anymore anyway," Nate said, handing her his key.

"You might. You're more than welcome to stay with me tonight if you want," Anise offered. "I know I wouldn't want to be alone. Just let me in with yours. I'm sure my key is in the room somewhere. I'll find it."

He let her in without a word, walked by Boy Scout, and entered Kent's room. Kent's clothes in the closet and shaving kit on the sink waited for him, ready for their next use. But he wasn't coming back. Neither was Lorelei. Nate perched on the edge of a chair, still in a fog. Five seconds or five hours later, he began packing up Kent's things. Luckily, it didn't take long. Now he had his own room, but there was no way he could sleep here. As numb as his mind and heart were, he could still feel the ghost.

He found himself in the hallway, not sure what to do with Kent's travel bag. *Maybe I could leave it in Anise's room for now.* He knocked on her door, and when she opened it, her eyes pitied him. Pity glance aside, he missed her and wanted nothing more than to go to sleep with her in his arms. He thought about apologizing to her again, but it made him think of Grace's apology to him. Neither were well received. Both were completely futile. He found the connection disturbing but profound.

"It's okay for you to use your key," Anise told him. "That's why I wanted you to keep it."

He slightly lifted the luggage. "Can I leave this in here for now until I can find somewhere to donate it?"

She opened her door wider. "Of course. Come in. Is there anything I can do to help?"

He stepped in, dumped the bag in the closet, and looked at her. "I want you to know I get it."

She raised her eyebrows in question. "You get what?"

"Grace apologized to me when I found her in the cave," he began. "And I don't care. After everything she did, I can't bring myself to give a shit at all that she's sorry."

"That's understandable," Anise replied.

"So I get how you feel," he continued. "You've had enough of me. No matter how much I apologize, it's not going to matter. I never want to see Grace again even though she's different now. The old Grace would never have apologized. But it's too little, too late. It's the same with us. Even though I never would knowingly help Grace escape or let her hurt you, it doesn't matter. I still kept something from you, and now it's too late. You never want to see me again, and I get it."

Anise opened her mouth but closed it again and looked at the ground with a small sigh. Her brows narrowed and her eyes welled up.

"I don't know if I've seen the last of Grace," Nate frowned, "but I want you to know I have no intention of causing you any more pain. I've made some decisions. I'm happy to help you find the Plate of Destiny. But once we get back home, I'm going to put my condo up for sale. I'm going to move out of the city, state, maybe even country. You won't ever have to see me again, just like you want."

He looked at her standing there, twisting her garnet ring around her finger, tears streaming down her beautiful face. He wished he could comfort her, but she wouldn't want that. She wanted nothing more to do with him. Hopefully this would be the last time he'd ever make her cry.

Feeling a sudden need to be anywhere but there, Nate left the room, quietly closing the door behind him. His legs walked him down the stairs to the lobby while his brain stayed in a comforting fog. Realizing he didn't actually have anywhere to go, he sat in a chair across from the front desk and stared into oblivion.

JONATHAN STEPPED UP TO THE FRONT desk to grab a warm cookie that the evening staff baked fresh nightly. He chatted for a moment with the front-desk clerk about nothing in particular and turned to head back to his room to watch movies until he fell asleep. He saw Nate sitting in a chair by the revolving door, his arms crossed, his body slouching down in the seat, and one knee bouncing up and down like its life depended on it. Jonathan knew he could walk on by as if he saw nothing. He wanted to.

"Hey," he said, walking over to Nate. "What are you doing?"

Nate looked up as if he were startled to see another

person there. "Nothing."

"So you're just sitting here." Jonathan felt a wave of annoyance and then felt guilty about it.

Nate shrugged. "I wouldn't want to stay in Lorelei's room even if I could. Don't want to stay in Kent's either. Or Anise's."

Jonathan nodded. "I get it. My room has two beds. You can stay with me."

Nate gave him another surprised look. "Thanks, Boy Scout." His eyes drifted to the floor and his knee continued its frantic dance.

Jonathan took a few steps away and looked back. "Are you coming?"

"I'll catch up with you in a while."

Losing someone wasn't something Jonathan had ever experienced. Even all four of his grandparents were still alive. But the mere thought of his mother passing away made him feel sick. Hanging out with Nate wasn't how he'd choose to spend an evening, but he couldn't stop himself from saying, "There's a sports bar a few blocks from here. Wanna go get a drink?"

Nate slowly raised his head and nodded. "Yeah."

ANISE HADN'T MEANT TO CRY IN front of Nate, but the tears had come anyway. His sudden decision to move so far away that they'd never have a chance to run in to each other felt so final. And like a dramatic overreaction. But his mother just died; she wouldn't call him out on that, not now. Maybe he'd come to his senses after a good night's sleep. Sitting cross-legged on the bed, she built a nest of pillows including one that still smelled like him. Hiding there with her pencils and sketchbook, her dropping tears smudged her drawing of him riding away on his motorcycle. "Stay," read the caption.

Tomorrow she'd tell Nate and Jonathan that she, Raina, and Selina had found the second map and then had it stolen by Dromly. They'd find a way to get it back, somehow figure out how to read it, and find the Plate of Destiny. Maybe in her wildest dreams it might be that easy. It was still early, but the sun was setting, and crawling under the covers felt so good. She put the pillow Nate had slept on behind her head and back as if he were there. Breathing in his scent made sleep come quickly.

IT WAS THE SPORTS BAR OF Jonathan's dreams. A stage for bands, or like tonight, karaoke. Giant flat screen TVs on leather-paneled walls. Oak tables, antique chandeliers, and bottles lined up like crown-molding on glass shelving near the ceiling. A well-stocked bar. Golf simulators in the back room. Another room for pool tables. And it was packed with beautiful women dancing to the songs the other patrons had chosen to sing.

He hadn't felt like going out, and his plan had been to buy Nate a beer, try to make some small talk to distract him from the horrors of the day, and go back to the hotel. None of that happened. After a few rounds of tequila shots and a lively debate about the fate of the upcoming football games on Sunday, Jonathan was happy to agree to a golf simulator competition that a couple guys had challenged them to. He and Nate surprisingly made a great team and beat their competitors at Best Ball. High-fiving each other and accepting beers as their prize, they sat at one of the oak tables to listen to the butchering of a classic rock anthem on the karaoke stage.

"You have a wicked swing," complimented Jonathan. "Did you ever play any other sports in school?"

"Baseball for a short while," Nate replied.

"You quit?"

"Grace thought it took up too much of my time that could be better used to serve her purposes." He raised his arm to the server who came over and took his order for another round of tequila.

"Sounds like her." Jonathan downed his shot when it was placed in front of him. "So...any big plans for after we find the Plate of Destiny?"

"Yeah. I'm moving."

"Selling the condo?"

"You interested?"

"Yeah," Jonathan scoffed. "I wanna be reminded of you everywhere I look when I'm at home." Jonathan shook his head. "Did you find a better place?"

"No. I'm leaving town. I need a new state. Or country."

Jonathan raised his eyebrows at him. "Why?"

Nate shrugged. "There's nothing for me there anymore."

"Because of Anise?"

"Not just her. I don't have my job anymore. No one'll hire a felon for a job I'd actually want to do. Only have a couple buddies left in town. Nothing's keeping me there."

Jonathan frowned, unable to keep the judgmental tone out of his voice. "Sounds like you're running away."

"Fuck you. I'm not running away." Nate signaled for another round.

"You might wanna slow down a bit."

"You can slow down if you want to. I'm fine."

Jonathan could tell Nate wasn't fine. Did he really have nothing to stay for in his own hometown? Jonathan had a band, a job he loved, family he adored, and more friends than he could count. He'd never dream of leaving. His detestation of Nate was slowly turning into compassion. "Would you be interested in playing on the museum's softball team next summer? We could use someone who can actually hit."

"Don't you have to be a museum employee?" Nate asked.

"No. It's open to employees and their family and friends."

Nate let out a low chuckle. "Are we friends now?"

"If you can help us win. The last few seasons have been humiliating."

Nate gave him a genuine smile. "Thanks for the offer. But like I said, I'm moving."

Jonathan shrugged. "Okay. Let me know if you change your mind."

Their shots came and Jonathan let his sit on the table. Not knowing what else to say to Nate, his eyes wandered through the room. They landed on a couple of women standing by the bar. They were well-dressed, looked sophisticated, groomed to perfection, and intimidated the hell out of him.

"Go," Nate said.

"Go? Where?"

"Go ask her to dance."

Jonathan felt his cheeks burning. "Who?"

Nate rolled his eyes. "Whichever one you were staring at."

Jonathan gave a half-shrug. "Nah, I'm good here."

"Yeah, I'm sure you're loving hanging out with me. Just go. I'll dance with her friend."

Jonathan shifted in his chair. "I said no. Let it go."

Nate gave him a confused look. "What's the problem, Boy Scout?"

"There's no problem." Jonathan looked at his lap.

"There's obviously a problem."

"I'm just shy, okay?" came Jonathan's annoyed response.

"Shy? You make friends with everyone you meet."

"Making a friend is different."

Nate flashed an amused grin. "Anise said you're in bars every weekend. Haven't you asked a woman to dance before?"

"I'm in bars every weekend because I'm performing,

not dancing. And yes, I've asked a woman to dance. But..."

"But?" Nate prompted.

"But only if I already know her."

"Seriously?" Nate laughed long enough to piss Jonathan off. "You're asking a woman to dance tonight."

Jonathan stared at the table. "I don't think so. That's not why we're here."

"You front a band, Boy Scout. Haven't you ever used that as an ice breaker?"

Jonathan shrugged. "What would I do? Go up to a girl and say, 'I front a band. Wanna dance?'"

"No," Nate replied, obviously suppressing a laugh. "I'll be your wingman and make it really easy for you since it's your first time. Here's what gonna happen. You're going to get up on stage and sing something. Pick a crowd pleaser and sing the hell out of it. I'll talk you up to those two girls. When you get off stage, join us, and ask one to dance."

Jonathan frowned, unsure of this haphazard plan. "Which one?"

"Whichever one you want." Nate shook his head. "Pathetic." He stood, motioned for Jonathan to get up, and pushed him toward the stage. Nate made his way toward the two women at the bar. "That's what you're drinking?" he asked them condescendingly after they'd downed their shots.

"What wrong with what we're drinking?" one asked him.

"If you don't know, then you've never had the good shit," Nate responded, motioning to the bartender for three shots of something expensive.

Up on stage, Jonathan picked a song he knew he could perform well. He saw Nate pointing toward him. While he couldn't hear him, he realized Nate must've said something nice because the two women directed their attention to the stage and smiled.

Performing on a stage was something that never

intimidated Jonathan. He belted the first few notes and was encouraged by the appreciative roar of the crowd. By the time he finished, the entire bar was cheering. He waved to his audience and stepped off the stage.

"I told you he was good," Nate said loudly, and bought four more shots, sliding one down to Jonathan as he stepped up to the bar.

The women downed their shots and agreed, one of them telling Jonathan how great his performance was, the other saying how impressed she was with his talent.

Jonathan saw Nate staring at him. Nate raised his eyebrows as if to say, "Do it now!"

Turning to the woman who'd originally caught his eye, Jonathan gathered his courage. "Would you like to dance?"

"Yeah!" she responded, grabbed his hand, and pulled him onto the dance floor as the next song started.

The elation Jonathan felt at conquering a fear was almost eclipsed by his surprise at how skillfully Nate moved to the music. No wonder Anise enjoyed going dancing with him. Next to him, Jonathan felt like a drunk bear on roller skates. His attention was brought back to his dance partner when she reached into his back pocket and grabbed his phone.

"Open it," she said, handing it to him.

He followed orders, and she grabbed it from him. He looked at the screen when she handed it back.

"We have to go. But see you guys later, hopefully," she said with a smile as she and her friend walked off.

"She put her number in my phone," Jonathan reported proudly.

"Same," Nate told him. He scrolled through his contacts and deleted the number of the girl he'd danced with.

"You're deleting it already?"

Nate shrugged. "I'm not going to call her."

"Yeah, neither am I, but I don't want them to see—"

"Gotta do it right away or else they'll accumulate. It

sucks to scroll through thousands of numbers to find the one you want." He smirked arrogantly.

Jonathan laughed. "Thousands. Yeah, right." For some reason Nate's grin wasn't as irritating as usual. Jonathan wondered how many shots he'd had. "You're a good wingman. And you can really dance."

"I know."

"Where'd you learn that?"

Nate shrugged. "I picked it up here and there. You know, you can really sing."

"Thanks! You should come out and hear the band play some weekend."

Nate put his phone back in his pocket. "Sure."

Jonathan thought about what he was saying. If he was making plans to hang out with Nate... "I'm pretty drunk. And you had more than I did. Are you ready to go?"

"Okay. Yeah."

They walked in silence through the crowded downtown street toward the hotel. Jonathan wondered how sorry he'd be later for mixing tequila with beer. His thoughts were interrupted when Nate walked right into a trash can and laughed at his predicament. "Your eyes are *open*, right?" Jonathan asked him.

Nate laughed again, and they continued walking. "Oh, look!" Nate pointed to the store window next to them. He put his hands and forehead on the glass as he stared inside. "Do you see that?"

"You drooling on the window? Unfortunately, yes."

Nate didn't move. "Not that, dipshit."

"What then? It's just a smoke shop," Jonathan commented as he looked more carefully through the window.

"I know, but look." He pointed to a sign in the window. "Gurkha His Majesty's Reserve."

"What?"

"It's a cigar."

"So what? Let's go."

"Wait, we need to get a couple of those." Nate tugged at the locked front door.

"It's like, midnight, dude," Jonathan reminded him. "They're closed."

Nate's eyes sparkled. "Not for us."

"Aw, fuck," Jonathan complained loudly. "You're not going to break in, are you?"

"Shhh," Nate hushed him. "*We're* going to break in." He grabbed Jonathan by the arm and pulled him into the alley along the side of the smoke shop. "Side door. See? No cameras."

"No way!" Jonathan hissed at him. "I am not going to prison for you."

Nate glared at him. "*I* went to prison for *you*." He whipped a lock pick out of his pocket.

"Bullshit. Anise might believe that, but I don't." Jonathan tried to watch what Nate was doing, but it happened so fast.

"That's 'cause you're not as smart as she is." Nate put the lock pick back in his pocket and slowly opened the door.

"You had no reason to go to prison for complete strangers," Jonathan said matter-of-factly as he followed Nate into the shop.

"Wait," Nate commanded, holding out his arm so Jonathan couldn't step in further.

"What's the problem?"

"I'm looking for cameras and motion detectors." Nate's eyes scanned the room. "The front area looks okay, but I'm sure there'll be an alarm when I go in the humidor. We'll have about fifteen minutes before the cops show up."

"I don't want any part of this," Jonathan proclaimed. He turned around quickly to leave and stumbled into a display of pipes. Several fell and skidded across the concrete floor. Trying not to giggle but failing miserably, they crawled around to pick them up.

"You grab a cigar kit from near the lounge," Nate ordered, pointing. I'm going to break in to the humidor, grab the cigars, and then we gotta run. Meet you back here by this door in thirty seconds."

"No!" Jonathan shook his head violently. "I'm not smoking anything you steal!"

"You gotta smoke this cigar!" Nate insisted. "It's one of the finest."

"No, I don't. What you're doing is wrong, and I want no part of it."

Nate groaned and looked at the ceiling with exasperation. "If I leave cash on the counter, will you smoke it? Then we've stolen nothin'."

"If these cigars are soooooo fine, do you have enough cash on you?" Jonathan asked.

"Good point." Nate opened his wallet and pulled out a stack of hundreds.

"Jesus." Jonathan's eyes opened wide. "How much are these cigars?"

"About twelve hundred a piece."

"What?!" Jonathan's jaw dropped.

Nate groaned as he counted his cash. "I don't have enough."

"Good! Then let's get outta here."

"No, I'll get some Opus X cigars instead. They're high end too. I have the cash for that." He showed Jonathan the money he was putting on the counter. "The cigars are about three hundred ten each. Plus you're going to get the cigar kit. Make sure it has a lighter, clipper, and punch, okay? That should be about thirty bucks. Total is about six hundred fifty. If I leave seven hundred, are you good?"

"Yes. If this'll mean we can leave after that, I'm good."

"Great. Go!" Nate grabbed his lock pick and opened the humidor.

Jonathan snatched one of the cigar kits from near the lounge and dashed back to the side door, cursing himself for allowing this situation to happen. When Nate joined him holding up two cigars with an obnoxious grin, they left out the side door.

"You're going the wrong way!" Jonathan called after Nate who was jogging down the alley. "The hotel is this way!" Realizing he was being ignored, Jonathan followed him. They quickly walked down the sidewalk that was filled with people going in and out of the bars and clubs.

"You're wrong, you know," Nate growled. "I had every reason to go to prison for complete strangers. I had to take Grace down or else you and Anise wouldn't be alive right now. I wasn't able to stop Grace earlier, so it was my fault the two of you were at the Springfield Museum for the earrings that night. And neither of you had any fucking idea what you were getting into, so it was my responsibility to keep you both from becoming more of Grace's victims. There was no way I'd let Anise get killed or locked up. I didn't know who the hell *you* were, but I was glad Anise wasn't alone. You risked your life to help her, and you didn't deserve to get killed or locked up either. I'm not a monster. I sacrificed my freedom for yours 'cause I wanted to help you." He turned to glare at Jonathan. "Self-righteous, judgmental asshole!"

"Okay," Jonathan said softly. "Sorry." The alcohol felt heavy sloshing around in his stomach. He dragged his body along after Nate who had way too much energy still. "Can we go back to the hotel now?"

Nate stopped at the entrance to a park. The metal barriers to block cars were closed, and he climbed over them.

"Where are you going?" Jonathan asked with exasperation as he climbed over the barriers after Nate.

"We can't smoke at the hotel," Nate replied. He headed across the green grass to a curved stone footbridge that crossed a large stream.

Jonathan laughed, having forgotten about the cigars. "Oh, yeah!"

They walked to the middle of the bridge and stood with their forearms resting on the railing.

"Why here?" Jonathan wondered out loud.

"It reminds me of a place I love back home," Nate said.

"And you still wanna move?"

"I can't go back there. Too many memories."

"Of what?"

"My mom. When I was a kid she'd take me to a park by our house. It has a bridge like this one."

"Isn't that a good memory though?" Jonathan asked.

Nate turned around and sat on the concrete deck of the bridge, his knees pointing to the sky and his back resting against the metal railing. "When I got her back, her eyes lit up every time she saw me. She hovered and fussed like I was a little kid and didn't let me get away with anything she didn't like. I couldn't stand it. But she was only trying to be a mom. She just wanted to make sure I was okay, and I was an ass to her." He ran a hand through his hair and his face tightened.

Jonathan looked down at Nate. "Yup. You were a fucking ass-dick bitchhead. Like usual." He laughed at his mixed-up insult.

"She was just trying to show me love. Now she's dead, and I wasn't there to protect her. We were supposed to travel the world together." Nate put his face in his hands and sobbed.

Jonathan stopped laughing and stared down at Nate, unsure of what to do. He sat next to him and let him rain out the heartbreak. A few minutes went by before the sobs began to quiet down. "It'll be...it'll be okay," Jonathan comforted softly.

Nate looked pitiful, his body slumping, shaking fingers wiping his eyes. "She was the only person who loved me."

"That's not true. Anise loves you."

"Not anymore. She made that clear." He frowned at

Jonathan unhappily. "*You* still have a shot though."

Jonathan narrowed his brows in confusion and slowly shook his head. "I've been trying to think about... thinking about trying to get back together with her, but I don't think I *ever* had a real shot. If you could steal her from me so easily, maybe she was never really mine at all. She *always* wanted *you*." Jonathan slumped next to Nate, feeling pitiful himself. "And I think...that I think I always knew that, deep down. Maybe something's telling me I should move on. Maybe that's why I can't stop thinking and thinking about Selina."

Nate looked at him with interest. "Really? What happened with Selina?"

Jonathan grinned. "She kissed me."

"That doesn't surprise me," Nate said, smiling too. "I've seen the way she looks at you. So what did you do?"

"Nothing." Jonathan shrugged.

"Idiot." Nate let a quiet laugh escape his lips.

"I still have feelings for Anise," Jonathan protested. "I can't..." He saw Nate giving him a look of disappointed disbelief. "Okay, I'm kind of an idiot."

"You don't get to choose when opportunity knocks," Nate told him. "She'd be good for you. I bet it's not too late."

Jonathan shrugged again. "I don't know. Maybe."

"Plus, she's hot."

Jonathan pointed a finger in Nate's face. "She's a sweet and incredible girl. You keep your filthy criminal hands...you keep your hands off her. You already took Anise—"

Nate held up his hands in surrender. "I wouldn't do that to you again. I promise."

Jonathan felt the heaviness and sleepiness getting stronger. "What time is it?"

Nate's eyes lit up. "It's time for the cigars!" He got to his feet and pulled Jonathan up by the arm.

Jonathan felt his mouth frowning. "I still can't believe

you made me break in..." He forgot what he was saying as he watched Nate open the cigar kit to prepare their tobacco treasures. He took the cigar when Nate handed it to him and let Nate light it. He watched Nate take a puff of his own cigar and Jonathan did the same—or so he thought. Overwhelmed with a heavy, thick, burning sensation, Jonathan broke into a coughing fit that made him wonder if he'd ever breathe again.

"No, no, no!" Nate exclaimed frantically, holding his hand out to signal Jonathan to stop. "You don't inhale cigar smoke. Haven't you ever had a cigar before?"

Jonathan shook his head, still coughing.

"You pull it into your mouth to taste it, then you exhale," he explained, demonstrating. "You okay?"

Jonathan let out a final cough. "Yeah."

"Try it again."

Jonathan followed Nate's instructions, managing not to cough this time. "Do you smoke these things all the time or something?" he asked Nate.

"No. This is my third one."

"Ever?"

"Yeah. They're for special occasions only."

"What's the occasion? Tonight, I mean?"

"I'm drunk."

Jonathan snorted a laugh. "Why is that...is that special? Is it your third time being drunk, too?"

"No. My second."

"What? That's it?" Jonathan asked in disbelief.

"Yeah."

"You're full of shit."

"I don't like losing control of myself," Nate responded.

"But you're so...so reckless," Jonathan argued.

"Maybe it looks that way to you. But I'm always in control of what's happening. I wouldn't have survived otherwise."

They stood in silence and watched people walking home from the bars and clubs on the city street from their perch on the bridge. It was a moment of quiet and peace that made Jonathan realize how stressed he'd been lately, and it felt so good that not even the strange fact that he was enjoying it because of Nate could ruin it for him. Jonathan wished it could last longer, but it seemed that lately nothing could be enjoyed peacefully. He put a hand to his stomach. "Nate, I don't feel so good."

Nate looked at him. "You're turning green, Boy Scout."

Jonathan turned away and stumbled around on the bridge without knowing where he was going, trying to walk off the squeezing sensations in his gut. He felt Nate grab his arm and lead him to the side of the bridge. Nate's hand gently pushed Jonathan's head forward over the side. He felt Nate holding his body fast so he wouldn't fall as he purged all the alcohol he'd had into the stream below. "Thanks," he said quietly, lifting his head and placing a hand on his forehead to keep the dizziness from getting overwhelming. "Let's go back to the hotel. I feel...like...I...just like...shit."

"You like shit?" Nate asked, making a face of both confusion and disgust. "Or you feel like you just shit?"

"No! I *feel* like shit. You know, like bad. So let's go back."

"In a minute," Nate agreed. "It's my turn." He grabbed on to the railing as he leaned over it to loudly expel his tequila and beer as well.

While Nate was busy, Jonathan thought about how alcohol wasn't the only thing that'd been purged on the bridge that night. Heavy guilt, heartbreak, insecurity, and repressed emotions had been poured out as well, leaving them feeling empty but also lighter from releasing a toxic load. "It would make a good...good, good song," he said out loud to himself.

"I don't think I wanna hear that song," Nate commented as he wiped his mouth with the back of his hand.

"No, not that," Jonathan tried to explain as he took a step forward and stumbled, falling to his knees. His eyes wanted to close, and the world was spinning. He felt Nate pulling him up.

"Can you walk?"

"Since I was ten months old," Jonathan announced proudly, stumbling forward again.

"Good," Nate told him. "Just hold on to me, and put one foot in front of the other until we get back."

"Okay," Jonathan said, nodding at the fantastic idea. "One front in foot of the other."

Chapter 19

The morning light squeezed its way through the space where the curtains didn't quite meet. Voices and footsteps from the hallway could be heard as hotel guests made their way to breakfast. Anise's eyes opened slowly. Her arms stretched over her head. She stood up to go to the bathroom, and a wave of nausea hit her. Sitting back on the bed, she breathed deeply until it passed.

Anise searched through her bag and all the drawers in the room but still couldn't find her room key. She wondered where the hell she had left it. This extra stress was not what she needed. Still feeling slightly queasy, she headed to the buffet in the lobby hoping that some food might settle her stomach. She turned at the sound of her name being called. "Raina, hi," she replied.

"I'm sorry to bother you so early," Raina said, "but you weren't answering your phone, and you need to see this." She showed Anise the screen of her phone and played a video.

"It's Dromly," Anise said. "Wait, this is last night in the cave!"

"This video went viral. It's on the world news," Raina told her. She fast-forwarded the video a few minutes. "Look at this flat stone tablet with carvings on it...it's the map!"

Anise squinted at the screen. The map looked like nothing more than a bunch of random drawings. "I can't believe it's so clear! Can you read it?"

Raina shook her head. "I have no idea what it means."

"Maybe Jonathan will know. Come on." Anise led Raina up to Jonathan's room and tapped softly on the door.

*** *** ***

THE LOUD BANGING ON THE DOOR made Jonathan groan as he put a hand to his head, hoping to swat away who-ever was pounding nails into his skull. He turned onto his side and saw Nate sleeping soundly in the next bed. Jonathan frowned as he tried to remember how they got back to the hotel. The loud banging on the door persist-ed. He forced himself to get up and answer it. "Hey," he mumbled, squinting in the bright light of the hallway.

"Hey," Anise answered back while Raina gave him a slight wave. "Are you okay? You look sick."

Jonathan nodded slowly. "I'll be fine. It was just a late night."

"You couldn't sleep?"

"Nate and I went to a sports bar and got back...I don't even know when."

Anise's eyebrows raised. "You...and Nate? Went to a bar? Together?"

"Yeah. He needed a friend. I was trying to be nice."

"That was kind of you." Anise gave him an inquisitive look. "How did that go?"

Jonathan thought about how best to answer that question. He hadn't wanted to hang out with Nate, but last night he'd won a golf tournament, got to be a rock star and earned the admiration of an entire bar, conquered a lifelong fear, smoked a fine cigar, composed a new song, lost an enemy, and maybe—maybe—even made a new friend. It'd been epic. "We had way too much to drink."

"Then you'll both want this," Anise said, reaching into her tote bag and handing him a bottle of painkillers.

He took it gratefully. "Thanks."

"Fred Dromly has the map," Anise told him, "and Raina found a video that shows it very clearly. Can you tell us what it says?"

"I don't know how to read this," Jonathan admitted after the women showed him the video. "But I'll do more research and figure it out. I'll have to hurry since Dromly already has it. And since we've seen it, I'm sure Dr. S. and Grace have seen it too."

"Thanks. We'll meet you downstairs when you're ready," Anise said before she and Raina left.

Jonathan sat on the edge of his bed and pulled up the video on his phone. The map didn't even look like a map. It had several small drawings on it of Jewelry, a ship, caves, and several things he couldn't identify. No writing, no specific places named. One part looked like it might have been a coastline because there was a ship docked next to it, but it could've been any coastline in the world. He watched the video a few times before throwing a pillow at Nate to wake him up.

"What the hell?" Nate grumbled with annoyance as he pulled the blankets over his head.

"Get up," Jonathan ordered. "Dromly found the map. We need to figure out how to read it."

"No we don't," came Nate's muffled voice. "We just need to find Dromly and follow him."

Jonathan frowned, feeling stupid. "Oh. Yeah. I guess that would work too. I can't think straight with this headache." He threw another pillow at Nate and set the bottle of pain killers on the nightstand by his head. "You still have to get up. We need to get going."

"Wake me up when you're done with the shower," Nate conceded. He turned over and pulled the blankets over his head again.

Jonathan hesitated by the bathroom door. "How'd we get back last night?" he asked. "I can't remember anything after the bridge."

"It's okay, I have pictures."

Jonathan could almost hear the obnoxiousness of Nate's grin in his voice. "What's that supposed to mean?"

"You passed out. I had to carry you like a baby."

"Bullshit." Jonathan closed the bathroom door behind him. A second later, he opened it and walked back into the room. "Is that why I still have my shoes on?" He pulled off his sneakers and dropped them on the floor.

Nate grunted. "No way was I going to touch your feet. I can smell them from here."

"And you actually have pictures?" Jonathan waited but rolled his eyes when the response was nothing but laughter. He turned and walked back into the bathroom.

"Hey," Nate said, sitting up. He winced and put a hand to his forehead. "I'm sorry about the cigar shop break-in. I shouldn't have done it, and I shouldn't have involved you. That's not who I want to be. It was never who I wanted to be."

"Forget it," Jonathan replied, realizing Nate's apology was for more than just the night before. Not that Nate had redeemed himself for his unethical actions, but at least he was sorry. And he was able to set aside his colossal arrogance to apologize. There was hope for him. "Pain killers are on the nightstand."

"How did you find the map, Dr. Dromly?"

"Can you confirm it was drawn by Wilhelm Schwartz?"

"Dr. Dromly, where does the map lead?"

Fred held up his hands to quiet the reporters who'd been waiting for him outside his hotel. "I had hoped to tell the world of my findings in a dignified way, not a viral video." He glared at a member of his army who hung her head in shame. "But since the knowledge is out, yes, we believe the map is the very one drawn by Schwartz. As far as where it leads, it'll need to be studied before more is known about it."

Fred answered several more questions as generally as he could until he felt done with the reporters. The reporters, however, weren't done with him. He walked through the crowd and was bombarded with questions as he made his way to the new rental car George had procured for him when they'd discovered the old one was missing along with Morty and Grace.

"Now that you've made the find of the century, what'll you do next?"

"What does this discovery mean to you, Dr. Dromly?"

"What made you keep searching your entire life?"

"Did your son's death motivate you to find the map last night?"

Fred stopped in his tracks and turned toward the reporter with horror strangling his heart. "Excuse me?"

"You found the map just hours after the death of your son, Dr. Dromly. Was his demise your prime motivation to live out your own dreams before it's too late?"

Fred felt George grab his arm and direct him to the car. He pushed through the crowd with an arm around Fred to protect him. "Dr. Dromly will answer no further questions!"

Fred sat in the passenger's seat feeling like he might die himself. "Please get rid of them and take me back to my room, George." The cuff he wore sparkled.

George's eyes glazed over. "Yes, Dr. Dromly."

"What happened to Kent?" Fred demanded as George started the car.

"I don't know." George grabbed his phone and brought up a news article. "It says he was accidentally shot while trying to save a friend from kidnappers yesterday afternoon."

"Yesterday afternoon? It must've been very soon after he visited me." Fred wondered how things might've turned out if their conversation had gone differently. If they'd talked longer, would Kent still be here? He buried his face in his hands.

Once back in his room, Fred sat on the edge of his bed, thinking about the questions he'd been asked by the reporters. "What made me search my entire life?" he asked himself out loud. "The memory of a woman who looked up to me and idolized me, but may or may not have actually loved me, while a woman who did love me but didn't idolize me waited for me."

Now that he thought about it, he wondered if he'd even truly loved Dot, the woman who'd idolized him. He'd always considered her to be the love of his live, but how fascinating that the evidence didn't support that. He could've captured Anise and been one step closer to spilling king's blood on the Plate of Destiny. One step closer to learning how to bring Dot back. However, he'd let Anise escape because he couldn't resist the glory of being on camera when he discovered the map. That wasn't love.

He paused and stared at his hands. "What does this discovery mean to me? That I have a chance to bring back this woman with the expectation of being idolized again. Idolized. Not loved. And while I searched for a way to be god-like and defeat death, I grew old and missed my life."

He traced the wrinkles on his face with his fingertips and gently touched the liver spots that had appeared on the backs of his hands without him noticing. He got up and stared at his face in the mirror. A lone tear rolled over each wrinkle. "So much time has passed." The tear dropped from the edge of his jaw and landed on his bare foot which ached from navigating the uneven cave floor the night before. "I eschewed every chance at love for every chance at fame and glory and status and worship. I'm still doing it."

He looked himself in the eye. "What'll I do next?" He stared at his reflection. "Mourn my son and all the moments with him I could've had but didn't. He was right. I should've tried harder. It's all my fault. It's all my doing." He allowed his self-pity to overtake him, sat on the edge of the bed again, and hung his head.

Suddenly, the bed collapsed underneath him, and after letting out a wail of surprise and fear, Fred found himself on the floor, looking at an old, splintered bed leg resting innocently next to him. The entire footboard had given out, and one of the legs had broken off in the fall. He couldn't help but laugh as he rubbed his lower back. "It seems you're just as old as I am and have seen some difficult times," he said to the bed leg. "You probably feel sorry for yourself, too, but was it really necessary to jettison me from—" His head snapped back up. "Wait..."

The thoughts in his mind were swirling in a vortex, and it took a moment for them to settle in an organized and understandable concept. They showed him a memory he hadn't thought about in a very long time. He closed his eyes and let the past play like a movie in his mind.

It was February 1941. Fourteen-year-old Etheldred stood in the hallway in the orphanage that'd been his home since he could remember, trying to hide his tears from the other children who enjoyed laughing at his misfortune. He'd been asked to carry a suitcase to the front office and had happily delivered it to the couple who sat there, believing them to be his new parents. He'd never known why the other children had been chosen over him, why he was the oldest child there, why no one had ever wanted him. When it was finally his turn, his heart had soared, but as high as it had flown, it'd sunk even lower when little Elizabeth stuck her tongue out at him. The couple was here for her, not him. He'd dropped the suitcase and run out of the office.

"Poor dear," he could hear the administrator telling the couple. "Such a kind, bright young man with the soul of an artist and the mind of a scientist. Those looking for a son adopted the boys who were loud and played with lorries and swords, not the quiet one who read poetry. Too sensitive, that one."

There was nowhere he could go to be alone, so he let his grief drop him to the floor. The dark green tile could pretend to be the mossy floor of an enchanted forest as it so often did when he was sad.

"I'm sorry, young man. My wife has her heart set on a daughter," said little Elizabeth's new father.

Etheldred looked up at the man's kind face. He wondered why the man had bothered to follow him out into the hallway and decided that he must be a very good person. He wiped his eyes and put on a brave smile. "I understand."

The man sat next to him on the floor in his perfectly tailored suit. "What's your name? How old are you?"

"Etheldred Loidsnool," he replied, wiping his nose on his sleeve. "I'm fourteen."

The man's eyebrows narrowed. "Loidsnool? What kind of a name is that?"

Etheldred shrugged. "I wouldn't know, sir."

"Hmm," the man said, nodding and handing Etheldred his handkerchief. "Dry those tears, now."

He took it gratefully. "Thank you."

The man stuck out his hand. "F. H. Dromly," he said, introducing himself. "There's something you need to know," he added as they shook hands.

Etheldred looked up at him and wondered if the nice Mr. Dromly would also prove to be wise.

"A man must take charge of his own life. And since you're old enough to turn into a man any day now, it's *time you took charge."*

Etheldred frowned at the useless words that he presumed were to give him hope. *"How? I'm stuck here."*

"Perhaps for now. But not for long. You need to realize that you don't have to accept what life hands you. You can choose the life you want. The secret is to not give up when times are difficult. In fact, I have a challenge for you that may help. Do you think you're up for it?"

Anything would be better than the monotony of daily life in the orphanage, even if this challenge was only an adult's way to trick a child into a smile. *"Yes,"* he responded.

"Good man," Mr. Dromly said. He reached into his pocket and pulled out ten pounds. *"Use this to make your fortune,"* he said, handing it to Etheldred. *"Everyone must start somewhere, and every man must have a plan for his future. See how far this'll take you. Make wise choices."*

"Thank you, sir! I will," Etheldred said as he took the money with gratitude. His excitement suddenly faded as he realized he had no idea what to do with it. *"Do you have any advice on how best to spend it?"*

"You'll need better clothes," Mr. Dromly said. *"You'll likely start an apprenticeship soon. No one would want you for anything but menial labor in the rag-and-bone worthy attire you're donning now. But you're too smart to settle for something menial, aren't you?"* he asked, pointing to the poetry book Etheldred clutched in his hands. *"You could put it in the bank and let it grow. Earn some interest and use that to get shoes and a hat, too. Put it toward a flat. Put it toward higher education. Step out with your future wife—show her a night she'll never forget. The possibilities are endless. If you make wise choices, you can have anything you want. What does your heart desire, Loidsnool?"*

Etheldred smiled. His heart desired so many things.

"I want to see the poetry in everything. I want to love a beautiful woman. I want to study the stories that are unseen."

"Unseen stories? Do you mean the metaphysical or something more like archeology?"

"Yes!" Etheldred said, *not knowing what either word meant, but suddenly having the desire to know everything. "I want knowledge. I want power." His eyes narrowed as he thought about the boys who'd laughed at his tears. "I want to be feared."*

"Those who are feared are powerful," Mr. Dromly agreed, *"but I promise being respected and idolized is far better than being feared."*

"Then I want all of it."

"And so you shall have it by making good choices. Taking control of your own life. Perhaps getting a better name will do also."

"What are you doing on the floor?!" cried Mrs. Dromly as she stepped out of the office with little Elizabeth.

Mr. Dromly stood and extended his hand to Etheldred. After helping him up, they shook hands again. *"Good luck to you, lad."*

"Thank you, sir."

"I'm going home," bragged little Elizabeth. *"I get to live in a house."*

"And it's time for us to be off," said Mrs. Dromly. *"You,"* she said, pointing at Etheldred. *"Be a good boy and bring my daughter's suitcase."*

Being pushed around wasn't in Etheldred's life plan anymore, but Mr. Dromly had been so kind to him, he couldn't think of any other way to repay him. He dragged the suitcase outside and placed it in the trunk of their car while the Dromly's finished the last of their business with the administrator. Little Elizabeth was going home and he...

Etheldred looked over his shoulder at the orphanage

door and was sickened by the thought of walking back through it. A man must take charge of his own life, Mr. Dromly had said. Etheldred had his book of poetry and ten pounds in his pocket. He decided that was enough to start over. His feet started walking.

After a few minutes of hurrying down the road in the direction of the rest of his life, a car pulled up beside him.

"Oh! What is that boy doing in the road?" Mrs. Dromly demanded, her voice carrying out the car's window.

"He needs to go back to the orphanage," added little Elizabeth.

"Loidsnool! What is the meaning of this?"

"I'm taking your advice, sir, and changing my life." He wrapped his arms around himself as the winter wind gusted.

Mr. Dromly frowned. "I don't recall telling you to run away," he said.

"I don't want to stay at the orphanage. I've decided to join the Merchant Navy," Etheldred explained. "I want to go somewhere far away." He left out his plans to jump ship once he got to wherever far away was.

"I suppose I did say you'll be a man any day now. Why not today?" Mr. Dromly said. "However, I must inform you that if you plan to enlist in the Merchant Navy, you're headed in the wrong direction."

"Oh. Thank you, sir." Etheldred turned around and began walking in the opposite direction.

"Do you know where to go? Have you ever left the orphanage grounds before?" Mr. Dromly called out.

"No, sir," Etheldred replied, a bit embarrassed at not being prepared. He shivered in the cold.

"Wait a moment," Mr. Dromly ordered. He stopped the car and got out. Reaching in to the backseat, he pulled out a long, black cape and placed it around Etheldred's shoulders. He buttoned the top two buttons *on the cape. "I was going to get rid of this. It hasn't been fashionable for a decade, but it'll keep you warm."*

Etheldred admired the coziness of the garment that almost felt like a hug. Or at least what he imagined a hug felt like as he'd never before experienced one. "Thank you, sir."

"Now, get in the car. I'll drive you."

Etheldred gratefully accepted the ride. He tried to listen to what Mr. Dromly was saying about him possibly being made a deck boy. But his mind was racing with what his future might look like, and his stomach was full of nerves.

After Mr. Dromly dropped him off in front of a building by the docks, Etheldred waved at him. "Goodbye and thank you again!" he yelled over his shoulder as he began to run. He could hear Mr. Dromly calling after him with words he'd never forget.

"Go forth, Loidsnool! Write your own story!"

Yes, *thought Etheldred.* I will write my own story. I've already started. *He pulled open the door to the building and entered, his nerves having turned into excitement. "I'm here to enlist," he told the man behind the desk.*

"Your name?" the man behind the desk asked.

Find a better name, *Mr. Dromly had told him. He said the first name that came to mind. "F. H. Dromly."*

"I need your full given name, young man."

Etheldred wondered what the F stood for in Mr. Dromly's name. He imagined it would be something sophisticated. Something respectable. Something that sounded strong. "Frederick," he said. "My name is Frederick Dromly."

"Eureka!" Fred cried, smiling with excitement at his epiphany as well as with amusement at how silly it sounded to say the word eureka out loud. He laughed with glee. "Destiny showed me how it works that day. I was simultaneously Etheldred Loidsnool and Frederick

Dromly. Two different people, yet the same. To become more like one than the other was not a change but a degree of adoption of traits from opposite ends of my personality. Mr. Dromly was half wrong. You do need to accept what life gives you. But he was also half right. You can decide what you want your life to be. Destiny is fated but also a choice. Destiny is a paradox," he told the bed leg, holding it above his head in victory. "I know what the Plate of Destiny says! Or rather, more importantly, what it doesn't say!"

Rummaging through the hotel desk drawer, he found stationery and a pen. "So what'll I do next? Turn down the traits of Frederick Dromly and turn up the traits of Etheldred Loidsnool. How? By giving humility an honest try. Attempting to make things right and dropping the need for idolization. Why? Because it's not too late for me, and I can finally follow my destiny." Sitting at the desk, he took some time to compose a letter and make a phone call. Then he stood up, grabbed his keys, cane, and cape, and walked out the door.

"WHAT ARE YOU DOING, GRANDPA?" SELINA asked Charlie as she stepped out of her bedroom. She stared at him as he walked back and forth, mumbling to himself.

"Nothing." He stopped pacing and cleared his throat. "What's wrong with your eyes? They're red and puffy."

"I've been crying."

He ignored her last statement. "Did you get the Armor Jewelry yet? We need a working set to get to the Plate."

"I know." She hung her head in shame, hating herself for her actions the night before. "And I feel awful about it, but I already swiped Anise's room key last night. You should know I hid in her closet sobbing silently until she fell asleep. She had the amulet around her neck so it was tricky to switch it out with your replica, but I got it. The rest of the Jewelry is still in her safe. Once I found the combination, I didn't have time to open it. She started stirring and was about to wake up. I had to leave." She reached into her bag and handed Anise's amulet to Charlie. "Wash this and charge it in the sunny window."

"Excellent job!" he praised. He stared at the amulet, turning it over in his hand.

"I want you to know I hate this. *Hate* this! I get that you're desperate, but Anise is my friend." Selina frowned at him and sat in a chair with her arms crossed. "And I'm your granddaughter! How could you blackmail me like that?"

He continued to admire the amulet. "I appreciate your help, Selina. I couldn't do this without you."

Flames of anger made her insides burn. He didn't seem remorseful at all. What happened to her sweet, loving grandpa? "Where did you get those replicas anyway?"

"I hired a Jewelry maker. Are you going to get the rest of the Jewelry now?"

Selina thought about her friend who hadn't even left for Springfield yet to pick up her dog. "I'm going to try. For Opal's life. And then I don't want you to ask me to do anything else like this ever again! And I want you to give Anise her Jewelry back after we find the Plate!"

Charlie grunted. "Fine."

"You know, I'm sure she's noticed that she lost her key by now and got a new one which would mean this one doesn't work anymore," she said, frowning at the key card she held in her hand. "I'm probably going to have to find another way in. So I'll be back as soon as I can...I just need a reason as to why I'm going over there."

"One of their group just died." Charlie sat on the couch, unable to take his eyes off the amulet.

"Yeah, I heard about Kent."

"No, the woman."

"Lorelei died too?!" Selina sat up straight.

Charlie nodded.

"Oh my god! What's going on?"

"Can you use it to your advantage or not?"

Her jaw dropped in horror. "That's so low, Grandpa! Please don't ask me to do that."

"We don't have time for this, Selina. Just do it," he responded gruffly.

"She was Nate's *mother*! I can't do that!"

"You know what'll happen if you don't."

She looked in his sad eyes. All he wanted was his wife back, and it was making him desperate. That part she understood. But being willing to devastate his granddaughter by killing her beloved pet? What had changed in him so drastically? There was more to this story, but she knew she didn't have time to figure it out. She hung her head in defeat. "Okay, I'll get the Jewelry." Agreeing to his demands made her feel sick.

"Be careful," he called out after her as she headed toward the door.

Stepping into the hallway, Selina closed the door behind her and ran right into Fred Dromly.

"Hello, Dr. Hanlon," he greeted her.

"What the hell are you doing here?" She snapped, staring down at the old man who was a couple inches shorter than she was and glared at the top of his bald head.

"I'm here to speak with your grandfather. Is he here?"

"You have some nerve showing up here after what you did!"

"It's really inconsequential now that the map is online, isn't it? Or is it the credit for the find that you wanted?"

"I'm not talking about the stupid map! You killed my grandmother!"

Dr. Dromly raised an eyebrow. "Is that what he told you? My dear young friend, let me remind you that affection and the trustworthiness of the object of said affection do not always correlate."

"How dare you?! He's been nothing but good to me my whole life!" Selina shot back. "I can trust my grandfather!" The words had been automatic but left a bitter taste in her mouth. They would've been true a day ago, but now...

"Have you ever heard about the time I smoked with a high ranking royal?" Dr. Dromly asked her. "We were in his palace, and I was showing him what I'd been able to excavate from his lands. He seemed pleased and invited me to dine with him and share a smoke afterward. I was excited to accept this honor of spending time with him. I told him how happy the university would be and how we intended to display the fine objects for our students. I was so proud of myself and my accomplishments and so enraptured by the kindness and attention of this royal. I thought it was flavored tobacco he'd given me, but before I knew it, I woke up in the middle of the deserted wilderness not knowing where I was. He'd stolen what I'd excavated and left me for dead."

Selina glared at him for wasting her time. "You know, I used to really look up to you and your sense of adventure. But it's all a bunch of bullshit, isn't it? What is up with you and your campy stories?"

Dr. Dromly looked hurt. "I'm a teacher. My students are far more likely to remember lessons delivered to them in the form of a 'campy story' as you put it. Especially when every word of them is true."

"So what's the lesson?" Selina asked, still annoyed.

"The lesson is that you should always know what's in the pipe before you start smoking."

She stared blankly at him.

"In other words, a true scientist would do her research and not just take someone for their word. Not even their grandfather."

"Whatever. I don't have time for your head games, old man." Selina stormed off.

***

FRED TURNED HIS ATTENTION BACK TO his mission and tapped on the door.

Charlie opened it and looked both stunned and enraged. "I've been trying to kill you for decades, and you mock me by coming to my door?"

"We need to talk," Fred began. "May I come in?"

Charlie took his phone out of his pocket and sent a quick text. "Sure, Freddie. What bullshit do you have to say to me?"

"Thank you for your willingness to hear me out. Frankly, I thought you'd slam the door in my face or try to shoot me again."

"Did you now?"

Charlie's eerily serene tone worried Fred, but he was determined to make his point. "You see, Charlie, I've had an epiphany."

"Oh?"

"Yes! We're old! Isn't that beautiful?"

Charlie stared at Fred for a moment before replying. "I don't follow."

"What I mean is I've been unsavory."

"I thought I already made that clear."

Fred sighed in frustration at not being understood. "I'm trying to say that I'm sorry for antagonizing you all those years. My reasons for doing so should never have existed in the first place. I should be at home with Helen and Kent right now."

"They're both dead, Freddie."

Fred sat on Charlie's sofa, tears forming in his eyes. "I know. And it's my fault."

"Dot's death was your fault, too." Charlie glared at him.

Fred thought about Dot Masser. He thought about Thomas Brevain. He thought about the redheaded women and Morty's brainwashed co-workers that had been lost along the way. "Old age brings such sight. Such powerful revelations. Why couldn't I have been older when I was young?"

Charlie narrowed his brow as his look of confusion grew.

"You know, Charlie, guilt is a flesh-eating parasite of our own making. A fascinating entity that we have complete control over, but we choose to allow it to devour us. Why do you suppose that is?"

Charlie shook his head at Fred.

Fred stood up. "I came here to offer my most humble apology to you. There is no expectation of forgiveness; I just wanted to let you know how sorry I am."

"I had a revelation too," Charlie told him.

"You did?"

Charlie nodded. "I know why I haven't been able to kill you. I know about the Armor Jewelry and the Plate of Destiny."

"You do?" Fred wasn't sure if he should be impressed or terrified. "Then do you know what I've been working toward all these years?"

A knock at the door put a smile on Charlie's face. "I know I'll never fall for those crocodile tears. I know you want to bring back Dot. I know I'm not going to let you have anything else to do with *my* wife. I know I can't kill you because you're wearing the amulet." He opened the door. "Dave. Shawn," he greeted the two men that walked in.

"The armed men you wanted us to hire, boss," said one of the men. He pushed the door open wider and the parade of men began.

Fred watched them all file in to the room, one after another after another. He counted forty.

"I know you can't fight all of them at once, Freddie. I know you're going to try and that the amulet will run out of charge. I know I can kill you then. What I *don't* know is what would be the most painful, torturous way to do it." Charlie looked at Dave and Shawn. "Let me know when he's ready for me. I have a few things I need to pick up." He left the room.

Fred's heart pounded as he looked down at his flashing amulet.

Chapter 20

"Don't try to stop me, Grace. My mind is made up."
Grace shrugged and wondered why Morty would think she'd object to him wanting to bring Jonathan along. "I'm okay with that. As long as Nate can come too."

"All right then." Morty held the car door open for her.

Grace stood up, brushed the grass from her long, gray skirt, and grabbed her cardigan from the tombstone that had been her headboard the night before. "Let's go."

"I'm going to need a vacation when all this is over," Morty said as he started the car and drove out the cemetery gates.

"What about a blood transfusion?" Grace asked him excitedly.

"Excuse me?"

"We have to spill a lot of Anise's blood in order to read the Plate of Destiny. If we're ready with donations that match her blood type, we could start an immediate blood transfusion, and she'd be fine!"

"No!" Morty cried, slamming his hand on the steering wheel. "We are not going to harm that girl any more than we already have!"

"Then how am I supposed to read the Plate?" Grace yelled. She'd waited for decades to be this close to reading the wisdom on the Plate. She wasn't about to let Morty stop her now.

"We probably won't ever get to read it."

Grace threw her head back to laugh. "That's not an option."

"It's the only option. Unless you can figure something else out."

She looked at him with confusion. "If you don't want to read the Plate then what the hell are you doing here with me?"

"I came to make sure you didn't harm Anise and to make sure that Dromly didn't harm you. I also want to help you get the Plate like we promised each other, but I won't help you hurt anyone."

"I'd never ask you to do that, Morty. But I *will* be reading that Plate."

Morty sighed. "I ask you to please let me help you think of another way before you do anything rash," he begged her. "Please."

"I need to read that Plate, Morty, and soon! If you haven't noticed, we're not aging backward!"

"I promise we won't stop until we find a way that's safe and not harmful to Anise. But if you try to harm her in the meantime, I will stop you."

Grace crossed her arms over her chest. She was sick of all the obstacles that stood in her way of seeing the words on the Plate, and now Morty was creating another one. On the other hand, she didn't actually want to hurt Anise or anyone. Just the thought made her feel guilty. Guilt was something she hadn't felt in a long time. Grace almost didn't recognize herself. Or maybe she was finally seeing the person she actually was instead of the rage-filled monster she used to be. She'd been exactly like her father. That was the last thing she wanted. "Fine," she grumbled. "I must be getting soft in my old age."

He took her hand. "You're getting more and more beautiful with every passing day."

She rolled her eyes at him but smiled to herself.

NATE JOINED ANISE, RAINA, AND BOY Scout at breakfast in the dining room near the lobby. He folded his arms on the table and rested his head on them. Lorelei's dead body invaded his mind every time he took a breath, yet some small part of him still expected her to come downstairs and join them. Everything felt like a dream except for the headache—that felt all too real. His heavy eyes closed, and he wondered if the grief would be worse when he couldn't blame everything that hurt on the hangover.

"Do you want some breakfast?" Anise asked him. "I can make you a plate."

He shook his head which still rested on the table. "No," he said into his arms.

"At least drink some coffee," Boy Scout said. He went to pour a paper cup full of black coffee and set it in front of Nate.

"Thanks," Nate mumbled.

"Dr. Dromly's team put the map to the Plate online," Raina told him.

"Really?" Nate lifted his head to watch the video and took a sip of his coffee.

"Jonathan, a word?" came a voice from behind Nate's head.

The four of them looked up and saw Dr. Smithton standing next to their table.

"What are you doing here?" Boy Scout looked surprised and confused at the sight of his former mentor and friend.

"Grace and I heard that Dromly found the map to the Plate of Destiny," Smithton declared.

Grace joined their table and moved her chair closer in order to view the video of the map on Raina's phone.

"She found the video," Grace told Smithton.

"Why are you here?" Nate demanded. He could tell by the way Anise stiffened that she was battling anxiety. She put a hand on the amulet he knew was under her shirt. It wasn't glowing, so Grace meant her no harm, at least not at the moment. "Stay away from Anise," Nate warned his grandmother.

"I told her on the plane we'd need to work together to get the Plate." Grace pressed rewind on Raina's phone and watched the video again.

"This is Nate's grandmother," Anise explained to Raina, as if that explained anything at all. She turned her attention back to Grace. "And no, we don't. You might need me and the Jewelry to find it, but we don't need you."

"I see," Grace said with a sly smirk. "So you can read this map? You know where you need to go next?"

Anise sighed. "No. But I suppose you do?"

"Of course. Are you ready? I want to leave now. We need to collect some supplies first, and I don't want to waste any more time."

"We're not going anywhere with you," Nate snarled.

Anise put a hand on his arm to get his attention. "We have no choice but to work with her, Nate. She's right. We don't know where to find it or how to read the map."

Nate pulled Anise aside. "And you're fine with going with her? After everything? After how afraid you've been?"

Anise frowned at him. "Like I said, we have no choice. I have to find the Plate, and it has to be now. It's not like Grace will find it on her own and then share it with me later. She'll just come after me for my blood, and then I'll never get to try to bring back Erin!"

"She's going to try to get your blood as soon as we find the goddamn thing," Nate reminded her. He worried about what his grandmother's plan might be and how he'd be able to protect Anise from her.

"The Jewelry has a full charge. I'm ready to take her on." She held a hand to her stomach. "In a minute. I need a soda. And to get a new room key. I still can't find mine."

ANISE REJOINED THE OTHERS MOMENTS LATER. She'd purchased a ginger ale and took a swig. The nausea was better, but not completely gone. "I got my key."

"Did you get the Jewelry?" Grace asked her.

"No, I only have the amulet. You said we need to get supplies. I'd feel better if we kept it in the safe until we're completely ready."

"That's a good idea," Morty told her. "We know Dromly is out there somewhere and he'll be coming after you. He still doesn't know that you've already awakened Grace's seer powers."

"Ohhh," said Anise as she saw Selina walk in the front door. "I don't think Selina would be a good person to bring along," she told Grace and Morty. She wanted to be able to trust Selina since she was so helpful the night before. But she'd known about the Armor Jewelry and didn't say anything. It could mean nothing, but it didn't sit right with Anise. "I'm going to let her know we're leaving. We'll meet you outside in a minute."

Grace narrowed her eyes, but left with Morty to wait by the lobby door.

"Hi everyone. I came over as soon as I heard," Selina said as she joined them. "Nate, I am so sorry about Lorelei."

"Thanks," he mumbled without looking at her.

"Selina, I'm sorry, but we're on our way out," Anise told her.

"Oh," Selina said with a look of disappointment on her face. "Are you leaving too?" she asked Nate. "I figured you could use a distraction, and I was hoping I might be able to help."

Anise didn't like the way Selina was smiling at Nate and felt her nose wrinkle in disgust when Selina's hand reached out to him.

Nate looked down at his arm that Selina was touching. "Just what are you offering?" he asked her with his mischievous grin.

She smiled coyly up at him again. "Whatever you need. We could discuss it further in your room."

"Let's go," he said. He put an arm around Selina and led her toward the elevators.

"Hey," Jonathan said, grabbing Nate's arm as he walked by. "What the hell are you doing? We have to go."

"I'll catch up with you later," Nate replied and continued walking away.

"Hey!" Jonathan said again, louder this time. "You promised you wouldn't do that again!"

Anise wondered what that meant.

Nate shrugged. "Sorry, Boy Scout."

"You're a dick!" Jonathan told him. His gaze drifted to the ground, and he looked defeated.

Anise stood there, stunned and horrified. "What the hell just happened?!"

"He's a jerk," Raina told her, frowning in Nate and Selina's direction. "So is she. They deserve each other."

"They're going up to *my* room," Anise complained, still stunned. "They're going to be in *my* bed."

"Fuck them both," Jonathan sneered, his face crinkled in anger.

"After everything, he has no intention of helping us get the Plate. He can't catch up with us later. He doesn't know where we're going. *We* don't know where we're going." Anise didn't know if she was livid, jealous, heartbroken, or all three.

"We don't need him," Jonathan said. "Come on, we have to go."

Not feeling reassured, Anise looked at Raina.

"He can always call to find out where we are, and I'm sure he will. Grief can make people do things they normally wouldn't," Raina reminded her.

"That's true," Anise agreed, feeling a little better. "Let's go."

"OH NO!" SELINA EXCLAIMED ONCE SHE and Nate entered his room. She hoped her distress looked convincing. "I forgot my sunglasses in the lobby. Would you be a dear?"

She grew nervous by the way Nate stared at her for a couple seconds before responding. "Sure. What do they look like?"

"They're wayfarers. White frames. I think I left them on one of the end tables near where we were all standing."

He hesitated another moment but left the room.

Selina tore through the desk drawer looking for the scrap piece of paper with three numbers written on it that she had found the night before. "Here it is!" she mumbled to herself. "Now as long as no one walks in this time..." She tried the combination on the safe in the closet. It opened. Grabbing the ring, earrings, and cuff, she put them in her backpack and replaced them with the replicas. With rushing, fumbling fingers, she closed the safe and the closet door. She opened the main door, darted into the hall, and ran right into Nate.

"Going somewhere?" he asked her.

"No," she said with a slight, nervous laugh. "You were just taking so long I thought I'd come help. Did you find them?"

"No."

She shrugged. "That's okay. They were old anyway. I'll take another look for them on my way out."

"So tell me more about this distraction you're promising," he said as he put his hand on her lower back and ushered her into the room. The door slammed shut behind them.

She forced herself to smile through her shame. Anise and Jonathan must absolutely hate her. She'd never *actually* seduce the friend of a man she really liked. Or worse yet, her new friend's just-barely ex. What they must think of her. Selina felt like crying but held back her tears. "I said whatever you need, and I meant it. Did you want to talk? Or maybe go get some coffee or food?" Her guilt forced her gaze to the floor.

Nate locked the door. He stepped up to her and tilted her chin up until she couldn't help but look him in the eye. "It sounded like you were promising more than that."

She forced another smile. "I was hoping you'd be up for that. I want you to relax and let me take complete control." She reached into her backpack and pulled out a pair of fuzzy pink handcuffs she'd found at a novelty store a few blocks away. "Come here." She stepped over to the bed, beckoning him to follow, and rewarding him with a seductive glance over her shoulder when he complied.

She attached one side of the handcuffs to the bedframe. "Give me your hand," she demanded. Once he was cuffed, she could leave.

He grinned at her. "Being handcuffed isn't my thing, sweetheart," he told her. "But maybe the other way around?"

Before Selina knew what was happening, he'd enclosed her wrist in the other side of the handcuffs. This hadn't been part of her plan, and she began to worry about what she'd gotten herself into. She looked him up and down, taking in all six feet of him, the definition of his form, the otherworldly eyes, the ridiculously mesmerizing expression. *Okay.* She'd never intended to actually go through with it, but if she *needed* to in order to keep up appearances, it certainly wouldn't be the worst thing in the world. Still, there was something about him that intimidated her, and not having any control was making her uncomfortable. "Being handcuffed isn't really my thing either."

His lusty countenance quickly morphed into something almost evil as he gave her an icy blue stare. "You don't have a choice."

Fear crept up into the pit of her stomach. "This isn't funny, Nate. Throw me my backpack so I can get the key."

He picked up her backpack, set it on the desk, and unzipped the small front pocket. "You mean this key?" he asked, holding it up.

"Yes," she said with relief. She held up her wrist so he could free her.

He dropped the key on the desk.

"Nate! Are you going to give me the key or not?"

"I think you know the answer to that," he told her, pulling out her wallet, passport, and phone from the same pocket of her backpack. He dropped them on the desk.

"Red! Red!" she cried.

He gave her an annoyed look.

"Isn't that what you're supposed to say if you're uncomfortable? You know, when the game gets too intense?" she asked nervously.

"Since you're too stupid to notice, let me clear things up for you. I'm not playing your fucking game," he said calmly while he flipped through her passport. "And I wouldn't fuck you if my life depended on it."

"Let me go *right now*," she demanded, "or else I'll scream!"

"Do it," he challenged her, taking a few steps toward her. "How long do you think it would take me to silence a screaming cunt?"

Her mouth opened in horror and shock. She violently pulled on the handcuffs, but they were too sturdy for her to break. "What do you want from me?"

He stood very still and stared at her. "I want to know

what you had to do with my mother's murder."

"What?! Nothing! I just heard about it today."

"From who?"

Selina didn't want to bring her grandfather into this. She began to wonder how *he* had heard about Lorelei's death.

"From who?" Nate demanded again.

"It was on the news," she said, hoping he'd buy that.

"You're lying!" His eyes narrowed.

"I'm not!"

Nate stormed over to her and grabbed her free wrist with one hand and her neck with the other. "Do you know how my mother was killed?"

Selina shook her head, tears forming in her eyes. *What is he going to do?*

His grip tightened on her neck. "She was strangled."

"I didn't do it! I didn't do it!" she wailed, frantically trying to wriggle out of his grasp.

He released his grip and walked back to the desk while she sat on the bed and trembled, her free hand touching her throat.

"No, you didn't," he confirmed. "But you know who did."

"No, I don't! I really don't! I swear! Please let me go," she begged, tears running down her face. Nate hadn't hurt her; his grip hadn't prevented her from breathing, and her neck sustained no injuries. She felt no pain at all, as if he'd never touched her. But would that change if he searched her backpack and found out she'd stolen Anise's Armor Jewelry? "Please, Nate. Please!"

He ignored her and opened her wallet. She watched him pull out her cash, two credit cards, her hotel room key, and an Illinois driver's license.

"I have nothing to hide," she told him with a sniff as she saw him reading her license. "Selina Dorothy Hanlon. Born October 8th, 1985. I just turned thirty. Resident of Chicago."

He picked up her phone which asked for a code to unlock it. He pushed a few buttons and smirked when the phone unlocked.

"How did you do that?" she asked.

"Like I said, you're stupid. You used your birthday as your code."

"You're not going to find anything on there," she told him. She desperately tried to think of a plan to stop him before he looked in the main section of her backpack and found the Armor Jewelry. "What are you looking for?" she demanded.

"Proof that you had something to do with my mother's murder," he said. "You have a lot of selfies with Boy Scout. And you've been hanging around us since we got here. Why? What the hell do you want?"

"Jonathan and I are friends. I helped him with his research."

"You and Boy Scout just met. No one is that good of a friend to someone they've known for a day."

"Why do you call him 'Boy Scout?'"

Nate ignored her and continued searching through her phone.

"Are you going to answer me?" she snarled.

"If you really want to know, then answer my question first."

She smirked at him. "I already know why. You call him 'Boy Scout' as if it were derogatory, a way to insult him, like he's a goody-two-shoes or something, because you're jealous of him."

Nate laughed and continued scrolling through her phone.

"You think that's funny? What's *actually* funny is that calling him 'Boy Scout' is really calling him honorable, helpful, and trustworthy. Everything you're not. You think you're degrading him when you're really praising his incredible character. You're so jealous of him that you can't even call him by his real name. You want to put him down so badly to make yourself feel better, but you can't even come up with a real derogatory word to call him because there's nothing wrong with him! Now, you, on the other hand—"

"Shut up!" Nate glared at her.

"Oh! It looks like I struck a nerve! Poor little Nate. You can't live up to Jonathan so you have to resort to childish name-calling, but you can't even do that right!" Selina forced herself to laugh loudly, hoping it would anger Nate enough to forget about her backpack. "I don't know why Anise would ever put up with that. Oh wait, she's not! She dumped you, didn't she?"

Nate stared at her but stayed silent. He unzipped the main compartment of the backpack.

Shit, shit, shit! Selina continued her tirade in a last-ditch effort to keep Nate from discovering the Armor Jewelry. "You probably didn't even see it coming! You probably thought she'd be enamored with you forever, didn't you?" She laughed again. "It's such a shame how the hot guys are always so dumb."

Nate pulled out the armor ring from her backpack and put it on. He twisted the base until the carnelian stone flipped over to reveal the poisonous side. "I'm guessing you know from your research what the Armor Jewelry can do?" he asked her. "Since you're trying to steal it."

Selina felt her stomach clench. "That's a replica," she said. "I bought it online. I just wanted to show it to Jonathan."

Nate took a few steps toward her. "Why don't I believe you?"

The room started spinning, and a bead of sweat ran down her forehead. "You're...you're not going to poison me, are you?" she asked in a wavering voice.

✳✳✳

NATE GAVE SELINA AS EVIL A smirk as he could in hopes of scaring her even more. Walking to the other side of the bed while she watched in petrified silence, he yanked the phone cord out of the wall. Returning to where she was sitting, he grabbed her free wrist.

Struggling against him, she yelled, "Stop! Let me go!"

He overpowered her and managed to avoid her kicking legs to tie her wrist to the headboard. Taking a moment to intimidate her further, he made a show of lifting the ring to look at it. He looked at Selina's pleading eyes and the tears streaming down her face, but he wasn't about to show any mercy. She was too scared. She'd talk before the ring touched her skin.

"Please! No!" she cried and fainted.

Nate sighed and stuffed one of Anise's dirty socks in her mouth. "Pathetic." It could be a while before she woke up and he didn't want to wait around for that. He twisted the ring so the carnelian flipped back over to its harmless side and returned it to her backpack. Slinging it over his shoulder, he walked out, letting the door slam shut. His mother had mentioned Selina's name in the text she'd tried to send him just before her murder. The dumb blonde knew something about it, and he was determined to find out what.

"IT'S JUST YOU AND ME NOW, Freddie," Charlie said to the tied-up figure sitting on the floor of his closet. He lifted the pillowcase off of Fred's head and removed the gag. "For once, you have nothing to say? No last words?"

"I do, actually. A question."

"Oh? What's that?"

"Don't you find it ironic that you believe *me* to be the bad—" Fred's words were interrupted by a knock at the door.

Charlie stepped in the closet and covered Fred's mouth with the t-shirt he used as a gag, tying it securely around Fred's head. They heard the door key being inserted into the lock and the door opening slowly. Charlie stayed in the closet and gently closed the door, leaving it slightly ajar so he could see who had entered the room.

A young, dark-haired man set a backpack on the sofa and began looking around the room. He must've realized there had been a struggle. A lamp had been overturned, and broken glass dotted the floor. As the man looked around with a bewildered expression, Charlie quietly grabbed the hotel room's iron that hung on the wall in the closet.

"Hello?" the young man called. "Is anyone here?"

Fred let out a muffled cry for help, and the young man opened the closet door. Charlie's reflexes were quick, but the young man still managed to dodge the iron that Charlie swung at him and turned his head to scan the room as he danced around with his hands in front of his face and chest. Before Charlie could swing again, the man kicked him in the gut and bolted for the door. Holding his stomach, Charlie threw the iron like he was making a Hail Mary pass and hit his target in the back of the head. The man fell forward, his forehead hitting the front door with a thud. Charlie scowled at the motionless intruder on his floor. He was one of Selina's supposed new friends. Why was he here with Selina's backpack, and where was she? Fred's torture and death would have to wait. Charlie bound the young man's limbs with rope and shoved him in the closet with Fred before leaving to find his granddaughter.

"EXCELLENT RECOVERY, SON! YOU WERE ONLY out about three minutes. Impressive!"

"I'm used to getting hit on the head," Nate replied, wondering if he was dreaming. His eyes wanted to stay closed, but he forced them to open. "Where am I?"

"Charlie Masser's closet," the other man replied in a muffled tone.

Nate groaned from the intense headache. "Who?"

"Selina Hanlon's grandfather. You must be Nate Brevain."

Nate squinted. It was difficult to see who was speaking to him in the dark. And whoever it was sounded like he had something in his mouth not letting him speak clearly. When Nate tried to move, he found that his arms and legs had been tied and that he'd been shoved haphazardly in between a suitcase and a pile of shoes. His neck was in an awkward position, and he could detect a distinct old-man smell. "Have we met?"

"No, but my son Kent spoke very highly of you and showed me your likeness on his phone. He thought of you like the son he never had."

"Fred Dromly," Nate said, finally realizing the other man's identity. "What the hell is going on?"

"An excellent question and one we'll address shortly. But first, you must answer two of mine."

"Okay," Nate agreed, still feeling sleepy. He figured he must still be dreaming and that Dromly was a troll who was about to ask him riddles before allowing him to cross the bridge.

"First, do you have an ingenious way to free us from our captivity?" Fred asked.

"If a pocket knife is ingenious, then yes."

"Good man. And second—now listen up, this is important—can you scuba dive?"

Chapter 21

Selina sat on the bed, tears streaming down her face. Her arms hurt and her wrists were getting sore as she tried to wriggle out of the handcuffs and phone cord. When she heard someone opening the hotel room door, her heart started pounding.

"There you are!"

"Grandpa! Thank god it's you!" She sighed with relief.

Charlie hurried over to his granddaughter. "What did that boy do to you?" he asked her, anger brewing in his eyes. "Are you hurt?"

She sniffed. "He found out that I'd stolen the Armor Jewelry. He tied me up and left me here, but I'm not hurt." Hanging her head she softly added, "He has my backpack with the Jewelry."

"Don't worry," her grandfather said. "I have the backpack. The kid is locked up in my closet with Fred Dromly."

"What?" Selina asked, the shock smacking her over the head. "You have people tied up in your room?! Grandpa, don't you think this is taking things way too far? You're obsessed, and it's scaring me." She looked at him, wondering why he hadn't yet untied her.

"This is something I have to do, Selina," he told her. "I think it'd be best if you stay here."

"You're not untying me? You're leaving me here?!"

Panic arose in her chest.

"It's for your own good." He turned to leave.

"Where are you going?!"

"My men have been tracking your friends. They've been picking up supplies. They're on their way to the Plate of Destiny, and I'll follow them the whole way there."

"Men? You have men?" Selina desperately struggled against her bindings. "What does that even mean? What are you going to do when you catch up to them?"

"I'll come back for you as soon as I can." He walked out despite her protests.

More tears started flowing, and she began yelling as loudly as she could. "Help! Somebody help me!"

✳✳✳

"THANK YOU SO MUCH," SELINA SAID to the maid, her cheeks burning with embarrassment at what she must be thinking at seeing the pink handcuffs. She offered her the biggest bills she had. "Please don't tell anyone about this." Grabbing her phone, wallet, and passport that Nate had left on the desk, as well the keys to Nate's motorcycle, she ran out of the hotel.

"Now to crawl into a hole and die. Or go to the airport and fly home as soon as possible," she said to herself as she mounted the motorcycle and played around with it until she figured out how to start it. She paused for a minute, but she wouldn't let her fear get the better of her. "How hard could this actually be?" she wondered. After stalling several times, she unwittingly took off at top speed and leaned hard to avoid hitting any of the parked cars. The motorcycle fell to the ground and slid on its side until a lamppost stopped it.

Selina groaned and crawled out from under the bike. Her clothes had torn, and she was grateful that she only had some scrapes on her arm, leg, and face. They were starting to bleed, but it wasn't anything concerning. As quickly as she could, she hobbled the several blocks to the café where she and Jonathan had had lunch.

After cleaning herself up, she sat and ordered some food. She used her phone to book a flight to Chicago. Since it didn't leave for six hours, she found her thoughts wandering back to her encounter with Fred Dromly outside her hotel room and how he'd recommended she not blindly take her grandfather's word. Images of her grandfather leaving her tied up in Nate's room and how he'd have willingly killed her dog if he felt it necessary entered her mind as well. "Okay, Dr. Dromly. I'll do my research." She picked up her phone again and created an account on a website where she could look at old newspapers. "Let's see what my grandfather doesn't want me to know."

ANISE STEPPED OFF THE ELEVATOR AND headed down the hallway toward her room. Purchasing scuba diving equipment with Grace and Dr. Smithton hadn't been as harrowing as she'd thought. They seemed to know what they were doing, and it gave her some hope that with them, she'd actually find the Plate of Destiny.

Anise paused in front of her door as her palm hovered over the handle. With any luck, Nate and Selina would be done doing whatever it was they were doing. She let herself in and was relieved to find the room empty. Then her relief turned to anger. If Nate wasn't in the room with Selina, where the hell was he, and why hadn't he called to find out where they're going?

She turned the dial on the safe and grabbed the Armor Jewelry. Spying something pink she didn't recognize out of the corner of her eye, she walked over to the bed. It had been made and everything looked clean.

The maid must've already been in. Turning her attention to the nightstand where the pink thing had been placed, disgust overtook her entire being. "Ugh," she said to the fuzzy, pink handcuffs. She picked them up using a towel so she wouldn't have to touch them directly and dropped them into the trash can.

THIS IS WHO EVERYONE'S AFRAID OF? Nate thought, finding it hard to believe. Dromly was tiny, no taller than Anise, and had a strange look in his eyes like he knew something you didn't and liked it that way. "I'm not going anywhere with you," Nate proclaimed defiantly, wondering why Dromly would want his company anyway.

"That's your choice to make," Fred told him as they exited Charlie's room and headed toward the elevator. "But I'd rethink it if I were you."

"Why should I?"

"Because I'm going to get the Plate of Destiny right now. When I arrive at the Gulf of Mexico, Anise, Grace, and Morty will be waiting there."

"And?"

"And I'll be there to offer my assistance, same as you." Fred stepped into the elevator and pressed the button for the lobby.

Nate stepped in with him. "And by 'assistance' you mean using them to find the Plate for yourself."

Fred shook his head. "Not at all. I'll be there to help only."

Nate furrowed his brow in confusion. "So all this time..."

"All this time I've wanted the Plate for myself. Now I don't. Like I told Charlie, I had an epiphany. The beautiful part about aging is, if you'll let it, it'll bring you inspirational flashes of wisdom." His eyes sparkled.

Nate stared at Dromly. The old man might be losing his mind.

Fred gave him a knowing glance. "Have you spent any time in a dumpster?"

Nate narrowed his brows again. On second thought, maybe his mind was already lost. He humored the old man anyway as he recalled the time Anise's ex threw him out like a sack of garbage. "Yeah, actually I have. Why?"

"Wonderful! Perhaps you can relate. Did Kent ever tell you about the time I found myself in a dumpster? The second time, mind you, not the first."

"No."

"I'm so grateful for the experience. It was back during my Army days when I was still very young and learning much about the world. Do you know what I found in there?"

"What?"

"Trash!" Dromly gave Nate an excited smile.

Nate raised an eyebrow. "Good for you."

"You don't understand." The doors opened with a ding. Dromly stepped out of the elevator and started making his way toward the lobby. He stopped and turned around so suddenly that Nate almost walked right in to him. The small, old man looked up at him. "Let me put it this way. Did you climb in voluntarily, or were you thrown in against your will?"

Nate wasn't sure why he was still humoring this old crack pot. "Thrown in."

"Perfect. It was the same for me." He walked past the reception desk with Nate next to him. "I don't know about you, but I deserved it."

"So did I," Nate admitted.

"Then you do understand?"

"Understand what?" Nate wondered why he had let himself get so invested in this stupid story. For some reason, he was interested in whatever point this old man was going to make. He followed Dromly into the parking lot.

"Think about it. What is trash? Something that's unwanted and deemed useless. By throwing you in a dumpster, someone assigned you those adjectives, and you accepted them. Even now, you're still agreeing to it. You became the trash. You looked awful, felt awful, and likely smelled awful as well. My dumpster was next to a fish market. I had a feral cat following me for a mile afterward. But I digress."

"Is there a point?" Nate asked in annoyance.

"Yes. I know you don't believe it's possible that I had a change of heart about the Plate. But the message of the dumpster is clear. It shows you where you are in your life. One minute you're doing what you think is going to be right for you. The next minute, you're enveloped in waste, agreeing that you belong there. *Reality* and *perception* can change from one moment to the next."

"Maybe so," Nate agreed. "But it's more probable that you're a manipulative piece of shit. Why do you care if I come with you? What's it to you?" He looked toward his own hotel's parking lot and squinted to try to sharpen his vision. Was that his bike wrapped around a lamppost? *Shit.*

Dromly looked up at Nate. "Your anger bursts from your eyes like a geyser, much like your grandfather Thomas," Dromly said. "But you're very different from him. Thomas hated me, and I don't blame him. But his one and only motive was revenge. You're better than that. You have more in common with Grace, but you're better than she is, too. This I know."

Nate looked at the small man and started to feel like he was floating outside of his body which happened anytime someone compared him to Grace.

"I know because both of your grandparents would've left me tied up in Masser's closet," Dromly continued. "But you freed me without thinking twice about it." He beamed at Nate. "Not to mention Kent cared for you. He would want me to help you. Charlie Masser is a murderer who wants the Plate, and I will join you and your friends in stopping him."

Nate stopped listening to the old man as he thought about how Masser must be on his way to wherever Anise was going. He'd need transportation to find Anise now that his bike was destroyed. He saw the rental car in the parking lot, but Kent was the last one to hold the keys. They no longer had Kent's room and he didn't remember seeing any keys when he was getting Kent's things together. Where would the keys be? He looked down when he felt Dromly grab his arm.

"I understand we're at an impasse of sorts. There're many things I need to do before it's too late. I need to help find the Plate for Ms. Viston. I need to impart wisdom to you that I should have given to Kent. But you don't believe me and understandably so. I want to give you something as a measure of good faith. Perhaps if I give something, then you will give something, and we can learn to trust one another." Dromly handed Nate his car keys. "Anise, Grace, and Morty are at the Gulf of Mexico. Why don't you drive us there?"

Nate took the keys, wondering what kind of a game Dromly was trying to play.

"The ball is now in your court," Dromly continued. "You can steal my car. You can drive me to a remote location and abandon me there, leaving my fate to the elements. Or you can take a chance and offer me something in return. Offer me a ride and listen to what I have to tell you. So, what'll it be?"

Nate looked at Dromly and then at the keys in his hand.

FRED SIGHED AS HE STOOD IN the parking lot watching

Nate drive off. It was going to be harder than he thought to get someone to listen to the wisdom he needed to impart. He pulled his phone out of his pocket. "George, I need a ride."

***

"SO WHERE EXACTLY ARE WE GOING?" Jonathan asked from the backseat with Anise to his left and Raina to his right. As intimidating as being in the same car as Dr. S. and Grace was, he couldn't wait to find out more about the Plate of Destiny.

"The coast," Morty replied from the driver's seat.

"How do you know the Plate's there?" Anise asked. "The map didn't look like much of a map to me."

"That's because it's not a geographical map," Grace replied. "It's a timeline of Wilhelm Schwartz's life."

"How so?" Jonathan asked, pulling up the video of the map on his phone and pausing it.

"Schwartz began as an archeologist in Germany," Grace said. "On the map, you'll see a picture of a cave with a 'D' in it."

"I found it!" Jonathan said, getting excited. "So that represents the time in his life that he was an archaeologist in Germany?"

"Yes," Grace told him. "The 'D' is for Deutschland. He also found the Armor Jewelry, the Plate of Destiny, and then sailed to the United States."

"Found Armor Jewelry, found Plate, sailed to U.S.," Jonathan said, moving his finger over the map on his screen. "The pictures that represent these events plus the cave with the 'D' in it form an 'X' pattern on the map when I trace it with my finger."

"Very good," Grace said.

Jonathan looked over when Anise's phone rang. "It's Nate," she mumbled with a look of disgust, muted her phone, and put it away.

Jonathan followed along as Grace led him through the other events in Schwartz's life that led to him hiding the Plate. Every group of four events were laid out chronologically in an 'X' shape on the map.

"The last pictures show that he found hiding places for the Armor Jewelry and the seer's wand, and that he disguised the first map as ancient cave art," she concluded.

"Okay, but wait," Jonathan said. "That doesn't complete the last 'X' pattern. There are only three points on the last 'X.'" He looked at his ringing phone and also muted it when he saw that it was Nate.

"Are there?" Morty challenged him. "If there was a last point on the 'X,' where would it be?"

"I'm not sure," Jonathan said. "It should be here where all these caves are, but the picture for where his ship docked is in the way." Then he understood. "The Plate is in one of these caves by the coast!"

"Yes, it is," Grace told him.

"Grace, you're a genius!" Raina exclaimed.

"That's great!" Anise said. "All we have to do is search the caves for the Plate. I should be able to see the special sheen on it with no problem because I have the Jewelry!"

"Unfortunately, it's not that simple," Morty said.

"Why not?" Jonathan asked.

"Those caves by the coast aren't on the shore," Grace explained. "They're underwater."

Raina picked up her ringing phone.

"RAINA! THANKS FOR PICKING UP. ARE you with Anise?" Nate asked frantically as he sped down the highway.

"Yes, is everything alright?"

"No, where are you?"

She explained which beach they were headed toward. "Grace and Morty know where the Plate of Destiny is."

"Is that Nate you're talking to?" Nate could hear Anise ask.

"Yes," Raina replied.

"Listen, Anise is in danger," Nate tried to explain. "Hello?" He realized he'd been hung up on. Afraid of what might happen to Anise if Charlie Masser or Dromly caught up with her, he drove as if he'd just robbed a museum.

He arrived at a clean, sandy beach and spotted Boy Scout right away. He ran as fast as he could. The Gulf of Mexico was big, beautiful, and cheerfully waved at him, but he barely noticed its existence. "Hey Bo...Jonathan," he called out, panting.

Jonathan was standing alone on the shore watching the waves. He turned in Nate's direction and glared at him. "What are you doing here?"

"Where's Anise? And the others?"

"They got a boat. The Plate is in an underwater cave... it's a long story. I never learned how to scuba dive...or swim...and I get sea sick."

"Shit."

"You know, you have a lot of nerve showing up here," Jonathan told him with a scowling face.

"Shut up," Nate told him. "Anise is in danger."

"What do you mean?"

"My mother tried to send me a text just before she was killed," Nate began, and filled Jonathan in on all the details of his encounter with Selina, her grandfather, and Fred Dromly.

Jonathan paused for a moment. "You're accusing Selina of some pretty terrible things," he snapped. He looked at the ground and a look of agony crossed his face. "Oh, shit. I remember now. I was excited to tell her about the legends of the Armor Jewelry, and I let it slip that Anise named me Jewelry engineer. Somehow Selina must've figured out the legends were real and used it against me. My kidnapping was a set-up by her and her grandfather, wasn't it? And I blamed it on you. I'm sorry. This is all my fault."

Jonathan looked so genuinely sorry that Nate didn't feel angry anymore. "Forget it," Nate said, dismissing it. "Anise won't answer my calls. Call her and tell her the Jewelry set she has is fake."

After a few tries, Jonathan put his phone back in his pocket. "She's not answering." His eyes focused on something down the beach. "Look," he said, pointing.

Nate turned to look. "It's Dromly," he said, watching a small boat leaving the shore.

"And George," Jonathan added. A group of several others were also boarding small boats and following Dromly. "They're all my former co-workers. Dr. S. told me that they'd either retired or were working on a project in Europe or Florida. But the truth is he brainwashed them and sent them to Dromly."

"Try Anise again," Nate suggested. "She needs to know Dromly's on his way."

Jonathan frowned at his phone. "She's still not picking up. Neither is Dr. S."

"Neither is Grace or Raina. I'll go find a boat." Nate put his phone in his pocket and ran toward the boat rental shops.

SELINA JUMPED OUT OF THE TAXI and headed for the water. Grateful that she'd put a tracker on her grandfather's phone ever since he got lost the year before when he visited her, she looked around for him. He was nowhere to be found, but she spotted someone else she'd been hoping to see.

"Jonathan!" Selina called out as she ran toward him.

She'd fantasized about being alone with him on a beach, but not under these circumstances.

"What do *you* want?" he asked her.

His tone told her he was upset with her, and she couldn't blame him. "Nothing happened with me and Nate," she assured him.

"I don't care about that," Jonathan snapped. "Nate's here. He told me everything."

Selina hung her head and let her tears flow. "Look, Jonathan, my grandfather lied to me. At first he said he wanted to find the Plate of Destiny to piss off Fred Dromly who'd had an affair with my grandmother years ago and then killed her by driving while drunk. I had no reason to not believe him. When I discovered that the legends of the Jewelry were true, I thought maybe if I could help him find the Plate first, he'd be able to bring back my grandmother and be happy again. But now I don't think that's all he wants." She took a tissue out of the pocket of her jeans to wipe her eyes and blow her nose. "Otherwise he wouldn't have threatened Opal when I told him I didn't want to steal the Armor Jewelry from Anise."

"So what is it that you think he wants?" Jonathan asked.

"I think he wants to kill Fred Dromly. And I think he's going to try to kill Anise."

"What do you mean?"

"My grandpa's still bent on finding the Plate. He knows he has to spill Anise's blood on it for the writing on it to appear. We need to help her!"

"You need to leave," Nate said, coming up behind them.

"Where's the boat?" Jonathan asked Nate.

"I went to every boat rental shop. They're all out. Dromly and his army got them all. We're stuck on shore."

"I want to help," Selina said. "What can I do?"

"You can leave," Nate repeated.

"No one believes you're here to help anyone but your

grandfather," Jonathan added.

"I'll prove it to you. I'll show you why I won't help him anymore." She pulled out her phone, ready to show him the newspaper articles she'd found.

"Not interested," Jonathan said.

"But please, just listen!"

"Go!" Jonathan demanded.

Her lower lip starting to quiver again, Selina turned on her heel and found a small dune to sit behind to think. Where the hell was her grandfather?

GRACE LOOKED AT THE APPROACHING WATERCRAFT from her perch on the edge of the boat. She removed her goggles and took her regulator out of her mouth. Squinting, she realized who was trying to get her attention.

"Stop!" Dromly shouted, waving his arms. "Stop!"

"I thought you'd have been long underwater by now," Morty said to Dromly as his boat pulled close.

"I...got tied up," Dromly said. He cut his engine. "But since you're all here, I have a proposition for you."

"We're not interested," Grace sneered. Dromly's arrival had created extra waves, and she held on as her boat rocked back and forth.

"I'm offering my assistance," Fred told her. "In exchange, all I want is to film this momentous occasion."

"We have everything we need to find the Plate," Grace told him. "We don't need or want your help."

"Let me put it this way," Fred replied. His army of co-workers pulled up behind him in several more boats. "Which of you knows how many caves are below these waves? Which of you knows how large each of these caves are? Which of you knows exactly which cave holds the Plate and exactly where in said cave the Plate has been residing?"

"There are several caves," Raina replied. "Many of which are very large and interconnected."

"Yes," agreed Fred. "And what about the exact location?"

"Nobody can know that from the map Wilhelm Schwartz made!" Grace snapped.

"Nobody except for you, Grace," Fred told her. He took the map out of a satchel. "I assume you've figured out how to activate your seer abilities by now. You probably also know you have to touch something to have a vision about it. Hold the map. Tell me what you see."

Grace leaned forward and snatched the stone map from his outstretched hand, careful not to drop it in the water. Her boat tilted under her weight. She felt like she was falling, saw swirling colors, and suddenly she was floating outside a three-story high underwater wall of stone. She noticed a large hole in the rock and passed through it. A short way inside, several more pathways opened up. Grace realized she had to make a choice of which one to enter, and something drew her to the largest one. Making her way through the natural doorway, she floated down the corridor. The sun didn't reach this part of the cave, but somehow, she could still see clearly down her chosen path. Grace noticed the other pathways were dark. Following the light, she entered a passageway that opened up into a large space. This great hall stretched far and had corridors leading off in every direction. She was startled to see a man in an old-fashioned diving suit with a window on his helmet in front of his face. Guessing he must be Wilhelm Schwartz, she watched what he'd do next. He held a metal box tightly in his gloves and headed down one of the corridors. Grace followed him into a room that was full of cracks and crevices in the walls.

Wilhelm looked around as if he wanted to make sure no one was watching. He appeared to look right through her. With a confident stroke of his arm and kick of his legs, he swam quickly to a far corner that lay behind a pile of rocks.

Wilhelm removed some rocks to reveal a small aperture. He placed the box inside. Grace tried to take a quick peak, but Wilhelm shoved a large rock in front of it and Grace jumped at the noise, finding herself back in the boat.

"You saw it, didn't you?" Fred asked her.

"That's none of your business!" she snarled. She wasn't about to give up the location of the Plate to Dromly.

"And you're not coming with us!" Morty added. "I've spent my life trying to protect Grace from you, and I'll be damned if I fail now!"

"Dromly's been searching for the Plate of Destiny for most of his life. He's not going to let us go on our own," Anise said, glaring at Dromly.

"That's where you're wrong," Fred told her. "If my leaving is what it takes for the Plate to be found and protected by the one person destined to have it, that's exactly what I'll do."

"How stupid do you think we are?" demanded Grace. "You killed my Thomas over this! You coerced Morty into brainwashing all his colleagues. You were ready to harvest my eyes to possess them!"

"I did *not* kill Thomas. I've never killed anyone. And when I told Morty we needed to possess your eyes, I meant for him to strike a bargain with you, not to harvest anything," Fred huffed, looking offended. "Perhaps a trade such as an agreement that we own your eyes, and in exchange we share the interpretation of the Plate with you. Or perhaps we bring back Thomas for you. Why are the opinions of those who know me best reflecting a complete misunderstanding of everything I am?"

"Save your breath, and spare us your self-pity, you candy-ass!" Grace spat.

Dromly sighed. "Regardless, I must tell you about my epiphany. You see, I realized that with destiny, there comes a truth—"

"Oh, shut up!" Grace shouted. She wondered what it would take for him to go away. "If you're going to leave, then go already!"

"How strange that truths can only be heard by those ready to listen." Fred hung his head. "Very well, I'll leave. But first, I have something for Ms. Viston."

"For me?" Anise asked, looking wary.

"I'm doing this as an act of faith, so that we can perhaps begin to trust one another." Fred took off the amulet he wore around his neck. He had attached the ring and earrings to the chain so it would all stay together. Gently, he tossed it to her. "Your Jewelry is fake," he informed her. "Currently, the real Jewelry is with Charlie Masser who is likely on his way as we speak. Be warned." He then tossed her his cuff.

"Wait," Anise said, confused. "I thought there was only one cuff."

"No," Dromly informed her. "Back in the Bronze Age, no one knew the Jewelry could be recharged when it stopped working. Therefore, several copies were made, even of the cuff. The king never wanted to be without one. So...good luck to you! Let's go, George."

"Yes, Dr. Dromly." George turned the boat and headed back to shore while the fleet of brainwashed army members followed.

"What the hell was that?" Grace asked, annoyed at the interruption.

"A trick," Morty replied. "It must've been. I know for a fact that he has at least one more set of Armor Jewelry if not more. I'm sure he's carrying it with him now."

"I don't understand," Raina said. "What would Dr. Dromly have to gain by giving Anise a set of his Armor Jewelry?"

"That's a good question," Grace said.

"My Jewelry isn't fake," Anise added. "I've had it for years. I would know."

"I can't believe that he would turn around and leave. This is the moment he's been waiting for nearly his entire life," Morty said. His brows narrowed in disbelief.

Grace watched as her old professor sailed away. What game was he trying to play? She almost let herself wonder about it when she remembered that she didn't give a shit. *Good riddance.*

Anise shoved Dromly's gift into her small, waterproof bag that was hooked to her weight belt. "Let's dive."

Once the group had submerged, Grace led the way through the winding paths of barnacle-covered stone walls. There were plenty of openings in the rocks, but none looked like the one in her vision. Morty followed closely behind her, and Anise and Raina brought up the rear. Grace marveled at the underwater scenery. Colorful fish swam with her and one nibbled at her scuba gear.

Grace's heart started pounding when she realized she recognized the cave mouth she'd just passed. Backtracking quickly, she floated through the large entrance and headed straight for the largest corridor. Morty, Anise, and Raina followed her into the great hall and down another corridor. Grace swam directly into the corner where she'd seen Wilhelm. She pointed at the pile of rocks. Wilhelm had somehow moved very large stones in front of the opening—perhaps using the strength of the Armor earrings. Morty got there first and pulled on the largest one but couldn't move it. Anise swam up and tried, but the stone still wouldn't budge.

Grace wondered why the young woman wasn't strong enough. She'd been charging the Jewelry in the car. Anise reached into her pocket and pulled out the set of Jewelry Dromly had given her. She draped the amulet over her neck, tucking it underneath her swimsuit so it wouldn't float away. Carefully, she put on the ring, earrings, and cuff. This time, she barely had to try. The rock was moved aside with what looked to be the most minimal of effort.

Grace pointed inside the aperture when she realized there wasn't just the one metal box in there but a large pile of many metal boxes. She held out her hands to ask Anise which one. There seemed to be close to a hundred of them, and they all looked exactly the same.

One by one, Anise picked them up and opened them for a closer inspection. Each one had a round metal plate inside that had developed a greenish patina from being underwater for ninety years. Morty made the signal that it was time to return to the surface. Grace, Anise, and Raina responded with the "okay" signal. Anise set down the plate she'd been inspecting and they all turned to leave. Suddenly, Anise swiveled her head over her shoulder, and her hands started digging furiously through the pile of boxes.

Morty tapped on his watch to signal they were running out of time and air. Anise refused to stop digging, however, and Raina joined her. Grace started to help as well and gave Morty a dirty look. He rolled his eyes in exasperation and helped the women.

Anise squinted and turned her head away from the box she had unearthed. Peering at it from the corner of her eye, she opened it and took out the plate that was resting inside while everyone watched her in anticipation. She held the plate in front of her with one hand and peeked at it through the fingers of her other hand. Grace wondered if this could be the Plate. *Thomas. Soon, my love.*

Like the others, this plate was made out of bronze, about a foot in diameter, and had a greenish patina. Anise made the "okay" signal, and they swam out of the cave. As soon as they had open water above their heads, they headed straight for the surface, going as quickly as possible without risking the bends.

Once at the surface, they began swimming toward their boat.

"That was a fine stunt you pulled," Morty reprimanded

Anise. "We could've run out of air."

"But we didn't; we're fine, Morty," Grace reminded him. "Is that it?" she asked Anise.

"Yes!" Anise said with an excited smile. "It's the Plate of Destiny!"

"Are you sure?" Grace asked. "It looks exactly like all the other plates we saw down there."

"I'm *so* sure!" Anise still wouldn't look directly at the Plate she held.

"How can you tell?" Grace demanded, climbing into the boat. "You've barely looked at it."

"That's because I see the sheen," Anise explained. "It's like looking at the sun!"

"Is it heavy?" Morty wanted to know.

"It feels like it's about five pounds," Anise replied.

Grace wasn't about to let this girl make the final decision on whether this was the right Plate or not. There was too much riding on this. "Your other set of Jewelry," said Grace, hoping Anise would fall for her plan. "Do you think it's fake like Dromly said?"

"Maybe it is," Anise replied. "I couldn't move the large rock until I put on the set that Dromly gave me."

"Give me the original set," Grace demanded. "The one you brought with you today. We're going to have to fight Fred off when we get to shore, and we'll need to know what resources we have."

"I'm not giving you anything," Anise said with a glare.

"I'm just going to test it to see if it works."

"I said no."

"Then *you* test it out," Grace prompted her. "Try it on."

Anise glared at her. "As soon as I take off the set Dromly gave me, you're going to snatch it."

"We don't have time for this, little girl!" Grace snapped. "Give the set you have on to someone you trust, and try on the original set." She motioned to Raina.

Anise looked toward the shore. Grace knew she

could see Dromly and his army on the beach. Judging by the look on her face, she was taking Grace's words into consideration which is what Grace was hoping for.

"Fine." Anise took off the Jewelry Dromly had given her and handed it to Raina. She put on the set she'd originally brought with her that day.

"Well?" Grace asked her.

"I don't see the sheen anymore," Anise replied. "This set doesn't work."

"That's what I thought," Grace said. In one quick motion, she pressed her fingers near Raina's neck and grabbed the Jewelry out of her hand.

Raina let out a cry of pain as Grace hurriedly put on the amulet to prevent anyone from snatching the Jewelry back.

Anise checked to make sure Raina was okay and then stood up angrily. "Give it back!" she demanded of Grace as the boat rocked back and forth from Anise's sudden movement.

"Oh!" Grace exclaimed after she looked at the Plate that Anise was gripping in her hand. An unearthly sparkle was radiating off of the Plate. The brightness was almost blinding but even the intense glow couldn't make her look away. *Soon, Thomas.* She noticed Morty frowning at her.

"What? I'll give it back," Grace assured Morty and Anise. "When we get to shore. I just needed to make sure that this was the right Plate!"

Anise sat down with a huff and looked to the quickly approaching shore. Grace saw the girl's veins pulsing in her neck.

"Remember your promise to me," Morty whispered in her ear. "Don't even think about taking Anise's blood. We'll come up with a plan together that won't involve hurting that girl."

Grace frowned back at him. "I remember," she said, annoyed.

"And you still promise?" he prompted her.

"Yes," she assured him. "Anise's blood won't touch that Plate—as long as you find me another way to read it. And you better be quick about it."

Nate and Jonathan helped pull the boat to shore.

"We found it!" Anise exclaimed to them. "We found it!"

"That's great news," an old man shouted as he bounded down the beach toward them. His rapid strides were fifteen feet each, and he reached Anise within seconds, just as Grace realized that only the Armor Jewelry could allow someone to run like that. Searching her memory, she recognized him as Dromly's brother-in-law who'd worked as Chief of Security at the university when Thomas worked there. "Charlie Masser," she said out loud, recalling his name. Dromly had just warned them about this. He'd been telling the truth all along.

In one quick motion, Charlie grabbed Anise and sliced her throat open with a knife, her life's blood pulsing from her jugular onto the Plate in her hands. He caught the Plate as she dropped it and let her limp body fall in a crumpled heap onto the sand.

Chapter 22

During the shouts and commotion that drowned out the sound of the waves, Grace gawked at Anise on the sand—pale, limp, and covered in blood.

"Grace, the Armor Jewelry. We need it," Morty told her.

"Yes," she replied, but her attention had already shifted to the Plate of Destiny. She barely felt Morty removing the Jewelry she wore. She was too busy wondering if enough blood had been spilled on the Plate for the words to show. Eyeing the Plate in Charlie's hand, her fingers itched to touch it to see if the words of wisdom would appear to her. She began making her way over to Charlie.

The young blonde woman that Grace had seen entering Anise's hotel earlier came running from behind a dune. She screamed when she saw Anise's body. "What have you done, Grandpa?" she asked Charlie in horror.

"You!" Charlie shouted to Grace as she approached him. "You're the seer." He held up the Plate of Destiny. "What do you see?" he demanded.

Now's my chance! Grace couldn't keep her eyes away from the Plate. "I have to touch it to see the words," she explained.

Charlie wiped some of the dripping blood away with

his sleeve and held the Plate a little closer to Grace. She reached out and touched it with her index finger. Golden images began to appear on the Plate that weren't there before. The gold vividly contrasted with the green patina and Grace felt herself sharply inhale in wonder.

"You see something, don't you?!" Charlie asked urgently.

"Yes," she responded. There were many wavy, curly symbols in the language of Mallandia she hadn't seen before. She snapped a picture of them with her phone since there was no way she'd be able to remember them all. Grace knew that since she was the seer, only she would be able to see them whether in person or on the photograph.

"Well? What do you see?"

She sneered at him. "You kill an innocent young girl and make demands of me? Who the hell do you think you are?"

His look of surprise was quickly replaced by a snarling face. "You better start talking if you know what's good for you! I could squash you like a bug, you decrepit old bitch!" Charlie shouted.

"Oh, I would *love* to see you try!" Grace shouted back to the man who was twice her size. Morty had removed all of her Armor Jewelry, but she didn't care. No way would she let this overstuffed gorilla speak to her that way.

Charlie reached for Grace's neck.

"Stop!" Charlie's granddaughter ordered, coming between them.

"Get out of the way, Selina," Charlie warned her.

"I won't let you hurt anyone else!" Selina shot back.

While Masser and his granddaughter squabbled amongst themselves, Grace turned toward Anise. Jonathan's flannel shirt had been wrapped around her neck in an attempt to stop the bleeding. Grace watched as Morty put his hands on Anise's neck gently and focused his attention. The cuff didn't sparkle. He looked up at

Jonathan's and Nate's distraught faces. "I'm trying to heal her with the Jewelry," said Morty. "I injected blood from Anise's mother into my arm. I wonder why isn't it working?"

Jonathan's strained voice was barely audible. "Blood cells get replaced within a couple days, Dr. S. The blood you took from Anise's mom a couple years ago isn't there anymore. The cuff can't work unless you have willing, royal blood."

Grace watched Nate's face contort in anguish as he stared at Anise's motionless body. She remembered that feeling all too well. "Jonathan's right," said Grace as she joined them. She scooped up some of Anise's blood in her hands and held it up to Morty's mouth. "You need more. I have no doubt this would be willing blood."

"Yes," agreed Morty. He turned green as he looked at the blood in Grace's hands and passed out.

"Candy-ass," she said under her breath. She had a flashback to when she was a homeless teenager. *I stayed alive by swallowing worse things*, she reminded herself. *The strong do what needs to be done.* Holding her breath, she guzzled the blood, took the Armor Jewelry off of Morty's unconscious body, and put it on. She removed the blood-soaked flannel shirt from around Anise's neck and rested her hands on the wound. "What do I do now?" she asked Jonathan.

"You have to want her to heal," Jonathan explained in a weak voice as he pushed on his glasses that were sliding down his sweat-drenched nose.

Nate stepped up to her. "Anise said it's about intention," he told Grace. "You need to will the Jewelry to help her." He dropped to his knees beside Anise, his body visibly shaking. "Come back to me," he whispered.

Come back to me. How many times had she whispered that exact phrase to the night sky when thinking of Thomas, wondering if she'd ever find the Plate of Destiny? Now she'd seen the Plate and the wisdom it had to offer. She and Thomas were going to get their second chance! Nate deserved the same. Her grandson's devastation, the way he trembled, the color draining from his face, was too much for her to take. Empathy wasn't something she'd felt for decades, but it was back now. Guilt was back too. The things she'd said and done to him, the things he felt he had to do to survive her wrath that were completely against his nature...her chest ached. Knowing she couldn't change any of that, she pushed it from her mind. The only thing she could do for him now was to give him the one thing he wanted and needed more than anything—the love of his life.

Grace focused her intent on helping Anise. It was difficult to focus purely on love, giving, and healing without any negativity popping into her mind. She was accustomed to negativity as her default state of being, but the sheer force of her determination alone was enough to amaze her as she watched Anise's neck wound close on its own while the cuff sparkled.

✳✳✳

"YOU DID IT!" JONATHAN EXCLAIMED WITH relief. When Anise didn't move, however, panic took over. "Why isn't she waking up?!" Anise was very pale, and Jonathan's fear made him think he'd lose his mind. He knelt down next to her. He glanced at Nate who was kneeling on her other side, then at Grace, hoping anyone might have an idea of what to do.

"Don't worry, she can't die," said Fred Dromly, walking briskly toward them. "I know you have my trip journals; didn't you read the legend of the curse? Since she's the only one with king's blood, she can't die until she procreates."

"She's not the only one with king's blood. She has a brother," Nate hissed with a glare so only Dr. Dromly and Jonathan heard.

"What?!" Dr. Dromly said with surprise. "Then her life force is too far gone. Even the famed Mallandian Armor Jewelry has its limits on what it can do."

"There has to be *something* we can do!" Nate cried, grabbing Anise's hand and bringing it up to his lips.

"Do you have any ideas?" Raina asked Jonathan.

"No," he choked out, feeling like he might be sick. He tried to think but was distracted by Selina yelling at her grandfather.

"Do you want to get arrested for murder?" Selina demanded of Charlie. "Go wait for me at the car. I'm going to see if I can help fix your mess."

"I'm not going anywhere until she tells me what's on this Plate!" Charlie said, pointing a finger at Grace.

"And what are you going to do when she doesn't?" Selina asked him.

"She will when I get through with her."

"Fine. But she's trying to save the life of Anise and you need to let her. What good will it do if you bring Grandma back and can only see her if she visits you in federal prison? And that's a big if. I wouldn't visit you."

"Shut up, the both of you!" Jonathan shouted over their argument. "I need to concentrate!"

"Hey, does this look like it's trying to ignite?" Nate asked, staring at Anise's hand that he held.

"What are you talking about?" Jonathan demanded.

"I thought I saw a spark from this ring," Nate replied.

"What is that?" Dr. Dromly asked, pointing to Anise's finger on the hand Nate held. "Is that a garnet?"

"Yes," Nate told him.

"Has anyone here been named a Jewelry engineer?" Dr. Dromly asked.

"I have," both Jonathan and Nate said in unison.

"Engrave that ring! Hurry!"

"I already did," Nate explained. "We wanted to see if a garnet had any powers."

"There've been many cultures with beliefs that garnets protect against injuries. The garnet can heal her." Dr. Dromly looked at Jonathan and Nate expectantly. "Put her hand on her heart!" he commanded. Nate did as he was told.

"Bend her fingers so the garnet feels her heartbeat."

Jonathan reached over to help move Anise's hand. He couldn't feel her heartbeat and hoped the garnet would have better luck. "Will this help?" he asked.

"Let's hope so."

Dr. S. groggily sat up. "Are you sure?" he said, looking doubtfully at Anise's stationary form. "The incantation is Mallandian, but that's not one of the cultures that used garnets for injuries. How can they work together?"

"Culture, nationality—this matters not," Dr. Dromly replied. "All that matters is intent."

"Nothing's happening!" Nate yelled in frustration.

"It needs a chalcedony anchor," Selina said, coming up behind them. "All the other pieces of Jewelry have a stone in the chalcedony family. Here, use my bloodstone." She offered her bloodstone ring to Dr. Dromly.

Of course! We even talked about that. Jonathan silently scolded himself. He sat back on his heels to get out of Dromly's way. *Why didn't I think of that?* He let himself start to hope again.

"You could be right," Dr. Dromly agreed. He pulled off a piece of his frayed shoelace and tied the bloodstone and garnet rings together tightly before putting both rings on Anise's finger. "I never noticed the chalcedony family presence on the Jewelry before. A brilliant observation, Dr. Hanlon."

Mere moments passed that seemed like an eternity.

"Look!" said Grace.

The garnet on the ring Anise wore emitted a soft glow. Jonathan leaned over to hover his hand over the garnet. He could feel the warmth coming from the tiny stone and entering Anise's body. Color came back into her cheeks, and her lungs expanded, taking in a deep breath of air. Her eyes fluttered and opened. She tried to speak, but only a labored sigh emerged from her lips.

"Anise!" cried Jonathan excitedly. His racing heart started to calm down.

Nate silently rested his forehead on hers.

"I'm okay," Anise told Nate, tapping his shoulder until he moved, and trying to sit up. Groaning, she relaxed back on the sand.

"You should rest," Dr. Dromly told her.

"This will help," said Dr. S., taking the set of Armor Jewelry from Grace and handing it to Anise.

She put it on. Some color came back into her cheeks immediately. "I feel it helping already."

"I told you I'd give it back," Grace said snidely.

"Looks like the girl's going to be okay," Charlie said, grabbing Grace by her shoulder-length white hair and lifting her off the ground. "Now tell me what's written on the Plate!"

Grace shrieked and kicked and punched at Charlie.

"Let her go." Dr. Dromly took a second set of Armor Jewelry out of his bag and put it on. He then took out a third set and tossed it to Dr. S.

"Let her go," Dr. S. echoed. Wearing the Armor Jewelry, he stepped up to Charlie. Dr. S. was the only one tall enough to be able to look Charlie straight in the eye. Jonathan was proud of his mentor's bravery until he remembered how angry he still was at Dr. S.

Charlie looked down at the amulet around his own neck. "Why is it flashing? What does that mean?" he asked Selina.

"It means you're going to lose this fight," she told him. "Badly. Please, put her down and come with me," she begged.

Dr. Dromly stepped closer to Charlie, and Charlie's amulet flashed quicker.

"Grandpa, trust me!"

Charlie looked at his granddaughter's terrified face. With a grunt, he hurled Grace toward the Gulf of Mexico, picked up Selina, and ran away with strides the length of school buses.

Everyone watched as Grace landed with a large splash at least fifty yards into the water. Jonathan scrambled to his feet while Dr. S. let out a noise that was a half yell and half gasp.

Raina began pushing on the beached boat toward the water. "I can't move it. It's stuck."

Dr. S. tried to assist, but the boat moved barely an inch. "The tide is withdrawing! Come on, you look strong. We need your help!" he called to Nate.

"I'm not leaving Anise," Nate replied firmly over his shoulder.

"Please! It won't take long," Dr. S. begged. "Help me push it in. I'll need help pulling Grace out of the water, too."

"Help them," Jonathan told Nate. "I'll stay with Anise."

"There's no time to waste!" Dr. S. pulled desperately on Nate's arm until he stood.

Nate frowned but turned and went with Dr. S. "I'll be right back," he promised Anise.

"I'll follow Charlie," Dr. Dromly told Anise. "I will reclaim the Plate for you."

"I'm coming with you," Anise declared, standing up. Her knees gave out, and she fell back on the sand.

Jonathan reached out to steady her. "No," he said, as Dr. Dromly hurried off without them. "You lost a lot of blood and you have to rest until your body can make more. It shouldn't be too long since you're wearing the earrings. But until then, you're going to stay right here."

"Okay," she agreed. She put her head on the sand and relaxed in a supine position with her hand on her forehead. "But I'll be fine. You could've gone with Dromly to help. Or with Dr. Smithton."

Jonathan squeezed her hand. "I wouldn't leave you."

Anise flashed her beautiful smile at him. He wanted to hold her tightly and take her away from all this, but he knew she wouldn't go.

"What happened to me?" Anise asked. "I remember a sharp pain at my throat and then I woke up feeling like shit with everyone huddled over me."

"Charlie Masser, Selina's grandfather, cut open your jugular."

Anise put a hand to her throat. "Because he needed to spill my blood on the Plate so the words would appear."

"And get this," Jonathan added. "Grace, Dr. Dromly, and Selina are the ones who saved your life."

"Really?"

He told her how the three of them had worked together. "Without each of them, I don't think you would've made it."

"That's amazing," she admitted.

Jonathan could tell by her quick breathing that she was starting to get anxious. "You wanna hear something else weird?" Jonathan said in another attempt to distract her.

"Not really. There's too much to worry about already." She sat up slowly and wiped her sandy hand on her clothes before rubbing her face.

He ignored her refusal. "Nate called me Jonathan."

Anise looked at him with her brows narrowed in disbelief. "Really? To your face?"

"Yeah! What do you think that's about?"

"I have no idea. But I don't want to talk about him."

"You should know nothing happened between Nate and Selina," Jonathan told her. "He was only trying to get information from her about Lorelei's murder. She knows something about it. And she stole your Armor Jewelry."

"Selina?!" Anise gave him a look of disbelief.

"I was shocked, too. So maybe cut him a break?"

Anise let out a small laugh. "Since when are *you* Nate's biggest fan?"

Jonathan gave her a half-shrug. "I may not like his methods. Or his way of doing...anything at all. But he wasn't trying to hurt you when he took her upstairs. I just thought you should know the truth because you were really upset about it, and I don't want you to hurt anymore."

Anise looked like she was about to say something before they were interrupted.

"Are you okay, honey?"

Anise looked over her shoulder when Nate's voice drifted up behind them. "I will be." Her gaze didn't leave his face. "You're back already? I thought you went to help Grace."

Nate's expression almost looked insulted. "No. I had to help Smithton with the boat or he wouldn't have left me alone. But I'm not leaving your side for Grace or anyone." He sat next to her, and they looked at each other.

The silence went on for a while until Jonathan decided to fill it. "Dr. Dromly went after Charlie. He says he wants to help us, but...obviously we can't trust him, right?"

Nate shook his head. "Dromly's been after the Plate for himself longer than we've been alive."

At hearing the sound of a boat, Jonathan, Anise, and Nate turned their heads toward the Gulf.

ANISE WATCHED FROM HER SEAT ON the beach as the boat returned to land.

"I'm fine," Grace insisted in between coughs when Dr. Smithton and Raina brought her ashore. Bruises were starting to form all over her arms and legs. Anise wondered how hard Grace had hit the water.

"Please?" Dr. Smithton begged Anise as he had Grace sit down on the sand. "Heal her?"

"Of course," Anise said. She put her hands on Grace's arms. The cuff sparkled as Anise willed her to heal.

Grace's coughing stopped, and she took in a deep, cleansing breath. "Your turn," she told Anise. "The garnet saved your life, but you're still not completely healed."

"I hear you played a big part in saving my life as well."

"Well, hand over the Jewelry so I can do it again. I still have your blood in my system."

"Jonathan told me all about it. Thank you, Grace." Anise gave her all four pieces of Armor Jewelry, and while the cuff sparkled, she felt her heartbeat getting stronger, her lungs taking in more oxygen, and her weakness disappearing.

Grace handed back the Armor Jewelry with the exception of the cuff. "I think I'll hold on to this," Grace said, keeping the cuff on her wrist. "Just in case you need my help again. Charlie isn't done with either of us yet."

Dr. Smithton checked his phone. "I just got a text message from Dromly. He says he and George are following Charlie who's headed west. Look, he sent a photo of the highway signs because he knew we wouldn't trust him."

"Let's go," said Nate. "I still have Dromly's car." He held up the keys.

Grace insisted that Anise, Raina, and Jonathan ride with Nate in Dromly's car. "You and I have some things to discuss," she said to Dr. Smithton, shoving him toward their car.

"And I have something I want to discuss with you," Anise said to Nate. She turned to Jonathan and Raina. "Could you two give us just a minute? We'll be right behind you."

"Of course," Raina told her.

"We have to get going," Jonathan said impatiently. "What's more important than getting the Plate?"

"We won't be long," Anise promised him.

"Here," Nate said, tossing the car keys to Jonathan.

"Pull the car around. Silver Buick." He looked at Anise intensely. "Honey, I want to explain about Selina."

"Jonathan already did," she told him as she pushed aside her hair that danced in front of her face in the sea breeze. "That's not what I wanted to talk about."

"Okay," he said while she took a pause and stared at him. "What did you want to say?"

Ignoring the butterflies that had invaded her stomach, she summoned all her courage and let her truth overtake her. "This." She grabbed his shirt with both hands, pulled him toward her, and kissed him. If he was shocked by her actions, he recovered quickly enough to kiss her back until she pulled away.

"I had some time to think while I was recovering on the beach," she explained. "You were right. I would've told Jonathan that you went to visit Grace in prison and what she told you. He would've gone to Dr. Smithton, and it would've caused big trouble for us. I know you had my best interest at heart by not telling me you visited Grace, even though you went about it the wrong way. But beyond that, I finally understand the deeper reason as to why you lied to me."

"I told you my reason—" he began.

"You did, but besides you worrying about my big mouth, the underlying reason is that you don't trust me."

"I do trust you," he said, wearing an expression of confusion.

"Nate, shut up and let me talk."

He looked at her without a word.

She took his hand, and they began walking toward the parking lot. "You don't trust me because you don't trust anyone. And I get why. The people who raised you—who were supposed to have loved you the most—betrayed you over and over again. I know something about that. I understand that when you lied to me, you were just trying to protect yourself with a method that worked for you when you lived with Grace and Dan. You lied because you didn't trust that I could still care about you if you decided to do something that I didn't like. Does that sound right?"

His head nodded gently, and his eyes looked down at the ground.

"I understand that. I tend to lie to myself about how I'm actually feeling when I'm having emotions I don't want. And when I lie to *myself*, how could I possibly expect *you* to know what I'm feeling and what I need and want? The truth is, I'm not angry with you anymore. I haven't been for a while. It was just easier to stay angry than to challenge my method of protecting myself that I've been using for as long as I remember. But I want to work on that."

"I've been trying to work on mine, too," Nate said.

"I know," she said, squeezing his hand. "I want to apologize to you for something. That night we went out after you got released from prison I practically ordered you not to see your own grandmother or else I wouldn't be your friend anymore. I shouldn't have done that."

Nate looked confused. "She tried to kill you. You had every right."

"Yes, but I mishandled the situation. I knew you wanted nothing to do with her and never had any plans to let her back in to your life. I know if it came down to me or her, you'd pick me every time. I know you'd never let her hurt me. If I had just asked you to let me know if you went to see her, or to keep me updated on her or something, which would've eased my fear just as much, would you have told me right away that you went to see her? Even though you were worried about my big mouth?"

"I would've told you *before* I went to see her."

"And if I'd explained how scared I was of her and how disruptive to my mental health it would be if you were in contact with her?"

He frowned. "I wouldn't have gone at all."

"I know," Anise said. "See, this is why I'm partly responsible. We both messed up. I should've communicated better. I also shouldn't have told you what to do or threatened to take away my affection if you didn't do what I wanted. I was just scared, and I have a bad habit of letting my fear dictate my actions. By not being completely open with you, I didn't make it easy for you to be completely open with me. But I don't want to do that anymore. I'm working on it. No good relationship of any kind ever started with an ultimatum, and I'm sorry. What should've happened was a discussion instead. We could've come up with a good solution together."

"Thank you," he said, the surprise still showing on his face. "I'm sorry too. I didn't want to keep anything from you. I don't want to have secrets from you. I only wanted to help you and protect you."

They stood where the beach met the parking lot. "I believe you. But that's not all I wanted to say. Dromly gave me a set of real Armor Jewelry before I dove for the Plate because he knew the set I had was fake. He called it an act of faith, and its purpose is to build trust. Grace and Dr. Smithton weren't impressed by it, but I have to admit that I was. I thought it was inspiring, and I want to give you an act of faith now, if you're okay with it."

She paused to take a deep breath and gather her words. "Nate, you wandering this earth without me next to you isn't something I even want to imagine. Because ultimately, when I think about our relationship, the happiness I've felt far outweighs any unhappiness we've gone though, and I'd really like to hold on to that. But if we're going to stand a chance in hell at being together, we have to have complete trust and faith in one another. That means full disclosure, especially for any decision that has the potential to affect both of us. We need to discuss things, work as a team, and make our decisions together. We need to be partners. Can you do that?"

She wanted this, so much. She just wished she knew

with more certainty that he understood how much he'd hurt her and that he wouldn't keep things from her anymore. All she could do was try though, and they were too good together to *not* try.

Nate looked at her, and she could see his hope and excitement for their future heighten as she watched his eyes getting misty.

"Yes," he said softly. "Absolutely!"

The car horn interrupted their kiss. They both turned to see that Jonathan and Raina were in the running car waiting for them.

"So, in the interest of full disclosure, I need to tell you something," Nate said, his discomfort reflecting in his voice.

Anise grabbed his hand. "It's okay," she assured him. "What is it?"

"It's about Les."

"I'm listening." They climbed into the backseat.

"I had to tell Lorelei, Kent, and Bo...Jonathan about Les."

"What do you mean you had to?" she asked.

Nate continued. "There's a curse Dromly mentioned in his trip journals that you haven't read about. The reason there aren't more descendants of your royal line is because of that curse. Only one descendant can live to procreate—and they won't die until they do. But once that happens, all blood relatives besides the parent and child die. The parent will die before any grandchildren come along. They all thought you'd be safe until you had a child, but I knew better."

Jonathan chimed in. "Nate thought Les might have had a family before he got sick and we were worried you might..."

"Drop dead at any moment?" Anise finished for him.

Jonathan looked at her in the rearview mirror as he headed toward the highway. "Well, I wasn't going to say it so morbidly, but yeah. Nate didn't want us to think you were invincible and not do everything we could to protect you when Dromly or Charlie Masser came after you."

"So I'm going to die early?" Anise said. Her stomach started to ache as she wondered how much time she had left.

Nate grabbed her hand. "I won't let that happen. We'll do everything we have to do to break that curse."

Anise squeezed his hand, still feeling disturbed.

"I'll do everything I can to help, too," Jonathan assured her. "I'm sure Dr. S. will also help."

"I don't know what you're talking about exactly," Raina added as she turned around from the front seat to look at Anise, "but count me in to help with whatever I can."

"Thank you all. I don't know what I'd do without you," Anise said gratefully to her friends. Even with the threat of an early death, their words and promises comforted her somewhat. "And thank you for telling me," she said to Nate. "And for always wanting to protect me."

"I always will."

"I love you," she told him softly.

"I love you, too."

"So cute!" Raina mouthed silently to Jonathan, smiling happily.

Jonathan gave her a small nod, turned the radio on, and kept his eyes on the road.

"WHAT'S WRONG?" MORTY ASKED AS HE tried to watch the road and her at the same time. The expression on Grace's face worried him.

"Nothing's wrong," Grace said. "But I saw the writing on the Plate. You know how to read it." She took out a pad of paper and a pen from the glove box. "Together we can know the secrets of life and death! I can finally bring

Thomas back to me!"

Morty sighed hesitantly. "I don't know how comfortable I am doing that. Who are we to know how life and death work?"

She looked up at him with horror on her face. "Morty! I've been working almost my entire life to get to this moment, and I can't do it without you! Please! I beg of you!"

Grace had never begged in her life as far as Morty could recall. He knew if he didn't help her now she'd never forgive him. Besides, he'd never forgive himself if he caused her any more pain. "Okay," he said, reluctantly voicing his agreement.

"Thank you!" she cried into his chest as she wrapped her arms around him, causing the car to swerve into oncoming traffic.

He straightened the car out quickly and wrapped one arm around her, hugging her back.

She pulled a notepad from her purse, carefully drew the symbols that she'd seen on the Plate, and showed it to him. "What does it say? Morty? What does it say?" Grace asked him frantically.

His eyes darted back and forth between the pad of paper and the windshield. "It's so simple and yet so complex," he said in wonder.

Grace rolled her eyes. "Oh, stop being so dramatic," she scolded him. "What does it say?"

"I'm not being dramatic; I'm serious," he replied. "I don't think I can explain what this says, at least not to the extent where the full meaning would come across. I've spent a lifetime studying languages, especially ancient ones, and they had words and ideas that would be foreign to people of our time. There's absolutely nothing in modern English today that can capture what the message says in these symbols you drew. What the Plate is showing is not a group of words in a sentence structure but a series of ideas or concepts that would also take a lifetime of study to understand. Furthermore, they're put together in such a way to create an entirely new and different meaning than if you thought about them separately. I've never seen anything like it. It's so beautiful."

"Whatever," Grace said, brushing away Morty's words with a wave of her hand. "Can we bring Thomas back or not?"

"I'm not sure, but—"

"What do you mean you're not sure?" cried Grace impatiently.

"I read the secrets of life, but I stopped there. It's very clear that the secrets of death are not for humans to know."

"Who the hell cares?!" Grace's wild-eyed response was almost a scream. "I have not come this far to stop now! Morty!"

"All right," he agreed softly. "Let me see the paper again."

She handed him the pad with the symbols she'd drawn.

"The dead can come back," Morty told her, his eyes slowly scanning the symbols. "But only if they haven't completed their destiny in the life they were meant to live. Whether or not Thomas completed his destiny in the time he was here is not for me to know. We also don't know where his destiny will place him, if indeed he hasn't completed it. He could reappear anywhere, and it could take a long time to find him. He could be older or younger. And he may or may not remember his old life." He looked deep into Grace's eyes, and they were looking back at him expectantly. *Anything for her.* "I don't know what result we'll get, but we can try to bring him back."

"Thank you, Morty." Grace gave him a smile.

"There's one more thing. According to the Plate, one cannot give another a second chance at fulfilling a destiny without accepting a new one for themselves."

"What does that mean?" she asked.

"When Thomas passed away, and if we assume he didn't complete his destiny before the time of his death, the destiny he was meant to fulfill was passed to someone else to complete. If he comes back to fulfill that destiny, we must accept the responsibility of taking on a second destiny as a balancing force for the changing energies and the lives we're affecting. In other words, it's not just Thomas and ourselves we're affecting by bringing him back. We're also affecting another person who has taken on the responsibility of Thomas's original destiny and is now giving it back to him. The second destinies we accept will help to balance that person's life and every action that will be changed for them as a result of what we're doing. I have absolutely no idea how that will come to manifest for us. And there's no way for us to ever know who that person is or how we're to create balance for them."

"I don't care," said Grace. "And I'm not afraid. Change can manifest however it wants to as long as Thomas can come back."

"Okay," Morty said. His doubt created worry lines across his forehead.

Grace looked at his expression. "You've done so much for me, and I love you for it. Are you okay with helping me do this?"

He was taken aback at first. It wasn't like Grace to put his feelings first, especially when she wanted something so desperately. She had come such a long way from the angry young woman he had met all those years ago. "Yes," he replied. "And I love you too."

"I know," she told him. "Thank you."

"I just have to warn you again before we do this. Thomas isn't who you thought he was."

Grace leaned back in her seat and closed her eyes. "Soon, Thomas," she said softly. "I don't care what Morty says. I know you loved me."

Chapter 23

C ome along, now. This is the place," Charlie said
over his shoulder as he stepped off the forest trail
and started walking through the trees. He hadn't
felt this excited since he was a little boy and just received
his first bike. He heard the footsteps of his granddaughter trotting after him over the brush, twigs, and fallen
leaves.

"Do you even have a plan, Grandpa?" Her voice
sounded desperate and scared.

"We wait here until Dromly and the seer arrive. We
fight, we win, we bring back your grandmother."

"And why are we in the forest?" Selina demanded.

"Your grandmother always loved the woods," Charlie told her. "And we don't want interruptions when we
bring her back. This is perfect. Remote." He looked up
at the canopy of cypress trees that pointed toward the
dusky sky. "I can't wait to see her again." For the first
time in decades, his heart felt open.

"There's no 'we' in this anymore, Grandpa," Selina
snapped at him. "I did my research and discovered the
truth. *You're* the one who killed Grandma. *You* were the
driver that hit their car. The article I read said that the
driver, a *female*, was killed and that Frederick Dromly,
the male *passenger*, went to the hospital with life-threat-

ening injuries."

"Selina—"

"I'm not done! The accident was a hit-and-run. They never found out who caused the crash."

"So why do you think it was me?" Charlie gruffed.

Selina was silent for a moment before she softly asked him, "Because you also killed my father, didn't you?"

Charlie made a show of scoffing at the notion. "Dean Hanlon died in prison."

"Yes, and you were there with him. According to the articles I read, you were incarcerated at the same prison for attempted murder! You never told me you were in prison!"

Charlie scowled and said nothing. He'd always been so proud of his highly intelligent granddaughter, but did she have to be *this* smart? It would be so much easier if she hadn't discovered all of his secrets, pulling them out from their hiding spots and announcing what she'd found to the world as if she were still a child on an Easter egg hunt.

Selina continued. "But it wasn't for killing Grandma with the car. They never caught you for that. It was for trying to kill Fred Dromly at his office at the university. You failed to kill him during the accident, and you tried and failed again in his office. Then you were arrested. It's not a stretch to believe that my father, an otherwise healthy and strong man, died by your hand when you *happened* to be at the same prison at the same time."

"Dean was a piece of shit!" Charlie grumbled over his shoulder. He stomped on the sticks that had fallen off the trees, breaking them in half as he continued deeper into the forest. Old memories stirred like a toxic soup in his gut. "The way he treated your mother, especially when she was sick...and his failure to provide for the both of you..." Even though Dean Hanlon was dead, Charlie's hatred of him wasn't. He could still picture the towheaded devil with the soulless, pale blue eyes strutting around town with suits he didn't need and a car he couldn't afford, strutting down the aisle with Charlie's innocent daughter, strutting through the prison hallways after getting caught. Always and forever strutting when his head should've been hung in shame.

"He went to prison for embezzlement. Why did he feel the need to steal money?" Selina asked.

"Because he was a piece of shit!"

"Or was it because he felt he had no other option? Like you said, my mom was sick. Medical bills can put families into huge debt. Where were you during this time?" she spat at him.

He looked at her over his shoulder. "Dot and I gave Barbara and Dean as much as we could. He spent most of it on liquor and whores. So when he was bragging to his jailbird friends about the tail he'd gotten on the side, I..."

"So you admit it?" Tears streamed down Selina's face, and her words came out in hiccupping sobs. "At least my father never killed anyone! He never tried to use me for his own gain! If what you're saying about him is true, then you're worse than he was! You never wanted the Plate of Destiny at all, did you? All you ever wanted was to kill Fred Dromly for revenge."

"That's not true!" he shouted, stopping his stride and spinning around to face her. "I also wanted to bring back your Grandma. I want to bring her back to our wedding day so we can start over. Get married and move away from Springfield so we can change everything that happened. And I didn't want Fred to do it first."

"But that's not how the Plate works!" Selina looked exasperated.

"What are you talking about?" Charlie felt his stomach growing sick with the sudden realization that he'd been had. That goddamn pipsqueak Thomas Brevain had fed him lie after lie when it came to the Plate and how it worked, and he was just finding out about it now.

Selina stood in front of him and gave him a glare. "It supposedly brings back the dead, but there's nothing in any legend that says you get to decide how and where the dead come back. And nothing about you being able to travel back in time with them. Why would you even think that?" She cocked her head at him. "And you didn't even know about the Plate's powers until I...wait. I was shocked that you immediately believed me when I told you about the powers of the Plate and the Jewelry. But that's because you already knew, isn't it?"

There was no point in trying to hide anything from Selina anymore. Charlie nodded at her.

"Why didn't you tell me?!"

"Would you have believed me?"

"Honestly...no."

Charlie laughed sadly. "No. Of course not. What sane person would? You would've locked me in a padded cell or forced medication down my throat."

"Why did you bring me here?" With tears still rolling down her face, Selina sat on a stump and looked up at the setting sun broken up by the silhouettes of the trees.

Charlie leaned his back against a tree next to her. "I needed you. I knew about the Plate of Destiny and the Armor Jewelry, but I didn't know enough, and if I was going to bring Dot back to us I'd need to know everything there was to know. You're better at research than I am. I tried but found nothing. Look at everything you found in just a few days' time. Besides, my body is old. I needed your youthful strength."

"You needed help, but you didn't need *me*."

"I always need you, Selina. You're the only light in my life."

She frowned at him. "Grandpa, you killed two people and you're waiting for your third victim to arrive. What do you expect me to do with that information?"

"You're a smart girl; you know that you have to fight for what you want in this world."

"Or you can just be grateful for what you already have. And we have each other. Please Grandpa, let's go home. Move to Chicago and live with me." She got up and took his hand, trying to pull him back toward the path to the parking lot. "Please! Let's go!"

Charlie didn't budge. "I'm so close to getting everything," he told her. "Then we'll go home. The three of us."

"This isn't you," Selina told him. Her arms crossed in front of her. "You're completely obsessed. I don't even recognize you anymore. I want my grandpa back."

Charlie wasn't in the mood for her pouting. "You're thirty now, Selina. Grow up." He began walking again, his eyes drawn to a spot about the size of two baseball diamonds that had been cleared from trees. Several short stumps dotted the ground and the dusky light was just bright enough to illuminate a picnic table near the center. The edges of the clearing were thickly lined with trees.

"I won't help you," she spat, stepping in front of him to glare at him once again.

Her light blue eyes looked just like her father's when she was angry. It was almost as if Dean was looking at him through her. Charlie shivered at the thought. "Then you best stay out of my way," he warned.

"CHARLIE IS IN THAT CLEARING," FRED whispered to his army above the singing frogs and the last bird calls of the evening as they hid behind trees. He looked at them as they nodded with glazed eyes, ready to do whatever he said. There were many people in their 60's and 70's as well as younger people that still worked for Morty at his museum. They were all heights, shapes, and sizes. All of them had many good years left. They still had time for beautiful things like love and adventure. Unless, of course, he endangered those years for his own purposes. This group didn't want the Plate of Destiny. If they weren't brainwashed, all they'd want would be to go home and live for themselves. Perhaps, like him, they had sons who felt ignored by their absences. For the first time, Fred saw them as people. He realized how many lives he had impacted, and he felt a pain in his gut. "And you're not coming with me," he told them. "Charlie and I each have a set of the Jewelry. When Anise arrives, she and I will team up to get the Plate of Destiny from him. No one gets hurt, and we all get a happily ever after. Now, off you go. Go home. Thank you for everything you've done for me." He saw almost fifty sets of eyes glaze over.

"Yes, Dr. Dromly," they whispered in unison.

Fred watched them walk away. "George."

George turned back around, his hazy eyes staring at Fred. "Yes, boss?"

"Before you go, send over the two large gentlemen that brought Morty here on the plane."

Lines formed on George's forehead. "Sorry, boss, who?"

"You know, the ones he calls Big Ears and Crooked Nose that I'd sent to escort him here. I asked them to be on standby in case I needed them again."

"Yes, Dr. Dromly."

"And you," Fred said, looking at the oak tree that loomed before him. "Wish me luck."

GRACE GOT OUT OF THE CAR and looked around. Visiting hours at the park were over. A chain hung across the trail head. Darkness was falling over the forest. The city lights shined from miles away. She joined Nate, Anise, Raina, and Jonathan as they looked at the thickly treed area before them.

"Where are they supposed to be, exactly?" Anise asked.

"Dromly didn't say," Morty replied, coming up behind Grace. "I'm texting him now to let him know we've arrived."

"We'll find them," Nate declared with confidence.

Jonathan headed toward the trailhead. "Let's go."

Grace held Morty back by the wrist as the younger people ran ahead. "Let's do this now," she said.

He gave her a look of disbelief. "No, not now! They need our help."

"I can't wait anymore!" she snapped. "It shouldn't take long, right? The Jewelry works instantaneously. Why not the Plate of Destiny?"

"They need our help," he repeated, more firmly this time.

"Thomas can help, too!" she insisted. "We'll find a quiet, secluded place in these woods, bring him back, and then find the others. You know it'll take longer to argue with me than to actually do it."

Morty sighed. "Fine."

FRED HID BEHIND A LARGE OAK and peered into the wide clearing where the last dim rays of sun shined down on Charlie's head. From the safety of the shadows, Fred made sure all four pieces of Armor Jewelry were securely in place on his body. To ensure he'd be prepared, his mind reviewed what he knew. He had a full set of Armor Jewelry, Charlie had a full set, Morty and Grace had a full set, and Anise had an amulet, ring, and earrings but no cuff. Moments earlier, he'd received a text from Morty that everyone had arrived and were on their way through the woods. He checked his watch, ready to start fighting.

Peeking through the branches once more, he saw

Charlie sitting at a lone picnic table in the middle of the clearing, his back to Fred, looking at the sun disappearing into the horizon. Selina had walked a distance away from her grandfather, her fingers constantly wiping tears from her eyes as she kept stealing glances at Charlie, heading toward him, and then turning around again to walk away.

Fred checked his watch again. *Where is Anise?* There was no time to waste, and the sense of urgency to finish Charlie was building up strongly. He decided not to wait anymore. With as much stealth as he could muster, Fred first charged on Selina, taking care to have barely audible footsteps. What little noise he did make was covered by the squawking birds singing their song of dusk. Giving her a shove at the edge of the clearing, Fred watched as she landed face first in a tuft of underbrush, screaming. The Armor Jewelry allowed him to easily overpower her and tie her limbs together with a rope he'd brought.

"Hey! Dromly, let her go! You're a dead man!" Charlie grabbed the back of Fred's collar just as he finished immobilizing Selina, and Fred felt himself being lifted off the ground. Charlie's fist flew toward his face. Charlie landed a few good punches on Fred, but he took a few to the face as well. Charlie was larger, but Fred was quicker and in better shape.

"Where are you?" Charlie called out to the sky. He smiled when two men scrambled down a nearby tree and dropped to the ground. "Shawn. Dave. It's time!" Charlie shouted excitedly.

Three against one. Fred held his own against Charlie's henchmen, concentrating on them one at a time. One push sent Dave flying into a magnolia tree, and he came rolling back down, branches tearing at his skin, and blood splattering in all directions. One kick sent Shawn flying backward, taking down Dave who had just stood back up. Seeing that Charlie was trying to free his granddaughter from her ropes, Fred leapt toward Charlie and attacked him from behind, jumping on his back and pushing him onto the forest floor.

THE TWO NEARLY NINETY-YEAR-OLD MEN FOUGHT, fists flying in the dark so quickly that they were barely visible. All Anise could see for certain through the trees were the glowing amulets that seemed to dance like fireflies with every movement. Her own jaw ached as she watched Dromly take several of Charlie's punches in a row and fall.

"Dromly needs help. I'm going in," Anise announced, as she, Nate, Jonathan, and Raina stood at the edge of the clearing watching the fight. Not giving the boys a chance to stop her, she made a beeline for the two older men.

"Right behind you," Raina told her.

Anise headed to where Dromly lay in the grass and brush, about a car's length from where Selina was struggling to free herself from ropes. Dromly's body appeared defeated with broken bones. Anise's fingers brushed her amulet. She could heal him with the Jewelry, and together they'd take down Charlie.

A light-haired man stepped in her way, making her stop dead in her tracks so suddenly that Raina collided into the back of her. He pointed a gun at Raina's head, grabbed her by the arm, and pulled her toward the picnic table where he forced her to sit. Anise turned around and saw a dark-haired man pointing a gun at Nate and Jonathan who hadn't been far behind her. *Shit!* Obviously Charlie had brought back-up.

"Look what I found in your room, Freddie!" Charlie called out as he walked toward the picnic table to hand something to his light-haired henchman. "Here, Dave. You know what to do." He then set out several camping lanterns on the table that he pulled from knapsacks.

Anise watched as Dromly winced when he sat up and squinted in the dark. In the light of the lanterns, she could see that Dave was clutching the obsidian seer's wand and was forcing Raina to hold it to her heart and her head. "That won't work!" Anise shouted. "You can't turn her into a seer!"

"Let her go, you dolt!" Dromly yelled. "She's not a redhead!"

"According to my granddaughter, all I need is a beautiful woman with hair of flame," Charlie shot back. He stepped over to Raina and grabbed her by the chin. "The beauty she has. The hair of flame she'll have soon enough." He took a clear bottle filled with an amber-colored liquid out of Dave's pack and poured it over Raina's raven hair. It dripped down her petrified expression and onto her shoulders and arms. "Flaxseed oil," he announced. "Highly flammable."

"No, Grandpa!" Selina yelled, still struggling in her ropes. "Please! She's my friend."

"Let her go!" Anise demanded. She began heading toward Raina.

"Stop her, Shawn!" Charlie commanded his dark-haired henchman.

"I wouldn't do that if I were you," Shawn warned her, still pointing his gun at Nate and Jonathan.

Anise stopped in her tracks, not sure what to do.

"For your sake, you better tell me what you see as soon as possible," Charlie informed Raina.

"No, her seer powers haven't been activated! Stop! It won't work!" Selina yelled, but it came too late. Charlie had already taken a match to Raina's hair.

Raina screamed, and Anise began running toward her. Her strides were long and quick from the strength the earrings gave her, but everything happened so fast.

"What do you see?" Charlie demanded, holding the Plate in front of Raina's face.

"Nothing!" Raina cried. She smacked her burning hair to no avail. The fire engulfed her head in flames.

Determined to not let her friend burn, Anise pushed Raina to the ground and covered the flames with damp moss and mud as quickly as possible. Raina's screams of pain were deafening.

NATE USED THE HORRIFIC DISTRACTION TO surprise Shawn by wrestling the gun out of his hands and shooting him. He aimed at Dave and shot at him as well. The bullet only grazed his arm, however, and Dave shot back. Nate shot again and planted a bullet in Dave's leg. As Dave hobbled away to hide in the trees, Nate tried to get his bearings. He saw Jonathan and Anise attempting to put out the fire that had overtaken Raina as she rolled frantically on the ground. Charlie shoved his way in between Anise and Jonathan, pulled out a revolver, and shot Raina point-blank in her charred face to silence her screams.

One.

"Move!" Nate shouted to Anise and Jonathan. He shot once at Charlie who ran and pushed over the picnic table to use as a shield.

"Those were my two best men," Charlie sneered at Nate as he hid behind the table and looked at Shawn and Dave on the ground. Charlie aimed and shot at him.

Nate ducked.

Two. Not even close.

Nate ran, hoping to lure Charlie away from Anise.

Three. Nate almost laughed when the bullet flew far over his head.

* * *

WITH JONATHAN ON HER HEELS, ANISE ran over to Dromly who still sat near the edge of the clearing, immobilized by his broken bones.

"I need to help Raina, but I don't have a cuff," Anise told Dromly once she reached him, holding out her hand in expectation.

Dromly replied, "She's dead. To save her life now, we'd need the Plate."

He's right. Her heart wanted to shatter, but that would have to wait for later. "I'm going to heal you," Anise told Dromly.

Selina was about ten feet away, struggling in her ropes, begging for help. "Anise. Jonathan! Please..."

Jonathan turned his back to her, and Anise ignored her.

"Take his cuff," Jonathan said, pointing to Dromly who was trying to breathe through his pain.

Anise put on Dromly's cuff, knelt in front of him, and put her hands on his arms, willing him to heal. They watched his bones grow back together as the cuff sparkled.

"Thank you for your act of faith," he said, looking surprised.

"You say you're on our side, so prove it," she challenged him. "We need your help."

Dromly stood. "If we're to get the Plate, we must both attack Charlie at the same time. It should be simple enough; it'll be our seven pieces of Jewelry to his four. We'll have to take out his two combatants-for-hire as well. Or possibly just one," he added, pointing to Shawn who hadn't moved. "Are you ready?"

"Yes," Anise agreed. She looked around the clearing but didn't see Charlie anywhere. She couldn't spot Nate either. "Let's go find him," she said, leading Jonathan and Dromly into the trees.

***

"WHERE WERE YOU?" SELINA DEMANDED OF Charlie as he stepped out of the woods behind her.

"That kid is fast; I couldn't catch him," Charlie replied with a snarl, speaking of Nate.

"Even with the Jewelry on? You got lost, didn't you?" Selina challenged him.

Charlie snorted. "And then I had to hide from Dromly and Anise. I need to break up their little gang so it'll be easier to take them out."

"Grandpa, please, you have the Plate. Just go and stop hurting my friends!" Selina begged Charlie as she continued to struggle against the ropes that bound her limbs. She wriggled on the ground, unable to take her eyes off of Raina's dead body still smoldering by the picnic table as her grandfather loomed over her.

Charlie flicked the Plate of Destiny with his index finger, and it answered back with a sharp metallic *thwack*. "This piece of tin is worthless without knowing what's written on it!" He bent down and pulled at one of the knots in her rope.

"What are you going to do?" Selina asked, tears running down her face. She dreaded his answer.

"I need another seer!" Charlie shouted at her. "What went wrong with your friend?" He pointed toward Raina.

Selina didn't answer. Everything was too overwhelming. When Charlie finally freed her wrists, she put her face in her hands and sobbed.

"I don't have a problem lighting everyone else on fire until I figure it out," he announced, shaking her by the shoulders. "If you want to prevent more needless deaths, start talking!"

The man glaring down at her was no longer the man who'd raised her. Something about his need to find the Plate of Destiny had changed him. Her face was wet with tears, and her pants were wet with urine. Fear forced her to open her mouth, and she stumbled over her words as her head spun. "The...the blood on the Plate needs to be fresh. The blood was...was too dry."

"Then I need more of Anise's blood!" He turned around and began walking away.

"It's not just that!" Selina shouted at his back. "A seer's powers needed to be activated, too, before she can read the Plate. And you can't do that because you don't have king's blood!" She frowned as he continued his quick, long strides. "Grandpa, did you hear me?" He didn't answer. "Grandpa!" she yelled, frantically trying to free her ankles from the ropes.

Selina saw Anise and Dromly step out of the woods and back into the clearing far to her right. "Anise! Anise, run!" She hoped Anise would run back into the trees, but she headed toward Charlie instead.

"Dave! Where are you? We need to get the Jewelry off that girl!" Charlie roared, squinting in the dark.

"I'm in a bind, boss," Dave called out.

Selina looked to her left in the direction of Dave's voice and saw Nate pointing a gun at Dave's head while Dave stood behind Jonathan with his gun pointed at Jonathan's temple. Selina turned her head to the right and saw Anise and Dromly bounding to the picnic table—straight for Charlie.

Finally managing to free herself from her ropes, Selina raced up to Dave and gave him a hard shove. She, Nate, and Jonathan all pounced on him in an attempt to pry the gun from his hands. They jumped back when he fired, giving him time to run and hide in the trees.

Selina's head swiveled back toward her grandfather. Fred and Anise landed blow after blow on him, and Fred easily took the Plate out of Charlie's hands. Selina started toward them, tripping over stumps and large tufts of grass, almost blinded by the tears that just wouldn't stop. Charlie lay perfectly still, bruised and bleeding. Anise and Fred stood over him, and Selina heard them talking.

"I won't kill him," Anise told Fred. "I won't kill anyone. I feel awful enough having hurt someone."

Selina heard footsteps behind her. She turned around and saw Dave zooming past her. Dave grabbed the Plate out of Fred's unsuspecting grip and ran.

Jonathan and Nate emerged from the trees behind Selina where they'd been searching for Dave, and Jonathan pointed at him. "There he is!" He ran after him.

Fred took the cuff from Anise and took off after Dave as well.

Anise began to follow him but turned around and stared at Raina's body.

"Anise, run!" Selina called out.

Anise dropped to her knees and sobbed into her palm.

"Anise!" Selina shouted again, running over to her. "Get away from my Grandfather! He wants more of your blood!"

Selina glanced toward Charlie and let out a cry. Her grandpa's arm was broken and bent in the wrong direction. Even though he was no longer the kind, loving grandfather she'd once known, seeing him mangled was more than she could bear. She gasped with dizzying fear and surprise when she felt a strong hand grab her and pull her backward.

NATE COCKED THE GUN HE'D TAKEN off of Shawn's motionless-but-still-breathing form. He saw Dave heading for the trees again, trying to outrun Jonathan and Dromly. Dave didn't stand a chance with that bullet in his leg, but Nate still yelled, "Call back your dog, Masser!"

Charlie pushed himself to his feet at the sound of his name. Nate stood behind Selina with an arm binding her torso and the gun to her head. She struggled, but he easily held her fast. Nate watched as Charlie let out a loud, angry yell and took aim at him. Grazing his wrist, the bullet caused the gun to fall from Nate's hand.

Four.

DROMLY HAD MADE FUN OF CHARLIE'S bad aim many annoying times. However, today, Charlie had managed to hit Raina directly in the head, and now he'd hit Nate too, almost where he'd expected. Impressed with his improving marksmanship, Charlie snarled at the young man that held his granddaughter captive. "Let her go!"

"Grandpa, stop! You could've shot *me!*" Selina yelled at him. "Let me go, Nate," she begged loudly. "If anyone can stop him from hurting Anise, it's me. Let me try!" She struggled against Nate's grip.

Charlie ignored them and looked around for Anise. *Where did the blood bag go?* Seeing her in his peripheral vision next to the dead girl, he clutched his broken arm, lunged at her, and she jumped out of the way.

"You can't stop me," Anise told him boldly. "We both have a set of the Armor Jewelry. That means all pieces cancel each other out."

"When was the last time you took a math class, little girl?" Charlie snarled. "I have four pieces and you have three." He pulled a knife out of the sheath on his belt with his good arm and swiped at her throat.

She wore a look of surprise as she barely leaned back far enough to miss the attack. "You missed me because I have something you don't—a new piece of Armor Jewelry."

What? He saw her garnet ring still attached to Selina's bloodstone ring. Cocking his head, he said, "Are you sure about that? Selina tells me the Jewelry is about intention. Was this ring made intentionally to work with the other pieces of Armor Jewelry?"

"Yes," she said confidently.

Charlie couldn't tell if she was bluffing. He scowled when he saw that Dave had somehow lost his weapons and was running from Nate who wielded Shawn's gun. Fred and Jonathan had reclaimed the Plate of Destiny from Dave. They were running back toward Anise and would be there in a matter of seconds. Everything was falling apart. He knew he'd lose if he had to fight both Anise and Freddie at the same time again. He had to get her blood *now*. Charlie lunged at Anise again and tackled her. As she tried to fight back, he easily removed her Jewelry, doing his best to ignore the excruciating pain in his arm. In their struggle, her Jewelry was dropped and got buried in the leaves, shrubs, and dirt.

"Looks like you were wrong," he sneered. "New piece of Armor Jewelry, my ass." He stood and aimed his gun at her as she scrambled backward in her seated position. *Finally. It's time to end this.*

"Stop! Grandpa!" Selina shouted. She jumped in front of him and grabbed the barrel. "Stop! I won't let you do this!"

"Selina, let go!" Charlie demanded, trying to shove her away.

FIVE.

Nate had heard Anise struggling and gave up pursuing Dave to help her. He was running toward Anise as Charlie's gun went off, and he looked up in time to see Selina take a large, wheezing breath and fall. *No!* He knew he shouldn't have let her go. He pushed himself to run even faster.

Charlie let out a scream, dropped to his knees, and held his dead, limp granddaughter in his arms.

"Let me try to save her!" Anise offered as she stood and took a few steps toward Charlie and Selina. "Just give me back my Jewelry—"

"You use her death to try to get the Jewelry from me?!" Charlie stood and pointed the gun at Anise while his finger pointed at Selina's body on the ground. "Look what you made me do!"

Anise backed away from him with her hands raised, shaking her head and saying something Nate couldn't quite hear. He aimed Shawn's gun at Charlie and pulled the trigger as he ran. Nothing happened. *Fuck!* Out of bullets.

But he was almost there. Nate continued running toward Anise as fast as he could go, unsure of how he'd save her now, but determined to do so nonetheless.

Anise continued to back away from the revolver pointed at her face, her footsteps picking up speed. Charlie hurried after her.

"Run!" Nate shouted to her as he finally reached her. He turned to wrestle the gun from Charlie's grasp but was too late.

Six.

For a moment, Nate had no idea what had happened. He then watched as Anise screamed, dropped to her knees, and looked at him, horrified. Her hand clutched her stomach.

Did Charlie shoot her in the gut? Still disoriented, Nate instinctively put his hand on his aching chest. He wouldn't be able to handle it if something happened to her. "Are you okay?" Nate asked Anise in a weak voice as her face made the most pained expression he'd ever seen.

Jonathan reached them and knelt next to Anise.

"He stepped in front of me!" Anise cried to Jonathan.

Relieved that Anise seemed to be okay, Nate wondered why his hand felt so wet. He looked down and saw that it was covered in his own blood. Only then did he realize that he was on his back on the ground.

"I'll get the Jewelry!" Jonathan shouted, already on his way.

"Damn it! Now I have to reload," Charlie muttered to himself. Nate lifted his head to watch Charlie head back to the picnic table and begin rooting through his backpack.

Out of the corner of his eye, Nate saw Dromly digging furiously with his hands through the underbrush and dirt. He dug up the set of Armor Jewelry that Charlie had removed from Anise and accidentally dropped. Fred then attacked Charlie once more. Both amulets he wore glowed as Fred flattened his opponent. Jonathan reached Fred and pointed back at Nate.

"Why did you do that?" Anise asked Nate, her tears landing on his bloody chest.

"He was going to kill you. Go, now, before he reloads," Nate said to her.

"I'm not leaving you," she told him, caressing his hair.

Something in him knew what would happen to him next. But *she* was going to be fine. That's what mattered most. Nate took her hand. His words came out in the loudest whisper he could muster. "Honey, I want you to know that you've been—"

Anise interrupted him. "Please don't say goodbye. Dromly's on his way over with the Jewelry. You're going to be fine. And Jonathan found Charlie's bullets and threw them into the leaves. He won't find them."

"Good," Nate wheezed. He felt Anise grab his hand. She put the garnet and bloodstone rings on his pinkie, and even though he felt a warmth radiating from them, fear washed over him as he gasped for air and struggled to see her as his world turned darker and darker.

"Don't be afraid. Look right here," she said softly, pointing at her eyes. "It's just you and me. No one else, nothing else matters."

He felt her stroking his hair. "Just you and me," he repeated in a whisper as he focused on her gaze and remembered when he'd said that to her the night they met. For a moment, nothing else existed.

✳✳✳

"AND HERE'S DROMLY WITH THE JEWELRY. Nate?" Anise looked at Dromly and felt her heart pounding. "He's not breathing!"

"Quickly, now," Dromly said, giving Anise a full set of Jewelry to include the cuff.

Anise fumbled as she hurried to put on the Jewelry and grabbed Nate's hand again. His eyes were closed, and he was very still. She put her face on his chest and her hands on his wound and wished harder than she had ever wished in her life for Nate to heal, to live. The cuff sparkled, and the garnet that was still on his pinkie emitted a soft, glowing heat. Nate's wound grew back together, but his eyes remained closed.

"He needs more help," Dromly said, and he put a second amulet around Anise's neck and a second ring on her finger. Taking the earrings out of his own ears, he looped the hoops around the hoops already in her piercings.

The cuff sparkled but soon stopped, which made Anise feel a panic attack coming on. The next several minutes felt like hours. No matter how much she focused on willing him back to her, he stayed still. She gasped for air and asked Dromly in a frantic wail, "Why isn't it working?!"

Dromly knelt beside her and touched two fingers to Nate's neck. He shook his head. "I'm so sorry. He's gone."

✳✳✳

GRACE COULDN'T STOP SMILING. SOON, VERY soon, she was going to see the love of her life again. Thomas. She hadn't felt excitement like this since...ever.

"Grace, are you listening to me?" Morty asked her.

"What?" she said, startled out of her daydream. She grabbed on to the nearest tree to ground herself so she could do what needed to be done.

"I said if we're going to do this, we need to hurry so we can get back to the young people. We already wasted enough time walking around in circles."

"I had to find the perfect spot. This is it. This hill protects us from anyone who might be looking for us. There's a log to sit on in case his resurrection makes him tired. And there's no mud, just clean grass."

"Yes, fine," Morty agreed, not bothering to hide his impatience. "Let's get this done now. I'll explain how it works later. For now, just trust me, and do as I say." Morty handed Grace the ring and earrings while keeping the amulet and cuff. "Fight me."

Grace was slightly alarmed by his request but did as he asked. She turned the setting of the ring counter-clockwise ninety degrees and watched the stone flip over to reveal the poisonous mix of carnelian, cinnabar, and orpiment. She pressed the stone to Morty's arm with all the strength the earrings provided her.

Morty then began giving Grace orders in an attempt to use the cuff for brainwashing. "You will listen to everything I say. You will obey every command I give you." Since the Jewelry pieces were being used against each other, they cancelled each other out and neither felt anything. "You will fight harder!" Morty said to her.

"Morty, what are we doing?" Grace asked him, getting more and more concerned. "What if the opposing energies from the Jewelry being used against itself causes destructive forces like we always feared?"

"You will keep fighting!" he commanded her in order to keep using the cuff.

"But Morty, we never found out what kind of destructive force it is. We could destroy the Jewelry, ourselves, the planet, the universe—who knows?"

"You will keep fighting!" he said again, with a look that Grace knew meant she should trust him.

"Did you read about this on the Plate?" she couldn't help but ask.

"Yes. Just trust me."

"I do."

"Now intend for Thomas to return."

"Okay," Grace agreed, thinking about her husband. "What's supposed to happ...oooh," she groaned. The world was spinning and she grabbed the tree again so she wouldn't fall. Before she could wonder what caused the sudden dizzy spell, Thomas materialized before her. She felt her jaw drop and her knees shake. She squinted at him as she grabbed a flashlight and shined it at his face. He was just how she remembered him—young, handsome, and wearing the same clothes as the day he had died. Thomas was here so his destiny must be to be by her side! She dropped the flashlight, ran to him, and threw her arms around him. "Thomas!" she exclaimed with a joy she'd thought she'd never feel again. His body felt warm, strong, and comforting.

Touching him invoked a vision. She had the sensation of falling backward which made her close her eyes and grip him tighter. A multitude of emotions flooded her senses and overwhelmed her. It was surprising how dark and heavy they were when she'd been expecting joy and love. She felt Thomas's hatred for Fred Dromly and his overwhelming need for revenge. She felt his mediocre affection for her and his infatuation with a doe-eyed, chestnut-haired trollop he called Betty. She saw the boxes, duffel bags, and briefcases full of information about the Armor Jewelry and the Plate of Destiny that he never even mentioned to her.

Her eyes flew open and she took a few steps back. "How could you?" she asked him in a weak voice as he gave her a confused expression. "My whole life, my whole everything was for you! How could you?!" she yelled.

"What did you see?" Morty asked her.

Grace spun around to answer her friend. "You were right," she said. "He never loved me." In her whole life, she'd never felt so alone. Tears threatened to spill over, but she wouldn't let herself cry. She placed a hand on her aching chest firmly so her old, broken heart wouldn't jump from her ribcage to its death. Turning back toward Thomas, she raised her other hand to slap his face as hard as she could.

She became frustrated when his head seemed to go right through her assault as if he were just a ghost. She tried again and again as Thomas stood there looking at her face as if he were trying to place how he knew her.

"Ma'am?" Thomas asked, his cobalt eyes looking disoriented.

Grace turned to Morty. "What's happening?" She gasped slightly when she saw Morty's body fading and flickering as if it were about to disappear and then saw that her arms and the rest of her body was behaving in the same way.

"I'm so sorry," Morty said. "We're on our way to our new destiny. We won't be here much longer."

"Why isn't Thomas flickering too?" she demanded.

"His destiny appears to be here. You best say your goodbyes now."

"Gladly!" she declared. She turned her gaze back on her husband. "I'm sorry I brought you back! I hope you fucking die again, and I hope it's torturous! I'd end you myself if I could!"

"Ma'am?" he asked again, narrowing his brows in confusion.

Feeling dizzy again, Grace took a step back and stumbled.

✳✳✳

THOMAS FELT STRANGE, BUT THE STRANGENESS had an odd familiarity to it. He'd felt this before. But it seemed so long ago since he'd felt anything at all. What was happening?

The old man that stood flickering in front of him caught the irate old woman and gently put her unconscious, flickering body on the ground. The old man then sat next to her, leaned against a tree, and looked up at him. "Thomas," he said.

"Yes, sir?"

"May you rot in hell."

Thomas watched the old man pass out as well. What on earth was going on? Where was he and who were these people? And how did they know his name? Crouching down, he picked up the flashlight and looked at the old woman's face. A memory flooded his mind, and he let out a loud scream.

✳✳✳

"No! No!" ANISE SHOOK HER HEAD violently as she took rapid, wheezing breaths. "I have the Jewelry! I can save him!" She put her hands on Nate's chest and began giving him healing intentions once more. The cuff wasn't sparkling at all. Anise let out a wail that came from the widely opening cracks in her soul. "Why?" She looked at Dromly with tears in her eyes.

"He was too far gone," Dromly said in a quiet tone. Lines appeared on his forehead. "I'm so sorry."

"But the Jewelry saved *me*, and my wound was worse! My entire neck was sliced open!"

"The Jewelry is losing its charge," Dromly reminded her. "Think of all it's been through since saving you on the beach today."

"Charlie will never find his bullets where I hid them!" Jonathan announced proudly as he joined Anise and Dromly. "Oh, shit," he mumbled, seeing Nate. He dropped to his knees beside Anise and held her tightly as she sobbed.

Anise soon turned from Jonathan's arms, put her head on Nate's shoulder, and stretched out on the ground. Her eyes closed as she settled in. Nate's body felt warm. Her arm wrapped around him and her hand held his. Even though they were kneeling next to her, she barely heard Jonathan and Dromly discussing what to do next.

"Charlie got up. He's running away so he must know you're stronger than he is right now because you have two sets of Jewelry to his one," said Jonathan. "Did you get the Plate from him?"

"Right here," Dromly told him, patting the bag he wore over his shoulder.

"What about his Jewelry?" Jonathan asked.

"No time. I rushed right over here before I had the chance to take it from him."

"Charlie will regroup and come after us again," Jonathan predicted. "There's no way he'll let this go."

"Yes, we must pursue him and end this once and for all." Dromly agreed.

"Anise," Jonathan said in a soft voice. "Let me help you up."

She felt Jonathan caress her shoulder. "No," Anise said, not wanting to let go of Nate's hand. She put her forehead on his. "I know what you were going to say," she whispered to him. "You have been..." There wasn't a word that was good enough. "I know exactly what you meant."

"I know you don't want to leave him. I'm sorry. But we have to, Anise," Jonathan said.

Anise began hyperventilating and squeezed Nate's hand as Jonathan gently helped her up and pulled her toward him. Disoriented and tripping over her own feet, she let out a sob as Nate's hand dropped from her own and landed with a soul-crushing thud in the dirt. She turned her head and vomited loudly.

Dromly offered her his handkerchief.

"Thank you," she said, pressing it to her mouth.

All three turned their heads at the sound of a man's scream.

"That might be Morty. Where have he and Grace been this whole time?" Dromly said.

"I have to find out!" Jonathan said. "Come on, let's go!" He disappeared into the trees in the direction of the scream.

Anise took in a sharp breath and tried to center herself. As much as she wanted to rejoin Nate on their soft bed of moss at that moment, she knew she had to do everything she could to get the Plate and prevent any more unnecessary deaths. "Please, go after Charlie," she begged Dromly as she handed back one set of Armor Jewelry. "I know the Jewelry lost most of its charge, but it's better than nothing. Jonathan and I will find Grace and Dr. Smithton, and we'll all be there soon."

"I'm at your service." Dromly removed the garnet and bloodstone rings off of Nate's pinkie and handed them to Anise before he hurried off.

Anise ran after Jonathan and turned the corner around a hill. She stopped short when she saw Jonathan standing there. There was a man with his back to them, kneeling over something in the dark, the waning crescent moon providing just enough filtered light through the trees for him to be recognizable. Anise's heart leapt into her throat. "What?!" His build, his dark hair... She ran to him. "Nate! Nate, you're alive!"

Chapter 24

Sunday, October 11, 2015

Anise stopped short when she reached Nate and looked up into his cobalt blue eyes as he stood. "Oh!" She shook her head. "I'm so sorry. You look just like my boyfriend." Tears welled up in her eyes as her chest ached. This man was not Nate, but their similarities were uncanny. He looked like he could've been Nate's brother. Overwhelmed with guilt, Anise glanced down at her amulet and thought back to the day she first received it. She'd been so happy with it then. Now she couldn't stand the sight of it. It was nothing but a reminder of everyone she'd lost.

"Do you know what happened here?" the Nate-lookalike asked her, his voice trembling. He pointed to the ground behind him.

"Oh my god. Jonathan, look." Anise pointed as well.

"Grace and Dr. S!" Jonathan inhaled sharply at the sight of the unconscious bodies of Grace and Dr. Smithton leaning against the trees. "Are they dead?" He dropped to his knees and reached out to them. "What the...?" His hand went right through them as if they weren't there.

"So it *is* her." The man kneeled next to Jonathan, his

eyes fixed on Grace's face.

"What's going on?" Anise asked the man suspiciously. "Jonathan's hand went right through them. Are they there or not? And who are you?"

The man stood up and Jonathan followed suit. "I'm Thomas Brevain," the man said. "Grace was my wife."

"The Plate actually works!" Jonathan exclaimed.

"I'm Anise Viston, and this is Jonathan Casley," Anise responded, her wonder and curiosity growing.

"Do either of you know someone named Louis Stannell?" Thomas demanded.

"Louis Stannell was my grandfather." Anise replied. "You knew him?"

Thomas gave her a big smile. "No, but that's fantastic! Thank you for all you've done. Now I just need to figure out what my new destiny is supposed to be. Do either of you know what it is?"

Anise exchanged a look of bewilderment with Jonathan. She wondered what her late grandfather had to do with all this.

"No, sorry. But...are you...um...?" Anise wasn't sure what she was trying to say. "Grace told me about you, but she said you died long ago."

"I died in Morty's office," Thomas said.

"Yes, Grace said Morty Smithton shot you," Anise said. "Then later she and Dr. Smithton seemed to think that Dr. Dromly shot you."

Thomas shook his head. "Morty didn't shoot me."

"He didn't?" Jonathan asked. "Frederick Dromly, then?"

"No," Thomas said. He stared at his hands as he moved them in front of his face.

Anise exchanged glances with Jonathan again, wondering if Thomas would tell them the whole story. While Thomas seemed to be getting his bearings, Anise took the Armor Jewelry off Grace and Dr. Smithton.

Thomas pressed on his chest. He ran his hand

through his hair just like Nate used to do. "I feel... This is how it felt to be alive. I remember!"

"What's this?" Jonathan said, picking up a piece of paper from the ground and shining the light from his phone on it. "Maybe this has something to do with what's going on. It says 'Plate of Destiny' on it, and it's followed by symbols that look like a different form of Mallandian writing. These must be the words from the Plate of Destiny! Grace must've drawn them!"

"Grace and Morty found the Plate together?" Thomas asked, a look of bafflement on his face. "Interesting. May I see the paper?"

Jonathan handed it to him.

Anise stared at Thomas as he studied Grace's markings. "Can you read it?"

"I hope so!" Thomas replied. He looked at the piece of paper in his hand and glanced back at his unconscious wife. "We always believed the Plate could bring back the dead. Knowing Grace, she would've convinced Morty to help resurrect me. At least, that was the plan. I can't believe it actually worked!"

"That was *her* life's mission," Anise confirmed. "But what do you mean 'that was the plan?'"

"It seems that your grandfather Louis Stannell and your mother ignored their copies of the letter I wrote. I'm assuming you or a sibling of yours received my letter and that you gave it to Grace like I requested."

"How did you know I have a sibling?" Anise demanded of Thomas. "Wait, the letter!" she said, not giving Thomas a chance to answer her question. She thought back to the day of her college graduation when she'd first met her brother outside her mother's house. "That's what Les had come to see me and my mother about...before he collapsed and went in the hospital."

"So you've read it?" Thomas asked.

"No."

"No?" Thomas frowned. "You should've received your

own copy from my lawyer when you turned eighteen."

Anise frowned. "I was living with my mom at the time. She'd go through my mail before giving it to me."

"Why would she do that?" Jonathan asked.

"Probably because she was hiding Les's existence from me. If she saw a letter from a lawyer's office, it probably went in the trash." Her gaze turned back to Thomas. She saw Nate in every movement of his grandfather's face, and it made her eyes well up. Ignoring her grief for the moment, she asked, "What does the letter say?"

"It explains everything about how the Armor Jewelry works and how to find the Plate of Destiny. It asks you to help Grace bring me back from the dead because you have king's blood. If you didn't read the letter, how did you and Grace find each other?"

"That's a long story," Anise sighed.

The three of them looked over at the bodies. Their forms seemed lighter and were fading in and out of focus, like they were slowly disappearing.

"Does it say why Dr. S. and Grace are...like that?" Jonathan asked Thomas. "Are they dead?"

Thomas stared at the paper with the words from the Plate. "According to this, the secrets of life work in the same way that the Armor Jewelry does. The same way that destiny does!" He motioned to Grace and Morty. "They're not dead. They're in the process of going somewhere else, and this is their leftover essence that will be gone soon. Bringing back someone who has died has an effect on the person who brought them back. Grace and Morty must be experiencing that effect. They're receiving new destinies because they brought me back. It's about a balance."

"Will they come back from wherever they are?" Jonathan asked.

"They're still somewhere on the planet living their lives. They'll only come back to their current lives if that's part of their new destiny. There's no way for us to know that though." He knelt next to Grace and stared at her face.

"I'm sorry," said Anise, kneeling next to Thomas. "Grace would be so...disappointed that her plan didn't work. She devoted her whole life to finding you."

Thomas snorted a laugh. "Disappointed, no. She was furious. Age hasn't dampened her fiery spirit."

Anise put a hand to her heart, imagining how beautiful a reunion it must've been, even though it was short. She'd give anything to see Nate for a few extra moments. "You got to talk to her?"

"Not really," he answered flatly.

"We have to help Dr. S.! How can we find them?" Jonathan asked.

Thomas looked down at Grace's writing in his hand again. "I'll finish reading the secrets of death and maybe it'll tell us something." He began mumbling to himself as his eyes scanned the piece of paper in his hand while Anise shined a flashlight on it. "Cooperation through opposition...directing destruction of death by intention... new destinies." His face went pale, and the paper fell from his grasp. "I can't do this."

"What do you mean?" Jonathan demanded.

"I understand now," Thomas told him. "The secrets of life were intended to be shared with the world. But the secrets of death and resurrection aren't meant for human minds. They were always meant to be guarded and kept from humanity. Most humans couldn't handle this information. Myself included." He pointed to the paper on the ground. "I won't read the rest of this," he added.

"Grace did things you wouldn't believe in order to bring you back," Jonathan said, his eyes narrowing as he picked up the paper. "And you won't help her?"

Thomas sat down next to Grace's flickering form and said nothing. He had the same expression as Nate when he was deep in thought. Looking at him was agonizing, but Anise couldn't tear her eyes from his face.

"We don't have a lot of time," Jonathan said to Anise. "We need to get out there and find Charlie. I think we should give him the condensed version."

"Thomas, we found the Plate of Destiny in an underwater cave in the Gulf of Mexico," Anise began. "I'm the only blood relative left of the Mallandian royal line. Well, possibly *soon* to be the only one, so the Plate should rightfully be under my control. Many of the people helping us, including Nate, your grandson, have died in our mission to find the Plate."

"I have a grandson? Dan had a son?" Thomas beamed.

"Yes, and right now an enemy of Fred Dromly's named Charlie Masser has the Plate and is trying to escape with it."

"Charlie Masser?" Thomas laughed. "That idiot? He'll never be able to read it."

"Protecting the Plate is my responsibility," Anise reminded Thomas. "I need to get it from him, and I could really use your help."

"I'm sorry," Thomas said. "My answer is no."

"Boss! Boss!"

Fred turned around and saw a friendly face emerging from the darkness between the trees. "George! Thank you." George was flanked by Big Ears and Crooked Nose who were armed. "I'm hoping we won't need weaponry of any kind, but it's always better to be safe than—"

A stray bullet hit George in the chest, and he fell to the forest floor. Fred spun around, trying to determine the source.

"Over there!" shouted Big Ears.

Fred saw Charlie and Dave running through the trees toward them with Shawn looking like he might drop at any moment but still managing to keep up a few steps behind them. "Be ready!" Fred commanded. "Leave no man standing!"

"WHERE ARE YOU GOING?" ANISE ASKED as she and Jonathan hurried after Thomas, twigs snapping under their feet.

"The nearest city is that way, right?" Thomas said, pointing in the direction he was headed as he hurried through the trees and into a clearing. He stopped short and squinted in the darkness at the ground in front of him. He turned his head at the sound of Anise's sob.

"That's Nate," Jonathan said, motioning to the body.

Thomas knelt in front of his grandson and touched his face.

Anise turned away and tried to be comforted by Jonathan's embrace. Once she regained her composure, they looked around for Thomas. Seeing that he'd started walking again, they ran through the clearing after him.

"How do you know Charlie Masser?" Jonathan asked Thomas once they caught up with him.

"It's a long story," Thomas said, "but to make it short, he's the one that killed me."

"*Charlie* killed you?" Anise asked.

"Well, it wasn't him exactly. He was locked away at the time and hired someone to dress up as Fred Dromly and off me. He hated Fred as much as I did, and I suppose he figured he might be able to take both of us down this way."

"You hated Fred Dromly?" Jonathan asked.

"You either love him or you hate him," Thomas replied. "He's that kind of man."

"But why did Charlie have you killed?" Anise asked.

Thomas paused to pick up a large stick and used it to

help push branches and brush out of his way as he continued walking. "He found out about the Armor Jewelry and was blackmailing me into telling him everything I knew. I told him very little of the truth of course, and eventually he suspected I was holding back. He threatened my life, and I tried to run, but his associate found me before I had the chance. I assume they also stole the research that I didn't have time to burn."

"You claim to know everything there is to know about the Jewelry and Plate," Jonathan said suspiciously. "But Grace doesn't. Why wouldn't you tell your own wife? Especially when you're telling us, two strangers you just met, everything we ask about?"

"Because it doesn't matter anymore. Grace was only a means to an end for me, nothing more. Don't get me wrong, I was fond of her, but it wasn't love. At least, not for me. Her desires surrounding the Jewelry didn't factor in anywhere for me. I knew I'd need a dependable redhead who'd be loyal to *me* and not Dromly to read the Plate once I found it. That's why I married her."

"That's not how *she* tells it," Anise said with disgust. Her heart broke for Grace. "That's despicable!"

Thomas shrugged. "I know. But Grace is now living out her new destiny and so must I."

He turned to look at Anise when she put her hand on his arm. "Are you alright?"

"Yes," she said, taking her hand away quickly. "It's just that...you were dead, and now you're not. I was wondering if maybe my hand would go through you like Jonathan's went through Grace and Dr. Smithton, but you're solid. How can your body be here like you were never gone?" She wanted to know exactly what Nate would go through when she used the Plate of Destiny to bring him back.

"Your body is an energetic form of who you are," Thomas answered.

"I'm not sure I understand," she said.

Thomas took a thoughtful pause. "Let me see if I can think of a better way to explain it. What you think of as your solid body is actually a projection of your own conscious state—some people think of it as a soul—into a physical form. When my soul left this planet, realm, dimension—whatever you want to call it, my body wasn't needed anymore and it decomposed. Now that my soul is back, my consciousness is being projected into the same form because my soul hasn't changed. My body is just a way for me to be here physically and be able to experience events in this world. Grace and Morty read the secrets of death and figured out how to change the projection of my conscious state back into what it was when I was alive on Earth."

Jonathan wore his fascination prominently on his face as he trotted next to Thomas who kept a quick pace. He couldn't take his eyes off Thomas and rammed his shoulder into a tree.

"Best watch where you're going," Thomas told him.

"Where did you go after you died?" Jonathan asked, rubbing his shoulder.

"After you die, you go where you *expect* to go," Thomas said. "Some people believe they'll end up sitting on clouds in a heaven-like location, so they do. Others expect to burn in fire, so they do. They might tell themselves that they believe good things will happen to them when they die, but if their souls don't truly believe it due to guilt or lack of self-love, they'll go to a place they think they deserve. That place can be something similar to what people think of as hell, or it might be a place a little less frightening, but wherever they go, they're there for their soul to learn. Others think that death is the end of everything and that they won't go anywhere, so they don't. They end up in a void and stay there unless they decide to project their soul in another way. The soul can decide to do that without having the same kind of consciousness that we experience when alive."

"So if your soul still exists in some form after death," Jonathan said, "is it just the body that dies?"

"You could think of it that way. Death isn't really death," Thomas told him. "Death is just the end of your existence as you know it. Death is a change. But your beliefs, be they limited or insightful, have the final say on what happens to your soul. Everyone creates their own afterlife, and it's wherever their souls believe they will go and what they believe they deserve. Everyone manifests their own reality."

"And so, when you die—" Jonathan began.

"Stop," Thomas requested, hitting the end of his stick on the ground. "You're asking the wrong questions. You're focused on the death secrets when you should be focused on the life secrets. I'll answer no more questions about death or resurrection."

"But I need you to tell me how the Plate works!" Anise exclaimed, tears forming in her eyes again. "I want to bring back Nate and everyone else who died trying to help me. Don't you want to meet your grandson?"

"I would've loved to meet him, but I refuse to read that part," Thomas said, shaking his head. "I now know that the Plate of Destiny tests us as soon as we decide we want it. It'll keep testing us until we stop wanting it and we learn the secrets of life instead."

"You just read the secrets of life, so you should be fine," Anise insisted.

"I read them, but I haven't *learned* them. I haven't lived them. I'm not on the right path toward my destiny and never have been. The Plate tested me, and I failed. Therefore, I can only conclude that the secrets of death are not meant for us to know. Or at least not meant for me to know."

"What do you mean the Plate tests you?" Jonathan asked.

"Events happen in your life that throw you off course. Push you off the right path to your destiny. You become obsessed with the wrong things," Thomas tried to explain. "The Plate will find the darkness inside of you and exaggerate it. My darkness was revenge, and I dedicated my life to it when I could've been doing something that made me happy instead. Grace's darkness was her misplaced need for me. Morty's was his infatuation with protecting Grace. Dromly needed glory. And Charlie... he's full of hate." He pointed at the piece of paper with the symbols on it that Jonathan held in his hand. "But if you want to read it for yourself, go right ahead."

"I would, but I don't know the language. I need your help!" Anise begged.

Thomas sighed. "Please understand. This is my second chance. I'm grateful for it, and I'm not going to blow it this time. I want to go home and see Dan. I want to apologize to Betty."

"Betty?"

Thomas ignored the question, stopped walking, and turned around to face Anise and Jonathan. "I'm washing my hands of this. I no longer want the Plate, and therefore, it'll no longer test me. But the rules are different for you, Anise. As someone with king's blood, you have a stronger bond to the Plate. Whether you want the Plate or not, it's your responsibility to be its keeper, and the Plate will always test its keeper. You must protect the secrets of death and share the secrets of life. And if it's in your destiny to know any of the secrets, you will." He turned and started walking up a steep hill.

Anise felt sick again, and her chest tightened as she felt her last chance to bring Nate and Erin back to life slipping from her fingers. "You said you're grateful for your second chance," she argued, hurrying after Thomas. "Don't you want to give others the second chance you've been given?"

"My second chance is about me, no one else," Thomas replied.

"That's the most selfish thing I've ever heard!" Anise

exclaimed, horrified. She huffed and puffed trying to keep up with Thomas as he took long strides up the steep ground.

"Now that I know the secrets of life, I fear knowing the secrets of death, and so should you," Thomas scolded. "We don't know what's going to happen to Morty and Grace. They're getting a new destiny, but who knows what that'll look like for them. They could end up anywhere, at any age. They may or may not remember their old life. It'll be whatever works best to restore the balance for resurrecting someone. It'll be whatever condition is best for them to have the greatest chance to live out their destiny."

"I used to let my fear make my decisions for me," Anise told him. "But I don't want to do that anymore." She stopped to rest at the top of the hill, panting.

"Then I admire your bravery," Thomas said. "But take it from someone who's lived it—when you want something from the Plate of Destiny, you start to obsess. The obsession takes over your mind and spreads to other areas of your life, and I don't want that anymore. That's what I just learned from the little that I read. My obsession ends here." Looking around, he pointed to a road in the distance. "I'm headed that way, and this is where we part." He turned and began walking away.

"At least tell us the secrets of life!" Anise called out after him, still out of breath.

"Read my letter," Thomas called back. He jogged down the hill and was gone.

"I can't believe he won't help us," Anise choked out. She sat on the grassy ground and felt her face crinkle in agony as her pain pushed out an involuntary sob. Nate and Erin were gone, and the one person who could bring them back just walked away.

"Over there!" Jonathan said, pointing his finger down the hill toward a large clearing in the distance. "Directly across from where the sun is about to rise!"

On the horizon in the dim light of the dawn, five dark figures could be seen lunging, turning, shoving, attacking, retreating, killing, dying. As they hurried in that direction, Anise's eyes moved constantly, searching for Dromly. "Dromly only has the amulet, ring, and earrings," she said. "I hope he's okay. Charlie has the full set to include the cuff."

She scanned the scene again, looking past the fighting in all directions. She could just barely make out some movement of a rock about a quarter mile to the left of the battle. Not knowing what she just saw, she stared until she saw the movement again. She pointed in that direction. "I think Dromly's hiding behind that boulder."

"You have two full sets of Jewelry now, right?" Jonathan confirmed with her. "You can give him one of your cuffs when we get to him."

Anise frowned. "The set I originally had needs to be charged. That means Dromly's set is probably about to run out of charge as well. The set I just took from Grace and Dr. Smithton is still working at least. But both cuffs are completely out of juice. Charlie's set seems to still be holding a decent charge for some strange reason, so Dromly and I will have to work together."

Hand-in-hand for support and balance, they bounded down the hill, slipping on the wet mud and grass on their way. They dashed through the trees in the direction of the battle. When they got close, they dropped to the ground and crawled the rest of the way through the trees, bushes, and underbrush to get to Dromly unnoticed. Anise arrived first and made sure he was okay.

"Yes, my Jewelry is very weak, too," Fred confirmed to Anise. "That's why I'm cowardly crouched behind this rock hoping the civil twilight is dark enough to protect me from someone even darker."

"That's not cowardly, it's smart," Anise told him. She sat down next to him. The wind picked up and she pushed her blowing hair out of her face. "Charlie would've destroyed you. Why isn't his Jewelry losing its charge like ours is?"

"Do you have a plan?" Jonathan asked him as he eyed the fighters who seemed to be evenly matched. "Looks like we could use some more help."

"Indeed. Did you find Morty and Grace?" Dromly asked.

"They're off to their new destiny," Jonathan said.

"What does that mean?" Dromly asked.

Before Anise or Jonathan could answer, Charlie stepped into view, placed a hand on Jonathan and with one quick motion, shoved him into the rock. His body hit the boulder with such force that it knocked him out. Charlie took a step toward Anise who looked at him with horror. "Your men may be large, but they don't have the intelligence or strategy that mine do. You can't win."

"You're not getting the Plate," she sneered at him while scrambling to her feet.

"I will never stop coming after you until I have it," Charlie informed her over the wind that had started to howl.

"Then you leave us no choice but to stop you now." Dromly stood beside Anise.

Jonathan woke up in time to see Charlie let out a small laugh. Someone of Charlie's height and girth would never be intimidated by Dr. Dromly and Anise, two people half his size who moved like their Armor Jewelry was losing its charge. Jonathan would bet that his passing out on the ground was also less than impressive to Charlie. He reached up to gingerly touch the growing lump on his head.

"You can't stop me," Charlie said, swinging his arm toward Anise.

Anise jumped back but wasn't fast enough. She let out a small cry when his knife slashed her arm. Blood rushed down toward her fingertips and dripped on the ground. Relief overwhelmed Jonathan when he saw Anise's garnet ring emit a soft glow and the gash grow back together as if it had never occurred.

Jonathan tried to get up, but his head was spinning. As he slowly pulled himself to his feet using the boulder as support, he figured Charlie knew Dr. Dromly's Jewelry must be as weak as Anise's. One right cross from Selina's grandfather caused Dromly's face to hit the ground.

Selina. She'd been invading Jonathan's brain ever since they met, and now her ghost was haunting him. As much as he didn't want to think about Selina at that moment and everything she'd done, Jonathan's heart still hurt knowing she was gone.

Pushing Selina from his mind, Jonathan knew he needed to do something, but nothing that came to mind seemed like it would do any good. Nevertheless, he charged at Charlie.

Anise joined him. The two of them jumped Charlie, knocking him over. Jonathan was relieved that Anise's Armor Jewelry still had enough charge left to fight. However, to his surprise, Charlie's instinct to shove them off resulted in the two younger people flying in opposite directions.

Jonathan landed face first on the grass, and his world started spinning again. He raised his head and looked around, but the world was blurry. His hands felt around in the grass for his missing glasses. He found them not far from where he'd landed and put them on. Anise hadn't flown as far as he had. She seemed to be okay, but Charlie came after her, picked her up, and slammed her down head first on a large rock. He dropped her body to the ground and she stayed there, motionless.

Jonathan saw something shiny near Anise's feet. He squinted to try to make out what it was. *Anise's Armor*

Jewelry! He realized that when she'd jumped on Charlie, her cuff had caught in the chain of her amulet, ripping them both off. No wonder Charlie had been able to free himself so easily. Jonathan tried to get up but was too dizzy and fell again.

Waiting for the world to stop spinning, Jonathan watched Charlie and Dr. Dromly. While Charlie loomed over Anise's unconscious body, pulling his gun from his belt, he looked behind him and saw that Dr. Dromly was trying to get up. Stepping closer so it would be easier to aim, Charlie shot him. Dromly fell back on the ground once more, grabbing his gut. "It's your turn next," Charlie said to Anise who was still out cold. They way he said it made Jonathan shiver. Reaching inside her backpack, Charlie grabbed the Plate of Destiny.

Moving quietly, and acting purely on instinct, Jonathan grabbed the back of Charlie's jacket and lifted it over his head, covering his eyes. He tried to hold Charlie's arms fast, but with the strength of the earrings, he easily shoved Jonathan off. As Charlie rustled through the long jacket, fighting the growing wind to get it off of his face, he took a step back and tripped over something. He finally got his eyes free of the jacket just in time to see a rock hurdling toward his face. Unalarmed, he remained still and watched the rock stop in midair and land gently by his feet in the clearing's long grass. Charlie dropped the Plate inside the knapsack he wore.

Jonathan scrambled to his feet and threw another rock, knowing full well it wouldn't hurt Charlie, but he hoped it would serve as a distraction until he could come up with a better plan. With Dr. Dromly incapacitated, Jonathan was the only barrier between Charlie and Anise. The old man had working Armor Jewelry, and Jonathan knew he didn't stand a chance, but he couldn't stand back and watch Charlie kill her.

Charlie stood and headed toward Anise, swatting Jonathan away like a fly when he charged. Jonathan ducked and was able to avert Charlie's swing. Jonathan charged again and felt how strong the earrings made the old man. The heel of Charlie's palm hit his chest, and wheezing, Jonathan flew backward only to have his motion stopped by the boulder. He heard bones cracking but stood up anyway and ran to Charlie who was headed toward Anise. Charlie's fist met Jonathan's cheek which caused him to spin around and cry out in pain. Stars were all Jonathan could see as he fumbled around in the dark for something to hold on to. As he went down, Jonathan reached for the bright glowing object he saw out of the corner of his eye and held on tightly to it. The amulet's chain broke away from Charlie's neck under Jonathan's weight as he fell, was dropped onto the ground, hidden by the tall grasses, and promptly covered by blowing leaves and dirt.

Out of frustration, Charlie kicked Jonathan out of the way. "I don't need the amulet to kill this unconscious girl," he grumbled. As he took a step toward Anise, Jonathan tried to stand up. Kicking him again and making him roll a few times, Charlie reached into his jacket. Grabbing his gun, he then made his way to where Anise lay. "It's time to end this!" he snarled.

"Stop and think!" Jonathan yelled, desperately trying to reason with Charlie. "If you kill her for her blood, you can spill it on the Plate, but there's no one around to be your seer! By the time you find another woman to set on fire, the blood will be too dry! And Anise will be dead so you won't be able to get any more fresh blood from her!"

Charlie glared at him. "Nice try. But I have a plan for that. I found an early morning hiker. A woman who I have tied to a tree. All I have to do is set fire to her hair, and I have another seer."

Jonathan forced his broken body to move. He then did the only thing he knew would make the old man leave Anise alone. In one swift motion, Jonathan reached inside Charlie's knapsack, grabbed the Plate, and ran.

Charlie let out a surprised grunt and hurried after Jonathan as he hobbled away as quickly as he could. After a few long, quick steps, Charlie caught up and grabbed Jonathan's arm.

Jonathan held the Plate over some nearby rocks with his other arm. "I'll scratch it all to hell!" he warned. "You won't be able to read it!" He felt his arm being released, and he turned to face Charlie, clutching the Plate to his chest and breathing heavily. He saw a hand flying at his face and felt a tremendous force on his forehead. His head snapped backward, and he found himself lying supine on the ground, staring up at the trees swaying heavily. The Plate was harshly removed from his grip, and a gun was pointed at him.

"This ends now!" cried Charlie. His long jacket flapped around him in the wind.

Jonathan watched with shock as Charlie's body seemed to rise and levitate a few feet off the ground. Jonathan caught the Plate when the old man dropped it out of surprise. Charlie looked around as if trying to figure out what was happening and let out a groan when his body flew forward and hit the earth, his face scratched by thorny plants.

Jonathan looked up and saw Anise standing there, wearing the entire set of her Armor Jewelry plus Charlie's amulet that she'd found in the dirt. "You're okay!" He cried with relief.

ANISE KICKED AWAY THE GUN THAT had fallen from Charlie's hand. It landed in front of Dromly who was trying to sit up. "I'm fine." She helped Jonathan to his feet, and he handed her the Plate. She looked behind her when she heard Dromly calling her name. He lay on the ground, reaching out to her, as the morning's first light dawned behind him and filtered through the trees. Anise and Jonathan hurried over to him.

"Bent, broken, defeated. This is not how Frederick Dromly dies!" Dromly groaned as Anise and Jonathan reached him. He lifted himself to a seated position with a moan. "There's just enough time for one more legend, one more adventure, one final heroic act..." Dromly held out a key to Anise. "I've added your name to a lockbox at my bank," he told her. "Make sure you retrieve the contents."

She took his Armor Jewelry and placed her hands on him, willing him to heal. Both cuffs sparkled for a few seconds only. Nowhere near long enough. "The cuffs need to be charged," she told him, wishing she could save him. "I'm so sorry. But maybe the garnet can help." She put the garnet and bloodstone rings on Dromly's finger. The garnet stayed cold.

"It also needs to be charged," Fred said.

"I'll carry you somewhere and hide you from Charlie until we can charge the Jewelry," Anise suggested. She tried to pick him up, but found that she wasn't strong enough.

"I'll help," Jonathan offered.

Dromly waved him off. "No. Never mind that. There's no time."

It was obvious he was struggling to breathe, and Anise's guilt grew. *He fought so valiantly for me. Now he's going to die too, and it's my fault.*

Anise turned around when she noticed Dromly's eyes peer behind her. She saw Charlie slowly get up and start to make his way over.

Dromly touched her arm to get her attention. "I have one final legend to tell you. Descartes believed that the earth is really just an encrusted sun..." He paused to pick up Charlie's gun that Anise had kicked over near him and planted three bullets in Charlie's chest.

Charlie looked down at his wounds, but with the

strength of the earrings, it barely slowed him down. He kept heading toward them.

"For its possessor, obsidian has another purpose..." Dromly wheezed and slumped onto his back. He let his last breath escape, and his eyes closed permanently.

"He was talking about the seer's wand," Anise said to Jonathan. "It has an obsidian on it."

"Yeah, but Charlie has it," Jonathan reminded her. He picked up Charlie's gun that was still in Dromly's hand. It was out of bullets, and he shoved it in his backpack. "I saw it in the inside pocket of his jacket when the wind blew it open."

"Isn't obsidian volcanic glass?" she asked. She thought about how strong of a charge the Jewelry Charlie wore had. It was almost as if it wasn't losing its charge at all. Having an idea, she slipped one full set of the Armor Jewelry in her pocket.

"Yes," Jonathan told her, "but we have bigger problems to worry about."

"Get behind me," Anise told Jonathan.

He followed her instruction and Anise stood tall as Charlie aimed his gun at them. She and Jonathan backed away from Charlie who kept stepping toward them. They stopped at the edge of the clearing where the thick forest began.

"Our men killed each other," Charlie announced to her. "It's just you, me, your four-eyed friend here, and my future seer, who shouldn't have been hiking after hours," he said, motioning to the frightened female hiker he'd managed to tie to a tree in the distance. "Your only working piece of Jewelry is that amulet you're wearing."

"The sun is coming up," Jonathan said. "Soon we'll be able to recharge our Jewelry and—"

"You don't have time for that, kid. I'll shoot you long before that happens."

"Shoot us with what?" Jonathan challenged him. "I have your gun."

"And I have several more I took off of my dead men and yours," Charlie informed him, pulling another gun out of his knapsack.

"I want to make a deal," Anise blurted out. "I know you could easily shoot us both right here and now, and I want to prevent any more deaths. I will give you the Plate of Destiny. All I want in return is the seer's wand."

"Anise, no!" said Jonathan, horrified. "What are you doing?"

"Trust me," she mumbled back to him.

Charlie glared at her. "You're in no position to be offering a deal. Here's the deal—you give me the Plate and all your Armor Jewelry, and because Selina liked you, I won't kill you."

"You expect me to believe that you'll just let us walk?" Anise scoffed.

"Take it or leave it."

Anise was silent for a moment. "Fine." She took off the Armor Jewelry and tossed it in a bush behind Charlie who glared at her again. She took the Plate of Destiny out of her backpack and with all her strength, threw it as high as she could. It smacked against some branches, tearing off a few leaves that took their time floating downward. As Charlie looked up and held out his hands to catch it, Anise charged with Jonathan following her lead. Reaching into Charlie's jacket, she grabbed the seer's wand and ran. Jonathan jumped in front of Charlie and caught the Plate. He took off in the opposite direction from Anise.

Anise took the cuff and the rest of the Armor Jewelry she had hidden in her pocket and quickly put it on. She poured some water on the cuff from the canteen in Jonathan's backpack and touched the obsidian wand to the wet lapis lazuli and jasper stones. *Volcanic glass,* she told herself. *A cooled, hardened piece of the encrusted sun. A sun that holds the solar ability to charge gemstones.* Within seconds, the cuff began to sparkle. Anise did the same for the rest of the Jewelry. Now she had more fully charged pieces of Jewelry than Charlie.

Charlie easily caught up to Jonathan and punched him in the face, breaking his glasses. He snatched back the Plate while pushing the barrel of his gun against Jonathan's forehead. His finger touched the trigger.

"Charlie, stop!" Anise watched Charlie's eyes glaze over. "Put down the gun, and give the Plate to Jonathan."

Charlie did as he was told. Jonathan brought the Plate to Anise.

"Now give Jonathan all your Armor Jewelry."

Charlie took off the earrings, ring, and cuff and handed them over. Jonathan brought those to Anise as well. "You wear them," Anise told him.

Feeling safe and confident now that she wore two sets of charged Jewelry and Jonathan had one, she was sure she could end this without any further harm coming to anyone. "Now, Charlie, I want you to completely forget about the Armor Jewelry and the Plate and..." Anise stared as Charlie slumped forward and fell to his side.

Jonathan rolled him over. "He's dead!"

"What?! How?" asked Anise. Her hand covered her mouth in shock. "I didn't...did I?"

Jonathan shook his head as he saw blood pouring down Charlie's torso. "No, you didn't. Dromly did with the three bullets he planted in Charlie's chest. He should've died instantly, but the earrings kept him alive."

"But...shouldn't the earrings have protected him from the bullet wounds?" Anise asked. "Made him resistant to injury?"

"They did while he was wearing them," Jonathan explained. "Dromly knew that if he lodged the bullets in Charlie's vital organs, and if you got him to take off the earrings, he'd die. They look like they probably went into Charlie's heart and lungs."

Anise didn't know how much more guilt she could take. She opened her mouth to say something, but nothing came out.

"You didn't kill him," Jonathan told her again. "Charlie would've died as soon as he took the earrings off or when their charge wore off, whether we were around or not. This was Dromly's doing."

Anise was quiet as she stared at her dead enemy. They were safe now, but nothing felt right.

"You saved our lives," Jonathan assured her.

Frowning, she looked around at the new morning rays shining brightly on the dead men dotting the grassy ground. A Pyrrhic victory. "I have to brainwash this poor woman into believing this was all a dream," she said, motioning to the frightened hiker still tied to the tree, struggling and trying to scream through the gag in her mouth. "And law enforcement when they show up. But after that, I want to go home."

Part 4

DESTINY IS A PARADOX

Chapter 25

Friday, October 16, 2015

Anise pedaled as hard as her legs would allow. The wind blew her hair back as her bike flew through the downtown streets. She stopped in front of Johnny's Bar and chained her bike to a lamppost. Then she ran around the corner and down a flight of concrete stairs. Following the sidewalk, she continued at full speed under the freeway and beyond.

The last time she'd been here, she was holding on to Nate's arm, and the trees had the beautiful, fragrant flowers of early summer. Now she was alone, and the trees were dropping their dried, brown leaves that crunched when she stepped on them.

Reaching the park at the end of the sidewalk, she shoved through the wrought iron gate and darted along the paved path around the pond. She raced over the bridge where she and Nate had once stood and headed straight for the bench where they'd sat on their first date. Where they'd talked about so many things. The place she'd begun falling in love with him.

She dropped onto the bench and leaned back, trying to catch her breath. Her head turned to the empty place on the bench next to her where Nate had sat that night. She reached her hand out and placed it where he'd been, where she wished he was now.

"I just came from your condo," she said aloud. "Your friends Scott and Peter seem to think that if you'd had the time, you would've changed your will to leave everything to me. They encouraged me to look around and take anything I wanted. They offered me everything—your motorcycle, your car, the condo itself. It was so thoughtful of them. But all I wanted was this." She snuggled up inside Nate's black leather jacket and zipped it closed.

She shut her eyes and wrapped her arms around her own waist. The jacket still smelled like his woodsy cologne, and its weight made it feel like he was there, hugging her from behind. And for a moment, he *was* there. She could feel him. His breath on her ear, his grin easily detectable in the words he whispered to her. *I love you, honey.* Words from a voice that she'd never hear again.

She put her hands in the jacket's pockets to see if he had a tissue in there. One hand closed on a firm piece of paper and the other on a napkin. Pulling out the napkin to wipe her eyes, she stopped when she realized it had something written on it in her handwriting. It was from the night they'd met. She'd jotted down her name, email address, and a note that read, "Thank you for a night I'll never forget." She looked at her other hand. It held the affirmation card she'd given him on their first date, right there on the very bench she sat on now. *He kept them. And not only that, he carried them around with him wherever he went.*

Completely forgetting about finding a tissue, she covered her face with her hands and sobbed.

Monday, October 19, 2015

ANISE PUT HER HANDS ON HER stomach and closed her eyes, grateful that the car was now parked.

"Are you sure you're feeling better?" Jonathan asked her. "I can take you back to the hotel if you want."

Anise shook her head. Spending more time in a moving vehicle was the last thing she wanted. "I'm fine," she said. "It was just a little motion sickness."

"I know," he said. "I've just never known you to be motion sick on planes before. Or in cars."

"I still have heartburn, and it escalated from there." She changed the subject to not have to talk about it anymore. "Are you excited?"

"I'm out of my mind," Jonathan said with a huge grin. "Being asked to lead this dig is the biggest honor I've gotten at work so far. It's strange though. Dr. S was supposed to have been here to help the archeologist lead this dig. Nobody's asked about him or mentioned him in any way. It's almost like he never existed."

"Dr. Smithton has a new destiny now," said Anise. "Maybe part of the whole process is the people in his old life not remembering him."

"Maybe." Jonathan frowned. "It's hard though. I miss him. At least, I miss the person I thought he was."

"I know." Anise took his hand in an attempt to comfort him. She looked out the windshield at the excavation site in front of them. "I didn't realize that curators went on digs."

"We don't," Jonathan replied. "This is a unique situation. Dr. S. had been doing some research on the kind of artifacts that might be found here, so he sponsored this dig with the hopes that the artifacts would be found and brought home to be displayed at the museum. We haven't had as much business lately, and this was his way of trying to drum up interest in the public." Looking at his watch, he opened the car door. "We'd better get over there. I promised I'd arrive early."

They got out of their rental car and walked over to

the site where Jonathan would be meeting select students from various universities around the country. He and the local archaeologists working at the site would be leading a dig, and the students would get to help. Anise took in the surroundings as they walked. She saw a flat section of dirt the size of a large house that was marked off in a grid and ready to be explored. Some students were starting to arrive. The archaeologists were preparing their tools and waved at them as they walked by.

"I bet the students are as excited as you are," Anise told him. She wished she hadn't forgotten her sunglasses as she squinted in the hot, bright sun.

Jonathan wiped away the sweat that was already forming on his brow. "It was an honor for them to have been chosen for this project. I hear the competition was fierce."

"Thanks again for letting me tag along," Anise said.

"You don't have to keep thanking me," Jonathan told her. "I'm happy to have you with me."

"I wasn't sure you would be."

He gave her a confused look. "What are you talking about?"

"Well...when I tried to tell you about what you mean to me at the hotel in Florida, you didn't want to hear it." She shrugged, not completely sure how she wanted to express her thoughts. "Even though we said we'd be friends, we never really talked about what that would mean or what that would look like for us. I was thinking that you might want some distance from me, but that you might be feeling obligated to be around because of everything we've been through lately. It's okay if you want some space. Just tell me."

Jonathan looked at the ground. "It was hard for me to listen to what you were saying."

It was her turn to feel confused. "What do you mean?"

He frowned and shuffled his feet on the dirt ground. "When you told me you still had feelings for me...at the time, that gave me hope, and I didn't want to hear it. The way you were talking about Nate and how upset you were about your breakup...I could tell you weren't done with him yet. The thought of us getting back together and then me losing you to him a second time...I didn't want to think about it."

She knew he was right. If they'd gotten back together, it wouldn't have ended well. As much as she loved Jonathan, Nate had been the one. Anise looked at Jonathan but said nothing.

Jonathan looked down and dug the toe of his shoe into the ground. "I feel like an ass for not finishing that conversation with you. But I want to tell you the truth now."

"Which is what?"

Jonathan opened his mouth and it took an extra moment for the words to come out. "I still want to be in your life, and I've been thinking about this a lot. The thing is, I'm not sure a romantic relationship would work between us. But I could be wrong. I don't know. We don't have to decide anything now—"

"I think you're right," Anise agreed, glad he brought it up. "We make better friends than lovers. And I hope we can always be as close friends are we are now."

"Of course we will," Jonathan assured her. "So...this won't happen anytime soon, but how would you feel if I asked out someone else one day?"

Anise smiled at him. "I'd be happy for you," she told him honestly.

A middle-aged man in a light blue shirt and khakis gave a big wave and started walking toward them. "Hi folks," he said. "Bill Turner. Lead archaeologist. You must be Dr. Casley." He shook Jonathan's hand.

"Yes, I'm Jonathan. This is Anise."

"Pleased to meet you," said Bill as he shook Anise's hand as well. "Come with me, and I'll show you around."

Bill introduced Jonathan and Anise to his team who

were waiting by the dig site.

Anise suddenly felt queasy again, and her hand went to her stomach. "I think I need to sit for a minute," she said.

"Are you okay?" Jonathan asked her with a concerned look on his face.

"I just need to sit."

Bill pointed to a location behind them. "There are some chairs over there underneath the tarp," he told her. "Drinks are in the cooler. Help yourself."

Jonathan walked her the thirty yards to where the chairs were located and grabbed a bottle of water for her from the cooler.

"Thanks," she said quietly.

"I'm sorry you're still not feeling well," Jonathan said. "The students are starting to arrive, and I have to take roll and get them started, but I'll be back to check on you right after that."

She sat quietly with her eyes closed and did some slow, deep breathing while the nausea faded. She could hear Jonathan doing the roll call.

"Andrew Myers?"

"Here."

"Bethany Compton?"

"Here."

"Julie French?"

"Right here."

"Morton...Smithton?"

Anise's eyes flew open and her head popped up in time to see a college-aged man with a long face and wavy blond hair raise his hand.

"Present," he said.

Jonathan stared at the next name for several seconds before he was able to say it in a wavering voice. "Grace Polk?"

Anise felt her jaw drop when she saw a young woman with flame red hair raise her hand.

"Here," the young woman said.

Rising from her chair, Anise stared at Grace. She couldn't stop herself from slowly walking over to her. Jonathan gave the students directions before joining her, and the two of them looked on without knowing what to say.

Grace stopped unpacking her supplies, turned her head, and gave them both an annoyed look of confusion. "Hello," she said. "You're one of the leaders of the dig," she added, directing her comment at Jonathan. The man with the wavy blond hair looked over at them and smiled.

"Yes," Jonathan replied. "Where are the two of you from?"

"Springfield University," the blond man said. "I'm Morty. This is Grace." He shook hands with Jonathan.

Jonathan introduced Anise. She took a step forward and stuck her hand out to shake Morty's but stumbled and almost fell over. Grace caught her.

"You're not okay," Jonathan said. "I'm taking you back to the hotel."

"No, you're working," said Anise. "I'm going to sit in the shade. I'll be fine."

"Jonathan, you're needed over here," Bill called out from across the site.

"I'll help her into the shade," Grace told Jonathan.

Anise nodded at Jonathan to let him know it was okay. She felt embarrassed as Grace helped her to the chair. "It must be this heat," she said.

"Bullshit," Grace snorted. "You're pregnant, aren't you?"

Anise looked at her with wide eyes.

"Don't worry, I won't tell." She made sure Anise was comfortable.

"Is it that obvious?" Anise asked.

Grace shrugged. "No. I can just tell. But I'm sure no one else can."

Anise took that opportunity to try to find out more

about Grace. "Your family must be proud of you for being selected for this opportunity."

"My family's dead," Grace said matter-of-factly as she handed Anise her bottle of water.

"I'm so sorry!" Anise said.

"It was a long time ago," Grace replied.

"How long have you and Morty been dating?" From the look Grace gave her, Anise knew she was annoying the younger woman with all of the questions, but she couldn't help herself.

"A few months."

"I bet you knew as soon as you caught me that I was pregnant. You see things, don't you?" Anise asked her.

Grace looked at her with alarm and suspicion.

"Do you see anything else? Do you remember me?"

Grace took a few cautious steps away from Anise. "I have to get back. Are you going to be okay?"

"Yes, of course. Sorry for keeping you. And thank you!"

Grace turned to leave, but stopped and looked at Anise as if she were trying to decide what to say. "Take care of that baby."

Before Anise could respond, Grace hurried away. Putting her hands over her navel, Anise thought about how she'd have to tell Jonathan eventually. The thought made her a little nervous, and she wondered how he'd take the news. "I hope you have Jonathan's heart, integrity, and enthusiasm, and Nate's charm, brilliance, and intensity," she whispered to her belly. "No matter who your father is."

"MORTY DOESN'T REMEMBER US," ANISE SAID sadly to Jonathan when they were driving back to the hotel that evening. "I think Grace might have, but she looked at me like I had three heads when I asked her."

"Yeah," Jonathan agreed. "It's weird though—Dr. S's history as he tells it is still the same as it was before. He has the same old stories about his parents he used to tell me when I worked for him. But I looked up the names of his parents online," he said, holding up his cell phone, "and they were still born at the same time they were before. The dates in his story are off, but he doesn't seem to know that. It's like his memories have been altered.

"He's still his incredibly smart self though," Jonathan continued. "I almost told him to apply for a job at the museum in our town after graduation if he's interested in moving out there to work and attend grad school."

"Almost?" Anise asked.

Jonathan shrugged. "I liked talking with him today. Like I said, I missed him. But the more we spoke, the angrier I got. I just don't know if I can forgive him for how he betrayed us."

Thursday, October 22, 2015

ANISE WALKED INTO THE SECURE ROOM at Frederick Dromly's bank in Springfield with Jonathan right behind her. The box was handed to her by the man with the keys who then left them alone.

"I didn't know if Dromly was telling the truth when he said he had a safe deposit box in my name," she said, as she put the box on the table and sat down.

"Let's see what he put in it!" Jonathan said excitedly, sitting down next to her.

Anise opened the box and pulled out a list of names and contact information. "What's this?" she wondered aloud.

"That's a list of buyers in case you want to sell the

artifacts he put in here," explained Jonathan.

Anise pulled out several pieces of Jewelry and hair accessories made of gold and silver that featured lapis lazuli, jasper, carnelian, bloodstone, and onyx gemstones.

"Wow! These look Sumerian," Jonathan said, telling her about each piece with excitement.

Anise only half listened to what he was saying. She thought about how she'd driven past Nate's condo before leaving on this trip. It was completely empty now, as if Nate had never existed. She took a deep breath and resisted the tears that threatened an appearance.

"Anise?" Jonathan said. "What are you thinking about?"

"Sorry," she said, "I just don't feel right about selling these. They belong in a museum. Let's donate them."

Jonathan smiled at her. "I'm behind that decision one hundred percent. Although I couldn't blame you if you wanted to sell at least one piece. Since you got fired for not coming in to work when we were in Florida, and you haven't been able to find anything else..."

"I know," Anise said, slightly annoyed at his constant worry about her financial state. "Please stop reminding me. I'll find another job eventually. Besides, I have the money I inherited from my parents, so I'll be okay for a little while."

"I know, I'm sorry," Jonathan said, backing down. "I just want you to have everything you need."

"So do I," she replied, putting her hand on her abdomen. "But I don't want to sell. All these pieces belong in the museum."

"I agree," he said, his face lighting up at her statement. "Is there anything else in the box?"

"Just this," she said, pulling out a white envelope with her name on it. She opened it. "It's a letter from Professor Dromly. Judging by the date, he wrote it while we were all in Florida."

"What does it say?"

Anise began reading to him.

"Saturday, October 10, 2015

Dear Ms. Viston,

If you're reading this, it means I am deceased and you are honoring one of my last wishes—that you use the contents of this safe deposit box in the way that will best suit you, to include the wisdom I shall impart here. I'm composing this missive as I feel you are owed an explanation.

Let me begin by admitting I wanted to know the secrets of death in order to have love in my life. However, the very pursuit of the Plate of Destiny made me abandon my wife and son, both of whom loved me. I lost what I was searching for by looking for what I already had. In the past, I've always considered irony to perhaps be a sort of poetic justice. Now, I've come to the dolorous conclusion that I was absolutely correct. With this sickening realization, paired with a betrayal of my hotel bed, came another realization. I finally understand destiny."

"A betrayal of my hotel bed?" asked Jonathan. He wore a look of confusion. "What do you think he meant by that?"

Anise couldn't help but laugh. It was the first time since Nate died. "Nate and I broke it accidentally. We were jumping up and down on his bed. I tried to fix it, but it must've collapsed under Dromly too."

"You were jumping on the bed? *Why?*" Jonathan looked at her, completely baffled. "Weren't you there to get the keystones?"

Anise shrugged. She knew he wouldn't get it even if she tried to explain. "You had to be there," she said and turned her attention back to the letter.

"As we go through life, we have ideas of who we are, of who we'll be, of what we'll do, of what we'll get, of what we deserve. Many follow these ideas through life and into the grave, sometimes getting what they want, sometimes not, but in either case, never truly understanding why they're there in the first place.

You see, life gives us the beautiful gift of aging. The most beautiful gift anyone could ever receive, and no one wants it. What's even more beautiful is that no matter how much effort, time, and money a person may spend to avoid aging, the gift is never taken away, at least not from the lucky ones. With each wrinkle carved into the face, a memory is carved into the heart. Each age spot is simply another dot to connect that makes the big picture more vivid. With each experience comes knowledge. And if we truly pay attention, with that knowledge comes wisdom.

The wisdom I've gained is that destiny is a paradox. It's a plan laid out for your future that's meant to happen—yet, it's completely changeable. Why? Because your true destiny is not only the ultimate destination, but in how you get there, and there are infinite ways to do that.

You may be wondering – what does this mean? We know the Plate of Destiny can bring back the dead, and the secrets of death and how to reverse it is why anyone who's ever searched for the Plate has desired it. That, or to further their own selfish agenda. However, no one has ever wanted the Plate for its true secrets of life—a grave error (pardon the pun).

"That's what Thomas said," interjected Jonathan. "We should be focused on the secrets of life, not death."

I realized that a universal truth lies within destiny itself—due to its <u>infinite</u> nature, it's never about an <u>ending</u> to your story, it's about <u>continuation.</u> Second chances. This is why I know without having to read it that the Plate of Destiny will explain how important a universal balance is, that one must focus on life itself (without obsession of resurrection), and how to bring someone back from the dead but will impart no other knowledge. The biggest realization I've ever had is in what the Plate purposely doesn't say, and what it doesn't say speaks volumes. What someone who has aged enough to have gained the necessary wisdom will realize from the Plate's silence is that you create your own destiny and your own truth by the way you get to your final destiny. The final destiny determines your path while your path determines your final destiny. And although you can get second chances, such as returning from the dead, these chances are better taken when you're still alive because you can have as many as you need. These second chances are opportunities to learn and gain wisdom. They are not meant to be used to try to control destiny, for the only thing

you can control is your reaction to occurrences and how you adjust your path
accordingly. You must walk your path to
gain wisdom, and you must use wisdom
to choose your path. As an aged person who has gained said wisdom, and a
teacher by trade and by nature, it's my
destiny to pass along the knowledge to
younger people like you who may not
have aged enough for this wisdom, but
already possess the maturity to listen to
and understand the wisdom of the ages.

"The only thing you can control is your reaction to
occurrences..." Anise repeated. "I have something like
that on one of my affirmation cards." She was enjoying
the letter and the way Dromly saw the world. Eagerly,
she continued reading, looking forward to what other
wisdom he might impart.

So how does one use this knowledge
in the real world? You must accept your
destiny and not try to adopt someone
else's. Your destiny isn't just about you.

Everyone's destinies are linked together as in a jigsaw puzzle, and every piece of a jigsaw puzzle is equally important. We must discover, accept, and embrace our own roles whether we're a gray edge piece or a colorful center. Believing any one piece is more important than another is incorrect because the puzzle would be equally incomplete without any of them.

I'll use myself as an example. I am a gray edge who wanted to be a colorful center, and I tried everything to become what I thought was better than what I was. I learned from experience that when one places more importance on attempting to control destiny than on learning the wisdom that accompanies the lessons of every life event, mistakes are inevitably made, sometimes with devastating consequences. The good news is that although you may not get to decide every detail of your life, after every mistake you make, you can humbly and respectfully give yourself as many second chances as you need. Today, I accepted my role as the gray edge. This doesn't mean that I failed at being a colorful center. It means that I finally realized that a gray edge is equally as important to the entire picture of the puzzle as a colorful center. By living my best gray edginess, I will be able to complete my destiny. We're all linked, and what we do affects the other pieces. If you are not yourself, the entire puzzle is compromised. Our differences are what bring out the beauty in each other. The gray edges enhance the vividness of the colorful center, and the colorful centers bring out the profound depth of the gray edges. By doing what you're best at, you serve the puzzle as a whole. Once you discover your place in the puzzle, you'll be on the right path to your destiny.

Jigsaw puzzles aside, it will take time to discover your right path which is what makes the second chances I discussed earlier so important. What I've found is that forgiveness of the self and using your knowledge and wisdom to move forward without ego, although difficult and lengthy conquests, are the secrets to completing your destiny, and I don't need to read the Plate to understand that now.

You may now be wondering how destiny is a paradox if all we must do is accept it. The answer is that accepting is one side of the coin. Choosing our destiny is the other side, and we must do both. Your destiny, your place in the puzzle, is waiting for you, but you must also manifest it – choose to bring it into existence by stepping onto a pathway that leads you there. It's meant for you, destined for you, but you must also choose it. <u>Unrealized potential</u> and the <u>fulfillment of your destiny</u> are the same thing on opposite sides of the scale of choice – and there lies the paradox. Just like turning up the thermostat turns cold into heat, making choices and taking new pathways turns our unrealized potential into a fulfilled destiny.

"I'm not quite sure I understand that fully," Anise said, her brow wrinkling. "Do you?"

Jonathan shook his head. "I'm not sure either."

If you remember nothing else, remember this – we are not born knowing our place in the puzzle. To live your best life, you must try different locations in the puzzle to determine where you fit, and once you find that place, you'll know your destiny. You must choose it as it chooses you. You won't get it right the first time. You must allow yourself the second chances which will lead you to a new path toward your place in the puzzle, your destiny, but you won't get to those second chances unless you create a new path to lead you there. If you find yourself on a dead-end path, ask yourself: what's holding you back? Use your wisdom to discover the answer to that question, and pass along your wisdom when you can.

There's a saying that goes something like, 'You enter school blind but come out seeing.' How appropriate for the theme of this letter, and how very sad that I denied myself of my sight until now. My motives were avaricious and selfish, and I want to offer my deepest apologies to you and everyone else who has had a painful and devastating role to play in this endeavor.

My original plan was to obtain the

knowledge of the Plate and that immediately afterward, my highest priority
would be to return to life those who have
passed on because of my actions as well
as restore to health anyone who has
suffered. During the darkest time of my
life, I desperately lied to myself, telling
myself that my morality would remain un-
blemished as long as I "fixed" everything
in the end. I realize now that I was trying
to control destiny. Trying to change my
place in the puzzle. Absolutely nothing
I do between the date of this letter and
the date of my death can make up for
what has occurred, so all I can do now
is attempt to make atonement as best I
can and live with the remorse for having
hurt so many.

Anise, the only comfort I feel is from
this vow that I will do everything in my
power to ensure that you end up with
the Plate of Destiny, and I must remain

roseate that I will accomplish this task as I have nothing left to hold on to. The Plate must go to the one person born in the bloodline that was meant to protect it. It will be your responsibility to keep it safe from that moment on, and I'm sure you've already realized this, but part of keeping it safe will mean having an heir as soon as possible to keep the King's bloodline alive. This choice is of course yours, and you will not be judged by me should you decide that being child-free is the best life for you. However, I do ask that you seriously contemplate the role you could play in preserving this priceless knowledge. Please, though, balance it with the knowledge that this would also be a large legacy to place on a child who didn't ask for it or for a child who was only born for that purpose alone. Only you can make this decision, and from what I've seen of your intelligence, bravery, and sense of morality, I have no doubt you will choose your correct path.

I thank you for your time and consideration, your devotion to the Plate, and for being a friend to my son.

Yours truly,
Frederick Dromly"

"Wow," Jonathan whispered.

Anise nodded. "He's wrong about one thing though."

"What's that?" Jonathan asked.

"King's blood doesn't only flow through *my* veins."

"That's right," Jonathan agreed. "Les. I'm glad Nate told us about him. That knowledge made us all work harder to keep you safe."

Anise watched Jonathan's face as he looked at the ground and narrowed his eyebrows. She knew he was thinking about something, and she couldn't help but feel curious. "What is it?"

He blushed. "I was a little jealous that you told Nate about Les and not me. But just now it made me realize why you kept trusting Nate even after everything that had happened and how much he'd lied to you. If Nate hadn't been completely on your side, he could've gone to Grace with the knowledge that you had a sibling with King's blood. They could've easily taken Les's blood. But Grace never knew because Nate never told her. He made a lot of mistakes, but his loyalty to you was unquestionable. And his decision to tell us about Les when he did was a good one. It may have saved your life."

"He saved my life more than once," she agreed. *But I couldn't save his.* Even though a wave of guilt threatened to make her sick, she squeezed Jonathan's hand. "And so did you. I know you battled Charlie by yourself while I was knocked out. You were so heroic and brave."

"You saved my life, too," he reminded her. "You're the hero here, I was just along for the ride."

She started putting the lock box contents in her backpack. "I'm sorry I never told you about Les. I told Nate really soon after we met and then he turned out to not be who I thought he was. I didn't want to go through that again, so I waited to tell you until we knew each other better. Then my parents died, and I had a lot to take care of. Then you started acting strangely from the brainwashing—"

"It's okay. I understand."

"Thank you. I'm glad you know now."

"So, Dromly brought up a good point at the end of his letter. How do you feel about having an heir someday?" Jonathan asked her with curiosity. "I know the one time we talked about it you weren't sure you wanted to have kids."

"I never really thought much about having kids because my own childhood wasn't great," she answered truthfully. "But I know now that I would like to have one." She softly touched her abdomen. "I'll tell him or her about the Plate and its knowledge. But whether they want the responsibility of protecting it will be their choice, not mine."

"That's great!" Jonathan said, smiling happily. "Are you ready to go?"

"Almost. First, I have something to tell you. Speaking of having an heir...I'm pregnant."

Jonathan's eyes widened and his jaw dropped in stunned silence. His face lit up, and he gave her a hug. When their embrace broke, his face turned serious. "Is it...?"

"It could be yours," she said, "or it could be Nate's."
He took her hands. "Either way, you're not alone."

Sunday, October 25, 2015

THE HOSPITAL ROOM WAS WHITE, STARK, and smelled like it had been cleaned with strong chemical disinfectants. Anise closed her eyes and concentrated on the hand she held. The Armor Jewelry she wore was fully charged, but the cuff wasn't sparkling at all as she sent healing intentions.

The man had been deathly still when Anise had entered his room, but now he stirred slightly. With a great effort, he blinked open his eyes, and looked around with an expression of confusion and mild anxiety. His eyes met hers, and he smiled. "Anise?"

"Hi Les!" She patted his hand and wiped the sweat from his brow with a cloth. "How are you feeling?" Opening the drapes, she let the sun brighten up the dark room. It was strange the cuff hadn't sparkled, but he should be fine now, right?

His eyes scanned the room and then looked out the window. "I'm okay," came his breathless response. "It's good to see you."

Anise frowned. Why didn't he seem better? "I'm sorry I didn't come sooner. Your mother made it clear that she didn't want me around you. I recently learned from the nurses that she's here all the time except for Sunday mornings."

"She never misses church." His eyes drifted to her wrist. His hand tried to lift to point a finger but fell back to the bed, not having the strength. "It's the cuff from the letter."

She nodded. "I now know what you were talking

about when you mentioned the letter the first time we met in front of my mother's house. Thomas Brevain wrote it, and he meant for us to have it." She told him the entire story about the Jewelry, the Plate of Destiny, and her adventures in obtaining them. She gave him a demonstration of the strength of the earrings by bending the metal side rails of his hospital bed with her bare hands.

His eyes tried to jump out of his skull, and they glued themselves to Anise's face while his fingers grasped the bedsheets. "So you were trying to heal me just now?" he asked as she carefully bent the bed rails back into place.

"I know this is a lot to take in," she said. "But yes, I tried. I failed you, though. You don't seem any better. But I have another idea." She took her garnet ring and Selina's bloodstone ring off her finger and put them on Les's. They waited a few minutes. "Garnets are supposed to heal injuries. But I don't think this is working either."

He shook his head. "I don't feel any different."

She took the garnet and bloodstone rings back. "I'm so sorry." Her tears flooded her cheeks. "I thought for sure one of those methods would work."

"Tell me about our family," he wheezed.

"What?"

"My mom didn't want me to know my birth family. But I'd love to know more. Tell me."

"Okay, well, Deb and Ben were our parents as you know."

"I wish I'd gotten to meet them. What were they like?"

Anise twisted the garnet ring around her finger. "Honestly, what I remember most is that dad was distant and mom was angry."

"Okay. We don't have to talk about them."

"I wish I knew how to break the curse," Anise said softly. "I'm pregnant, and once this child is born, you won't have much time left. I'll have a little more time, but I won't ever meet my grandchildren."

"Don't worry about me. I don't think I'd have much time left anyway. These unconscious spells have been happening more often than ever now. I'm very sorry you won't get to live as long as you should either."

Anise hung her head. "I'm sorry for both of us. I really thought I could help."

"Did Deb ever talk about her parents?" Les wanted to know.

"A little. Her mom seemed like a sweet lady. She was an artist and taught painting, drawing, and sculpting at an art school. Mom's dad passed away when she was in high school. She said for years before then he didn't spend much time with her. He slept a lot, sometimes for days at a time until one day he didn't wake up."

"Days at a time?" Les asked.

"Like you!" Anise exclaimed, in shock at her revelation. "I never thought about that!"

"Deb had me when she was in high school," Les pondered. "So her dad...what was his name?"

"Louis Stannell."

"So Louis passed before I was born. Before he could meet his grandchild."

"You're not sick at all! It's the curse!" Anise realized. "So that's why the cuff isn't helping. It can't help with a curse."

"It wouldn't have helped if I had been sick either," Les said. "I reread the letter that Thomas sent me several more times while I've been lying here trying to make sense of it. It says the cuff can only help with physical injuries or mental injuries like brainwashing."

"I don't suppose the letter explained how to break this curse?" Anise said, trying not to let hope build up in her chest. She didn't feel like she could take being drop-kicked in one of hope's cruel tricks again.

Les's eyebrows raised in excitement as his eyes lit up like they always did when he had an idea. "Not specifically. But it explains a lot about the Jewelry and Plate, and from that explanation plus what you just told me, I know that the key to breaking the curse is the poison ring."

"What do you mean?" Anise looked at the carnelian ring on her hand and then back to her brother to listen to his explanation.

Les continued. "The knowledge on the Plate is like a reset button. You can use it when you want to undo something, like death for example."

"Or a curse?" Anise asked. This "undoing" concept Les was talking about must've been Thomas's way of explaining the second chances that Fred Dromly mentioned in his letter.

"Right. The Jewelry and the Plate both use a kind of universal knowledge to work. And in that way, the Jewelry is a tangible representation of the knowledge on the Plate of Destiny. Thomas Brevain had never read the Plate when he wrote the letter, but somehow he had figured out that universal wisdom is dualistic."

Anise thought for a moment. "In his letter to me, Professor Dromly said that destiny is a paradox."

"That's a good way to look at it, too," Les said. "Even though destiny is set, you can 'undo' it or change it. So although it's one way, it's also the opposite way, because opposites aren't really opposites."

Anise narrowed her brow in confusion. "Okay, I think you lost me there."

"Pick a pair of opposites," Les told her.

"You mean like...up and down?" Anise asked.

"Sure. So, it seems like up and down are opposites. But when you think about it, up and down are both just words to describe elevation. They're the same thing on different ends of the same scale. Up can change into down and vice versa very easily only by changing your degree of elevation."

"I never thought about it like that before!" Anise said, understanding. "In the letter Dr. Dromly wrote me, he has a line in there that says, 'Unrealized potential and the fulfillment of your destiny are the same thing on opposite sides of the scale of choice.' I wasn't quite sure what that meant, but now I get it! By changing your choices, you can either fulfill your destiny or not. It's pretty simple."

"That's how destiny works," Les told her. "As well as the Plate. It can give life back to someone, but it also takes life away."

Anise nodded, already understanding. "I see that," she said. "It doesn't kill anyone, but Grace, Dr. Smithton, Thomas, Professor Dromly, and Charlie Masser all became obsessed with finding it. They each gave up most of their lives in order to do so. That's all they lived for."

"And that's how the Jewelry works, too," Les told her. "Take the cuff, for example. When used one way, the cuff can cause brainwashing, or loss of the self. But it can also bring back the self through healing when it was stolen by mental or physical injury."

"I always thought it was interesting that the cuff can both harm and heal," Anise said. "Now I know that it's supposed to be that way."

"Exactly. The other pieces work the same way. The earrings give you great physical strength, but they also can bring about weakness of character. Have they ever really been used for anything other than fighting?"

"Not that I know of." Anise thought about Les's explanation. "What about the amulet?"

"The amulet protects you, but it can also bring you harm if you become too dependent on it," Les answered.

"That's true!" Anise agreed. "I've had anxiety for years, but it got worse after I got the amulet and had to fight Grace. I've been having agoraphobic symptoms when I try to go anywhere without wearing it," she admitted. "If I try to leave the house without it, I get panic attacks. I've been depending on the amulet to make me feel safe, but I'd like to find a way to feel better without using it. Just thinking about confronting my phobia though is scary, so I've been putting it off."

"Could the Armor Jewelry be helpful with this?" Les wondered. "Maybe you can use it to heal your anxiety and then put the amulet away so you won't be dependent on it anymore," Les suggested.

Anise frowned. "I would love to stop the panic attacks. Unfortunately, it's not that easy. I learned from Grace that the Jewelry can't change your emotions. I can't brainwash anyone into feeling an emotion with the cuff, and I can't rid myself of unwanted emotions either. But even though it'll be challenging, I do plan on trying to stop depending on the amulet. It would be so nice to be able to go places comfortably again without it."

"Let me know if I can help in any way," Les offered.

Anise thanked him before her eyes drifted to her hand. "You said the key to breaking the curse is the ring?"

"Yes. The ring is poisonous, but it can also eliminate poisons."

"Oh!" Anise said, understanding. "Not necessarily physical poisons, but any kind of poison. Like the toxic energy of a curse."

"Exactly. The only thing is that Thomas's letter doesn't say how specifically to do it. Do you have any ideas?"

Anise nodded. "I do. The ring delivers poison when you turn the setting like this and the stone flips over. Then you press the poisonous side to someone's skin." She showed him the bands of red cinnabar and yellow orpiment in the carnelian by turning the setting. Then she turned the setting back and the stone flipped over again to the non-poisonous side. "I think we need to leave the ring with the non-poisonous side showing." She held the carnelian stone in the ring to her brother's arm. "The Jewelry works on intention. I'm now mindfully intending for the curse to be gone."

They watched as the ring sparkled. When it stopped, Anise removed it from Les's arm. "It never sparkled like that before!" she said excitedly. "How do you feel?" She watched in amazement as his ghostly pale skin warmed. His dark eye circles disappeared, and his shallow breathing deepened.

He sat up. His legs swung over the side of the bed and he stood. Anise laughed with delight as she watched him dance in circles, getting twisted in the tubes stuck in his nose and arm. He pulled out the cannula and IV and laughed along with her. "It worked!"

Anise held the ring to her own arm and repeated the process. When the ring was done sparkling once again, she smiled.

He smiled back. "Now we have the rest of our lives to continue to get to know each other. And our children, nieces, nephews, and grandchildren."

Anise didn't know if she wanted to laugh or cry. She did both. "The rest of our *long* lives."

Tuesday, October 27, 2015

ANISE SAT ON HER COUCH PUTTING the finishing touches on a sketch of Nate's father behind bars. Her depiction of Dan had the same devastated look on his face that he'd worn when she and Nate had visited him in prison. The caption read, "There's so much you still don't know." Her tears fell on the paper, smudging the lines of Dan's face.

Jonathan let himself in to Anise's apartment and rushed over to her.

"Are you okay? What's wrong?" he asked, grabbing a box of tissues on his way. He sat next to her and took her hands. "Are you feeling okay? Is it the baby?"

She grabbed a tissue and dabbed her eyes. "How am I going to tell Dan?"

"Dan?"

"How can I face him and tell him that his mother, son,

and ex-wife are all dead because of me?"

Jonathan squeezed her hand. "They're not dead because of you. Grace isn't dead at all, just...different."

"They were all in Florida to help me."

"Grace kidnapped you. She may have teamed up with us at the end, sort of, but she was there to help herself, not you."

Anise sighed. "Regardless. What will I say to Dan?"

"You don't owe Dan anything. You and I almost died because of him."

"I know, but Dan was a victim of Grace's as much as we were, and we let *her* on our side."

"We needed her. And besides, Grace's behavior wasn't her fault," Jonathan argued. "She was brainwashed by the cuff."

"The abuse that Grace inflicted on Dan wasn't *his* fault," Anise insisted. "And that's why he behaved the way he did."

"I really admire your compassion," Jonathan told her and gave her a long embrace. "That still doesn't make you responsible for him. He's an adult who made his own decisions. You did what you had to do."

Anise looked him in the eye. "I've thought long and hard about this, and I want to try to bring back everyone that died because of me, the Armor Jewelry, and the Plate. Professor Dromly wanted to make things right, and I do too. In his letter, he told me I should live my life according to the knowledge from the Plate, and that's what I want to do. Starting with giving them all second chances. And if it doesn't bring anyone back, I'll put away the Plate and Jewelry forever. I won't get obsessed with it. But I do need to try."

"How?" Jonathan shrugged. "I know we saw Grace's drawings of the words on the Plate, but we still have no idea how to bring back the dead. Thomas wouldn't read it for us."

"He read enough. I think he unwittingly told us how

bringing back the dead is done."

"I don't remember that," Jonathan said, narrowing his brow in confusion.

"I was replaying everything in my head that he had said about the Plate," Anise told him. "Remember when he mentioned something about cooperation through opposition and the directed destruction of death?"

"Sort of," Jonathan said. "He said a *lot* of things."

"Okay," Anise said. "Now think back to when we were in Dr. Smithton's office three years ago, and he was telling us about the Armor Jewelry. He told us the pieces were meant to work together, and if they were used to oppose each other, the result could be destruction."

"Right," Jonathan said.

"We usually think of destruction as a bad thing," Anise continued. "But I believe that the Jewelry can work together when it's used against itself. It's another paradox. Like Thomas said: 'Cooperation through opposition.' When intentionally used in that way, the destruction isn't a bad thing. It isn't destruction of the world. It's destruction of death. It literally destroys what death has done and brings people back to life."

She let Jonathan ponder that thought while she got up and brought over a wooden box she took from underneath her kitchen sink. Sitting back on the couch, she opened the box, took out the amulet, ring, cuff, and earrings, and put them on. After giving him a big hug, she said, "You might want to stand back. I don't exactly know what to expect, and I don't want this to affect you."

Jonathan paused as he looked at her. "Are you sure this is what you want to do?"

"Yes," she said. "If someone wasn't able to live out their destiny because of me, and I have the power to correct that, then that's something I have to do. So I need to try to bring back everyone, not just our friends and my parents. I also want to bring back Brian, everyone that died fighting in Florida, any of your brainwashed co-workers who died, the security guard at the Spring-field Museum, Dromly, and even Charlie Masser, too."

"They might not all come back," Jonathan warned her. "And you would be getting a new destiny, too. There's no telling what could happen."

"I know," Anise said. "If they don't come back, then they've lived out their destiny. But I have to take responsibility for those who missed out on their opportunities because of me. I'm at peace with getting a new destiny. I firmly believe that the right decision isn't always clear. But sometimes what's right and what isn't *is* a black and white decision. Like a very wise person once told me: When you know what the right thing to do is, do you really have any other choice?"

He laughed, remembering how he'd said that to her years ago. "Nice try. But you might come back at a different age or in a different place. You might not remember your old life at all. Do you want to risk that?"

"Things might be different for me," Anise agreed, "but if I don't do this, I'm going to forever feel guilty about everyone who got killed. If I can give them second chances, I want to, no matter what happens to me."

"In that case, I want to help you," Jonathan told her.

"That's not necessary. I can do it by myself."

"I have no doubt you can. But it's going to be pretty hard to fight yourself in the way you need to when wearing this Jewelry. It'll be much easier if I help you."

Anise shook her head, uncomfortable with the idea. "You would get a whole new destiny, too. I don't want you to have to go through that because of me."

He surprised her by taking her hand and holding it in both of his. "We're in this together. We always have been. Let me help you. Okay?"

After more convincing, she finally gave in. Something was gnawing at her stomach though. "Thank you. But you had a good point about not remembering our old lives. What if we forget each other? I don't know if I could handle that. Grace and Morty don't remember us at all."

"But they found *each other*. And we will too. I have no doubt. I know in my heart our destiny is to be in each other's lives, one way or another."

When they were ready, Jonathan wore the ring and cuff while Anise kept on the earrings and the amulet.

"Obey my every command," he told her while pressing the poisonous side of the ring to her skin. The amulet glowed as she pushed him away with her supernatural strength.

"Use your intention to bring them all back to life," Jonathan said.

They continued using the Jewelry against each other. Besides Jonathan's voice giving her commands, the apartment seemed to be getting quieter. The hum of the refrigerator faded, and Anise heard no outside traffic. The lights started to dim, and she felt like she might be floating.

"Jonathan, look!" Anise said after several minutes had passed. They both tilted their heads downward. "It must have worked! But I don't see anyone."

Their bodies were flickering in and out just like Morty and Grace's had after bringing back Thomas.

"I guess whoever came back isn't going to live out their destiny in your apartment," he joked. "If we're meant to know who it is, we'll find out soon enough."

"I'm dizzy," Anise told him, putting a hand to her forehead and squeezing her eyes shut.

"I am too," he said.

Anise and Jonathan leaned back on the couch and held hands, staring at each other while awaiting their fate.

"You know you're amazing, right?" Jonathan asked her as everything faded to black.

Chapter 26

Saturday, November 30, 2019

The sunlight on her face gently woke Anise. She opened her eyes and saw the familiar paisley sheets she had bought on sale several years ago. Her bed felt so good that she closed her eyes again. Then they flew open.

Wait.

She sat up straight in bed as everything came back to her. Florida, the Armor Jewelry, the new destinies. What had happened? She remembered the Plate was in a safe under the floorboards in her bedroom closet. She and Jonathan had been wearing the Jewelry, but where was it now? She touched her chest, but the amulet wasn't there. She had a strange memory of practicing sleeping with the amulet next to her bed instead of around her neck, but when would that have happened? This was the very next moment after receiving her new destiny. She grabbed the amulet from her nightstand and put it on. But that wasn't her nightstand. She also wasn't in her apartment.

What the hell?

Breathing heavily and frantically turning her head

to find something familiar, she saw her phone blinking. Picking it up, she saw she had a text from Jonathan.

Jonathan: Are we still on for this afternoon?

She let out a sigh of relief, suddenly feeling much calmer.

Anise: Yes. See you then.

Looking around the room, she remembered she'd moved out of her apartment. There was a view of a fenced backyard outside the window. A memory of purchasing a house rushed into her mind. Several pictures hung on the wall, and she got up to study them.

There was one of her friend Vanessa in her bridal gown and Anise standing next to her as one of her bridesmaids. A flood of new memories about Vanessa's wedding day invaded her mind. It was surprisingly easy to remember the details of an event she had been to but never actually experienced. But maybe, in a strange way, she *had* experienced it. The memories were so strong. In her mind, she was there—the excitement, helping her friend get ready, watching her walk down the aisle, and the inexpressible joy she felt.

Smiling, she looked at the other pictures. The next one was of her standing next to Les during one of their visits, his wavy brown hair brushing the tips of his shoulders. Many of the other pictures were of Anise with her friends—Jonathan, Vanessa, Erin, Joy, Doreen. She touched Erin's face on the photograph, leaving a fingerprint on the glass. Then she looked more closely. "Wait, this is a new picture!" She let out a happy cry, tore the picture from the wall, and hugged it. "She came back!"

Anise felt another memory emerging and grabbed her day planner to ensure that she was, in fact, meeting Erin, Joy, and Vanessa that evening. *Yes! Seven o' clock tonight.* She decided to tell them everything. And she'd tell Doreen tomorrow when she'd visit the thrift shop. It might take some time for them to believe it like with Jonathan, and she'd have to drill it in to Joy to not tell anyone. That was a risk. But it was too scary not to tell them. What if Grace came back and tried to hurt one of them to get to her? They needed to be prepared.

Her eyes scanned the other pictures on the wall. One was of her and Selina when she visited the year before. Another memory popped into her mind, this time of Selina tracking her and Jonathan down to apologize for having stolen the Armor Jewelry and to thank Anise for bringing her back. Jonathan and Selina then spent some time together and...

"Selina?!" she exclaimed under her breath. If both Erin and Selina came back... Anise dove for her phone, wondering who else she may have brought back with the Plate's knowledge. Opening a browser, she typed "Nate Brevain." When nothing pertinent came up, she tried "Nathan Brevain." A flood of silent tears made their way down her cheeks when the results again came up negative. She scrolled through the contacts in her phone and on each social media account, reading every name carefully, but he wasn't there. Choking back sobs and holding her stomach, she brought up a picture of Nate she'd taken when they'd gone riding and stared at it while wiping her tears away. Somehow, the grief felt both fresh and older at the same time.

After the tears stopped falling, she typed "Kent Dromly." Pictures of Kent at his medical practice in Springfield popped up. His brief biography on his website mentioned that he was married with one son, Kent Dromly, Jr.

Anise put a hand to her heart. "He finally got the family he wanted." She went back to the picture of Nate on his motorcycle and thought about his voice, sweet things he'd said to her, how he felt when he wrapped his arms around her. She was startled out of her daydream when she felt something touch her knees.

"Hi, Mommy."

Without thinking, Anise picked up her three-year-old daughter and gave her a kiss on the cheek. "Good morning, Natalia! Did you sleep well?" She carried the girl to the end of the bed and sat there with her.

The child nodded. Anise pushed some of the girl's almost-black hair out of her sweet, smiling face while she stared up at her mother with cobalt blue eyes.

Natalia grabbed her mother's phone when she saw the picture on the screen. "That's my daddy."

"That's right."

"Is he still in heaven?"

"Yes." Anise stroked her daughter's hair.

"What's that?" Natalia asked, pointing at the screen.

"That's his motorcycle. He loved it. He'd take me for rides on it, and we'd go soooo fast!"

Natalia's eyes grew as wide as her smile. "Can I have one?"

Anise laughed. "Not until you're much, much older."

Sunday, February 11, 2024

"GRACE AND MORTY?" ANISE SAID WITH surprise as she opened the door to see who'd been ringing her bell incessantly. It was strange to see them so young. Anise guessed they'd be about thirty now. She took the card that Morty was handing her. It said he was a curator at the Springfield Museum.

"You actually remember us?" Morty said with a laugh. "It's been nine years since we met at the dig."

"I remember," Anise said, staring at Grace questioningly.

"Aren't you going to invite us in?" Grace demanded, her long red hair dancing in the breeze.

"Grace..." Morty muttered, shaking his head. "We're here due to a conundrum that Grace believes you can help us with. If you're willing, perhaps we can meet somewhere for dinner at your convenience?"

Going out to dinner with Grace wasn't on Anise's to-do list, but she was curious as to why these two would track her down. She opened the door wider. "Come in. What is this about?"

They stepped inside. "I want him to remember. I think you can help make that happen," Grace said.

"So you *do* remember," Anise said to her.

"Of course I do. I didn't at first, but I remembered as soon as I caught you when you fell. I saw everything." She narrowed her eyes and stared at Anise.

"If the way to make someone remember is to turn them into a seer, then I can't do that for him," Anise said.

"There's always more than one way with magic," Grace insisted. "For instance, remember how a seer has to have hair of flame? We all thought that meant she had to have red hair. But Charlie Masser found a way around that by setting your friend's hair on fire."

"Yeah, I know," Anise snapped, not wanting to relive the gruesome memory.

"She won't tell me what she's talking about, Anise," Morty said softly. "And she keeps refusing my marriage proposals. She says I'm not completely myself anymore and that I won't be until I can remember. I haven't the faintest idea of what she means. Do you?"

"I do," Anise told him.

"Is that..." Grace said looking over Anise's shoulder.

"Yes." Anise reached behind her. The little girl took her hand and stepped forward. "This is my daughter, Natalia."

"Hello," Natalia said with a grin that was missing a front tooth. "Talia for short."

"Hello, my dear," said Morty, smiling back. "How old are you?"

"Seven and a half," Natalia replied.

"She looks just like him." Grace stared at the girl.

Anise wasn't sure if Grace meant Nate or Thomas. "Yes." She turned to her daughter. "This is Grace and Morty."

Natalia's eyes lit up. "From the stories you told me!"

"You told her?" Grace said with a look of shock. "She's a child!"

"She's both intelligent and mature," Anise said. "And I don't keep secrets from my daughter. She knows everything about you, the Jewelry, and the Plate of Destiny."

Morty sat on a chair and put his head in his hands.

Grace rolled her eyes at him. "He thinks he has dementia," she muttered to Anise.

Anise grabbed Grace's arm and pulled her aside, out of ear shot of Morty and Talia. "What the hell is wrong with you?" Anise hissed at her. "You're getting a second chance! You get to do it all over again! Why the hell are you still being a raving bitch?!"

"Because I don't want to do it all over again without him!" Grace hissed back, her eyes glancing back at Morty. Her face crinkled and her lower lip quivered. She quickly put a hand over her mouth and took a deep breath. Her hand lowered as she composed herself. "Do you know how to help or not?"

Anise looked at Morty and felt sorry for him. "I don't, but I have an idea." She grabbed her phone. "Jonathan would want to be here for this."

JONATHAN'S NERVES MADE HIM HURRY UP Anise's walkway, but the conflict between his heart and mind made him slow his steps. The possibility of being able to talk to his old mentor again was a thrilling notion, even though he still felt betrayed by Dr. S.'s lies, not to mention his unethical and shocking behavior. "Where are they?" he asked after Anise let him inside.

"Getting lunch. They'll be back."

"They went out?" he asked, confused. "Now?"

Anise shrugged. "I had a little fight with Grace. She needed some time to cool off."

"What do you mean a fight?"

"I wouldn't tell her my idea about how to get Morty to remember without you here. I knew you'd want to see this. And...well, you know Grace. I told her if she wants my help that we'll do this my way or not at all. She had choice words for me that she said in front of Talia. So I kicked them out."

"So they're gone?"

"No. Grace wants Morty to remember. They'll be back."

"Can you get them back soon?" Jonathan asked. "Selina wasn't thrilled that I dropped everything and left her alone with the kids when you called. People are going to start coming over in just a few hours and we still have to prepare the food and do some cleaning."

"Oh, right, the game. I almost forgot." Anise picked up the business card Morty had given her and typed his number into her phone. "I'll text them now."

"You're still coming over tonight, right?"

"That's the plan. But let's see how today goes with Grace and Morty."

Jonathan shifted nervously in his chair. "If you can bring back his memories, what will I say to him?" Jonathan asked. "I don't even know if I can forgive him."

"You don't have to forgive him," Anise said. "I can't forgive Grace for everything she put us through or for everything she did to Nate when he was a child. And I think if she had helped us that night with Charlie instead of selfishly attending to her own agenda, Nate might have lived."

"So why are you helping her?" Jonathan asked.

"Because of what Fred Dromly said in his letter. All our destinies are connected. Grace is like a loose cannon. If someone doesn't show her some kindness and love, she's going to turn into a bitter and angry person, worse than she already is. And with Grace, that's a dangerous thing. She and I are never going to be friends, but I'm still going to help her because Morty will love her. He might be the only one who can. And Grace being loved is the best thing for her and everyone around her."

Jonathan slowly nodded his head and looked at the ground. Anise's words made sense, and he agreed. "That's really noble."

Anise shrugged. "But also I'm a little afraid of what she might do if I don't help her."

"Understandable." Jonathan could sense Anise's nervousness, and he tried to come up with something better to say. But he couldn't stop his mind from racing, still thinking about what he might say to Morty or if he should say anything at all.

"Maybe you can forgive Morty eventually," Anise said, as if reading his mind. "You forgave Selina."

"Her grandfather blackmailed her. And she didn't know what he was planning to do."

"You even forgave Nate," Anise reminded him with a smirk.

Jonathan let out a small laugh. "Sort of, yeah. Even *I'm* shocked by that one."

"Even if you don't forgive Morty," Anise said gently, "you can still talk to him. Maybe it'll help you put everything behind you."

"Maybe." Jonathan was quiet for a moment. "Oh, I meant to tell you. I saw Raina."

Anise raised her eyebrows in surprise. "Really?"

"I was in Tallahassee with Selina for a symposium she wanted to attend," Jonathan explained. "We saw her at the park where she still works. She walked right by us like we'd never met."

"So she doesn't remember," Anise said, frowning. "I searched for her online but couldn't find her."

"She has a different last name now."

Anise sighed and her eyes welled up. "I spent so much time online looking for any little sign. Hours and days and months. I found nothing."

Jonathan's heart ached for her. She wasn't talking about Raina anymore. He watched a tear run down her face. He stood and opened his arms to her.

She wrapped her arms around him and rested her face on his chest. "I'm glad you're here."

"Me too." He held her for a moment until the doorbell rang three times in a row.

"Ugh," she said. "That would be Grace."

"WELL, WHAT DO YOU THINK?" ANISE asked. She couldn't tell what was going on in Grace's head from her expression, but knowing Grace, she had something to say about it.

"Really? The Armor ring? This is your great idea?" Grace scoffed.

"Give it a chance!" Jonathan demanded.

"Yeah!" Talia piped up, narrowing her eyes at Grace. "I don't hear any great ideas coming from you."

Anise suppressed a laugh. Nate would've said something like that.

"That ring is incredible," Morty said, grabbing Anise's hand to get a better look. "Not to mention the rest of the Jewelry you're wearing. You said it came from Mallandia? I'd love to know more."

"If this works, you'll know far more about it than I do." Anise pressed the ring's carnelian stone to Morty's arm.

"You're using it wrong!" Grace said. "Did you forget you have to twist it?"

Anise shook her head. "If I did that, I'd poison him."

Morty's eyes opened wide, and he pulled his arm away.

Anise gently pulled his arm back. "This side of the stone is harmless," she explained to him. "The other side delivers poisons; this side takes them away. Right now, you can't remember much of your life, and it's causing toxic emotions in your relationship with Grace. Your false ideas about what's true and what's not must also be causing some kind of toxicity in your heart and mind. How can they not when the real memories are in there somewhere conflicting with everything you believe? I'm sending out the intention to remove these toxins from your life, and the way to do that is to restore your memory."

Morty looked at her as if she'd told him that unicorns and leprechauns were real. She felt a ray of hope as the ring began to sparkle and made a plan to visit Raina to restore her memories if this worked. "How do you feel?" she asked.

Grace stared intently at Morty, waiting for him to answer.

IT ALL CAME BACK IN BITS and pieces. Every second, he had another memory fill his mind's eye. As the fragments of times long ago ripped through his brain like bullets, Morty grabbed on to the edges of his chair and stared at Anise. The amulet. The fight in his office. Her deceased parents. "I'm so sorry," he whispered. He turned his head and saw Jonathan. His protégé with the rumpled clothes and the brilliant ideas had grown up and was looking at him with an expression of judgment that made Morty uncomfortable. The brainwashing. The lies. "I'm so sorry," he repeated.

Feeling a hand on his arm, his head turned to Grace, and he saw the most beautiful woman in the world looking at him expectantly. In her wild brown eyes he also saw all the pain and hurt he'd caused everyone else because of the love he felt for her that had never been returned. He brushed away her touch and stood up angrily. "We were old!" he informed her loudly. He narrowed his eyes in disgust. "And my entire long life was lived for you and you alone!" He was now yelling. "I did despicable things, and it was all for you! Well, no more! Do you hear me, Grace?! Never again will I betray myself for you!"

He watched with surprise as her face radiated joy. "You're back," she said, her voice vibrating and a happy tear running down her cheek. He'd never seen her cry before, not in this life or the last one. Her arms wrapped around him and squeezed. "I missed you!" she said, crying into his chest. "I love you so much."

Morty stood there motionless for a moment. He felt different. Better. And *she* was different, too. Not that he wanted to her to cry, but she was finally showing her true self to him and letting him in fully. So much better. He returned her embrace and mirrored her tears. "I love you, too."

ANISE FELT GRACE GRAB HER ARM.

"Thank you," Grace said. Her eyes began darting back and forth just like when she'd had visions on the plane.

"What did you see?" Anise asked her when Grace's eyes stopped moving.

"Go see Kent Dromly."

"I already did. Kent didn't remember me when I tried

to visit him at his office. He didn't believe anything I told him and had no interest in the Armor Jewelry. I must've made him really uncomfortable to say the least. I was basically thrown out of his office and was warned not to come back. I don't think he'd let me get near enough to him to restore his memories."

Grace gave her a frown. "Go see Kent Dromly!" she repeated forcefully before grabbing Morty's hand and pulling him out the door.

Tuesday, February 20, 2024

ANISE WALKED THROUGH THE DOOR OF Kent's surgical practice and wandered the lobby. *How will Kent react? He warned me never to come back.* She put a hand over the amulet she wore under her coat.

"Ma'am, do you have an appointment?" the receptionist asked.

Anise stepped up to the front desk. "Yes, I'm here to see Dr. Dromly." She looked to the wall next to her where photographs were prominently displayed in frames. "Is this Dr. Dromly's family?" Her heart wanted to stop as she took one of the photos off the wall. Her hand grasped the front counter as the room began to spin. Her hyperventilating gasps grew quicker as she stared at the photograph.

"You? I thought I told you not to come back!" Kent had stepped into the lobby and was hissing at Anise under his breath.

"Is this your family?" Anise demanded of him as she held up the photograph. "Is it?!"

"Keep it down," Kent whisper-demanded and waved her through the door with a sign that said "Staff Only."

"Start explaining!" Anise growled as she followed

Kent into a small exam room. "Why are *Nate* and *Lorelei* in this photograph?"

"It's an old picture, Anise. We took that when we were all in Florida."

Anise took another look and felt her rage exploding. "This is *not* an old picture! All three of you look older than you did nine years ago! And the last time I was here you said you didn't remember me... Why did you lie?!"

"I had to." He put a hand to his forehead and sighed.

"For god's sake, why?!"

"Okay." Kent paced the room. "I assume it was you who ended up with the Plate of Destiny and brought us back from death?"

"Yes..." Anise confirmed impatiently.

"We're grateful. Thank you. And you're right, I didn't forget my old life."

"I already know that! Where is he? I want to see him!"

Kent sighed again. "Wait here for a minute. You caught me in the middle of something. I'll be right back."

"See that you are," she called out as Kent left the room.

Anise fumed as she stared out the window. There was a motorcycle that looked just like Nate's in the parking lot. *Is he here too?* The thought that Nate might be in the same building as her caused her to drop the photograph and sob into her hands. She wanted to run out of the room and search the office for him, but what if he wasn't there? And also, what if he was? Either way, it was too much. Feeling dizzy, she tripped over a small raise in the carpet and fell to her hands and knees. Letting her head hang low and her tears drench the carpet, she stayed there, crying silently, until she felt a pair of arms wrap around her.

A soft female voice spoke to her. "Anise, I'm so sorry you had to find out like this."

Anise looked behind her. "Where is he, Lorelei?"

"He's here today. In his office. He's a physician's assistant."

Anise got up and headed straight for the door.

"Where do you think you're going?" Kent asked her, blocking her path.

"I want to see him! He would want to see me!"

"He doesn't remember his old life, Anise," Lorelei said gently. "And we think it's better that way."

A wave of horror chilled Anise so strongly she could swear her marrow was frozen. "How can you say that?!"

"He has new memories," Kent explained. "He remembers growing up with Lorelei. And with me as his father. We were good to him. He didn't have to suffer the abuse from Grace and Dan. He doesn't remember them either."

"He doesn't have a criminal record," Lorelei added, her expression full of happiness. "He can do whatever he wants."

"If he can do whatever he wants, then why isn't he working in finance?"

"We're all a product of our environment and upbringing, Anise," Kent told her. "There are bound to be differences now that he remembers a different background."

"Okay, but I know him. He would want to see me. He has a daughter, too. He'd want to know her. This is Natalia." Anise showed Lorelei a picture.

Lorelei shed a tear looking at her granddaughter. "She's beautiful!"

"So it's settled then. I know how to restore his memories!"

"That's what we were afraid of. We don't want you to do that," Lorelei told her.

Nausea squeezed Anise's stomach. "But—"

"There's more," Kent said. "Nate has a community. A good job working with his family. And...he's engaged."

"Engaged?" Anise felt her heart shatter inside her chest.

"He's happy, Anise," Lorelei insisted. "Please let him stay that way. If he remembers all the trauma he had to go through...He did *not* have a good life, but he does now. He deserves it. Wouldn't you agree?"

A knock at the door interrupted the conversation. It cracked open. Anise gasped when Nate stuck his head in.

"Sorry to intrude, but I—" Nate stopped when he saw Anise.

The ticking clock in the room was suddenly deafening, and Anise opened her mouth to speak. Nothing came out except his barely audible name. "Nate." Her eyes flooded with tears again.

"Are you okay, ma'am?" he asked her. He grabbed a tissue box from the counter and held it out to her.

She took one. "Yes, I...I just received some upsetting news." She looked him up and down. He was wearing an orange sweater. It tried dutifully to cover up a small beer gut but looked horrible on him just the same. The color made his complexion look sick, and it wasn't something he'd ever pick out. At least, not in his old life. It would've reminded him of the orange jumpsuit he'd had to wear in prison. He'd sworn never to wear orange again.

"I'm so sorry to hear that." Nate gave her a somber look.

"This is my son," Lorelei said, introducing them, "Kent Dromly, Jr. And this is Anise Viston, uh, our newest patient."

"Nice to meet you," Nate said.

Kent Dromly, Jr.? With a new name, no wonder she hadn't been able to find him online. Anise hated everything about this conversation. The connection he'd always said they'd had...there was no trace of it in his eyes. Wanting to find even a glimpse of him in there, she pointed out the window to the motorcycle in the parking lot. "I think it's a Harley Davidson Night Rod Special," she said, hoping he'd react. When he didn't, she continued, "Is it yours?"

He smiled politely at her. "No way. Those things are far too dangerous for me."

She held her breath. She had to, or else she'd scream.

"There you are!" came a sing-song voice that Anise already hated. "I need to borrow my fiancé! Can you please help me finish these files?" The woman's face was a blur through Anise's tears, but it was easy to see that she wore a matching orange sweater.

Gross.

"Be right there," Nate told her with a warm, loving gaze. He turned back toward Anise. "I know my dad will do everything he can to help you. You're in good hands here."

"Are you happy?" Anise blurted out. "Is your life everything you want it to be?"

Nate nodded. "I have a job and a fiancé. What more is there?"

The real Nate would be bored as hell. This, all of it, was so disgusting, she thought she might puke. "A lot, actually. What about hobbies and friends and adventure and excitement?"

He gave her a pitying look. "I understand. Exploring regrets is something I see a lot in this office. But my dad is the best. I promise you he'll do everything he can to get you well again. I wish you the best, Ms. Viston." He held his hand out to shake hers.

That hand. The one that'd held hers. Comforted her and protected her and loved her. This was her chance to hold it again. She took it and they shook. He paused and stared at her for a moment, still holding her hand. His hand turned hers over, and his eyes took in the sight of the carnelian ring that Anise had hoped to use to restore his memories.

"That's a very unique ring," he commented.

"Yes, it is," she agreed, staring into his eyes. *Is he remembering?* Her thumb stroked his fingers.

At the touch, his hand dropped hers like a hot pan. "Sorry for the interruption," he mumbled. He backed away, then turned and hurried out the door.

Anise felt her jaw clench as she pointed to the door. "That's not him."

"Did he tell you he was having nightmares about prison?" Lorelei asked. "He couldn't sleep. He didn't know how to deal emotionally with his problems. He was struggling. Now he's not. He's happy, Anise. Please, don't ruin it for him. If you truly love him, you'll let him be."

Something didn't feel right about leaving without Nate. Anise opened the office door and saw Nate and his fiancé down the hall. Her annoyingly melodic voice said something that made him laugh, and he gave her a kiss. He really did look happy. What if Lorelei and Kent were right? If she gave him back his memories, he'd have to deal with the trauma of his past life. This was a way for him to not have to. Was it selfish of her to want to upheave the peace he'd found? And if she did, would he hate her for it? Would he suffer the rest of his life because of her? He was still smiling at his future wife when Anise turned around to look at Lorelei and Kent. "Okay," she agreed weakly. "I won't contact him again."

Thursday, January 9, 2025

"IT'S YOUR BIRTHDAY, ANISE. YOU'RE SUPPOSED to be happy," Joy informed her.

"I know," Anise agreed. She *should* be happy. She was in her cute house she'd taken care to decorate in a modern and cozy style. Talia was with Vanessa's daughter and Jonathan and Selina's two sons playing board games in her bedroom, and their laughter could be heard throughout the house. All of her friends were there. Erin, Vanessa, Joy, Jonathan, Selina, and Doreen had helped her decorate or prepare the food. Raina had flown in from Florida. Les was visiting from Philadelphia. They'd all brought gifts, cake, and well-wishes. "I'm sorry."

"Don't be sorry. You can feel however you want," Erin said.

"You're not feeling *old* already, are you?" Joy demanded.

Doreen sighed wistfully. "I'd take thirty-seven in a heartbeat."

"No, not old," Anise replied, although she *had* found a few more gray hairs in the mirror that morning. "It's just...it's getting worse."

"What is?" Vanessa wanted to know.

"Thomas Brevain warned me that the Plate of Destiny would be testing me. He said that the Plate takes your darkness and increases it to the point of obsession."

"Are you obsessing about something?" Jonathan asked, giving her a worried look.

Anise frowned. "I finally figured out what my darkness is—it's letting my fear make my decisions for me. I was afraid Grace might come after any of you because I have the Plate...what if she still wanted it? So I told you all everything and now you have the burden of keeping this secret. And I was afraid to not help Grace when she asked me to give Morty his memories back—what if she wanted revenge if I didn't help? But I wasn't sure I should do it because Thomas said that in your new destiny you'd either remember your old life or you wouldn't. It would be whichever way would be the best for you to carry out your new destiny. What if I ruined his new destiny?"

"But all that turned out fine," Selina argued. "It's not a burden for us to keep that secret at all."

"Not even for me!" Joy piped up. "I can do it when it really matters. Thank you for trusting me with it."

"And the last time I talked to Morty, he was doing great. He's loving his new life with Grace and is grateful to you for restoring his memories," Jonathan added.

"I also was too afraid to give Nate back his memories,

even though my instincts said I should." Anise looked down at the ground. "I didn't want to ruin his new destiny. And he did seem happy. So I let Lorelei and Kent talk me into the idea that leaving him alone was the right thing to do."

"Do you not agree?" Raina asked.

"I don't know. And that makes me feel selfish. But it's more than that," Anise explained. She felt herself getting agitated and spoke quicker and louder than she meant to. "Fear and doubt are starting to fill my every waking thought more and more. I've been reprimanded at work for mistakes that I've made by listening to the wrong people. I spent six hours at the grocery store last Saturday because I was afraid to buy the wrong canned soup. Some have less salt, some are organic, some have too much cream...I couldn't leave until I asked another shopper which brand *she* recommended. I don't even like canned soup, but I'm afraid to not stock up on canned goods because what if something happens?"

She felt Erin take her hand, and Anise squeezed back, grateful for the comforting.

"Thomas also said you can break the bond to the Plate by not wanting it anymore," Jonathan reminded her. "Do you still want it for some reason? Is there anyone else you were hoping to bring back?"

Anise shook her head. "I'm not going to bring anyone else back. I'm trying to live by the secrets of life like Dromly said to. The one about giving yourself second chances by using your wisdom to choose a new pathway, for example. But it's impossible to use my wisdom to choose new paths when my darkness makes me unable to make my own choices. Plus, I'm the keeper of the Plate, and I have the bond of king's blood to it, so it's going to keep testing me, and I'm going to keep failing. You can't break a blood bond."

"I could take the Plate and be the keeper of it," Les offered.

"No, I don't want you to have to deal with this," Anise said. "And I don't ever want this burden to fall to Talia either. I've been trying to come up with a solution, but I don't know what to do."

"Maybe there *is* a way to break the bond..." Les looked thoughtful. "From Thomas's letter, we learned that the Armor Jewelry and the Plate of Destiny are dualistic... how the ring poisons but also removes toxins, for example. But what about the seer's wand? We never discussed how it might have dualistic powers."

"A redheaded woman has to connect to the wand to have visions," Jonathan said, crinkling his face with doubt. "How can that be dualistic?"

"It's the connection!" Anise exclaimed as she began to understand what Les was thinking. "If the wand can make connections, maybe it can break them as well!"

"But Anise doesn't have red hair," Doreen pointed out. "Will that matter?"

"Maybe it's a good thing," Selina speculated. "Maybe to break a connection, the person would have to have the opposite of red hair, which is *not* red hair."

"But using that logic, if the wand makes connections only for redheaded women, it might only break connections for non-redheaded men," Raina countered.

"There are too many maybes," Erin commented with a frown.

"Yeah!" Joy stuffed a bite of cake in her mouth. "How did the ancient Mallandian people figure all this out anyway?"

"I talked about this once with Dr. S...Morty," Jonathan answered. "He said they'd get visions about the Jewelry and how it should work. It was explained in the visions how exactly to make the Jewelry in order to get the effect they wanted."

"You're a descendant of Mallandia," Vanessa said to Anise. "Have you had any visions of the wand?"

"No," Anise told her. "But it wouldn't be me getting

the visions. It would be the person responsible for making the Jewelry. The Jewelry engineer."

All heads swiveled toward Jonathan.

"Have you had any visions?" Les asked Jonathan.

"Visions, no. But I dream about the Jewelry all the time," Jonathan replied. "At least once a week ever since Anise named me Jewelry engineer."

"Maybe a dream is what the Mallandians meant when they spoke about visions!" said Selina.

"What did you dream?" Anise asked Jonathan. "Anything about the seer's wand?"

"This is kind of creepy, but I had a dream about you and the wand last night," Jonathan told Anise. "You held it to your heart, then to your forehead, and then you moved it away from you. Held it at arm's length as far as you could. It's the opposite of what redheaded women have to do to become seers."

"Try it!" Joy cried.

"Do you think it'll work?" Anise asked. Apprehension prickled her skin. *What if something goes wrong?*

"I think it'll work because Jonathan dreamt it," Selina said, matter-of-factly. "That's how the Jewelry engineers created the Armor Jewelry, right? That's how the curse was created that was making Les sleep. A Jewelry engineer got the information he needed from his visions to create what he wanted to happen. As long as Jonathan wants this to happen, it will."

"Of course I do!" Jonathan exclaimed. "As your royal Jewelry engineer, my intention with this new way of using the seer's wand is to allow anyone to break any connection they want. And specifically for you to break your connection to the Plate of Destiny so you're no longer being tested by it."

Anise felt encouraged by his excitement, but was still having a hard time making the decision to move forward. "So you think I should try it?"

"Oh my god, yes!" Joy said with mock annoyance.

"This is not the time to let fear stop you!"

"You're right." Anise went to her bedroom to fetch the wand from the safe. Rejoining her friends in the living room, she stood and stared at the wand. She was about to touch it to her heart when Jonathan spoke up.

"There's one other thing I just remembered from my dream. I heard a word: gesture."

"Like how touching the wand to my heart and head is a gesture?" Anise asked.

"No, not a physical gesture. A symbolic one. What I mean is...it's not enough to just intend to break the connection with a wave of the wand. You have to make a gesture to show your intentions."

"I'm not sure I understand," Les said.

"I think I do," Anise spoke up. "It's something I learned with my affirmation cards when I used them. When you want to change, it's not enough to simply read the affirmation and understand it, you have to act on it or it won't help. It's the same with the wisdom on the Plate of Destiny. It's not enough for someone to read and understand what the Plate has to say. They have to live it to truly learn it."

"Exactly," agreed Jonathan. "But I didn't dream what your gesture should be."

"Then it should be up to Anise," Raina concluded. "What do you think your gesture should be?"

Anise didn't know how she knew, but it felt right. "I need to give it all up. The Plate of Destiny, the Armor Jewelry, and after I use it to break the connection, the seer's wand as well."

"What do you mean, give it up?" Jonathan asked, a look of horror washing over his face. "Are you planning to destroy it?"

"No, not destroy it. I just need to not hang on to any of it. To not own it or be its keeper. I need to not *need* the Jewelry anymore. I have to go back to being who I am without depending on it. And I can still follow the

Plate's secrets of living without keeping the Plate locked in my safe. I can protect it by putting it somewhere safe, but not clinging to it. I think to truly be able to make decisions without fear, I have to let go of using it all as a safety net and trust myself instead."

"You could put the Plate of Destiny back in the underwater cave where we found it," Raina suggested. "We know it'll be safe there. I'll go with you, if you'd like."

"I would!" Anise replied with gratitude. "And I like the idea of putting it all back where it was."

"You could donate the Armor Jewelry to the museum," Jonathan said. "Well, except for the ring. It's still connected to the murder of Richard and Marilyn Woods. And the amulet was never in a museum." He thought for a moment. "Maybe some of us could take a trip to where Mallandia used to be and return the Jewelry to the site of the battlefield instead."

"Yes! Perfect!" Anise agreed. She looked at her hand. "I should let go of my garnet ring, too, since we engraved it with the incantation, and it has powers now. Brian gave it to me originally, so I should give it back to him. But...I don't know if he came back, and after how he treated me, I don't want to know."

"I'll take care of it," Jonathan said, stepping over to her and holding out his hand. "I'll find out what happened to him and return it to him one way or another."

Anise dropped her garnet ring in Jonathan's hand. "I appreciate it." Then she frowned. "But now what about the wand? Grace said the wand came from a cave somewhere in Europe. That doesn't narrow it down very much."

"Where was it after it left the cave?" Selina asked.

"Dromly had it."

"Maybe give it to Kent then?" Selina said. "I'm sure he'd take it if you told him why."

"That's a good idea," Anise said. "I'll mail it to him with a letter. I'm sure he'd appreciate knowing that without the Armor Jewelry I'll have no power to restore Nate's memories. Ever." Her stomach ached at the thought, but she'd given Kent and Lorelei her word, and Nate was happy in his new life. He must be married by now. Happy with his new bride and no past trauma. Happier than he'd been with her. And maybe without the possibility of seeing Nate again, she could finally start to heal her grief. Or at least *try* to start to heal.

Saturday, May 30, 2026

TODAY'S THE DAY.

A few nervous butterflies fluttered in Anise's stomach as she put on the dress she'd bought for today, but it wasn't an overwhelming flood of anxiety. Just a few nerves. Perfectly understandable. Anyone would feel the same.

She thought about how hard she'd worked against the agoraphobia. It'd been difficult and stressful to travel home from Europe without having the security of the Jewelry, and she'd had more than one panic attack, but it'd been worth it. As soon as she'd broken her bond to the Plate of Destiny, returned all four pieces of Armor Jewelry to where Mallandia used to be, and mailed the seer's wand to Kent, she'd started therapy. She'd slowly practiced leaving her home without having the amulet to rely on, going further and further each time until eventually she could comfortably go several places without having panic attacks. Her friends had accompanied her when she needed support and helped her celebrate each success.

Brand-new places were still sometimes challenging, but the fear was getting less and less the more she went out. She'd committed to living the secrets of life as per Dromly's letter and gave herself a second chance at everything she loved. It was leading her in the right direction. She'd become the star pupil in her art classes. She'd started teaching self-defense and kickboxing classes again and enjoying the freedom of participating in her world as much as she wanted. Going out was becoming fun again.

She'd practiced her drive back and forth to the art gallery and spent some time there whenever she could to let it become familiar and comfortable. "Today will be fun," she told her reflection in the mirror. "I won't be anxious, and the agoraphobia won't act up. The gallery is in my safe-zone. My friends will all be there to support me. I've been wanting this my entire life, and I'm going to enjoy every second of it."

Time to go! She dropped her keys, wallet, and phone in her bag and reached for the doorknob on her front door. The doorbell rang at that moment, startling her. *Who could that be?* After taking a breath, she swung the door open, wondering if one of her friends had decided to offer her a ride to the gallery. She looked at the man standing on her doorstep as he stared back at her. The room began to spin and she grabbed the door for support. She felt tightness in her chest and tried not to hyperventilate. A few streaks of silver now weaved through his almost-black hair, but his cobalt blue eyes looked exactly the same. "Na—um, Kent. Junior. Hello." She tried her best to look composed and opened her door wider. "Would you like to—"

His face crinkled in a pained expression as he brushed by her to enter her house. "Is this how *you* felt?" he demanded.

"Excuse me?" she asked while shutting the door.

"When you came to Kent's office two years ago and I saw that ring on your finger...I didn't know what to think. For years before then I'd had dreams—lots of them—about that exact ring. And some other very distinctive jewelry too."

Because I named him one of the royal Jewelry engineers, Anise realized. *Dreams just like Jonathan had.*

"I thought someone was playing a joke on me. Or like the dream world and reality were merging somehow."

He must be so confused. She opened her mouth to speak, but didn't know what to say.

He continued. "Since that day, I couldn't get you out of my mind. It wasn't just the Jewelry and the dreams, though. You'd asked me if that motorcycle in the parking lot was mine. It wasn't, but I have a tattoo on my arm of a very similar bike, and I couldn't for the life of me remember getting it or why I had it. I couldn't fathom why you'd think that bike was mine, either. I asked Lorelei and Kent about you over and over, and they fed me some story about you being a patient. But I couldn't find any of your patient records. And I kept dreaming about the Jewelry and some magic wand with an obsidian on it. Then one day, a package came to the office. It had your name on the return address."

The seer's wand. He looked angry, and Anise wondered where he was going with this. She started to worry about what she should do but said nothing as he continued his story.

"I opened the package thinking it was something for the office. It wasn't the first time a grateful patient send a thank-you gift to the practice. Then I saw the wand and the letter to Kent. The same goddamn wand I'd been dreaming about! I couldn't help but feel like I had a connection to you that went beyond logic and reason. So I read the letter."

Anise swallowed nervously. "And?"

"And I thought you'd lost your mind. You talked about how the wand can break connections, and how you broke your connection to the Plate of Destiny because it had some magical hold on you. You said that giving the wand to Kent was a gesture—your way of returning it to the universe so you could be free. You said you'd keep a promise you made to never give Nate his memories back. I had no idea who that was. Weirdest fairy tale I ever read. I was about to suggest to Kent that he recommend a psychiatrist to you when I remembered that you'd called me 'Nate' that day you came to the office."

"Kent Jr., look, I know you're upset—"

"I couldn't shake the dreams," he interrupted. He began pacing back and forth in her living room. "I started dreaming every night about holding the wand to my heart, then my head, and then drawing it away from me. *Every single night.* For months. I couldn't think about anything else. I kept oversleeping. I made mistakes at work that I normally wouldn't have. And I kept pushing back the date to my own wedding because I couldn't think about anything else."

Anise couldn't help but feel how tortured he was. "I...I..." She sighed with exasperation at the absence of her words.

"So I thought maybe you or the Jewelry or the wand were representations of something deep in my subconscious that needed to be resolved. Some kind of connection that I wanted severed. I wasn't sure what that might be, but I hoped that if I made that symbolic gesture by using the wand the way I had in my dreams, I might get over whatever it was that was haunting me."

Anise nodded at him to continue, hanging on his every word. He'd always said they had some indefinable connection. Did he manage to break it? Was he happy with his fiancé now? And if so, why had he come?

"I tore Kent's garage apart looking for the wand." He paused to take a deep breath. His jaw was rigid and Anise could see the pain clouding his normally bright eyes.

"Did you find it?"

"Yes. But first I found something else." He frowned at her.

"What was it?"

"Fred Dromly's trip journals. I read them all. They

talked about the Jewelry and the wand that I'd been dreaming about. He had *sketches* of them in his journals, and they looked exactly like the ones in my dream! He had a sketch of the ring you'd worn that day in Kent's office. And the most recent journals mentioned you by name. They also mentioned someone named Nate Brevain."

"So you came here because you want answers." Anise's stomach clenched. What could she tell him that he'd believe?

"No. I came here to tell you that I know I was lied to," he growled. "The truth was kept from me by people who thought they knew better. My right to make choices about my own life was taken away from me. It's infuriating. Humiliating. No one treated me with the *fucking* respect I deserve but instead acted like I was too fragile to handle the truth! I couldn't believe anyone would think so little of me." He faced the wall and placed a palm on it, closing his eyes for a moment until he turned to face her. "So I ask you again: Is this how *you* felt when I lied to you?"

"Yes." Anise felt her eyes start to flood. "You remember." She covered her mouth with her hand, not sure if she was trying to suppress a sob or a laugh. Her heart pounded in her ears.

Nate stared at her, barely blinking. "I used the wand with the intention to break the connection I had to the Jewelry, the Plate of Destiny, and to you. I wanted to move on with my life. As soon as I did, I saw a flash of green in the obsidian, and I remembered. Everything."

"Nate, I'm so sorry! I didn't want to leave without you that day I came to Kent's office, but I—"

"No, *I'm* sorry," he interrupted. "If this is how I made you feel when I lied to you—and I know I did it more than once—then I owe *you* an apology. Why you ever forgave me, I'll never know."

He finally understands. But was he only here to offer

an apology and then go back to his life? She couldn't tell if she was angry or heartbroken at the thought. Her stomach felt sick. "I have to know...why are you here?" Anise demanded. "You have the truth now. And if you broke your connection to me, now you can move on. Why come all the way out here?"

"Two reasons. The first one is that Lorelei told me about Natalia after I remembered everything."

"Yes. We have a daughter. Talia's going to be so excited to meet you. But I'm going to need to sit and talk with her myself about it first when she gets back from summer camp. It's going to be a shock."

Nate nodded. "Of course."

"What's the second reason?"

"The second reason is that we had that strong connection the entire time we knew each other. And then we were separated by death and kept apart by unexplainable ancient magic. I used that magic to break all connections I had to you and my former life."

Here it comes. She braced herself for another apology, sincere but torturous, for lying, for her grief, for the shock of him showing up at her door, for falling in love with someone else along the way. For choosing a path that didn't include her, and for everything that could've been but now never will be.

He ran a hand through his hair and stared at the floor for a moment before looking her straight in the eye. "...And yet here I am next to you, not wanting to go."

But...he broke our connection, right? Her heart leapt. "What do you mean?"

"I mean," he said, taking a few steps closer to her, "that some connections are more powerful than magic. Would you agree?"

"Yes!" she blurted out, and wondered if this was actually happening. Was Nate really in her living room saying these things to her? "But you have a...life in Springfield."

Nate shook his head. "The first thing I did when I

remembered everything is talk to Lorelei and Kent. They confirmed it all. Next, I broke off my engagement. It wasn't real. Nothing about that life was real, and I didn't want to live a lie. And I can't imagine being with anyone else but you."

Anise opened her mouth, but no words came out.

A nervous expression crossed his face. "Do you feel the same?"

Anise nodded her agreement, too overwhelmed to speak but basking in the grin he was giving her. *Is this real?*

"Then I threw out all the god-awful Easter-egg-colored sweaters in my closet. What the hell was I thinking?"

Anise couldn't help but laugh. "The one I saw you in was pretty terrible."

"I used to be strong and fit," Nate grumbled as his cheeks turned red. "And I want to get back in shape. But I had more important things I needed to do first. Right after I got rid of my sweaters, I bought a new motorcycle."

"Another Night Rod Special?"

"No. I got a touring bike. It's a little slower, but I wanted something more comfortable that I can take on long-distance trips. Then I rode out here."

"...And now?"

He took her hand. "And now I'd like to kiss you."

She intertwined her fingers with his. "I'd like that too." He leaned in until their lips softly touched. It felt like he'd never been away.

Nate gave her a serious look when they pulled back. "If this is going to happen, if we're going to possibly be a 'we' again, it has to go slowly. We have Talia to think about."

"I couldn't agree more," Anise told him, happy that he was planning ahead and putting their daughter first. "And we have to start this relationship from the beginning, not where we left off. We don't know each other very well anymore."

"That's easily fixed. Let me take you out. The Concert in the Park is on Tuesday."

Anise grinned at him. "Perfect. But I also have an art show featuring my works. I'd love you to be my date."

"You have your own art show?!" His smile showed her how proud and impressed he was. "When is it?"

"Right now. And we'd need to hurry."

"I'd be honored, honey."

Honey. He said it! Her pleasure turned up the corners of her lips. "I never thought I'd hear that again."

"Get used to it." He offered her his arm.

She took it. They walked out her front door and stepped onto a pathway together. She could see it was lined with petunias and led to her car, the art gallery, and after that, in every imaginable direction. Anise looked forward to finding out where they'd choose to go.

Epilogue
LIVING YOUR BEST LIFE

Les stood there in a suit, his pride evident in his stance. "Thank you all for coming. I have the great honor to introduce the woman of the hour, the reason the art world has become all the more beautiful. My sister, Anise Viston."

Anise smoothed her hair and stepped up on the small stage to hug her brother and accept the applause that echoed off the gallery walls. She said a few words of appreciation and watched the audience disperse around the large room to enjoy her works. Nate was waiting for her as she descended the few stairs back into the crowd.

"This is incredible! I'm so proud of you, honey," he told her.

She squeezed his hand and gave him an appreciative grin.

While Nate took his time to gaze at each of her pieces, Anise ambled slowly around the room to greet everyone who had come out to help her celebrate. Vanessa, Erin, Joy, and Doreen had brought their families to enjoy the event. Raina had flown in from Tallahassee and was catching up with Selina by the refreshments table.

Jonathan waved as he walked over to her. "You know, your date looks a lot like..."

"I have a lot to tell you. After the show."

"Okay." He pointed to one of her paintings. "I just can't get over how real this looks."

Anise turned her head to look at the painting. "I took my time with that one."

"It looks exactly like him," he said, his look of wonder growing with every second he started at the painting entitled 'Dromly.' "If we didn't have all the history with him that we do, I'd buy this one. But we'll definitely be taking at least one painting home today." Jonathan gave Anise a hug. "You never cease to amaze me."

"You're the artist," a young woman said to her. "Can I ask you a question?"

"Certainly," Anise said and allowed the woman to lead her to a painting in the corner.

"All of your art is either a portrait or a landscape and uses a lot of color except for one. This one on the round canvas is abstract and is all gray, black, and white, except for the purple puzzle piece in the center. Can you tell me more about it? Why did you call it 'The Plate of Destiny?'"

Anise noticed others had heard the woman's question and had gathered around to hear the answer. "There really wasn't any other way to paint what I wanted to get across. I've learned there's not just one pathway for your destiny, and the routes you choose ultimately change how you get to your destiny while your destiny can affect the routes you choose. They go hand in hand in a circular fashion. You see, these," she said, pointing at a part of her painting, "are pathways through life. As you travel them, you might find that one is better for you than another."

Her finger traced one of the pathways that was above the others like a bridge linking one side of the canvas to the other. "Or you might discover that there are some connections that simply can't be broken." She glanced at Nate and saw him flash his sideways smile at her. "You'll notice that sometimes the decision to take one path is black and white, and sometimes the decision is grayer. But if you think about it, black, white, and gray are really all the same, they're all colors, the only difference is in their degree of saturation of light. To turn a hesitation into a decision, you have to use wisdom to know how much or how little to adjust the pathway to make it right for you. Just ask yourself, 'Who do I want to be in this situation?' And we don't need to be afraid to make these decisions, because if you happen to take the wrong path, there are always several more pathways of varying directions to offer you a second chance. All you have to do is step on to one and let it lead you to your destiny, to where you fit." Her finger traced a path to the purple puzzle piece. "Because everyone fits. We're all part of the same puzzle. I believe that inherently, we all know that. But sometimes we have to stand back and see the big picture to remember it."

She motioned for everyone to join her in moving back several large steps. When they had, she flipped a switch on the wall and a light shined on her painting, revealing formerly unseen gold and silver outlines of puzzle pieces that fit together over the entire canvas. Anise smiled at the woman and at the delighted sounds coming from the crowd. "And that's what living your best life is all about."

About the Author

Katarina Kyde grew up in southern Illinois where she constantly made up stories using toys, photographs, markers—anything—as characters. She has a degree in psychology from the University of Illinois and fosters a nerdy love of neuroplasticity, herbalism, and anything with a touch of magic. Currently, she lives in Colorado with her husband and enjoys hiking, kickboxing, and reading. *Strength of Sight* is her third novel and follows *Protection of Beauty* and *Poisoning of Minds* in the Armor Series.

katarinakyde.com

Acknowledgements

Thank you Ed, Tyler, and Jude, for the editing and support, the discussions about plotlines and characters, making me laugh when I felt stressed, and encouraging me to remain confident when it was exactly what I needed to hear. You worked so hard to help make my dream of becoming an author into a reality. I adore you all.

Thank you so much to James and Bestie for your invaluable help with a certain scene.

Thank you, Gavin, for everything you taught me about video editing and for sharing in my excitement for the creation of all the trailers. Your support and encouragement means so much.

Thank you, Mom, for portraying a favorite character in the trailer and your support throughout the creation of this series. It means the world to me.

Thank you, Ellen, for the fun we had creating stories together when we were kids. Echoes of that will forever reverberate through the stories I write as an adult.

Finally, thank you to everyone who took a chance on a new author and read my series through to the end. I am so happy and grateful you joined me on this journey.